Edwin Mullins was born in 1933 in London, where he still lives. He has been a publisher, magazine editor, travel writer, journalist, art critic of the *Sunday Telegraph* and sale-room correspondent of the *Financial Times*. He is also a regular broadcaster and television presenter: his recent TV series include *100 Great Paintings* (BBC) and *A Love Affair with Nature* (Channel 4), and he is currently at work on a new series for Channel 4 called *Paradise on Earth*. He has written numerous books on painting and sculpture, including *The Painted Witch* and *The Pilgrimage to Santiago*, both of which drew widespread critical acclaim.

The Golden Bird, his third novel, is set at the dawn of the Age of Chivalry; its successor, *The Lands of the Sea* (Collins, 1988), is set in its dusk.

G000256947

THE
GOLDEN BIRD

Edwin Mullins

Fontana/Collins

For
GWEN MULLINS
my mother

First published by William Collins 1987
First issued in Fontana Paperbacks 1988

Copyright © Edwin Mullins 1987

Photoset in Linotron Sabon by
Ace Filmsetting Ltd, Frome
Made and printed in Great Britain by
William Collins Sons & Co. Ltd, Glasgow

ONE

THERE WAS A SOUND of axes throughout France. If you could have had a buzzard's eye on that midsummer day the land would have looked like an emerald carpet spread between sea and sea. The expanse of forest was broken only by the threads of a thousand rivers which caught the sunlight, and here and there by uneven patches of open ground where invisible creatures had nibbled. Swooping lower, on the fringes of the forest you would have spotted trees lying felled, and figures like ants bustling around them – lopping branches, sawing trunks into manageable lengths, then levering them until they rolled clumsily down the slope towards one of those silver threads of water where a barge awaited them, to be half-submerged by the weight of so much wood.

Every so often the ring of axes would cease within the dense canopy of forest, branches begin to quiver and slide and, amid a frantic scattering of pigs, another oak tree pitch on to the verge of the clearing. Then the ants would re-gather and the sound of axes be resumed. Veils of smoke filtered upwards through the reed-thatch of wooden cottages; and if you circled low enough to set the geese into a raucous alarm you would have caught the smell of heavy black bread newly baked in mud-ovens, blending with the acrid tang of pigswill.

This was France, northern France somewhere between the Channel and the River Loire – it would be hard to say precisely where since all this mottled carpet of green looked so remarkably alike at this time, touched only lightly by man until recent years except as outlaw, predator, scavenger, pirate, invader. In Roman times it had been quite different, but they were long past. The Roman cities of northern Gaul had gradually dwindled into squalid market-towns half their former size, the prouder mansions invariably the most decayed, their stone quarried for meaner shacks and hovels where the survivors — well! — survived as best they could, praying for insignificance whenever the fury of the Norsemen struck at dawn from their flotillas of agile boats. Farms the Romans cultivated so assiduously had become deserted out of fear, or fire, or death, or all those things: the forest crept over them; bears and wolves did the rest. Only the roads the Romans cut through the forest had remained — rutted and overgrown — and they did so largely because patrols of bandits heading for the next town or farm or monastery found it convenient to use them. Few others dared and, if they did, often died for it.

But all this, too, was past or mostly so. The Norsemen, tiring of pillage (or perhaps tired of having no regular base, home, woman, food), had finally settled, had even opened their eyes to Christ. The Peace of God, if not always godly, had begun to descend upon the land, at least sufficiently so for wary men to venture out of their shattered towns, axe in hand, to do battle with the forest, drag a simple plough across the wasteland. And in doing so they made a discovery; that during all those years of emptiness — the forgotten years — the rivers had burst their untended banks every spring and flooded the dead fields with nutrients; the forest floor was mulched deep with centuries of goodness; wild boar, deer, partridge, bustard, these and other provender were seen to ratify God's peace with God's plenty. Crops grew as if by His blessing. A net, a trap, an arrow, a hoe — nothing more was needed to eat, and to eat well.

Not that it was quite so easy. The fury of the Norsemen had created a need for men powerful enough to withstand it; men who could call up an army and equip it; who could build bastions to which a family could scuttle when the pirates sailed up the river; who could fortify the mill because the Norsemen too needed bread. Oh, it was good to be free, but in the years of terror it was the free man who was found in the morning bleeding into the embers of his crops, and whose wife amused some longboat crew drunk on loot for a few hours until her terrible body was discovered by fishermen in their river-nets. Without protection you died; and *for* protection you paid – with your freedom, your corn (some of it at least), your service whenever and for whatever the lord required it – and therefore sometimes you paid for protection with your life. Because the lord, of course, had his enemies as well as his allies, and the most decisive means of weakening an enemy was to burn and pillage his lands – precisely as the Norsemen had once done, except that now you did not always know who your lord's enemies were or from what direction they might appear. In other words, it was a brave man in these times who ventured out into the forest with his axe to clear a new life for himself and his young family. At best, he hoped that the soil he scratched lay well off the paths of revenge. But who could be certain where these might be?

The year, then: Anno Domini 996. And on the longest day of that year two men on horseback were riding southwards from Normandy through that interminable forest. At least, so it appeared to one of them who was a stranger to the county of Maine, in fact a stranger to almost everything life had to offer outside the walls of the great monastery of Jumièges which had been his home and his workshop for as long as he could remember.

His name was Rollo, which from the ring of it will tell you that he was a Norman. From his looks alone you could have guessed this. He was tall; Rollo did not realize how exceptionally tall he was until he noticed the astonished expressions on the faces of villagers they had passed since leaving

9

the boundaries of Normandy. More than this, he was fair — even for a Norman. His hair stood out in a brilliant torch of pale curls, and a beard of the same form and colour was sufficiently thin in growth not to mask the rather delicate features of his jawline and mouth.

But it was his eyes that caused the villagers to stare and wonder more than his height and Viking looks. You could have called them blue, rather as you call the sea blue, knowing it not to be; and like the sea Rollo's eyes seemed to take on the prevailing shade of light around them. They could be a dead grey, or a bright silver, greenish sometimes; but, most extraordinary of all, when the sun left his face they became an intense violet hue as if they were windows on to some luminous cavern where you knew immediately that secrets lay, and were troubled by what they might be. So surprising were those eyes that Rollo's companion, on their first meeting, had enquired laughingly whether his famed skills as a master-mason included the lighting of a lantern within his skull to shine out through those astonishing orbs.

'You must be able to see things others can't,' he said with an expression of slightly mocking amazement.

But then his face had taken on an anxious look.

'Mind you, my friend,' he went on, lowering his gaze, 'if your great gifts include seeing in people what other people can't, you could find yourself in hot water where we're going.'

And he swept a mop of dark hair from his eyes and gave an uneasy laugh.

Rollo had wondered what he might mean. All the same, from that morning beneath the great octagonal towers of Jumièges he had warmed to this jovial emissary from the Count of Anjou. He was a slight, little man with a look of permanent amusement on his face, which was clean-shaven and youthful under thick black curls. Rollo imagined him to be perhaps four or five years the younger of the two, say about twenty-three. He had introduced himself in the monastery courtyard simply as Sebrand. His handshake was powerful, though his hands were small compared to Rollo's. A swordsman's hands, Rollo thought: his own were the large calloused hands of a stonemason.

Meanwhile the monks, his fellow-masons, lay brothers, servants, cooks, gardeners, stable-boys, they had all gathered round the two men as Rollo's bags were strapped behind the saddle. The rest of his belongings were to follow in a day or so, including – Rollo had insisted – his precious chisels and measuring equipment. The aged abbot, shrunken under his cowl, had emerged with tears in his eyes to say a final farewell, embracing Rollo as the mason prepared to mount his horse.

'Peace on your journey. St Philibert be with you,' he said quietly.

Then the abbot had turned to the young Angevin.

'Care for him, sir; he has been like a son to me. May he build you houses of God as fine as he has built here.'

And with that the abbot gazed with watery eyes at the towers of Rollo's church. Never would he have believed that anyone could have raised such a ladder to heaven, that here in his own mason's yard there should have been a man with so extraordinary a vision. It was, as it seemed to him, nothing short of a miracle: invariably all eyes that gazed upon those towers became transfixed as if in contemplation of the divinity. He marvelled at how this great church had risen from the dead in his own lifetime, its towers like hands raised in blessing above the wounded land. God was indeed good that He should have implanted such a gift in one of His own flock. The abbot sighed. Rollo felt tears on his own cheeks as he embraced the old man: it was like embracing the bones of a dying bird. Rollo's voice choked as he tried to thank the abbot: he could hear inadequate words mumbling from his lips. Then he and Sebrand had mounted, turned their horses, and with hands raised in salute they passed over the cobbles and out of the monastery gates. Those gates closed behind them on sixteen years of Rollo's life. Before them lay the silence of the forest.

So, by that midsummer day the two men had now ridden for two days. It was further than Rollo had ever travelled, and he marvelled at how the forests he knew so intimately along the valley of the Seine, where he had so often hunted or chopped wood, should continue from morning till night, morning till night again, always with a never-changing horizon of more forest. Here and there were expanses of heath and marshland which they skirted, and as they did so they were inspected by huge bronze dragonflies. Every hour or so a break in the trees revealed a scattering of low wooden houses amid small fields where corn was beginning to turn a pallid gold. Rollo came to recognize when a settlement was near by the pigs rooting in the undergrowth on either side of the track. And when they reached a clearing villagers would stare anxiously, or vanish. Sebrand, who was riding in front, paid them no attention beyond raising his hat in greeting. Black kites were perched on thatched roofs, following the movements in the farmyard with scavenging eyes. The two men rode on. Just once or twice Sebrand would dismount and lead his horse over to one of the larger farmhouses, leaving Rollo to wait in the shade of the forest. He would watch Sebrand disappear inside the house, and reappear some ten minutes later carrying bread, cheese, pork sausage and a pitcher of ale; and the farmer would emerge and watch him depart, standing at his door open-mouthed and glancing down at the cluster of silver coins in his hand.

Rollo felt admiration for the way Sebrand exuded confidence in the midst of what seemed to him an eternal wilderness. He missed the great bulwark of the monastery, never out of view, like a tethering-post. Sebrand always appeared certain which track to take, with just a glance at the sun. And as the light began to fade, and they could hear a howling of wolves across the valley, the Angevin would suddenly sniff around him and — sure enough — by dusk they

12

would find themselves being led by tallow candles into a spacious barn deep with new-mown hay, and a flagon of ale set down beside each of them, while their horses were led by the farmer to an adjoining stable, and they could hear the sound of animals being watered, hay being munched, saddles removed, coats brushed. And in the morning there would be fresh cheese and milk and dark bread on a wooden platter. Sebrand would stretch himself contentedly, feel the black stubble on his chin, and begin to talk.

He felt freer to talk now they had left Normandy, Sebrand explained. The county of Maine, which lay between Normandy and Anjou, was an ally: the lord of Maine was a vassal of the Count of Anjou. Normandy – begging Rollo's pardon – felt alien to him. There might be peace now, but he could remember his grandfather telling how bands of Normans would cut a path of destruction through the villages of Anjou with no warning. They would burn, pillage, rape: nothing was spared, nothing was sacred. You would see the plumes of smoke rise, and you knew they were coming. It made him, Sebrand, uneasy riding through that country.

Rollo felt happy to listen. He enjoyed the younger man's openness, and the way he would switch rapidly from intensity to laughter, and back again. He had a habit of thumping his fist into his open palm to make a point, and then the mood would change and he would throw his arms wide with a grin as if to embrace the world. As they rode on through the morning Rollo began to learn about his companion. The tracks were broader now, and they could ride abreast and talk. He was, he said, Sebrand de Chemillé. His father Barthélémi was the lord of Chemillé. He was high in the service of the Count of Anjou – his constable, as he had also been to the Count's father and as Sebrand's grandfather had been to the Count's grandfather. And so on. If he outlived his father he too might be High Constable of Anjou. That was the way it was. It was the Count, Sebrand said, who had sent him to ensure Rollo safe conduct, insisting he travel alone so as not to attract attention.

'You see,' said Sebrand, rather solemnly, without turning his head, 'the Count has a lot of enemies...' Whereupon the serious tone broke: '... many of whom are now dead' – and Sebrand let out a laugh – 'or if not they might as well be. The Count, you'd better know, is a man to be reckoned with.'

Rollo had heard as much. Count Fulk. Often known as Fulk the Black. The abbot of Jumièges had not known why 'the Black', but had suggested it might not be due to the colour of his eyes, though these were indeed black. The abbot had refused to say more, in a manner that suggested he knew a great deal more and did not choose to think about it.

'You don't talk much, Rollo.' Sebrand turned in his saddle to face his companion. 'Yet everyone talks about you.'

It was Rollo's turn to laugh.

'And what on earth do they talk about?'

'Well! Maybe you aren't aware of these things, locked up in your monastery. You know, I'd expected a much older man, because what they say about you is that you understand how to build in a way unknown in Anjou, or indeed anywhere else. That you know about stone. That for other people it's just lumps of rock, and for you it's ... like fine clay. As though it's soft. You can mould it, bend it, hollow it, even give it human faces. And yet you can make it hold tremendous weight. Is that true?'

But Sebrand didn't give Rollo a chance to answer.

'My father told me a story,' he went on. 'The abbot of Corméry was visiting Jumièges, and he saw you at work in the mason's yard. He just watched. You were giving instructions, though they were all older than you. D'you know what he said? That you were like Christ in the carpenter's shop. He couldn't forget you. And he asked your abbot. What he was told was that when you were a boy – just an apprentice – you'd had a vision of Jumièges, and how it would look. And when you'd told the abbot about it, he'd spoken to Duke Richard because he was so astonished. And the Duke placed all the finest craftsmen in Normandy in your charge to rebuild the monastery in honour of St Philibert. And paid everything himself. That's what my father said.'

It was true. Rollo just nodded. He had no idea that the story had spread, or that there was anything so remarkable about it. There had been so many mysteries. Often he had only felt part of this world when he was in the mason's yard: it was as if he came to life only through employing his hands. He looked at them – huge rough hands – and showed them to Sebrand by way of an answer, letting the reins dangle from his wrists.

'That's what I am, I suppose. A builder. Not like you; you're a swordsman.'

'How can you tell?'

'Because your hands dance.'

Sebrand looked puzzled. Then he laughed and looked pleased. He kicked his horse into a trot as the path they were following passed under a handsome avenue of trees towards a shaded river that Rollo could just glimpse some half a mile beyond, winding through a shallow valley. Sebrand broke into a song as he rode ahead. Rollo could catch enough of the words to know that it was a song about women and, to judge by the number of verses, a great number of women. Sebrand had the air of a man going home.

Rollo on the other hand was leaving everything he knew behind. His home had been Jumièges – only Jumièges. He had even been named there. Where he came from was another mystery. He remembered nothing before being a young boy handed a chisel in that mason's yard. No name. No parents. No childhood. No one knew anything. Only that he'd been found wandering, with no memory. The monks said he must have been concussed. They had asked everywhere but nobody had ever come forward to claim him. He must have been twelve then. Perhaps his parents had been killed in the same accident. There were so many accidents; many people got killed, or just vanished. For a while he was just 'the lost boy', or 'the fair one' because of his hair. Or 'the boy from the sea' because of the colour of his eyes: people put it about that he had drifted ashore from a shipwreck. But nobody ever knew. He had begun to learn who he was only through the work he was given to do; as if his chisel held the answers. He felt he understood himself as he began to understand stone – the grain and texture of it, how to cut it, carve it, raise it. Wood, too. He built a hall for the monks, a refectory with enormous arched timbers of oak. Nobody had taught him how: he just knew. Just as he had 'seen' how the abbey church might be, with a lantern tower supported by four huge arches at the crossing of the nave, the stout walls of ashlar, the carved columns, and the twin octagonal towers at the west end. Then the Duke had come. Richard the Fearless, the abbot told him it was, son of William Longsword, grandson of Rollo, the first Duke of Normandy. The Duke had asked him how he had conceived all this, and he had not known what to reply. He had just 'seen' it: it was there before his eyes, finished. The Duke informed the abbot that he did honour to the dukedom, and when the abbot said the boy had no name the Duke bestowed on him the name of Rollo, after the first Duke of Normandy, his grandfather. And everyone at the monastery was silent, and looked on him strangely.

From then on, the abbey absorbed him entirely. Year by year it grew around him, stone bringing to life his dream of it, block by block, each stone shaped and set under his eye. He supervised everything. As the towers grew the undermasons began to grow scared to climb the scaffolding. It was sinful, some of them muttered, to build proudly towards heaven like that. God would strike without any doubt. So Rollo would shin up the ladders ahead of them, haul on the pulleys until they felt ashamed and began to help him heave the stones into place. He acquired a reputation for great strength. One of the older masons given to ale challenged him to wrestle. A huge barrel of a man. But Rollo seized his hand and spun him like a top: and when he got up and hurled himself at Rollo in fury and shame, the young master-mason ducked under him and hoisted him on to his shoulders in the monastery forecourt. Then he carried him ceremoniously out of the gates and, as the villagers gathered around, tipped him in the stream. The following day news was brought that the man had died of heart failure, which upset Rollo, but the other masons pronounced it to be the punishment of God and seemed to forget that God was supposed to be striking Rollo for invading the heavens with his stonework. He had no further trouble with his workmen nor – to his knowledge – with the Almighty.

Sebrand's mounting good spirits began to unloose Rollo's tongue. He began to talk of his life at the monastery, how absorption in his work had left him little time for much else, how company had never greatly mattered to him, or marriage, how he had been content to live and feed with the monks who saw to it he had all that he needed – it had not occurred to him to want land, or riches, or a position at court. He asked only to be free to be what he was, a builder.

Rollo could see a puzzled look clouding his companion's face, and noticed him fingering the hilt of his sword as if his words were arousing in him an irrepressible itch for action. They had reached the end of the long avenue of trees and were approaching the river bank. Rollo could see how the water hurried as it swept across the shallows of the ford, and beyond it the track cut diagonally up the wooded slope. Sebrand reined his horse by the water's edge and turned to Rollo as if exasperated.

'Building! What is the joy of it? Tell me.'

Rollo said nothing. Sebrand watched him gazing about him, searching as it seemed for an answer. Suddenly Rollo gave an agile leap from his horse and, still without saying a word, began to stride along the river bank. Alder trees leaned out over the dark water. Rollo paused. He looked up into the branches, and with both hands felt the surface of the trunk, caressing it – Sebrand thought – as if it were a living body.

'The coil of rope behind your saddle – could you throw it over?' he called out.

Sebrand did as he was asked: the rope landed accurately at Rollo's feet. He picked it up, placed his head and one arm through the coil and secured it with the heavy leather belt around his waist. Then he stepped back a few paces from the tree and with a spring reached the first branch with both hands. Sebrand's look turned to astonishment as the Norman proceeded to clamber up the alder tree like a lanky cat. He was already five times higher than a man. The trunk became thinner, and Rollo's weight was beginning to bend the whole tree even further out over the river like a bow. Sebrand dismounted in horror as he saw him kick out with one leg, grasping the uppermost stem of the tree in both hands above him. He was pulling at the tree, treating it like a spring, forward and back, so that it propelled him wider and wider over the river until the tree all but touched the branches leaning towards him on the farther bank. Sebrand rushed forward into the water as he saw the figure high above him launch both feet outwards from the tree until for a second he seemed to be floating horizontally with two arms outstretched, two legs outstretched. The next moment the two legs were clenched round a branch opposite and he was hanging between the two trees, holding them together in his arms as if they were a sheaf of corn. Lower and lower he pulled them – his legs round one tree, his arms round the other – until the two trunks that crossed above his body were as thick as a man's legs. Sebrand stood spellbound, water swirling past his thighs, arms extended in a futile gesture of rescue should the Norman fall. Staring upwards he saw Rollo carefully disengage one arm, work the rope free of his belt and toss one end of it over the join between the two trees. Over and over he passed it, working with extraordinary deftness and speed, until he heaved his body up on to the join and sat there as if he were merely straddling a fence, with the ends of the rope in either hand, which he proceeded to tie and tie again. Then he clambered down on to the farther bank as effortlessly as he had climbed up from the near one.

Sebrand was still standing in the shallow water as if transfixed. Sixty feet above him the two alders were joined in a perfect arch. Rollo was brushing greenery and twigs from his clothing and mopping the perspiration from his face and neck.

'That's how you build a roof,' he called to Sebrand who was starting to wade across the ford towards him. 'You tie the trees, and then you let them grow. You have to be patient. Ten, maybe twenty years: depends on the tree. By the time you cut them down they've grown that shape. And there's your roof, already shaped.'

Sebrand had recovered from the shock. He was now looking at Rollo as if scared of what he might do next. Water was dripping from his leggings. Flies were circuiting his surprised face.

'You mean that's how you build a hall in Normandy?'

'No,' said Rollo with a chuckle. 'Not as dangerously as that. If you start with young trees it's quite easy – except that you have to wait even longer.'

'So, who taught you?'

'Nobody,' Rollo answered with another laugh. 'I invented it just now . . .'

Sebrand gazed at him and shook his head, not knowing quite what to believe. It was the first time he understood why the lord of Anjou should have gone to such lengths to procure this man.

Still wringing with sweat, Rollo peeled off his clothing and plunged into the river. The chill water stung his body and he let the current carry him under his vault of trees.

How foolhardy, he realized, to have risked his life ... for what? To impress Sebrand? No, he didn't really feel the need. To prove something? All Rollo knew was that — as always — he could only understand who he was by what he did. Confronted by a man who understood nothing about him aroused his energies. Rollo could not have answered Sebrand's question 'What is the joy of it?' except by demonstrating it. *That* was the joy — inventing something, showing that it was possible.

He swam naked as he used to swim in the lakes around Jumièges. Trees. Water. Sky. Stones. After a day of dust up on the towers of Jumièges he would get away from the shrouded monks and walk through the forest to a pool blackened by the shadow of pines. The excitement of building, of making, was mirrored in the bright reflections of summer branches and fleeting skies. Sometimes Ebba would appear silently as he bathed, her body slip into the water beside him and his rough hands be softened by the touch of her breasts. Barefoot Ebba of the forest. Probably he would never see her again.

Sebrand had also bathed in the river, and now was drying himself in the afternoon sun. He watched the tall Norman wading back towards him and marvelled at the physique of the man, his biceps and chest muscles, his slender torso and legs that were matted with pale hair.

'Come, my friend,' said Sebrand after they had sat for a while in the sunlight, 'we have a few hours to ride yet.'

The two men carried their clothing across the ford, dressed, and untethered their horses to water them; then they mounted, recrossed the river and took the woodland track up the farther slope. The sun was beginning to sink into a luminous sky.

Sebrand had recovered his composure and was singing again. And on the crest of the hill he reined his horse. All day Rollo had noticed a gradual change in the countryside through which they were riding. The clearings in the forest had grown more frequent, the fields were larger and more fertile-looking, the farmhouses spacious and their occupants less suspicious. Now he saw before him a broad valley all but cleared of woodland, and his eyes caught the glint of a broad river winding away to the south-west in the direction they were taking. On the further bank spread open fields laid in patches of varied green under the evening sun.

'There!' Sebrand raised both arms in a joyful salute. 'See that river? The Sarthe. You won't be able to span that one like a squirrel, I can assure you. Beyond the Sarthe is my country, Rollo. And yours now. Anjou! Vines, d'you see? No more of your northern mists and northern ale. Wine, my friend. We'll drink like lords tonight.'

With that he spurred his horse and bellowed into song again as he rode ahead. Rollo cantered behind him along the broad track through heathland that was stained yellow with broom and speckled purple with wild orchids. A golden bird looped between poplar trees in the vale beyond them. A flute-like sound filled the air.

'There's the bird of Anjou,' Sebrand called out. 'Fulk's bird. The oriole. Nobody may hunt it. When it arrives in the spring he throws a feast. And some feast.'

'What happens if someone's caught hunting it?' Rollo called back.

Sebrand passed the edge of his fingers across his throat, and laughed.

'People just don't,' he said firmly.

The two riders were approaching the river. Through the screen of alders to the right of them the late sunlight flickered among the branches overhead. Already where they rode lay in shadow, and the shade deepened as they passed a decayed-looking barn hunched by the roadside. Grasses were growing tall from its reed-thatch, and blackened timbers had been pulled askew by nettles and long twists of bryony. Rollo was riding ahead now, and behind him he could hear the genial humming of Sebrand, the sound punctuated by ribald exclamations as yet another verse of his song ended naked in the sack. Rollo laughed.

Suddenly the laugh was stifled. He was falling. Twisting and tumbling in the air. And in that second as the world turned about him Rollo was aware of two figures. One was his shying horse. Of the other he could make out nothing but a blood-red jaw gaping with teeth and hurtling towards him; and even as his brain grappled with the identity of his attacker he knew that by the time words formed he would be as good as dead. Then the words came. Mad dog! Rollo hit the ground. Closed his eyes. Thrust an arm desperately above him. And in that instant he heard a stifled yell. He was aware of a tree-branch jabbing painfully into his shoulder, and as he opened his eyes he saw his own arm still raised before him.

Standing above him was Sebrand, sword in hand. The sword dripped red. Rollo could see nothing else until he raised himself to his feet. Sebrand was helping him with his other hand. Rollo could feel the Angevin's arm round his shoulder. He looked down. Across the track before them lay a lean grey creature – quite still. Its coat was matted and mangy, the long tail streaked with dirt. Flies were already settling on open sores along its back. But it was the head that Rollo was gazing at. Its lips were pulled back as if stitched, and the jaws even in death seemed to be devouring the ground on which it lay. From that wound of a mouth bubbled froth that was crimson with blood. Its eyes stared hideously, and they too were streaked with veins of red – and with rivulets of red that washed over them from a cleft across its forehead as deep as a man's hand. A glint of bone shone white within that dark trough of blood.

Sebrand let out a long whistling sound. He looked down at the sword in his right hand, then at Rollo standing there shakily.

Rollo could say nothing. Words tumbled over each other in his mouth and could get no further. He was aware that he had missed death by a second. His life seemed to be held in

22

Sebrand's hand – in his sword-hand. He could only imagine the speed with which the Angevin must have acted. At one moment he was ambling along behind Rollo, humming. At the next he had leapt off his horse, drawn his sword and struck the rabid dog a lethal blow clean across the forehead as it sprang at Rollo.

Rollo remembered how he had already noticed the hands of a swordsman.

'How can you tell?' Sebrand had asked.

'Because your hands dance.'

Sebrand's whole body must have danced in those two – perhaps three – seconds. A dance of death.

'Thank you,' he managed to say at last.

'That was close,' was all Sebrand replied. Then after a moment he added with a laugh, 'I hope you don't think that's how we always welcome strangers to Anjou.'

The two men remounted, and with a final glance at the dead creature they rode on.

The River Sarthe ran smooth and clear, and their track followed the northern bank for several miles. Sebrand's eyes were fixed on the further bank as they rode. The sun was setting right ahead of them, staining veils of thin cloud purple and green that deepened in hue moment by moment. Water-voles swam in and out of the banks below them, and frogs leapt as if on springs from patches of yellow iris. A squat stone tower rose above the poplar trees ahead of them across the river and, as they approached, the roofs of a town began to emerge in a tight cluster round the church.

'There's where we spend tonight. Malicorne. And now, my friend, after your escape you'll know what hospitality is really like in Anjou.' Sebrand chuckled happily. 'Count Fulk forgets nothing. You'll see. It's no fun if you're out of favour, I can tell you. But for friends and honoured guests' – and Sebrand glanced quizzically at Rollo with his head a little on one side – 'well ... Anjou's a good place to be.'

For the first time on their journey Rollo caught sight of a

bridge, a wooden affair wide enough to take an ox-cart, but no more. Roughly built. Timbers placed more in hope – Rollo fancied – than purpose. He would have chosen longer and stouter timbers, raised the bridge in the centre to give greater elevation for boats and distribute more of the weight on either side. They clattered across and entered the first town they had encountered on their journey. Sebrand made himself boldly conspicuous, one hand raised, as he led Rollo down the centre of a rough-paved street that was lined with wooden houses pressed and leaning together. People were gathering to stare. Sebrand shouted some words of command that Rollo did not follow, then wheeled his horse to face what appeared to be the largest of the houses around them. Several people scurried inside, calling excitedly. And as the two men on horseback waited in the open street a crowd whispered around them in a gradually narrowing circle. The fair curly head of Rollo was the centre of attention. There was much nudging and pointing. Some of them were putting their fingers to their eyes and turning to the others with looks of astonishment. If anyone in Malicorne had ever seen a lofty Norman like this, it was probably only the grandfathers among them and no doubt there were toothless elders in that crowd to whom the stranger brought back terrifying childhood memories. Rollo felt uncomfortable in the focus of all those querying eyes. Sebrand appeared to take no notice at all, merely turned his horse once or twice to press back the throng.

Lanterns were glowing within the inn and the sky turning a deep flush of sunset as the innkeeper hurried out to greet the two horsemen. He was breathless and heavily whiskered, and his roly-poly wife was scurrying after him making last-minute adjustments to what was clearly his best leather jerkin, before scuttling back inside. Her voice could be heard shrieking orders, and more lights began to appear through slotted windows. A boy groom hurried over to hold the heads of the horses, but Sebrand had already dismounted, tossing the reins to the boy and — as an after-thought — a couple of silver coins which the boy pocketed as though they were burning his hand. To Rollo's surprise Sebrand embraced the innkeeper who then bowed as low as his jerkin would permit, revealing white linen shirt-tails which Sebrand reached forward and tugged to the enter-tainment of the crowd.

They entered. It was the first night Rollo had ever spent in an inn. Often in summer he had slept under the stars, pine-needles for a pillow: sometimes Ebba would return as fresh as milk in the first light, and they would saunter with their arms round one another through the forest, she then running to the village with a wave as they approached the road, he wandering back towards the monastery. Otherwise he had spent every night within the walls of Jumièges since the day he arrived there as a lost boy.

The inn was dark, the walls stained even darker by the smoke of candles that were thrust here and there into tall stanchions. The lights flickered in a breeze from invisible windows. Heavy curtains were tied back to reveal a spaci-ous room set with long wooden tables where more candles were burning, and where a girl with her back to them was kneeling before an enormous fireplace, piling sticks and then logs on to a smoking heap of grey ash. Even on mid-summer's night the inn was cool, and as the fire began to blaze Rollo welcomed the warmth that filled the room and spread out into the draughty corridor.

Rollo waited while a boy carried in his belongings and then beckoned him to follow him up a rough-hewn stair-case. Sebrand could be heard giving instructions to the innkeeper somewhere down the end of the corridor. He could see the double shadow of the two men enlarged against the far wall. The boy led him up to a second corridor above and pulled aside another heavy curtain to reveal a handsome room where just a single candle stood lit on a wooden table in the centre, and in the shadows Rollo could pick out a plain bed on which a black bearskin rug had been thrown. The boy bowed and left him with his packages; then he returned a few moments later with more candles, a pitcher of hot water, followed by a basin, a rough towel and woollen slippers. Rollo was embarrassed to have no coins for the boy, but at that moment Sebrand appeared through the curtain wearing the broadest of smiles. He pressed a piece of silver into the boy's hand and told him to carry his own baggage to the next-door room.

'So, welcome to Anjou, my friend,' he said, grasping one of Rollo's hands in both his. 'Tomorrow night we'll be at Angers: you'll have better accommodation, I promise you. You'll be able to stand upright without grazing your skull. They're not used to giants in this town.'

Sebrand proceeded to tell him what he had fixed with the innkeeper. A reliable man, he said, a vassal of Fulk's. He, Sebrand, had stayed here many times. 'You get good treatment. A guest of Fulk is royalty – you'll see,' he said with a broad smile. 'You wouldn't believe it, but the old man was a fine soldier. Fulk's father gave him lands round here in thanks, for which tonight we shall benefit.'

As he spoke Rollo recognized the smell he had been aware of for some minutes. Above that fire the girl was coaxing as they entered there must now be a suckling pig turning on the spit. He realized he felt ravenous and desperately tired.

'And we'll have the finest Anjou wines. Fulk's command.'

Sebrand tugged back the heavy curtain and shouted, 'Wine'. Then he peeled off his jerkin and opened his shirt, running a hand across his chest.

'You're a stranger, Rollo,' he said becoming serious, 'and it must all seem unfamiliar to you.' Then he added with appealing courtesy, 'So I hope you'll forgive my own excitement at coming home. I want to tell you how welcome you are: I admire you and I hope we shall be good friends.'

Rollo felt touched by the formal little speech. He took Sebrand's hand again and squeezed it.

'But don't crush me to death, Viking.'

Rollo withdrew his hand with a laugh. He liked the young Angevin the more the better he knew him.

'And now I'll leave you. We'll dine in about an hour, Gaspard says. But first have some wine.'

The curtain twitched and a girl was standing at the entrance to the room, bearing a tray with a pitcher and a single pewter beaker. It was the same girl Rollo had seen preparing the fire. She had black – almost blue-black – glossy hair and bright dark eyes, and she looked straight at Rollo without expression and without fear. Her skin was of a strange smoky pallor he had never seen.

'We have the best slaves here in Anjou,' said Sebrand with a flicker of a smile as he moved to leave the room. 'How's your Arabic?' And he pulled the curtain behind him with a chuckle. Rollo could hear him whistling cheerfully as he made his way to his room.

The girl placed the tray on the table in the centre of the room and filled a beaker. Then without glancing at Rollo again she departed very quietly, a slim shadow in the candlelight. Rollo downed the wine as if it was ale. It was sweetish and pale, and it seemed to go straight to his eyelids. He stretched out on the bed, his head swimming with tiredness and wine. All his limbs ached from his exertions by the river. He could hear Sebrand still whistling enthusiastically in the neighbouring room, and the disembodied sound accompanied his mind into a haze of sleep.

Rollo had no idea who was shaking him, where he was, hardly who he was, but gradually the face leaning over him he recognized to be Sebrand, and he began to piece together the world about him.

'Eat!' said Sebrand.

Rollo grunted something, blinked, and gradually roused himself: he doused his face with water, dried it, and became aware that the pain in his body was hunger.

The innkeeper was waiting for them at the foot of the

stairs. He bowed again as he held back the curtain, and the two men entered the same room that Rollo had noticed on arrival where the dark-haired girl had been making up the fire. But now it was transformed. Never had Rollo laid eyes on such a spread. An island of light was created by a circle of candles in the centre of a large table, and around the candles were set countless tureens and platters laden with different meats and fish, steaming vegetables, cheeses, butter, bread, sweetmeats of various colours and descriptions, bowls of this and that (Rollo had no idea what), jugs of goat's milk, fruits heaped into mountains, sauces and spices, and God knows what else in smaller vessels that seemed to fill each space between the larger dishes. And, as if this were not enough to feast a troop of travellers, over by the fire and glistening and sizzling on its spit, was the suckling pig whose aroma had been filling their nostrils.

The innkeeper bowed once more and departed, and as he did so a serving-girl arrived bearing a large pitcher of wine: she had a frizz of brown hair and an ample body loosely covered by a coarse grey dress, and a reddish shawl that fastened where the mounds of her breasts met. And in the valley of her bosom she wore a flower the same colour as the shawl, a deep coppery red. Sebrand let out a bellow of pleasure: hurrying forward he bent over and picked out the flower in his teeth. The girl giggled and promptly undid the knot of her shawl, tossing the garment on to a stool; then she filled two tumblers of wine and advanced towards the two men in turn, holding each tumbler exactly where the flower had been, cradled between her breasts.

To a further whoop of approval from Sebrand a second girl entered the room, bearing another pitcher: Rollo saw with delight that it was the same Moorish girl except that now she had changed into a pale linen garment that fitted her form like a slim glove. Her feet were bare and she wore a silver anklet above her left foot, and another dangling on her dusky wrist. Silver for a slave? Rollo wondered. Her beauty was strange and distant, as if she belonged to the shadows. Without looking him in the eyes she refilled his beaker, and as she did so her hair fell forward, caressing her arm and seeming to play with the silver bracelet on her wrist. Rollo noticed a fine black down on her skin. He drank the wine in one draught and, still without raising her eyes, she refilled the beaker. Then she moved silently over towards the fire and began to turn and baste the suckling pig with a ladle grasped in slender hands. Rollo felt a spur of excitement.

The two men were brought steaming joints of pork on large platters along with innumerable sweetmeats, fruits and savouries which female hands constantly laid before them in bowls or pressed into their mouths with gentle fingers. The evening swam deliciously into the night: the promised hospitality of Anjou overflowed until every candle had a twin before their eyes and speech slurred into song and song into laughter. Rollo's eyes repeatedly flickered over the slim dark girl and he longed to touch her each time she came close to him carrying fruit or wine, but some invisible barrier of coolness seemed always to keep her beyond reach and she floated away into the shadows beyond the candlelight. Sebrand had now swept his plates aside and was standing rather unsteadily wiping wine from his lips. He had removed his jerkin, and the girl with the froth of brown hair was fingering his white loose-fitting shirt, unlacing it, running her fingers through the mat of hair on his chest. In a single movement Sebrand raised his hands to her shoulders and swept the girl's dress down over her breasts. It subsided on the floor leaving her quite naked. Rollo gulped. Then Sebrand grasped a pitcher from the table beside her and poured the wine over her bare torso. The girl gasped and leaned back against the table, her head thrown back, rivulets of wine tracing the broad curves of her flesh, candlelight framing the silhouette of her body with gold. Sebrand's head was buried in her heavy breasts, his hands grasping her bare thighs. Rollo felt dizzy. He saw the Arab girl gazing at the two figures with an expressionless face. Sebrand raised his head and called out to Rollo – 'Come on! Your turn!' Then he lurched over to the Arab girl and before she could step back seized her shoulder and roughly pulled at her dress. She grasped at it and held it to her bare shoulders. Rollo felt a flash of anger: he stepped forward and caught Sebrand's wrist. He crushed it until he felt Sebrand relax his grip, then let it fall. The Angevin stood there in silence for a moment, looking at Rollo with a perplexed expression and flexing his fingers, swaying. Meanwhile the Arab girl was moving silently away towards the curtain. The silver anklet glinted as she moved and he noticed the slender curve of her back under the linen garment. With one hand on the curtain she turned and for a second Rollo caught the whisper of a smile. There was a flicker of the curtain and she was gone.

For a moment Rollo moved as if to follow her. Then he checked, and while he stood confused about what to do he knew it was already too late and he had no idea where she now might be. That was it. His head swam with wine. He needed to sleep. Tomorrow they would be leaving for Angers: he would never see the girl again. He turned back to Sebrand who was looking sheepish. Then he held out a hand to Rollo, who took it in his.

'Forgive me,' he mumbled. 'I shouldn't have done that. I'm drunk. Drunk. Forgive me,' he said again.

And with one of his swift changes of mood he bellowed out 'Drunk!' once more. As he did so he turned to the naked girl behind him and hoisted her over his shoulder.

'Goodnight, my friend,' he bellowed again.

Muttering incoherently, Sebrand staggered past the curtain bearing the slumped girl on his shoulder, who was protesting happily, her breasts and hair dangling. Rollo heard their faltering progress up the staircase, punctuated by curses and laughter. Then he was alone with the chaos of the feast and the flicker of a dying fire. For the first time since leaving Normandy he felt depressed and lonely. The prospect of Angers and an unknown life filled him with uncertainty and foreboding. He sat blankly near the fire, for how long he had no idea; then a chill began to settle around his arms and shoulders. He rose and made his way past the curtain and up the stairs lit by a single guttering candle. He felt more sober than he had a right to. His own room was dank and unwelcoming. Rollo undressed by the window where a deep grey light told him of the approach of dawn. Then shivering he crossed the room towards the bed where a candle lit up the black bearskin rug and the pile of pale cushions for his head. What he saw sent a spasm through his body. The Arab girl was lying there gazing at him, her black hair spread over the black of the fur rug. Rollo leaned over and very gently, slowly, pulled back the bearskin.

In his sleep the landscape of Jumièges was vivid, and he moved through it as though it were a part of him. Roughness of stone, scent of pines, rustle of the wind in tall bracken, softness of the earth floor under foot, quietness of still water. The miraculous closeness of touch, smell, sound; experiences that grasped and shook his vitals. They belonged to his body. The tower reaching upwards through the embrace of branches. The hidden pool, dark reflections of reeds parting as he entered, enveloping him. Lying still, exhausted, immersed, by the soft bank. They used to call him 'the boy from the sea', then 'the builder'. Soft and hard elements conjoined. After some immeasurable time he was aware of stirring, of images detaching themselves from him, receding into pictures and memories – the abbey, the forest, the lake. Further and further away. He was stretching out an arm, but there was nothing. He opened his eyes. The girl had gone. Like Ebba. The sun filled the room with a shock of light. He could hear voices. Sebrand was talking downstairs. He heard the click of coins. Rollo rose and dressed.

*

The two men left the inn about mid-morning. Sebrand was subdued – after the rigours of the previous evening, Rollo imagined. Neither of the servant-girls was in evidence, though Rollo kept his ears and eyes open for any hint of the Arab girl. It was as if she had never existed except as a warm shadow that had vanished with the light. He realized he knew neither her name nor even her voice: the only sound of her lingering in his mind was the soft sigh as her body tautened in his arms. For a moment as they were leaving the inn Rollo imagined taking her with him. He had even said as much to Sebrand, who laughed dismissively.

'I paid the innkeeper: that's it. You don't have to think about it.'

Then he added, 'It was Fulk's orders that you should be provided for.'

They were riding through the marketplace. Suddenly Sebrand reined his horse.

'Look!'

Rollo saw a low platform with a cluster of men round it. Some of them were shouting and raising their hands. Young men were being led up on to the platform, arms bound, dressed in rags. One of them was dusky-skinned. There were flies clustered on his shaven scalp. The next man was almost black – Rollo had never seen anyone that colour, and at first he wondered if he were a human at all. One of the onlookers was climbing up on to the platform and feeling the black man's arm-muscles, then looking at his teeth.

'Have you never seen a slave-market?' Sebrand asked.

Rollo had not. In the monastery they did not have slaves; only servants.

'You'll see them all the time here. A lot of them are Arabs – they're brought from Spain. Look!'

Three women were being led on to the platform. They had the same skin as the Arab girl, but their hair was dishevelled and dirty and they were wrapped in stained blankets. Their eyes were cast down and they shuffled across the platform, but unlike the men their hands were not tied. One of them was old and very fat and one looked no more than a child: she was clasping her hands together in front of her face. But the third was tall and proud-looking. Rollo could not tell how old she might be: perhaps twenty-five. She looked up and gazed straight at the crowd of men below her, which had suddenly grown in numbers. There was a murmur, and some laughter. A man climbed up and stood in front of her. He was shorter than she was, and rather fat. He put his hand up to her face, tilting her head back. Rollo thought for a moment that she might bite him, but she stayed motionless. Then with a rough movement the man pulled the blanket off her so that she stood quite naked. There was a roar of approval from the crowd, mingled with bawdy laughter. The man turned with a grin as if to acknowledge the applause. Encouraged, he turned back to the girl and pinched one of her dark nipples. The girl took a rapid step back, whereupon he gave a deep bow in mock apology. The crowd laughed again. Two other men replaced him on the platform: one of them examined her hands, and her feet. Then with a slap on her buttocks he called out something Rollo could not hear, tossed a few coins to a man standing to one side, and led the girl off, wrapped in her blanket again. Rollo saw the young girl gazing after her with terror in her face. But she never looked back, and they disappeared into the crowd.

Rollo felt a chill of horror in his stomach, and he thought of the Arab girl at the inn. He remembered her standing by the fire with the same proud expressionless face as the woman on the platform, and he imagined that slender body exposed to the mockery of this crowd. He felt angry with Sebrand; but again the young Angevin surprised him.

'They're beasts, some of these people. Bumpkins. I hate them.'

They left the marketplace and the town, and rode on in silence for a while. The track led through vineyards and ripening cornfields where summer larks rose as if on invisible threads. They crossed a stream and entered yet another forest where pigs snorted in and out of the undergrowth, scampering away as the two horsemen passed. It was the fourth and final day of their journey: that evening they would be in Angers. What to expect Rollo had absolutely no idea. Sebrand, so young and impulsive, took for granted so much that he, Rollo, was having to learn like a newborn child. The monastery had guarded him, protected him, and in some respects *was* him, or had been until three days ago. He had, after all, conceived it and built it. He had come to feel that he had no identity beyond the practice of those gifts for which now – by a twist of fate – he was being led like some travelling bear expected to perform for masters he did not know. He was intrigued, excited and not a little apprehensive. He was a builder – he knew that and that only – but a builder of what, for whom, and why?

Sebrand, as so often, seemed to read his thoughts, and for the first time began to talk about his own country. It was a strange story, and it unrolled from him as they progressed through the forest of ancient oaks until each oak seemed like a milestone in the young man's tale. First he laid out his country before Rollo's eyes. To the north, where they had come, lay Maine and beyond that Normandy. To the south spread Poitou and Aquitaine; to the west Brittany; and, most powerful of all, to the east was Touraine. Anjou sat in the middle of these, a small state that had squeezed an independence for itself between the fat lands of neighbouring princes.

'We're a rich country because we fight,' Sebrand explained solemnly. 'All my life there's never been peace. Not one year's gone by in peace. The only way we survive, and grow, is by circling the country with castles. And that, my friend' – and he turned to look at Rollo – 'is where you come in; because we have castles of wood, and they must be stone. Or we shall be squashed.'

Rollo looked at the Angevin in amazement.

'Castles! Does the Count imagine I know anything about castles?'

'No. He knows about castles. *You* know about stone. And you can build them. Oh, don't worry,' Sebrand went on, 'that's not all he wants. Fulk's a man of God: I think you might call him that.' And he let out a rather cynical laugh. 'He wants to build the greatest churches too, and monasteries. And he will. But to survive – now – he needs castles.'

The thought disturbed Rollo. He said nothing more. He considered himself to be a builder for peace, for God, not for war. So how could he build castles?

The forest had thinned and the track was leading up towards a ridge of heathland. A flock of large birds ran ahead of them along the path, then took to the wing, sweeping low and white over the rough grass before vanishing one by one over the curve of the hill.

'Bustards,' exclaimed Sebrand. 'I'll take you hunting with dogs. Then we'll dine like kings.'

And he returned to his story. It was what his father had told him, he said. There had been a forester called Torquat: perhaps more of a bandit than a forester, but then everybody who survived in those days did so by stealth. That was one hundred and fifty years ago, or thereabouts. And Torquat had a son by the name of Tortulf, who managed to acquire – by whatever means – those same forests which were extensive and abutted on the lands controlled by the wild counts of Brittany. This was the time of piracy and brigandage throughout northern France, and Tortulf managed to gather together so effective an army to defend these borderlands that the king ennobled him for his services, giving him as his bride the daughter of the Duke of Burgundy as well as the castle of Landon and much of the surrounding land.

So the family began to rise in esteem and riches, which Tortulf's son considerably furthered by a heroic act which was talked of to this day. He was Ingelger the Bold, and it was he who assembled his own army and rode far beyond Paris, to Auxerre, where he seized the holy relics of St Martin of Tours from where they had been kept since the Viking invasions and brought them back in triumph to the saint's city. So high was his stock that the French king awarded him the castle of Loches and built him another at Amboise, which rightfully belonged to the counts of Blois. The King also saw to it that he took as his bride the niece of two powerful bishops, of Tours and of Angers, who were brothers. In reality she was certainly the daughter of one of them, but nobody could be sure which since both bishops availed themselves of the same mistress. At any rate the sees of Tours and of Angers matched one another in contributing handsomely to the dowry, so that wealth and possessions abounded, and in time these were passed on to Ingelger's son Fulk the Red. And it was not only these that were passed on: Fulk the Red outdid the exploits of his two episcopal uncles by seizing the opportunity to share his own wife with King Philip I of France – a most profitable act of generosity since it acquired him the title of Count of Anjou, and further lands which the King prised from the lord of Touraine, the Count of Blois.

Sebrand was warming to his tale with a gusto that surprised Rollo, coming from a loyal servant of the present count; but Sebrand, again reading Rollo's thoughts, assured him that this particular part of the tale was often recounted by Fulk the Black with gales of laughter, as proof of the political skills of his noble ancestors. 'We've always been very successful with our marriages,' Fulk would announce.

They had reached the crest of a hill, and Anjou spread away beyond them – a patchwork of fields and forest, threaded by rivers. Smoke was rising in the near distance. Angers itself, Sebrand explained, lay about an hour's ride beyond where the smoke was rising. The black city of the black count! It was perched above the River Sarthe, only a short distance from its junction with the mighty Loire where the Viking pirates used to bring slaughter in the dawn before Fulk's father built castles to protect the villages and the land. He was Geoffrey Greymantle, grandson of Fulk the Red, and was called 'Greymantle' because he always wore the coarse woollen tunic of an Angevin peasant. A man of enormous valour, Sebrand explained, and a loyal servant of the French King Louis, descendant of the mighty Charlemagne. Once when the Normans were besieging the gates of Paris, Geoffrey answered the challenge of the Viking champion, a giant, and crushed him in single combat. Geoffrey used to tell how when he stripped the dead Viking of his armour and clothing the man's penis was standing rigid and it was big as a man's forearm. Men and women poured out of the gates of Paris to gaze upon this extraordinary sight.

'Which is why Vikings have a certain reputation, you'll find. It may not only be your violet eyes that people wonder about in Angers.'

The result of Geoffrey's victory, Sebrand went on, was a treaty of peace between France and Normandy. A lasting peace. It also sealed the bond between Anjou and the French king. In fact he was the only ally Anjou had. Sadly, the French crown had become weak, and the enemies of Anjou were growing stronger – the Count of Blois, the Count of Rennes, the Viscount of Saumur, the Viscount of Châteaudun. Then King Louis died, and in the same year Geoffrey Greymantle died; that was just seven years ago. Now the French king was Hugh Capet, who was a schemer. He would change allegiances like the wind. Fulk had been scarcely more than a boy when Geoffrey died, and immediately the enemies of Anjou had converged. The slaughter, looting, burning, rape – they were terrible: Sebrand could remember those years as a boy. Nowhere was safe. But they had not reckoned on Fulk. The black count became a match for any man, in wits, in strength, and in anger. Rollo would see for himself.

The two men had almost reached the foot of the hill. Below them to the left another river meandered through vineyards and peaceful meadows. The smoke they had seen earlier on the horizon was drifting in a soft veil beyond a wood that masked the river directly ahead of them. Rollo gave it no further thought, but Sebrand appeared concerned. He said nothing, and spurred his horse into a quicker pace. Rollo kept up with him. They were on the fringes of the wood now. Suddenly Sebrand cried out and pulled on his reins. A figure was lying face downwards in the track ahead of them. They dismounted, and as they approached they noticed that his back was stained with blood. Sebrand rolled him over. The man was dead.

Sebrand stood in silence. Then his face puckered with anger and he looked ahead along the track to where a few wisps of smoke were still drifting among the trees in the distance. On the track itself Rollo noticed the grass was speckled here and there with blood that had already dried almost black. You could tell where the man had staggered by the swarms of flies that settled where his life had been spilling away.

'Follow me and keep to the forest,' Sebrand said in a quiet voice.

They remounted and the Angevin led the way through the trees, keeping the path in view. The silent forest closed around them and neither man spoke. Every now and then Sebrand halted and looked about him, listening. But there was no sound except the occasional clatter of pigeons' wings among the foliage. After perhaps a quarter of an hour the forest seemed to be lightening ahead of them. Beams of sunlight leaned in bright diagonals between the oak trees, turning opaque as drifts of dust and smoke passed across them. Now Rollo could see a broad clearing that widened out as far as the river only a short distance beyond. And in that space nothing moved: there was nothing alive to move. The eye took in the scene piece by piece, as the mind grasped what the eye saw. The clearing was strewn with mound after mound of smoking ash: from some of them timbers protruded at ungainly angles, edged with thin blades of flame that seemed to ripple and dance in the pervading haze. A flame brightened as a fragment of timber fell with a crack into the heap of ash below: they were the only sounds to be heard. And all round these burning mounds the earth was black: Rollo realized as they rode slowly forward that they were fields, had been fields, now flat and almost neat as if a carpet of charcoal had been rolled over them.

Then the eye took in the bodies. Round the edges of the burnt fields – on the river bank – near the fringes of the forest – around each of the smoking heaps of ash and timbers: everywhere the two men gazed lay death. Chickens without heads. Pigs with their throats slit. Dogs hacked wherever the blade struck. And humans – children, babies, young women, old men, grandmothers, youths: they littered the plain like so many spilled sacks. Some had been hacked down near their houses and lay scorched where they fell. The younger ones, some of them, had almost reached the cover of the trees and were sprawled as if still in flight. A child, not more than three years old, lay clutching some wooden toy in a pool of its own blood. Makeshift weapons were scattered around them – staves, sickles, bill-hooks, metal rods, vine-stakes, pruning knives, kitchen utensils, a chair, an adze. And keeping company with these implements of despair were scattered the most horrifying testimonies of carnage: heads without eyes, hands without fingers, legs without feet, bodies without any of these.

The two horsemen rode in a numbed silence across this butcher's field. They could not even look at one another. They reached the high bank of the river and gazed back. Then Sebrand lowered his head to his closed fists and sobbed, and the sob turned into a scream. He uttered only one word, over and over again, each time with greater ferocity.

'Odo!'

39

Rollo was too sickened and horrified to ask questions, but he placed his hand on the other's arm, and Sebrand grasped it. For the first time their eyes met, and through his tears Sebrand smiled. Then, suddenly calm, he said, 'There's something more yet.' And he turned his horse and began to follow the towpath upstream. Bodies littered the bank, some half-submerged in the water; one was caught in the reeds face downwards with an arrow in its back. A family of wild duck was feeding in the sedge around it. Then round a bend in the river they both saw what Sebrand had guessed. A round hill perhaps sixty feet high rose steeply from within a circle of ditches and low banks. At the top it seemed flat and covered an area maybe a hundred paces across, though this was hard to determine because the entire surface was an uneven pile of ash, as though someone had used the hill to build a gigantic pyre. The sides of the hill might well have been grass, but there was scarcely any grass to be seen. Sebrand let out a long gasp. Around the entire slope — ordered, in ranks, with much care — lay dead men head to toe, each one skewered by a spear. The hill bristled with death.

Rollo leaned over and vomited. Bewilderment and horror swept through him. He wanted to ride, run, anywhere, for no purpose except to be away from this scene. He was hardly aware of what was happening. Sebrand seemed to be leading, grasping his reins. They had forded the river; another forest enclosed them; then open pastures; then there were houses as though what they had witnessed earlier was only a nightmare; Sebrand had dismounted and was talking to a huddle of farmers; he was returning and they were riding again. The fields were green and comforting. Larks. Sunlight. Wild roses. Traveller's joy. Rollo realized he was weeping uncontrollably with the tremendous relief of tears.

It was Sebrand who broke the silence. He sounded calm and earnest.

'Now you know why we need you ... That used to be the castle of Durtal. ... You would have found a way of building it so it would have held.'

Rollo felt confused, and trapped. The unimaginable horror of what he had witnessed that morning had left him numb with revulsion. Nothing in his life had ever prepared him for such a scene. To be recruited and led here, to this barbaric land, so that he might help people fight this kind of war; the thought revolted him. He had imagined in his innocence that such brutality belonged to the past, that the world was healing its wounds. Even Sebrand revolted him at that moment: as a soldier, was he not yet another instrument of this barbarity? All his life he, Rollo, had been trained to be a man of peace, a man of God. And now ...!

Then, like a second wave breaking on the first, a tremendous anger caught him. He wheeled his horse and gazed back to where the smoke of Durtal was hidden now by the forests and fields rolling away from them. And in his mind he gazed far, far back – to those towers of Jumièges that rose like prayers lifted to heaven. He had built them in the love of God; he had followed a vision of that place like a servant, never doubting that it was good, because God was good. In that case *why – why* this carnage? If God was good why had He created humans so naked, so helpless? Where had God been when Durtal was plundered? A cord of faith seemed to snap within him. Welling up within Rollo was a burning anger of betrayal. He had, after all, built for a cruel God. Before his eyes rose the image of that dead child still clutching its wooden toy in a pool of blood. That little hand! And he looked at his own calloused hands. Tears were flowing down his cheeks, falling on to those strong hands of his held out. He could have caressed that child at this moment, washed away the blood with his tears. He wheeled his horse again to where Sebrand was waiting. Rollo barely noticed him. He stared at the path ahead, and knew what he must do. He would build – he vowed – for *men*. He would build castles such as not even God's thunderbolts could touch. Castles of stone that would rise up impregnable – like the towers of Jumièges, but linked by flanks of stone that no man could scale, no man could burn. Massive square fortresses guarded at all four corners. Why not? Already he could see them before his eyes. Then this slaughter would not have to be: these mason's hands would build so that people did not have to die like pigs within the cold sight of God.

Sebrand was staring at him in wonder.

'Your eyes. They're red! Like fire!'

'Tell me, Sebrand,' he asked quietly, 'who is this Odo?'

'I'll tell you.'

And so for the last stage of their journey Sebrand spoke more about his own country. Rollo listened in silence. By the time the two horsemen came within sight of the last river, beyond which Angers lay, he had in his mind a sketch of this new world into which he was riding. What Sebrand told him was this.

The most dangerous of Fulk's enemies was Odo, Count of Blois, lord of Touraine. He was grizzled, pock-marked, proud, ruthless. He strode the kingdom of northern France like an angry bear. His right hand held the throat of the king, his left hand was poised to crush Anjou. Fair Anjou. Before Fulk's time his father Geoffrey Greymantle, the man who struck down the Viking champion, had struck at Odo. He led an army against Tours and in single combat hacked off his left arm. None the less it had been Geoffrey who died. Some said that Odo's presence was enough to kill; and with that remaining arm he wreaked the most terrible vengeance. He never spared the life of an Angevin. As he grew up, the young Fulk watched the blood flow, powerless. But all the time a fury was brewing in him. The day came when he called his vassals around him and made a vow that he would never rest until he had brought Touraine under his heel. Then he too struck. Barely eighteen, he summoned his viscounts to call up their men and horses. And on his black stallion, Moro, Fulk led an army along forest tracks by moonlight until he was deep into Touraine. Before them lay one of Odo's strongholds, Langeais. At first light Fulk took four knights with him: they were Sebrand's father Barthélémi, the High Constable; Roger the lord of Montrésor – Roger the Devil; and the two noble brothers Archambaud d'Amboise and Sulpice de Buzançais. The five of them rode like a storm out of the forest. Before the alarm could be raised they overpowered and slaughtered the guard. Then they smashed open the gates with axes. Fulk himself was the first to break through. Within ten minutes his army had seized the town.

But Fulk was young and overconfident. That same day, while he himself held Langeais, Fulk dispatched a contingent of his army still further eastwards to pillage and menace Odo's capital itself, Tours. They were to draw blood and return that evening. It was foolhardy. Fulk had not reckoned on Odo's resourcefulness or his speed. The army was ambushed in a narrow stretch of meadow between the high rocks and the river; and as the sun sank Fulk saw barges floating downstream piled with human heads. Such was Odo's revenge.

That was Fulk's baptism. But he had other enemies. Chief among these was the Breton, Conan the Treacherous, Count of Rennes and lord of Brittany. Now Conan was the ally of Odo, and between them they would strike at Anjou alternately, one from the east, the other from the west. Conan was sly as a weasel. Geoffrey Greymantle had defeated him in battle and spared his life on the condition that he cede the city of Nantes to Anjou. Nantes commanded the Loire just beyond the territories of Anjou to the west. Conan agreed to Geoffrey's terms and was set free. For some years Nantes became Geoffrey's and then Fulk's protection against a stab in the back while grappling with Odo.

And then – Sebrand went on – Conan broke his word.

The Count of Nantes, Fulk's vassal, had died without an heir except a bastard nephew, Judicael, a mere boy. Conan drove out Judicael and appointed himself Count of Nantes. The lean and cunning Breton was poised to strike again at Anjou.

'Now you'll begin to understand what happened at Durtal, my friend.'

Sebrand reined his horse and turned to face Rollo. The young man's thin dark face was intense and stern.

'The day I departed from Angers, Fulk was gathering his army,' he explained. He had sworn to crush Conan for good. It was the greatest army ever seen in France, with allies from Maine, from Poitou and from Aquitaine. But Conan had his allies too – from Vendée, from Vitré, even from Normandy, from Cotentin and Avranchin where the Duke's power was still weaker than old hatreds, and where they still spoke the old language of the Viking pirates. Today, tomorrow, within a very few days at most, news would reach Angers of the outcome. If Fulk failed ... but Fulk would not fail.

'My father's there. My cousins. Friends. And I wonder who will come back.'

Sebrand's voice sounded bitter as he spoke.

'I would have been there too ... this sword would have spilt some Breton blood, I assure you. Instead, I've had to witness what happens when Fulk's back is turned. That was Odo's doing – Durtal! Now do you understand?'

Rollo felt like a man who had been baptized with blood. He gazed at the Angevin, at that passionate young face that was suddenly so much older, almost weary. No one Rollo had ever met lived his life like this. He thought of the calm monks, the old abbot, in the quiet garden of their forest, wreathed in God's peace. What did they know of this?

'These hands', Rollo replied, 'will do what they can for you.'

The two horsemen rode on. Then in a short while Sebrand

reined his horse again. They had reached the crest of the last hill.

'Look!' he said.

Rollo saw ahead of him the city that was to be his home. In a flash of gold, an oriole swooped across the river into the shadow of Fulk's fortress.

TWO

THE CLOSER YOU APPROACHED ANGERS the lower the city shrank behind its great walls, until only the dark bulk of Fulk's bastion loomed above them, keeping watch slit-eyed over the vineyards and the forest. It was hard to believe that almost three thousand people actually lived and worked in those invisible spaces between the walls and the castle; but once you were inside, those spaces seemed to expand into a bewildering tangle of buildings. Houses of red flintstone and brick, propped with timbers and faced with sheets of black slate, leaned and jostled against each other, their roofs parted by a ragged strip of sky barely the width of a man's reach. Below those ribbons of daylight lay a warren of streets that echoed with the cries and batterings of numerous trades: there was a street of the bakers, a street of the saddlers, another for the grocers, another for the butchers, and so on in a labyrinth of smells and sounds – smiths, shield-makers, wine-sellers, cordwainers, fishmongers, furriers, fullers, potters, basket-weavers, pewter-merchants, tinkers, cheese-makers. Along these alleys wandered itinerant vendors of leather and laces, knife-grinders, chair-menders, women carrying baskets of herbs, or leather belts slung from their shoulders, or linen and serge drapes, or beads, ointments, charms, love-potions, love-cures. Then there were the beggars – the legless and the blind, the halfwits and the maimed, the drunks and the crazed, the palsied and the starved; the ones who muttered, the ones who shouted, the ones who stared, the ones who plucked your sleeve as you passed, thrusting their wounds or their wares before your gaze.

Yet within this choking labyrinth every now and then a splash of sunlight broke upon patches of open ground. One such area was crammed twice weekly by country people bringing to market their fruit and turnips, pigs, goats, poultry and eggs. Another lay before the tower where the executioner lived — a tower that was linked by a stone platform to the city wall where gibbets and iron cages were perched high over the river bank. Another patch of open ground announced the house where the Count's agents collected their weekly dues, and in the centre of this space stood the stone cross where the Count's edicts were read. Nearby, the widest area of all linked the main city gate to the entrance of the Count's castle; and here on spring and summer days you could watch the spectacle of Angevin knights returning from their travels, riding haughtily past in their bright surcoats, and accompanied by their ladies with their wide sleeves of crimped linen and their flowing cloaks of fine cloth. The townsfolk would gather round staring, beggars rush or hobble towards them in the hope of a few coins tossed into the dust; and the huge gates of the castle swing open to receive them into the Count's stronghold.

Then there were the more regular to-ings and fro-ings. All day, each day, those gates would open just a foot or two to let in and out scores of the Count's *familia*, as they were known: trusted retainers who served and serviced the occupants of the castle — the cooks, the kitchen hands, the maids, the artisans, the attendants, the agents and provosts, chamberlains, guards, entertainers, musicians, provision merchants, apothecaries, priests, hunters, falconers, astrologers, wet-nurses, and heaven knows what other categories of humanity that supplied the wants and whims of that secret world within.

The castle was a labyrinth too. It had grown inwards from its walls. For every spacious hall or refectory there were a dozen small and dark rooms and almost as many small and dark passageways between them, and only the regular inmates of the place understood the geometry of so confusing a web. People could have lived separate lives for ever in the corners of this lamplit cavern had it not been for the urgent presence of the Black Count himself, who drew all inmates around him as if on strings and gave to all of them a sense of risky importance – importance because he might need their services at any hour of his choice, risky because any laxity in fulfilling that service could find them ejected from that formidable gateway and perhaps contemplating the sunset of their days from one of those cages that dangled over the flowing river. Count Fulk was not a patient man.

So, when the Count and his knights were away at war the mood of the castle was at once more tense and more indeterminate. An air of vulnerability pervaded: anxious eyes were to be seen scanning the landscape from the roofs and narrow windows for marauding patrols of the Count's enemies emboldened by the master's absence. There was the nagging fear that something might go wrong; that, instead of the triumphant return heralded by a hunting horn from far across the fields, some breathless messenger might stagger into the forecourt stuttering news of rout and death. It had not happened yet, and when Fulk was here barking orders no one even considered it a possibility. But now that he was away again, tremors of anxiety could be felt by everyone who walked along those passageways. They were apparent in the look of an eye as you passed, and in the tone of a greeting. This time, would he come back?

Something else surfaced too. It was as if the inner life of those who dwelt here was free to take over: hosts of separate ambitions, private quarrels, liaisons, jealousies, pettinesses and whispered confidences all began to occupy the place and to fill the silence left by the departed lord. The castle turned in on itself, watched itself, indulged itself.

If you could have been an invisible witness of events within the castle at this time, you would have been aware that, with Fulk away, the focus of attention was principally the Countess Elizabeth. This was for no better reason than the fact that her ears, after all, would select the first information of any private nature to be passed to the Count on his return: whatever she knew Fulk might soon know, and with a man like Fulk this could mean anything from ennoblement to a noose. Not surprisingly, then, people selected what they passed to her about the affairs of the castle of Angers, in the belief that she could be kept in the dark as it suited them. This was an idle belief since in fact no one possessed sharper eyes for seeing in the dark than the Countess, and in reality there was very little indeed she did not know about just as soon as it happened. She had a love of gossip so discreet that it was easily taken for polite conversation, so that people would impart news to her convinced that they were merely passing the time rather than giving intimate information. In her rooms in the sunniest part of the castle she spent her days much as she did when her husband was at home: she played with her little daughter, she sewed and embroidered, she sang, talked and laughed a great deal, and the people she saw most were those ladies and maids who had accompanied her from Vendôme when Geoffrey Greymantle led her to Angers seven years earlier to be the bride of his young son and heir. Then everyone in Angers had marvelled at her elegance and her looks: she was tall, red-haired, slender, with a pale skin, and the most beautiful hands which seemed to mime as she spoke. And such composure, they all noted; no one had set eyes on a woman of such bearing, or heard such elegance of wit. She in turn had found the court of Angers to be a rough and rural place after life at Vendôme where she had been accustomed to the company of so many brilliant visitors who came to discourse with her father Count Bouchard the Venerable. Elizabeth was his only child; moreover as a widower he had been happy to let his sparkling daughter become hostess to that learned company, and was pleased to note how swiftly she took that learning upon herself. Marriage to Fulk was a powerful alliance: she had accepted it without demur. But the Count of Anjou, two years younger than herself, was not a man such as she was accustomed to, and the core of her life remained that pocket of gentility she had brought with her from her father's court. Fulk was – quite simply and unquestionably – her husband and her lord: that was it. She knew her duty.

'How long is it he's been away?' she enquired of one of her maids without looking up.

'Seven days, my lady.'

'Ah!'

It would have been hard to detect in her voice any note of concern, beyond concern for the barest facts.

'Is the Chancellor here?' she went on in the same straightforward tone.

This was not so much a question as an order: the maid recognized this and departed immediately. Unlike Fulk, the Countess did not hurl commands like rocks, but she was his wife and had learned the art of authority in her own softer way. The maid could be heard talking to the Countess's chamberlain, Garnier. A short while later the latter entered accompanied by a tall man with a mane of white hair, but an expression of such vigour and alertness on his face that immediately you saw him as a young man grown old. The staff he carried seemed more for dignity than for support, even when he leaned on it. This was Audemand, who had been Geoffrey's Chancellor and was now Fulk's. It was said there was no shrewder figure in Anjou, and none who was more kindly. Apart from Sebrand's father Barthélémi, Audemand was the only man in Fulk's entourage whom Elizabeth felt able to regard as a friend; he was the only man in Angers to remind her of those sage figures she had grown to love in her father's circle at Vendôme. Often she seemed to communicate with her husband more through this elderly man than with him directly. His advice she had learnt to respect and to trust.

'My dear Audemand,' she greeted the Chancellor with the loveliest of smiles, 'is there no news?'

'Nothing, my lady. Not yet. Only that young Chemillé reports that Odo has been skirmishing again while your lordship's back is turned.'

The Countess appeared to be only half-listening. She was wearing the same look of polite concern with which she would listen to Fulk's detailed accounts of matters outside her experience of life: war had never been a topic of much discussion in the circle of her father Bouchard the Venerable.

'So Sebrand has returned with his Norman,' she went on, skipping over the news of Odo's treachery. 'Tell me about him, Audemand.'

'He seems a ... a remarkable young man,' replied the Chancellor in his most diplomatic voice.

'And what does he look like?' Elizabeth went on. Her face wore that look of amused enquiry which some of the ladies of the castle took to be outrageously flirtatious and were happy to embellish as rather more than that when it suited them.

'Exceedingly tall, my lady ... a Viking.'

Elizabeth's eyes took on a mischievous sparkle, and she raised her eyebrows.

'A *real* Viking?' And she gave that slightly husky laugh which Audemand knew well. The Countess looked quite extraordinarily pretty whenever she was being provocative. He liked her. The corners of his mouth wrinkled into a slight smile.

'That I ... don't know,' he said with slow deliberation. Elizabeth gave another laugh.

'I wonder who will be the first who does. But go on, tell me more about him.'

'Well, my lady, I can tell you he has a handshake like a vice. I think I have at least two broken fingers. Apart from that I only know his reputation. The abbot, as you know, is

51

of the opinion that he is the finest builder in France: he has
seen his great work at Jumièges. Sebrand tells me he's a most
excellent fellow. And brilliant. Apparently he's already
rebuilt the castle.'

Elizabeth's eyes widened in surprise.

'Where?'

'In his head, I believe.'

'I see. And shall I meet this handsome young Viking?'

'I didn't say he was handsome, your ladyship.' Audemand's eyes creased with humour. 'But I rather think
that were I a young lady I might find him so. And of course
you shall meet him whenever you wish. I may say I have
found him a most agreeable companion – for a Viking.'

Audemand's face had the teasing look of one who knew
the young Countess's susceptibilities, and knew equally well
how little these governed her actions. She was gazing at the
old man with an impish expression.

'I shall look forward to that. Kindly tell him so.'

For so long now had Audemand been at the helm of the
castle of Anjou that it had become automatic to seek his
advice and opinion on anything whatsoever that took place
within it. He was wise. And, most important of all in this
place, he was discreet. The trust which the Chancellor
inspired was the more remarkable for being a rare commod-
ity here. No one as a rule trusted anyone in Angers very
deeply or very far: there were a few exceptions, of course,
but none so notable as Audemand. As a result he most
probably knew (though he would never had divulged it)
where just about everybody in the castle was likely to be at
any moment and what they were doing. He would certainly
have guessed that not so far away a much sadder young lady
than the Countess Elizabeth would also be parted from her
husband. This was Adèle, a mere child of thirteen, an
orphan, and whose only two relatives in this world were at

present away at the war — the brothers Archambaud d'Amboise and Sulpice de Buzançais who were her uncles. It was they who had arranged with Count Fulk for their little niece — then nine — to marry his younger brother Maurice as soon as she was old enough. Thus it was that a bewildered Adèle had found herself led from her uncle's castle at Amboise this spring and given in marriage to a man who she decided looked like a fat fish, and who proceeded to ignore her altogether after a few frightening and painful nights.

Maurice, as Audemand would have known, was idling his time in a lofty part of the castle overlooking the river, where he was even more undesired than in his young wife's bed. Maurice, just two years younger than Count Fulk, possessed none whatever of his brother's warlike ferocity, seeing no purpose in riding to arms when softer pleasures lay around him. Fulk, for his part, took the practical view that his brother's presence on a battlefield would be a conspicuous liability; and having married him strategically to the niece of two trusted vassals, the Count was happy to leave young Maurice nominally in charge of the state in his absence. The arrangement fitted Maurice like a glove. He gave orders when it suited him (Audemand saw to it that they were rarely obeyed), he dressed lengthily and with fine attention to colour, he drank the good wine of Anjou, he ignored his trembling twig of a wife, and he made good sport with as many other women as possible in those hours remaining.

In this direction Maurice had one special weakness. Like many a young man who likes women, Maurice liked them with passion only when they failed to like him at all. And this was the case with the girl from Brittany, Hersende, in whose unwilling company Maurice chose to dally a great deal of his time. She became all too accustomed to his arrivals unannounced: her position in Fulk's court, on sufferance, made it impossible for her to insist even on common courtesies from the Count's brother. Maurice knew this, and with a bully's instincts importuned her the more, to the extent of pushing his way past her maid at an hour when he had good reason to think she might be dressing or undressing. Nothing in his wanton life gave him such a thrill of desire as to observe her snatch a garment before her body as he swept into her room; not even the flashes of hatred from her eyes blunted the pleasure he took at those stolen glimpses of breast and thigh.

Maurice laughed.

'What a waste. Can you really be a virgin still, Hersende? I tell you, every man in the castle lies at night with his wife dreaming of you. Including me.'

Hersende turned her back on the intruder while her maid hurriedly arranged a screen between them, throwing him a frightened look. By the inner door stood a younger girl, shy as a fawn. Maurice noticed how beautiful she was becoming. He took stock of her and leered – and she vanished.

The two girls were sisters, though you would never have guessed it from either their looks or their natures. Hersende was the elder sister. She was seventeen, fair-haired and buxom, with a roundish and pleasing face that was dotted with freckles. The appeal of her to men was doubtless the extraordinary shapeliness of her body – indeed, what man in Angers could have denied in his heart that she possessed everything he had ever lusted for? But women warmed to Hersende too – even those who felt compelled to count their own inches whenever she walked past them in her tight bodices and her dresses which seemed to emphasize rather than conceal what lay beneath. They liked her (at least most of them) because she had the sun in her nature. When she laughed it was like the bubbling of summer water, and when she smiled you felt warmed. The Countess Elizabeth would often send for her, and they would talk for hours on end, holding hands. Her eyes were green as a river and people called her 'the Breton girl'.

The dark, shy girl was her younger sister Milesende. No one knew her because she rarely spoke, but they became aware of her awareness of them – the way she watched with those moist black eyes, her mouth rather small and sad-looking, her black hair shining in the candlelight and in summer always pinned with a flower from the fields. No one knew how she got them. She seemed to be gazing at the world through the transparency of a dream, and it was the Countess Elizabeth who said that if that dream came true she would blossom into the loveliest woman in Anjou.

But there was a shadow over the two sisters. Their father was dead: he was Alain, Count of Nantes, that same count whom Geoffrey Greymantle had appointed to guard his western borders from the ravages of Conan of Rennes. He had died without a legitimate heir, and it was in support of Alain's deposed nephew Judicael that Fulk was at this moment leading his armies westwards. When Conan had seized Nantes on the death of Alain, his family had been forced to flee – not only the young Judicael but Alain's two daughters, who like their cousin were illegitimate, at least so it was believed since Alain had never troubled to acknowledge them. The late Count's wives had come and gone rather frequently, leaving dowries that became smaller with successive ladies. It was puzzling that the vagrant Count apparently had children by none of them, though there were these two beautiful creatures who grew up in his court and who – it was assumed – were his, though by whom and whether by the same mother no one had any idea. From looking at them the latter appeared unlikely, but neither Hersende nor Milesende had ever known any woman whom they called their mother; nor had Count Alain said a single word on the subject, and with his death the mystery was destined to remain locked for ever.

The arrival of the two ladies had been greeted at Angers with a mixture of excitement and concern – excitement mostly on the part of the male inhabitants of the castle, concern on the part of the females, and this was made worse by the knowledge soon imparted to them that the young beauties had neither lands nor titles and so were to all intents and purposes unmarriageable: they were not likely to be locked up safely in distant bastions under the jealous surveillance of this or that vassal of Fulk's. It was 'the Breton girl' with her fresh smile and prodigious shapeliness who invited the first arrows of jealousy along the corridors of the castle, until her charm and sweetness of manner won her friends even among those who felt inadequate next to her; as the months passed the more discerning wives began to view the dreamy beauty of the younger girl with the more troubled anticipation. Meanwhile the two sisters sat and did all there was to do for young ladies who adorned Fulk's court; they sewed in their rooms high over the river and waited — for what? They did not know. Love, certainly, but a love that demanded nothing more than what they were; and in Count Fulk's ambitious court such love was unknown.

The odious Maurice had departed, his daily offer to take Hersende's maidenhead having been received with the girl's usual silence. The two sisters were alone, Hersende sewing something or other, Milesende gazing out over the river and the fields.

'He's back, you know,' said the elder girl, breaking one of the lengthy silences the sisters frequently shared. 'I've seen him.'

Milesende registered no interest. She was accustomed to her sister's sighings over the young lord of Chemillé, who was so flirtatiously attentive and was so clearly going to obey his father and marry a nun-like widow from Maine. Milesende continued to gaze out over the fields. Soon Hersende would be called to the Countess, and she would wait to be alone, then wrap a grey shawl round her head and shoulders and slip out through the kitchens for an hour to walk by the river bank and pick flowers, watch the birds and the water-voles, and think about the day she might leave this place for ever. She would dream sometimes on her wanderings of those stories her maid used to recount to her as a child, about maidens dressed in rags who were really princesses though they did not know it, and how they would encounter wandering beggars who were really princes though they did not know it, and how their instant love for one another broke all kinds of terrible spells and miraculously castle gates opened to welcome them for ever and ever.

'And he's brought the Viking with him.' Milesende was not sure if her sister had been talking all the time, and she had only caught the first and last sentence. She shrugged her shoulders.

'He's very, very tall,' Hersende went on. 'Taller even than the Count, they say. Everyone is talking about him. And do you know, he has eyes that change colour like the river. And he climbs trees like a squirrel.'

'And why should he do that?' said Milesende. She wished the maid from the Countess would hurry up and call for her chattering sister.

'I don't know. But he can.' Hersende was smiling quizzically and wondering what effect her charms might have on the lonely Viking. Perhaps it might stir some jealousy in Sebrand and – who knows? – even divert him from marrying a grey stick of a widow who just happened to be the sister of the lord of Maine. A feeling of mischief crept upon her. Hersende was too good-hearted to wish Sebrand pain, but she was also in love.

Milesende was looking at her sister, and as usual had little difficulty in reading her thoughts. She felt a twinge of something she did not entirely understand.

'Nor is he married,' Hersende added with a little laugh.

'I know,' said Milesende almost to herself.

At this point a maid did appear, but to both the sisters' annoyance it was not to bring a message from the Countess Elizabeth. The girl announced the presence of a man almost as unwelcome as the odious Maurice. Standing in the entrance was a sallow figure in black, stooped, his face grey as ashes, his hair in lank strands sprouting between bare patches of scalp as if a mouse had gnawed at it fitfully. He smiled at the two sisters, and his teeth were rotten. He had protruding eyes that were never still, and as they wandered over whoever he was addressing he had a habit of gulping as if swallowing morsels of that person. This was Baudouin. Father Baudouin. He was Fulk's chaplain, who added to his responsibilities the spiritual well-being of Fulk's entire court, especially that of its women. He was a figure of dark corridors as he made his pastoral rounds, leaving behind him a smell of must and bad breath and the lingering sound of muttered sayings of the prophets.

Baudouin had come to inquire after some small ailment Hersende had forgotten she had. The inquiry was lengthy, while Milesende turned her gaze back to the open fields, leaving her sister to receive the ministrations of the priest.

'I am most well, Father, I assure you.'

Hersende remembered she had not kissed his hand, which still hung limply half-directed towards her. She decided not to kiss it.

'Both my sister and I are in excellent health. And I hear, Father,' she went on rather breathlessly, changing the subject, 'that Sebrand is returned from Normandy bringing with him the mason that the lord abbot of Cormery recommended.'

Baudouin's face took on a severe expression.

'Beware of the attentions of such men, my child,' he said between gulps. 'Women who do not have husbands to protect them against themselves may succumb to the sin of vanity. Men are easily tempted by what is presented to their eyes.' The priest gazed at her rather harder.

Hersende, who had dressed in light colourful clothing for her expected summons from the Countess Elizabeth, was uncomfortably aware that her neck and shoulders were uncovered, and that the bulbous eyes of the priest were roving disapprovingly over those exposed regions. She lowered her own eyes.

'Of course, Father,' she mumbled. She was torn between a wish to cover the line of her dress with her hands and a stronger impulse to unfasten it until her breasts tumbled out in front of his horrible eyes: that would really give him something to stare at, she thought. It was hard not to giggle, so she kept her eyes lowered. The priest cleared his throat and gulped.

'Remember the words of Our Lord: "No one knows the day nor the hour – neither the angels of heaven, nor the Sun, but only the Father."'

Hersende nodded, desperately willing the priest to depart, but aware that his eyes were still boring into her. She understood neither the meaning of Baudouin's words nor their relevance to herself, yet felt as always the uncomfortable sensation of being accused. The priest's obscure references to divine punishment invariably left her with a desire to hurry away and wash, as though her body were covered with some particularly odious slime.

Then, with a final stare at Milesende, who had said nothing and was still standing gazing from the window, the priest bowed and departed on his next mission. At that exact moment the long-awaited summons from the Countess arrived, and with relief Hersende rose. She took a deep breath and waited a few moments to give Baudouin time to disappear along one of the wood-panelled passageways before following the maid down the winding staircase towards the Countess's rooms. By the time she arrived Milesende had slipped down a narrower stairway towards the rear of the castle, grey shawl over her black hair. Her accomplice, the jovial and rotund cook, surrounded by her tribe of children, watched with a smile as she made her way to the gate of the city. The sleepwalker, the cook called Milesende; and her kitchen was always decorated with wild flowers that the girl would bring back without a word. The cook enjoyed imagining adventures that were a great deal more robust than Milesende's daydreams of fair princesses and princes in disguise. After all, she reflected contentedly, but for such adventures of her own, she would not have quite so many offspring playing round her aprons.

Two days passed and still there was no news. Sebrand had departed with a handful of knights for a reconnaissance in the direction of Nantes. Rollo watched him go, marvelling at the transformation from the soberly dressed companion with whom he had travelled from Normandy into this splendid figure with his glittering helmet and armour whom the crowds cheered as he raised his lance and rode majestically out of the city gates.

Rollo had begun to grow accustomed to this extraordinary place. He had only ever lived in a monastery. He had never known what it was like not to inhabit an exclusively male world — a world in which women were outside the walls and, barring a few scandalous occasions, stayed outside. The notion that women formed part of the fabric of daily life, were even a dominant thread of it, was entirely new to Rollo and he found it bewildering, disturbing and intensely exciting. He grew daily more conscious of living for the first time amid the sounds, glances and perfumes of love. And there was another experience quite new. Thinking back to all those years behind monastery walls he realized that one of the qualities of life at Jumièges was something he had taken for granted as being what all life must be like, namely that each member of that community understood precisely what he was there for, and what every other inmate was there for. There were no secrets, except of course those that belonged outside the walls when lay members visited families and friends, and those secrets did not count since they in no way impinged on the life of the monastery. Inside, everything was open. Every hour, every activity, every word was accounted for. Here at Angers it was quite the opposite. The castle seemed entirely closed, cave of mysteries. In two days Rollo had met numbers of occupants of Count Fulk's court and household, and with a few exceptions — notably the Chancellor Audemand — he had managed to form no impression of what the place was about, what people did, and why they were there at all. It was true there were a good many wives and children, most of whose husbands and fathers were away at the war; but there seemed to be an even larger number of ladies who drifted in and out of the deep shadows of the castle and who apparently led lives entirely separate from each other and from everybody else. And there were almost as many men, most of them somewhat elderly, who appeared and disappeared in much the same mysterious way. They all seemed as casual as the birds that would sit on the castle roofs, and you had no idea if they were the same birds you had seen yesterday, or why they had chosen to perch there in the first place.

How entirely wrong he was came to Rollo only a good deal later. No stranger could possibly have realized that each inhabitant of this dark labyrinth in fact occupied a role that was precisely understood by every other, or that all of them conducted their lives according to a code just as well defined and just as inflexible as the Rule of St Benedict which governed each minute of the monks' day at Jumièges. Angers was an edifice of unwritten rules. There was one man who imposed them, namely the Black Count. And there was one man who implemented and supervised them with an eye wrinkled with long practice at such a task — the Chancellor Audemand.

It was Audemand who took charge of initiating Rollo into the more accessible ways of the castle. In the absence of the Count and his knights it was as well — the Chancellor explained — for the Norman to become acquainted with some of those who graced the Count's court. He used the word 'graced' with a rather quizzical emphasis and the raising of a bushy eyebrow which Rollo noticed to be a characteristic of the old man's manner: it was like the subtlest invitation to conspiracy. Rollo caught his eye: he sensed that here he might have a friend and a mentor.

'The Countess expresses her concern to meet you.' The Chancellor was leading Rollo through a perplexing tangle of corridors that creaked underfoot and were lined with hangings of heavy serge. It was mid-afternoon, yet only the occasional blade of sunlight penetrated the patterns of deep shadow through which they walked.

'She knows of course of your reputation as a master-builder; and she is interested, furthermore, to make the acquaintance of a real Viking.'

Rollo detected that same quizzical inflection, and as they passed a narrow window on the staircase he thought he caught a flicker of a smile on Audemand's face. Then another figure appeared ahead of them descending the stairs, and as he stepped aside to make room he noticed that it was a nun. He saw her face only for an instant as she passed the window and glanced at him, but what he saw sent a shiver through him. He had expected a gentle face of piety: instead what he saw was wild, savage and mad. It was a face that had the look of a woman possessed. Then she turned away. Rollo felt burnt by that look. Another figure followed: it was a priest. He muttered a greeting to Audemand without raising his eyes, and passed Rollo without a word. The Chancellor turned and called after him.

'Father, you should meet our Viking.'

The priest paused on the stairs below and turned his head with an unwilling smile. Rollo noticed the sallow face and prominent eyes that seemed anxious not to look at him. He was clearly straining to leave. Audemand placed a hand on Rollo's shoulder and tapped his stick on the stairs, while the priest hesitated nervously.

'Our friend has built a house of God for the Duke of Normandy, Father Baudouin. The worthy Abbot Gervais is most anxious that he employ his skills for us. Perhaps,

Father, you should talk with him on some occasion when your duties are less pressing.'

Again Rollo caught the knowing tone of the Chancellor's voice. The priest's eyes were hunting in the corners of the stairway as he took a step backwards towards the waiting figure of the nun, with her back turned towards them some ten paces lower in the shadows. Rollo saw the lump in his throat rising and falling, as his mouth opened and quickly shut again. Then as if with an unnatural effort Baudouin extended a thin hand for Rollo to kiss. It was like the touch of a reptile: the priest snatched the hand back and was gone. Audemand's staff tapped on the boards as he began to climb the stairs again.

'Father Baudouin is the Count's chaplain. A man much engaged in spiritual labours.' Rollo looked to see what expression was on Audemand's face, but the old man's back gave away nothing.

The castle grew lighter: the passageway suddenly was wide enough for the two men to walk abreast. Rollo noticed how the muscles of the old man's face were constantly on the move as if registering a continuous flow of thoughts. He wondered if he would ever know Audemand well enough to be able to read what was going on in that face: to do so, Rollo felt, would be to read the entire history of Angers and indeed perhaps much of the history of the world. The Chancellor fascinated him, and he felt certain that Audemand was fully aware of it.

'Here we are,' he announced.

An attendant was waiting. He bowed and without a word led them through a double doorway and along a further passage that opened into the only large room Rollo had so far seen in the castle. It was flooded with sunlight. Several maids were busying themselves here and there and glancing furtively at the stranger. Three figures were gathered by the window as they entered. One was a slight, wiry-looking man of about forty who had the face of a ferret and seemed about to depart. To the left, a fair-haired girl in bright-coloured clothing had her back to the visitors and was talking and laughing with a slightly older woman seated in the centre. The seated woman had a pale, delicately beautiful face that was set within a cascade of red hair into which strings of jewels were looped. The Countess Elizabeth looked up and smiled as the two men approached. Audemand leaned forward and kissed her fingers, and as he did so she rose and greeted Rollo with both hands outstretched. Unsure for a moment what to do, he took one hand in each of his and kissed both of them in turn rather clumsily, and she laughed.

'What gallantry from a Viking!' she said with such a glint in her eyes that Rollo felt himself blushing. 'You told me he was handsome, Audemand, but I didn't expect such beauty. Or such a size.'

The voice was slightly hoarse and affectionately mocking, and her eyes widened as if in pure amazement. Then her tone changed to one of such warmth that Rollo felt entirely at ease.

'You're so very welcome, Rollo: we've all heard a great deal about you and I'm delighted you're with us. And now I want to talk to you.' She took Rollo by the arm and he was aware of the sweetish smell of her hair. 'You've built one of the marvels of our time – or so the Abbot Gervais tells me: I'm deeply sad not to have seen it. Perhaps one day we may make a journey to Jumièges together and you can show me. I should treasure that.' The Countess was still gripping his arm and steering him away from the others in the room. 'You know,' she went on, placing her free hand gently against her bosom, 'I was brought up near the great school of Chartres. And we have our own places of learning here: our monastery of St Aubin was founded by my Lord Fulk's father, as you may know; and of course the abbey of Cormèry where the famous Alcuin was abbot after leaving the court of Charlemagne. Oh, these things are dear to me,

Rollo, and there's so much I want you to tell me. I feel quite hungry.'

The Countess released Rollo's arm and turned towards the others, making it clear with a look that she wished them to leave. Then she added, 'But Audemand, stay a while. You can make sure I don't get carried away.' The gently mocking voice had returned. She nodded towards the ferret-faced man, who bowed and took his leave.

'Good day, my lord of Combourg.' Then the Countess extended an arm towards the girl who was still standing turned away towards the window.

'Hersende, come and visit me tomorrow, my beloved.' The kindly tone did not hide the Countess's clear intention to get rid of her lady visitor as quickly as possible; neither did she intend to delay the girl's departure by introducing her to the young Norman. None the less Hersende had to turn and make the short journey to the door, and in that brief passage of time a lot happened to Rollo. He was conscious of a pair of large green eyes, widely set, that questioned his gaze for an instance as she passed. He saw a radiant face from which she flicked back her pale hair as she turned away. She was wearing the colours of a summer meadow, and her light garment was laced tightly round the smallness of her waist and loosely round the fullness of her breasts. Her neck and shoulders were bare except for a silver chain from which dangled a purple jewel that rose and fell on her skin as she breathed. Rollo was aware of a humming silence around his head, and into that silence a voice penetrated seemingly from far away.

'Come and sit with me here. You Vikings are so tall it's like talking to God.'

If the Countess Elizabeth was aware that a bolt had struck her visitor, then she certainly never showed it. She had a way of talking that made whoever was with her convinced they were more remarkable than they realized, and that she was uniquely capable of appreciating their talents. She looked at

Rollo closely, her hands making elegant gestures of approval while he described to her his work for the abbot of Jumièges, his love of building, his hopes for his work in the service of her husband the Count, and his willingness to bend his skills to the construction of military forts. Only on the last subject did her close attention to his words waver, and she steered him back to the art of building and how stone could be made pliable to the human imagination and to the human vision of a better life. These, she said, were the kinds of conversation she had so enjoyed in the circle of her father the Count of Vendôme: alas — she could now say it — there were few men in Angers capable of perceiving the joys of the mind. Rollo wondered if she were referring to her husband, but he noticed that she made no reference to him at all, not even to the fact that he and his armies were perhaps at that moment engaged in a conflict whose outcome might shake the security of her delicate existence. She talked of her delight in her little daughter, adding that she fervently hoped the girl might one day have the companionship of a brother, but God had not yet willed it so. She would love, she said with a laugh, to have six sons, all of them as tall and as handsome as her present companion. Would that not be wonderful? But only the most evil people seemed capable of breeding a tribe of males, she had noticed, people like the Count of Blois and Conan of Rennes — who really did have six sons, not counting heaven knew how many unofficial ones of different shapes and colours which only showed the promiscuity of the man's taste. An impish look returned to her face.

As if the change of tone opened the conversation to include others, the Countess made a flattering reference to the Chancellor, whose presence Rollo had forgotten. Audemand, smiling in his most knowing way, took advantage of the moment to beg her permission for him to leave them for a while — he had some affairs to attend to — he would seek out Rollo shortly and continue their perambulations when her ladyship was fatigued. He kissed the Countess's hand and departed.

'There goes an exception to my rule about fathers,' said the Countess firmly. 'Audemand has six sons. He knows me well enough not to take offence. All six are with Fulk in Brittany.' Rollo thought of the dignified Chancellor and marvelled at such composure at a time when for all he knew his family might lie bleeding on a battlefield.

The Countess Elizabeth showed no signs of the fatigue Audemand had suggested. A maid brought pastries and a perfumed infusion of some sort. The Countess doubted if such delicacies could be had in Normandy, and surely not within the stern Rule of St Benedict. She became more inquiring in the absence of Audemand. Was Rollo married? She presumed this would have been difficult in the circumstances of a monastic existence. So what did he know of women? Aha! Well, he would soon learn. She herself could not have endured to be brought up in the company only of her own sex. Most of them thought only of one subject, and so few of the men here in Angers were worthy of such single-minded attention – except, she imagined, when it came to swordplay. And she laughed dismissively. Had Rollo encountered many of the women here? She then enumerated some of them, omitting – Rollo was disappointed to note – the sparkling creature who was with the Countess on his arrival. He did not even know her name. Was she some lady-in-waiting? Or perhaps a visitor who might already have departed to a distant city? But no, he recalled, the Countess had asked to see the girl tomorrow: so he might have a chance to inquire gently from the Chancellor who she was.

Rollo's attention was brought back to the Countess by an account of some of the ladies he might care to meet. Oh, this was perfectly permissible whether their husbands were away or not: the customs of the castle, though sometimes decorous, she stressed, were by no means strict on such matters. There was Adelaide, for example. Her husband was the bravest of Fulk's knights: Roger. A terrible man, she added lightly, known to all as Roger the Devil. Dark and hairy as a bear, and as strong. He and Fulk would wrestle in front of the whole court when filled with wine. Fulk was the only man who could throw the bear, but then Fulk was ... well ... an unusual man. And the Countess wrapped her arms round herself and raised her eyes: it was the only time that Rollo sensed her marriage might be rather more than a political alliance. But Adelaide – she went on – Roger's wife: how she suffered. She was older than Roger by some years and had been married to the nephew of the bishop – Bishop Renaud. Rollo would meet him, a most devout man, but so stern about it. His nephew had been the same, and this suited Adelaide to perfection. She wore her beauty like a veil that was never torn. But then the bishop's nephew died and she found herself married to Roger – not someone to enjoy veils. The Countess laughed huskily. There were not many veils in Angers when Roger was around, as Rollo would find out. Poor Adelaide was distraught – with distaste and jealousy both together. She was growing old amid piety and tears. And no children – which was not so surprising, the Countess added with another husky laugh.

Then there was Ermengarde. Rollo would probably meet her husband the Treasurer, Bouchard: the Countess had asked to see him about matters relating to the cathedral, a donation. She wished to mention that Bouchard was Ermengarde's husband since he might otherwise have thought it unlikely: marriages, he must understand, were not usually to do with love. In Bouchard's case, she suggested, the arrangement worked surprisingly well: it would be indiscreet to reveal intimate details concerning one of her husband's most loyal servants, but she could safely say that the success of their marriage rested on a shared taste for beautiful young men. Most convenient and economical – Ermengarde would doubtless tell Rollo about it, as she told everybody, often in considerable detail, depending on how much she had imbibed. For Ermengarde, the Countess volunteered without the slightest embarrassment, was a thirsty consumer of Angevin wine and Angevin men in roughly equal proportions: intake of the one tended to prompt intake of the other. Not that Normans were excluded: far from it. Vikings had a certain reputation – the Countess smiled impishly again – and Rollo should be on his guard unless of course the experiment appealed to him. He would see. Ermengarde was in any case a delight and an entertainment, and the Countess loved her dearly even when she was drunk. She often envied her the freedom of her life, the Countess sighed. But for her marriage and her faith she thought she might love to have been very wicked indeed: she leant forward confidentially and then broke into a peal of laughter. As a matter of fact, she added, on second thoughts she greatly preferred other people telling her about *their* wickednesses; it was all much safer when you did not have to do it yourself.

For instance ... and the Countess broke into another story. Rollo had never dreamed to hear such tales from the mouth of a woman, least of all from the regal-looking wife of the most feared man in Anjou. He imagined such conversations taking place in the abbot's company at Jumièges, and found himself smiling. In retrospect he could not help judging those interminable debates about the miraculous properties of St Philibert's relics to have been rather dry.

The Countess Elizabeth was reminding him of the small, wiry man who had been in her company when he arrived – the Viscount of Combourg. It was with the example of this particular gentleman that she wished to illustrate her preference for the quiet life of the listener, as Rollo would understand when he heard the Viscount's story. And the story was this.

There was a Viscount of Combourg – the present viscount's father – who had three sons. One day the father was killed by a bear while out hunting, or so it was said: the circumstances were suspicious since the viscount's bodyguard were also killed, all except one who claimed that a whole party of bears had attacked them. Now everyone knows that bears do not go around in packs looking for trouble; and after being questioned further by the three sons the surviving bodyguard suddenly disappeared. It began to seem likely that the viscount had in fact been murdered at the instigation of the Count of Rennes, the present Conan's father. The reason was that the lord of Combourg had switched his vassalage from the Count of Rennes to Geoffrey Greymantle, Fulk's father, thereby giving Anjou further protection on the borders of Brittany.

The three sons agreed to combine in vigilance against further assaults from the lord of Rennes, the eldest son taking the title of viscount and the principal reins of power. Then, only a few years later, he too died, under circumstances that were equally suspicious, leaving a young boy – Eble – as his heir, in the custody of his father's younger brother, Bernard, the very man Rollo had met. The two remaining brothers armed themselves even more assiduously against the Bretons, and over the course of many years Bernard became one of Geoffrey Greymantle's most valiant knights. Meanwhile the boy Eble grew up in the castle of Combourg into a young man of reckless pride, hated by all and bent solely on taking over his father's titles and wealth as soon as he came of age. When this day arrived Bernard and his remaining brother decided to refuse Eble his inheritance and to allow him only the castle of Combourg, constructing a second castle as their principal fortress at Fougères, to the east. Eble was incensed, hurling a multitude of dire threats against his usurping uncles, but he was a man quite incapable of implementing any of them and thus spent his solitary rage on the foulest fantasies of revenge that echoed round the walls of the castle of Combourg unable to find an outlet.

Then one day Bernard's wife, a niece of the Duke of Normandy, was being escorted back to Fougères by Bernard's younger brother to tend her husband, who had been taken gravely ill. The road passed not far from Combourg, where the party was espied by some of Eble's men. On hearing of this Eble gathered the few knights who remained loyal to him and sent them out to surprise the party. Bernard's brother was ambushed, he and most of his bodyguard killed, and the wife taken prisoner and led back to the castle of Combourg. Here in the hall of the castle Eble had her stripped and bound and publicly raped her. Out of shame the lady afterwards threw herself from a castle window and died instantly on the rocks below. Eble had her body thrown to the kites, except for her left hand with its wedding-ring which he despatched to Fougères with a surviving member of the bodyguard.

Bernard was on the point of death when the knight arrived and delivered his gory token. But at the sight of it he let out a long howl and forced himself to his feet. With a quavering arm he reached for his sword and, just managing to raise it, he ordered his physician to cure him on pain of death. The physician consulted apothecaries and herbalists, astrologers and purveyors of all kinds of magic, and miraculously within a month the sick man began to regain his strength. After three months he was entirely restored to health, and one day he called for his horse and set out alone for the castle of Combourg. His knights were fearful for his safety but he refused all assistance. Arriving within sight of the castle just before dusk Bernard drew his sword and proceeded to ride slowly round and round the walls taunting Eble with every known curse and insult in a loud voice. News of his uncle's appearance reached Eble at the hour when as usual he was beginning to float with wine; and hearing that the man he had longed to destroy for many years was alone he seized his own sword and rushed out to meet him. Seeing him, Bernard calmly dismounted, tethered his horse and waited while the outraged Eble hurled himself upon him. But he was too drunk to remember he was no swordsman and in less than a minute Bernard had wounded him grievously, disarmed him and thrown him to the ground. Then before the entire castle of Combourg he cut off Eble's offending member and cast it to the dogs, leaving his nephew dying in a pool of blood and screams.

'You see, my Viking, why I prefer a quieter life. We live in violent times.'

Rollo was looking at the Countess in amazement. To hear such words from so elegant a lady cast a shadow over his sweet bright notions of what women – as he thought – were supposed to be. Then, before the Countess chose to embark on any further revelations, the chamberlain entered, bowed low and backed away in favour of a papery-looking man who announced himself with an ingratiating smile and a whimper of greeting. This Rollo took to be the Treasurer of Anjou, Bouchard, of whose peculiar marriage he was promised such intimate accounts – but not, he hoped, just yet: the castle of Angers had already unfolded enough of its salacious secrets for one day.

Rollo rose and prepared to take his leave. He kissed the Countess's hand with more confidence this time and caught a twinkle in her eye.

'I shall ask my chamberlain, Garnier, to take you to the garden. Audemand will meet you there shortly before sundown – and that cannot be long.'

The Countess glanced at the window where the midsummer sun was already casting long streaks of orange across the brickwork. A white dove flew past the open window. The huddled roofs of the city squatted below them, and beyond the city walls lay the fabric of evening vineyards and small fields.

'I've learnt to love Anjou,' the Countess added, seeing Rollo follow her gaze. 'There's so much peace here, and yet sometimes it's hard to believe it.' And she sighed.

What a very beautiful woman, Rollo thought. And what an enigma. He took his leave and followed the chamberlain out through the double doors. At that moment he wished he were back at Jumièges in a familiar place with familiar people – the place that he had built and which was a part of himself. In this land he felt a child.

Rollo waited in the garden as the evening light softened from gold to violet. It was an area scarcely larger than one of the rooms of the castle, and like a room it was oppressed by huge walls, but with the sky for a roof. He was accustomed to the monastery garden with its row of beehives and its neat rectangles of herbs set between gravel paths, and monks shuffling in black robes carrying baskets on their arms. Here there was nothing but a single flowering tree whose branches, laden with blossom, almost brushed the walls. Looking up, all he could see was an expanse of blue embroidered with tiny white flowers. Then he noticed movement in the branches, and peering more closely he realized that the tree was crowned with white doves. Rollo moved his head and they rose in a tremor of wings, circling against the deepening sky until they settled one by one high on the castle wall where a series of ledges protruded beneath a pattern of spaces in the brickwork to make a dovecot. He looked down and saw the Chancellor standing by the entrance to the garden, his old hands clasped over the knob of his staff and his head on his hands. Audemand was wearing that familiar quizzical smile: Rollo wondered how long he had been there.

'The Count's white doves. The birds of peace: you might imagine they'd fly away.'

The Chancellor motioned Rollo to follow him. They made their way indoors along more corridors, moving from oil-lamp to oil-lamp, the sound of Audemand's staff echoing around them. They were making for the rear exit from the castle, he explained: it was used mostly by servants but it was the quickest way out to the cathedral. The Chancellor was anxious for Rollo to meet the Bishop, who would be waiting for them: Rollo would soon see why. The smell of roasting meat rose from what were obviously the kitchens somewhere to the right: Rollo could hear the sounds of laughter and raucous voices. Then the figure of a young woman passed them carrying a bunch of wild flowers; beneath her grey shawl Rollo caught sight of long black hair and a pair of dark eyes that were turned on him for a moment in the lamplight. He remembered the Arab girl in the inn at Malicorne.

They passed from the labyrinth of the castle to the labyrinth of the streets. Few people were about. The old Chancellor's staff tapped on rough paving-stones. Cats slithered between the shadows and dogs barked at them from within dimly lit houses. Rollo noticed how the black slate walls shone silver in the twilight and realized that a moon had risen somewhere behind the tangled roofs. Then ahead of them the street widened into an open patch of ground, and beyond it the moonlight lit up a jagged hunk of stonework that was fallen into rubble at one end and rose to a squat tower at the other. In between ran a line of mean windows, scarcely more than holes, some with plants sprouting from the broad cracks in the masonry. A faint light from inside picked out the silhouette of wooden props, and through one of the windows Rollo could see a shrine with the carving of some saint lit by a mean oil-lamp. So this was the cathedral.

They entered the west end by a narrow doorway that was no more than a rectangular space in the wall. A rat scuttled over powdered rubble into the inner shadows, and the floor was littered with dried excrement. Moonlight poured in from what Rollo at first imagined to be a window until he realized that the entire west end of the cathedral had collapsed and was open to the sky. Where they were standing

e ceiling was still intact, though slabs of stone from the
w roofing had become dislodged and had either fallen or
mained perilously wedged between their neighbours,
me of which were equally askew. Rollo noticed two rows
f squat round columns on either side of the narrow nave:
ese rested on hunks of rough-hewn square stone and rose
scarcely more than head height where they supported a
ries of battered capitals. Round the sides of these were
af-patterns carved with some primitive tool, and above
em various crude geometrical shapes — an endless knot
twined within a circle, loops cut to resemble twisted rope,
en scrolls, bulbous shapes that were mere blobs, some-
ing that might have been a flower, and on one of the
pitals the head of a pig turned sideways with its nostrils
st two lines and two holes and its eyes two further holes.
ll the carvings — Rollo thought — looked as though they had
en roughly moulded out of mud. He looked up, and saw
at the roof from where it had collapsed right up to the arch
hich divided the nave from the chancel was nothing more
an an extended stone lid: smears of light found their way
to it from the misshapen holes of windows on either side.

He heard Audemand's voice close to him.

'The Bishop is waiting for us.'

Rollo half-expected a figure as broken as his church and
as surprised to see a man as tall as the Chancellor and with
bearing that was upright and proud. He had a lean,
wk-like face, and he stood there as if he were a monarch in
s castle. He extended a long arm for Rollo to kiss the
shop's ring, but the face retained its aloof pose and regis-
red nothing. Audemand spoke to him and for the first time
ollo detected in the Chancellor's voice a note almost of
ference. The two men discussed various small matters of
e cathedral and then Audemand introduced the subject
the Countess's donation which, he affirmed was at the
press command of Count Fulk and was to be generous.
ll the Bishop's face retained its expressionless dignity,

though now his eyes were resting on Rollo, and while th
Chancellor elaborated on the gift it was as if the Bishop wa
reading the usefulness and competence of this strange
standing in front of him. He heard Audemand extolling th
work Rollo had done for the church at the behest of th
Duke of Normandy, and noticed the Bishop's eyebrows ris
and his face take on a look of disdainful surprise at th
realization that this visitor was a Norman. Rollo felt a sta
of irritation with the proud cleric and began to look poin
tedly around him at the squalid rubble of the cathedral whil
Audemand went on listing the good intentions of the Count

Rollo let his eyes wander over this downcast place, in suc
contrast to the haughty incumbent of its high office. What
difference from Jumièges where the church he had bui
raised the spirits of the inhabitants and yet rendered the
humble in the presence of something loftier than they. Hov
could you have a house of God which forbade men's spiri
to rise to God? Then suddenly the anger he had felt at Durta
welled up within him, and he recalled the image of tha
child's hand raised from the pool of its own blood. Had h
not resolved to build for man rather than for a God wh
could extend such indifference towards man's suffering
And yet here, all around him, was the evidence of *man*
indifference: this squalid place where rats were the natur
inhabitants and which was fit for little else. Perhaps, aft
all, the indifference of God was merely a response, an
people who showed they did not care deserved a God wh
did not care either. But then ... if this were true, God mu
be as vain and haughty as Bishop Renaud. Was it merely
flatter such a deity that he, Rollo, had raised the towers
Jumièges? And were those hourly chantings of the monk
mere sweetmeats offered up for His pleasure? Rollo thoug
of the old abbot and that lifetime of ritual dedication: it gav
him pain to consider it in such a trivial light, and he stampe
on the idea. Man's love of God was a finer thing than that
finer maybe than God deserved, certainly than God's pries

76

deserved. Perhaps that was all that mattered — to build a house of God that was worthy of that love.

'So you think you can teach us to build?' It was the first time the Bishop had addressed a word to Rollo, and his voice carried a note of contempt.

'Yes, my Lord Bishop!' Rollo saw the cleric's face stiffen, while on Audemand's he detected a flicker of amusement. Bishop Renaud turned to the Chancellor.

'Are we to believe that a Norman knows about matters of the Church?'

'I'm told so,' Audemand replied, resuming a tone of respectful dignity.

The Bishop's gaze returned to Rollo and he said nothing for a few moments. Then he cleared his throat with some solemnity.

'So what would you do, young man?'

Rollo looked around him — at the squat columns with their lumpy carvings, at the rough-hewn stone, at the heavy ceiling, at the gloom and decay.

'If ever I were asked, my Lord Bishop, I should build a church in which men's prayers might rise up and where all men might transcend themselves.'

The Bishop went on staring at him. Rollo was expecting a retort, but if any retort was in the Bishop's mind it was never voiced. Instead he simply turned and mounted the chancel steps where he paused and gazed back at the two men.

'Then I hope that with Count Fulk's generosity we may achieve many things,' he said enigmatically; whereupon without a word or glance of farewell he departed.

Rollo and the Chancellor made their way towards the narrow door through which they had entered. The nave seemed even gloomier now that darkness had fallen. The moon was obscured by clouds, and the wreckage of the western end was swallowed in shadow so that it was hard to detect where the masonry ended and the night began. It was a cathedral of darkness, Rollo thought. And before his eyes floated the image of the tree in the Countess's garden, spreading upwards into the light with its embroidery of flowers like stars and its coronet of white doves. Then he saw his own arch of trees bent over the river high above his head as he lay in the water. This was how he would build: stone as strong as branches, as light as blossom, bathed by the sun. He saw a cathedral whose arches seemed to embrace heaven itself, and he heard human voices that filled those lofty vaults with exaltation. If God wanted to be flattered, then he would show Him a church to make the angels flutter in amazement.

The two men made their way through the dark streets. As they approached the black walls of the castle Audemand paused and placed a hand on Rollo's arm.

'The Bishop is not entirely what you might think. He's an aloof man, but a man of God. It is hard for a bishop to be a man of God.'

They walked on and entered the castle by the same rear gate. They passed the stairway leading down to the kitchens and took yet another unfamiliar passageway. Then Rollo heard peals of laughter ahead of them and round a corner he saw a splash of light from a doorway. As they passed a figure staggered towards them and leaned heavily against the open door. It was a woman with dark dishevelled hair and a mouth that hung open as her eyes wandered over the two men. She was wearing nothing at all, and as Rollo started in astonishment she gave out a heavy laugh and called out something he could not catch. Then she slipped out of sight and Rollo heard the door slam behind them and the muffled sound of more laughter growing fainter as they continued down the passage. Audemand neither checked his pace nor made the slightest gesture of having noticed anything. At the end of the passage he stopped.

'This is where we part. Your rooms are up there in case you are lost. You must be hungry: a servant will bring some food up to you. When the Count is here we dine in the Great

Hall. Fulk likes to preside. But at times like this people eat as they wish ... and drink as they wish,' he added with a chuckle. 'That, by the way, was the Lady Ermengarde, wife of the Lord Treasurer. And now I must leave you.'

The Chancellor bade him good night and Rollo heard the tapping of his staff along hollow corridors. Then he climbed the stairway Audemand had indicated and found himself in a familiar part of the castle. He returned to his rooms, spacious and comfortable, to find that his servant had lit the candles and brought up the crates of his belongings from Normandy which must have reached Angers that day. Rollo looked at them stacked carefully along one wall and felt a surge of pleasure: here was everything he owned, all the small number of possessions he had accumulated during those sixteen years at Jumièges. And here, safely, were his chisels, his measuring equipment and the other tools of his trade with which he had lived for so long, many of which he had designed and made himself. Rollo looked through them quickly: they were complete, everything he might need. He would keep them here under lock and key.

At first light the castle was stirred by shouts and a pounding of feet along echoing corridors. Soon afterwards the cathedral bell began a dissonant clang that roused the city: people spilled from their houses and ran, strode, hobbled towards the main gate where urgent voices were already raised amid a forest of gestures. The city gate was open and a throng of men, women and children began spilling out into the vineyards, extending steadily further and further as if pressing back an invisible rope. All kept their backs turned to the city and their eyes fixed on the dark panorama to the west which the grey dawn was gradually sharpening into a pattern of fields and, beyond these, a black horizon of forest. Then, first singly here and there, soon in clusters and finally in a swaying mass, hands were thrust forward, pointing towards that far-distant ribbon of trees, as eyes began to pick out what the night-watch had already spotted from the roofs of the castle. Figures on horseback, no more than moving specks, could be seen emerging from some invisible track in the forest – three, ten, forty, then more and more; and seething round them as they advanced were the tinier specks of men on foot, growing and growing in numbers until the fields themselves seemed to be on the move. The surge of pointing and gesticulating figures before the castle gate began to give out a murmur of excited voices, and the voices rose in volume until they broke into cheering – cautious at first and then louder and wilder until the noise rolled across the lightening fields and reached the ears of the advancing army, which responded with swords, pikes, shields raised high in a greeting too tired for sound.

Then came the carts. In an ever-extending line they trundled out of the forest drawn by oxen, and as more and more of them threaded their way across the vineyards the voices of the waiting crowd sank to a whisper, because in each cart were the swaying, drooping heads of the wounded. Still they came, and as they drew closer even the whispers died away and the only sounds to be heard were the creaking of the wheels accompanied by a murmur of exhausted moans. Many were already dead, their heads pitched forward on to the barely living: legs, arms, carcasses lolled over the sides of each cart, and with every lurch these cargoes of blood and flesh trembled and slithered. No one spoke. The foot-soldiers trudged on either side like pall-bearers, their pikes and spears trailing, shields lowered. Many were limping, few of them raised their heads. The first shafts of morning sun gleamed dimly on dark blood staining their clothing and their weapons.

From the castle walls all eyes were on the knights: the splendour of Anjou was returning from the wars. At first it was only numbers they were able to count as the horsemen filled the distant fields. Then as the knights rode closer those dark silhouettes in the dawn became husbands, fathers, lovers, sons. Excitement and tension stirred among the figures gathered round the roofs and windows of the castle: eyes gazed anxiously, arms pointed, people embraced, wept, or held their hands nervously in front of their faces. Those still searching held their isolation from the others as they continued to scan the approaching horsemen for some familiar clue.

As the sun broke across the fields something else caught the eyes of all who were watching from the castle. For in the midst of the advancing knights they could pick out a trail of small carriages each drawn by a single horse, with a riderless horse tethered to each. There were ten, twenty, thirty of them. Cries of horror rose from the distant onlookers. Closer they came, and closer, until each could be seen to bear a figure slumped within – all, that is, except the front carriage in which a man was crouched, his hands gripping the sides. His head was raised and he was staring ahead of him in the direction of the castle. His face was long, his mouth set, his jerkin open. His body was red with blood. A gasp went up from the crowd on the castle walls and the massed throng in front of the gates. The foot-soldiers paused and the knights drew rein to let the single carriage pass. Forward it rolled alone across the last field. The voices of the crowd rose to a tumult – cries of fear mixed with joy. The carriage halted. No one moved. Now the figure in the carriage was pulling on the sides with enormous hands, his head bent low. Slowly, so slowly, he eased himself to the edge, swayed there for a moment, and inch by inch pivoted his body over the side still gripping the carriage with those powerful hands. One leg reached the ground ... then the other. The figure was standing bent almost double now. There was not a sound: thousands of people stood motionless around the fringes of this dawn field. Then the huge figure gradually straightened, pressing himself upright with the aid of his sword. He lifted his head and, step by slow step, made his way towards the city walls. Once or twice he halted and seemed to stagger, but always steadied himself, and went on. Finally, in the shadow of the great gates he raised the hilt of his sword to his lips, kissed it, and thrust it high in the air: then, still holding it aloft, he strode into his city. Count Fulk had returned.

THREE

No one who survived that battle would fail to tell the tale of it as long as he lived: his wife would tell it after him, his children to their children, and they to theirs, until the story would spread out across the land and legend of Anjou like a flood-tide. Conquereuil! The name itself tells you there had been battles here before — many of them. The reason? Because this wasteland between two rivers, the Chère and the Don, was like a passage through the forests separating Brittany and Anjou: here were those same bleak borderlands that Fulk's ancestor, Tortulf the Forester, had held against the Breton marauders in those years when no one was safe in his own house and the sound of oars in the dawn could mean death. Yet they were more than a passage between east and west. Cutting across the wastelands of Conquereuil ran the highway north and south between two great cities: so whoever commanded these plains also held the link between Nantes on the southern borders of Brittany and the Breton capital itself, Rennes. Alternatively, of course, those two cities could be isolated one from the other. In any case, either Brittany was menaced, or Anjou, depending on the control of this region of scrub, bog and heath which in all other respects was of no use whatever to anyone. Apart from a few shepherds, few people other than armies ever ventured here.

But in this place of many battles there had been none like this. They say that for centuries to come shepherds would catch the dim glint of iron or white of bone where the wind or wild creatures had scooped off a layer of sand; and that no one came here at all unless their animals had strayed, because of the sounds that inhabited the place. It belonged to death, and no birds ever sang.

This was a battle about the hatred between two men — a hatred that had bred and increased like a plague in the hearts of both. To each man the other bestrode the path that led to his destiny. Now, in the high summer of the year 996, these two men were carrying that hatred on their swords as they narrowed the distance between them. Riding from the east was Fulk — on that same black stallion, Moro, which had swept him to the gates of Langeais in the spring of his manhood: older now, with cunning added to that furious rage and swordsmanship to that titanic strength, and a pride swollen by the fear all had of him; a man certain that God and the saints were at his side, and whose eyes declared the irresistible force of will that had driven his ancestors upwards from the dark forests into the light of power and conquest. Fulk. Black Fulk. People followed him like a bright dark star, and where he stood the future was being born.

From the west rode Conan — lean greying figure of no age and a hundred scars: the silent Breton whose honour rested on a gilded past, carrying in his veins the blood of warriors who had brought their language, their saints and their songs over the seas from the ancient lands of the north; Conan could remember from his infancy the poems telling of King Gradlon who had built as his capital the most beautiful city in the world, the city of Is — so beautiful, they said, that the Franks could find no higher praise for their own capital than to name it 'like-Is', Paris — and how the Devil in his envy had opened the sea-locks and drowned it. Then there was the greatest of all Bretons, Nominoë, whom the Emperor Charlemagne created Duke of Brittany and who brought all Breton lands together into one kingdom which he ruled like a proud empire. This was the grandeur Conan would rebuild.

Fulk was the pursuer. By his side rode his High Constable,

Barthélémi de Chemillé, grizzled and wise, who had been with Fulk's father Geoffrey Greymantle fourteen years ago when the armies of Anjou met and defeated Conan, sparing his life in return for the city of Nantes. The two men rode in silence as the sun rose and set: around them on the broad forest trails were Fulk's nobles – Roger the lord of Montrésor, Sulpice de Buzançais, his brother Archambaud the governor of Amboise, the six sons of the Chancellor Audemand, the young Giraud Berlay, the viscounts of Beaufort, Craon, Baugé, Allonnes, Noyant, Basouges, Segré, Lude, Chalonnes, Champtoceaux, Gontier, Loudun, Loches, Montrichard, and many many more; and behind the horsemen stretched a trail of foot-soldiers – pikemen, spearmen, bowmen, soldiers with short-swords, soldiers from every town and village of Anjou, swollen by allies from Maine, from the Mauges, from Poitou and Aquitaine: in short the greatest army ever seen in the lands of the Loire. And the prize? The crushing of Brittany.

Conan, the pursued, could choose where to meet that army. He had been waiting for Fulk a great many years, nursing within him a deep pain of anger inflicted by that defeat at the hands of Fulk's father. He had waited and then had chosen his moment. When Count Alain of Nantes died without a legitimate heir he seized back that city which belonged to Brittany and which he had been forced to yield only on pain of death. This battle would remove for ever the threat of Anjou to the sacred lands of his ancestors. Conan knew Fulk to be headstrong and foolhardy, and without son and heir. With his defeat and death, the city of Angers would bend to him, Conan; then, with the Count of Blois as his ally, the splendour of Brittany would shine as far as the gates of Paris. All this he would achieve on that very place of ill memories – Conquereuil; and by reversing those fortunes he would exorcise such memories, wipe defeat from the story of the Breton race. With his pale eyes bright with the victory to come, Conan stood apart from his knights and watched the sun setting on the eve of Fulk's arrival: within two days it would set on the fortunes of Anjou.

Meanwhile, over the plain, Conan's huge army waited for battle, spread out across the warm summer night among a hundred points of fire; and as the light faded those camp fires began to spin webs of smoke between the clusters of yellow broom and the stunted oak trees. Horses whinnied and pawed the sandy earth. Foot-soldiers brought water in leather buckets from a stream hidden behind a line of poplars. A golden bird darted between the trees uttering a flute-like call, then crossed the open plain eastwards into the dusk: A bowman aimed an arrow at it as it passed, and his companions laughed. The lone figure of Conan stood outlined against the evening sky.

There is a terrible silence before a battle. It is the silence of fear. Friends no longer look at each other lest the message be read and its meaning be too hard to bear. Fear is a lonely pain, and in the cell of that loneliness rise sounds of old laughter and images of loved ones that are blurred with tears choked back. Sleep is held at bay because night is the last barrier against the dawn, and no one wants that barrier to fall. So people cough, stir, gaze at the stars, knowing that ten thousand other pairs of eyes are open to the dark. Owls monitor the passing of the hours.

Then almost mercifully the time is up. Suddenly the battle becomes a job to be done, and instead of lonely fear there is comfort in being one of so many. Confidence rises with the sun and warms the chilled heart of every soldier, and a great love for his fellows fills him like wine. By the evening it will be over, and there will be booty and loot, songs and wine, glory to take home.

The two armies were perhaps five hundred paces apart in the pallid morning light – the Angevins forming a crescent of mounted knights flanked by archers at the tips of the crescent to provide cross-fire from the verges of the forest on either side. The Bretons, with longer to prepare, were partly hidden behind a low sandy ridge built up by the wind and bound by thorny scrub. Between the two armies lay open country scoured by the seasons and cropped bare by goats and sheep.

There was a gradual build-up of sound drifting across the open plain – knights exhorting their foot-soldiers, a clatter of weapons, neighing of horses, a tide of voices carrying boasts and curses. Conan rode silently among his men, and all eyes gazed up at him as he passed, his hands folded calmly across the pommel of his saddle. Fulk swung his black steed to face his army, and silence fell. Then he began to speak – that great voice which bound men in loyalty and in awe; he spoke of simple things that people love and need and lose when wars are lost; he spoke of love of country and of his own love for all who lived in Anjou; and he spoke of a vow he had made to destroy the two men who had conspired to destroy him – today it would be Conan, lord of Brittany, next it would be Odo, lord of Blois. And as he spoke he raised his right hand to the sky and called on God and the saints to bless his army in this fight. Then, as cheering burst from the massed ranks of the Angevin soldiers, Fulk stooped and with one massive arm swept into his saddle the boy Judicael, and with two hands raised the youth above his head.

'Here,' he shouted, 'before God is the young lord of Nantes for whom we fight.'

He said no more. It was extraordinary, the effect on that vast crowd of men of this frail boy held up to them as if he were their own deprived son, and they his avengers. As Fulk returned the youth to the ground there was not a man in the army of Anjou who did not believe he could kill five Bretons with his bare hands that very moment.

Fulk wheeled his horse and gazed across that empty plain. There, quite still on that distant ridge, was Conan – waiting.

Fulk adjusted his helmet and his shield, and with the eyes of his army upon him drew his huge sword embossed with jewels, and raised it aloft so that to the soldiers behind him it shone like fire in the sun; then slowly, as if the arm that grasped it could never break, he brought it down in front of him until the point was held motionless towards the heart of Conan. Not a sound broke from the Angevin army. They waited. They knew, all of them, what the plan of attack was, and now they waited, straining like hounds. Not a movement.

The cry from Fulk when it came was swallowed by the pounding of hooves.

Within minutes there were five hundred dead on the plains of Conquereuil – most of them Angevins. Fulk was clever, but Conan cleverer. The lord of Anjou had divided his knights into three – so that, as the crescent of horsemen surged forward across the open ground, at a given signal two wings broke off to left and right along the verges of the forest to attack the Breton army in a pincer movement: one wing was under the command of Roger de Montrésor, the other under the young Sulpice de Buzançais. Meanwhile, the central body of Angevin knights, led by Fulk himself and the High Constable Barthélémi, converged to create a narrow wedge that struck straight at the heart of the waiting Bretons. Fulk's plan was to bewilder the massed ranks of Conan's army, which his spies had observed from the forest in the first light of dawn, by attacking them from these three points – left, right and centre – so that the Breton knights would never know which way to counter. The Angevin foot-soldiers would then surge forward and crowd in on their broken ranks. It was a tactic that demanded precision, speed, sudden changes of direction, and a constant barrage of surprise.

It was indeed clever. But the plan presupposed a simple

truth, that the battleground was exactly as it seemed to be. Barthélémi had fought Conan before, and he warned Fulk that the Breton was nobody's fool and would certainly have some hidden strategy – in fact the massing of the enemy army in the centre of the open plain made it appear deceptively vulnerable, as though inviting Fulk to come and get them. Fulk only half-listened to his High Constable: he insisted that a central thrust by his main force of knights would bring the quickest victory by splitting the enemy army into two right down the middle. Barthélémi argued that this could very well be folly, yet when Fulk pressed him for a reason the Constable could only reply that his long experience of warfare had taught him to suspect such an obvious move, however well disguised it might be. There was something wrong – he could not define what – he felt it in his bones. Fulk was not one to attribute such vagueness to wisdom. Perhaps, too, his urge to take the Bretons by brute storm overrode all other considerations, and Barthélémi knew the young count's impulsive nature would probably have its way whatever he might say.

And so, in a surge of horses and dust, the Angevin knights charged. A cross-fire of arrows from the forest verges seemed to pin the Breton army as the horsemen thundered towards the low ridge. Then, as Fulk raised his sword, Roger's contingent broke to the left, that of Sulpice to the right, while the central body of knights converged as though a current were sucking them inwards. It was like the stab of a trident, with Fulk at the point of the central prong. At first the effect on the Bretons was as Fulk anticipated: the impenetrable phalanx of Conan's knights occupying the plain was shaken apart by the threat of Fulk's pincers as the horsemen turned to meet these unexpected attacks from the wings. In the Breton count's mind rose consternation lest much of the Angevin army elude the trap he had set. Glancing anxiously to left and to right Conan fixed his eyes on that central prong speeding towards him. And it was at this moment at full gallop that Fulk's eyes caught something ahead which made him heave at his reins in horror and bellow 'Turn! Turn!'; his sword gestured frantically towards the forest and away from the ridge now a mere fifty paces before the careering horsemen. But it was too late. The knights immediately following Fulk were at full gallop, their heads lowered: he could no more have stemmed a river in torrent, and they swept him onwards. As for Barthélémi, he did not even see the Count swerve, but hurtled forward towards that central point where until a short while ago Conan had been standing motionless against the dawn sky.

What happened in the seconds to follow was precisely as the Breton had devised, and as Fulk in that hopeless moment feared. Suddenly that proud onslaught of Angevin knights became a tangle of limbs, iron and blood: horses' legs, arms, helmets, shields, lances, swords, all seemed stirred and mashed by some invisible force – and to that mêlée were added more and more horsemen powerless to halt before they pitched into the carnage. Knights were crushed beneath their own horses; those thrown clear were scythed down by the flail of other horses as they spun in the groaning air; and those who dragged themselves free were spitted by arrows from the Breton bowmen on the ridge above them, replacing one another in remorseless lines as each shot and retired, shot and retired, with the speed of hail. There died in those long few minutes almost one-third of the finest horsemen in Anjou, Maine and Poitou: somewhere in that hell of flesh lay the lord Barthélémi, High Constable of Anjou; besides him, the lords of Beaufort, Loches, Basouges, Craon, Loudun, Noyant, Gontier, and the sons, brothers, cousins, uncles of many more: barely a town would not mourn some of its proudest men, barely a noble family within the reaches of the Loire would not gaze in sorrow at a seat vacant when they dined.

And Fulk? He had never met disaster before, at least not on a scale such as this. Had he not been Fulk – had he heeded the words of Barthélémi — it might never have occurred. And yet, if he had not been Fulk this would have been the end — Black Fulk, Fulk the Rash, Fulk the Blind, who raised his pride too high against the lord of Brittany and fell alongside the corpse of his own country. Not so! ... What man but Fulk could have turned this battle, could have hoisted from the slaughterhouse of Conquereuil a banner that history would call victory?

Some who saw him there swear an archangel flew above him as he rode; others that his sword flashed fire, and that his black steed swept an avenue through the forest of Breton soldiers with the force of his hooves. All spoke of miracles of valour and strength as the Black Count hacked his way to where Conan stood within the garrison of his knights, and struck him down: they said that when the lord of Brittany fell a gasp of horror rose from the Breton ranks and that they stumbled back in fear, only to be slaughtered by the rage of Roger the Devil of Montrésor as he led his storm of knights from the verges of the forest to the south, and from the north by the two hundred horsemen who swept in behind the fair young Sulpice de Buzançais. They were crushed, those thousands of panicked Bretons: everywhere they turned a sword struck them; they were pressed — into each other, over each other, leaderless, down into the very ditch in which five hundred Angevins lay in their own blood. They stumbled into each other, struggled over each other, fought with each other, yelling out for direction, for support, for rescue, for escape; but they yelled in strange tongues — the Bretons with their language from the lands of the north clashed with their Viking allies who spoke in the tongue of the Norsemen, and both in their confusion heard their allies from the Vendée cry out in the French of their enemies from Anjou. All was chaos and murder and pain, and no one to cry halt because no one knew how or to whom. It was a sea of death on that desolate plain.

Fulk, somehow, had turned the tide. In that terrible split

second as his knights hurled their horses towards the ranks of Brittany he had perceived one thing. Ahead, in the sharpness of the early sun, he saw the patches of low scrub become suddenly a regular line of fresh branches already withering. And he understood – too late. Conan had dug a long ditch the entire width of the battlefield on the Angevin side of the low ridge that ran between the forest to the south and an area of swamp and stream to the north. Conan had calculated – correctly – that Fulk had the longer journey to make, and had seen to it that he arrived at Conquereuil a full two days before the Angevin army. His outriders kept him informed of Fulk's progress, and in that period the Breton count formed a huge workforce from among his foot-soldiers to dig this ditch several hundred paces in length and to a depth equal to the height of the tallest men in his army. The loose soil – most of it sand – he had carried behind the ridge out of sight (and here was one great weakness in the plan). When the excavations were complete Conan had staves driven into the base of the ditch less than a pace apart and sharpened to impale horsemen and riders who were to be lured there. Then, as the news reached him of Fulk's imminent arrival he had forest branches laid over the open ditch, with broom, scrub and fern wedged firmly among them: at the same time a short channel was cut between the north side of the ditch and the source of the stream so that during the night the ditch gradually flooded to the depth of several feet. Then Conan waited ... and in the dawn he calmly watched Fulk exhorting his army to their own destruction.

So nearly did the plan succeed: so close were the events of that summer morning to total catastrophe for the Angevins. How fortunes were finally turned became the subject of prolonged debate among the survivors in the more sober days that followed the sorrow and triumph. That more than half the knights of Fulk's army survived was due to the Count's strategy of despatching two contingents to the left and right under Roger de Montrésor and Sulpice de Buzançais. Roger's knights skirted the forest at a point where – to their good fortune – the soil had proved too stony for the ditch to continue to the edge of the trees; that very hardness of ground in fact aided the onward rush of horsemen so that they swooped upon the Bretons almost without warning. To the north the knights led by Sulpice, and who included the sons of Audemand the Chancellor, were slower since the lord of Buzançais was forced to circumvent the swampy ground, then leap the small stream beyond: but this too carried its own luck since their later arrival caught many of the Bretons already turned the other way to check the onslaught of Roger from the forest.

Moreover, Fulk's split-second forewarning, though too late to avert disaster to most of the main force of Angevin knights, gave him time to urge the black stallion, Moro, to leap the hidden ditch of death, and at least fifty of the knights following the Count managed to do the same, so that the central wedge – though thinner than planned – still drove into the heart of the massed Breton army, wreaking havoc among the foot-soldiers and archers who were assembled beyond the low ridge. And what Fulk's knights lacked in numbers they made up in fury, led by the Count himself who fought like a man possessed.

Even then the Bretons could – should – have rallied. Their numbers equalled those of Anjou, while their knights were more numerous now that so many of their foes lay writhing and impaled in that reddened ditch. And here, all agreed, the genius of Fulk tilted the scales. As he cleared the ditch on that swiftest of steeds Fulk could already hear around him the agony of his bravest knights. He did not know who, if any, were following him: he might, he believed, be quite alone as Moro stepped lightly over the ridge and plunged into that sea of Breton swords. He knew then that he would die, that he had perhaps one minute in which his headlong dash might keep him in the saddle. One minute, or less.

Time for ... what? For one thing! Treating the Breton foot-soldiers as ants he sped with head low and sword whirling like a wheel of blades straight towards the lean figure of Conan, mounted within a circle of Breton knights some fifty paces ahead. He would trade his own death for the destruction of that hated man.

Fulk did not remember those few seconds; but those following in the havoc of his charge swear he cut down three Breton knights like saplings. The next they saw was Fulk's huge sword held high – glittering red – and Conan's sword fall, and Conan fall, his horse with him; Fulk wheeled, yelled, then saw his knights in his wake; they swear he laughed; Conan lay somewhere under the crush of hooves as the Angevin knights formed a knot of horsemen round the Black Count. And now chaos broke. Where the Breton leader had stood, Fulk stood. To all Breton eyes the citadel of that battlefield had fallen, and they panicked: to the left they saw Roger's knights, to the right those of Sulpice, while in their very midst was Fulk. They tried to flee, but wherever they turned others were fleeing towards them: none could move far or fast in the deep sand piled up from the ditch, until all they could do was scream and die in their hundreds.

The sun was high. Suddenly a stillness fell upon the plain. Figures were running, limping, crawling away into the forests, dropping weapons in their haste. No one followed them. It was over. Numbness and exhaustion overtook those thousands of living men who were wandering among the thousands of the dead and dying. Very slowly, unresisting, the prisoners were rounded up. Carts that had brought provisions were loaded – piled rather – with the wounded. Already the kites were settling on the corpses: that night the wolves would howl, their eyes gleaming like phosphorus between the forest trees.

It was Roger de Montrésor, the tireless Roger, unscathed, who noticed the black stallion standing quite motionless with no rider, his head lowered. With a cry of horror he rode over the scattered dead and leaped from his horse. The sprawled form of Fulk lay still, face downwards, at the feet of his favourite steed. His neck and jerkin glistened with blood, and his hands were red. His knights crowded round him as Roger and two of the sons of Audemand bent to raise their lord; and as they gently turned him tears ran rivulets across the sand and sweat of their faces. 'He's alive!' was all Roger said.

They bore him back. And at the camp they cleaned him of the blood and bound his wounds with comfrey and healing herbs. He fainted more than once as the chill water touched those yawning gashes, and still the blood oozed and flowed. 'Get him to a monastery,' said Sulpice. 'Get me to Angers,' murmured Fulk. And there was no one who would dare disobey.

In the end it was through Fulk that Conan, too, escaped. The blow that toppled him had only stunned the Breton count, and he lay unconscious throughout the battle, saved from flailing hooves by his dead horse that bled over him as he lay beside its carcass until his fine armour and clothing were indistinguishable from those of any other poor soldier who had met his end that day. It was no more than a few paces from where they found Fulk; in fact it was a blow from Conan as Fulk charged that so sapped the strength of the Angevin lord that he fell among his knot of knights unnoticed as they fought to hold a ring around their beleaguered chief. So, the two men who hated one another with such poison lay almost together, each the victim of the other, united in oblivion. And when consciousness returned to Conan, it was to the sight of Angevin knights all around him standing over their fallen leader. Conan knew then that the war was lost; and when he heard the voice cry out 'He's alive!' he knew that all was lost. All but his own life. And yet even at that moment, feigning death on this field of carnage, half-drowned in the blood of a stallion, Conan could vow that all would *not* after all be lost. He watched as they bore Fulk away; then he rose and in the anonymity of his disguise guided his charmed life slowly and unobtrusively past the Angevin soldiers bent on spoil, and reached the forest. A wandering horse served him well, and he rode away.

He did not know, however, that among the prisoners even now being led towards the Angevin camp was the eldest of his sons, Budic, whom possibly he would never see again.

There was joy and sorrow within the castle of Angers. The battle was won, but the price heavy to bear. Count Fulk was alive, the Bretons broken and Conan assumed dead; yet the much-loved High Constable, Barthélémi, had perished in the slaughter, and alongside him one third at least of all the knights of Anjou. In this weakened state what could the Angevins hope to do against the other enemy, Odo of Blois? More powerful than Conan, and more deadly. In his fortress at Tours his spies even now would be relating to Odo the plight of Anjou: before winter settled he would surely attack again. Only castles – stone castles – thrown like a studded collar round the neck of Tours could hold him in. And Anjou possessed the one man in all the lands of the Loire with the skill to realize this – Rollo the Norman.

Fulk lay in the hushed room of his sickbed with these troubled thoughts drifting in and out of his sleep. For many days the faces that moved about him in the great panelled room blurred into the other reality of his delirium as night slid into day, then night again, beyond reckoning and beyond focus: colours of dreams and sounds from nowhere flowed between the inner and outer worlds without control or check, until he lost all sense of which life he inhabited or indeed if it was life at all. There were figures he seemed to know and recall, but whether he knew them from his dreams or from some existence outside himself he had no means of understanding. His constant companions – the

Countess Elizabeth, the Chancellor Audemand, Roger, Sebrand, his chaplain Baudouin, Bishop Renaud, the Treasurer Bouchard, his brother Maurice, his physicians and healers — began to recognize that the crisis was over when the Count's face began to lie still in sleep and his expression grew calm. It was then that his mind gradually took hold of those events before his collapse inside the city gates, and channels of memory served him sights that were all blood and terror, and an awareness of gentle arms supporting the last of his body's strength and laying him on soft linen in soothing shadow. He asked of friends — of Barthélémi whom he seemed to know was dead, but when at first no one answered for fear of weakening him further Fulk's face took on a pale fire of anger until Elizabeth, only Elizabeth, found the courage to tell him the truth; and he wept. Then they told him of the other knights also dead, and his tears moved all round him in that shaded room to a tenderness of love. The Countess held a huge bandaged hand and kissed him so that the others turned their heads. And he asked about Moro the black stallion, and when they told him he was uninjured and daily tended by two of the sons of Audemand, Fulk gave a weak laugh of pleasure. And one day all the knights of the court came to the great room to greet him and kiss his hand, and Fulk nodded to each of them: they swore they felt the strength flowing back into his body as they touched him, and that he thanked them with his eyes. That night the Countess Elizabeth shared his bed, and no one in the castle of Angers harboured any doubt that their lord was recovering.

Soon Fulk's room became a council of war, and the familiar voice barking orders was heard echoing down the labyrinthine corridors. Roger de Montrésor, Sulpice and his brother Archambaud, the elder sons of Audemand, Sebrand de Chemillé, numerous viscounts, marshals and local governors — all came and went at any hour of the day and night the Count chose to summon them. Among his first tasks was to see that all the offices of those killed at Conquereuil were filled by trusted men. Where the son of a dead viscount was unknown to him Fulk had him brought riding through the night to stand before those searching eyes: those who failed the test of the Count's gaze and questioning found themselves rudely placed under the overlordship of a nearby viscount, while those who impressed him favourably were expected to renew the bond of vassalage by kissing their master on the mouth, then placing their hands between Fulk's and swearing fealty over the holy relics of St Albinus brought from the monastery of St Aubin. Grants of fief were redistributed among the newcomers to the Count's *familia* under the watchful eye of Chancellor Audemand: scribes and notaries were at hand for the purpose, and after the Count had placed a cross to each document the Chancellor and several clergy (including the Chaplain) added their names in witness; finally Audemand applied the great seal of Anjou with due ceremony.

The Count sent for Sebrand alone. First he took him in his arms and sobbed. He felt a personal debt and a personal guilt, he said, concerning the death of Barthélémi, Sebrand's father – most loyal of men, to himself and to his own father Geoffrey Greymantle before him. Had he listened to the High Constable, Fulk admitted, Barthélémi would be here now with his son in joy and celebration, and scores of other fine men throughout Anjou would be lying in the arms of their wives and not in the soil of Conquereuil. The burden of that error would weigh upon him all his life, and he would seek forgiveness from the saints as soon as he was well enough to travel. He hoped Sebrand would soon accompany him to the monastery of Corméry to beg indulgence at the shrine of Saint Foy in the presence of the holy abbot Gervais. Meanwhile the only pleasure he could offer the bereaved son was to appoint him to his late father's office.

'You shall be our High Constable, Sebrand,' he said, raising himself on one elbow. 'And may you serve us as faithfully as your lamented father.'

Sebrand kissed the Count's hand. From the well of sadness within him rose an anguish that he had not seen his father alive just once more; for his arrival at Conquereuil had been only a few hours after the battle was over, and he had had the opportunity to do little other than escort his father's body from those bleak plains.

'And I hope, Sebrand, that you will marry soon,' added Fulk, 'in accordance with the wishes of your father.'

The rapid change of mood and subject was well familiar to Sebrand. The past was abruptly dismissed along with the sentiments attached to it. The phrase 'I hope' carried with it the authority of a command which he would find hard to disobey. His father's wishes had not in fact always been those of Fulk, as Sebrand knew, and there had been moments of complicity between father and son when Barthélémi, without displaying even a fragment of disloyalty to his lord, had suggested that the gain in lands and vassalage which Sebrand's marriage to the widow from Maine would bring to the Count might be outbalanced by another consideration. Sebrand had inspected his father's face closely for a clue, and the Constable without further comment had simply patted his stomach. Sebrand had gauged his meaning – that the lady in question might indeed be a sister of the Count of Maine and therefore an estimable match, but she was of some years and the birth of a son, let alone many sons, might well be beyond her; besides which her first marriage had yielded no children at all during the years of her bloom (if, Sebrand pondered, such a flowering had ever taken place).

He took his leave of Fulk with expressions of gratitude and devotion, while nursing the thought that the longer he could find reason to postpone such a fine match the stronger his late father's argument might weigh against the advisability of it in the Count's eyes. Marriage, Sebrand conceded, was a state which he was expected to have entered some years earlier, and he harboured no binding objection to such a commitment except that being without it was so utterly pleasurable and the only lady on offer struck him as the very reverse of pleasurable in anything. The Countess Elizabeth entered as he departed. Why, Sebrand thought, could not a lady of her grace and nobility be found for him? Perhaps the Countess herself, in whose company he delighted, could be persuaded to employ her skills to reveal such a one, and to impress on her lord the irresistible advantages of the match. He would choose his moment.

The Countess was a model of devotion during these weeks of Fulk's recovery. Her attentions were the subject of admiration of all at the castle except those few who, for their own intractable reasons, disapproved of Elizabeth's free spirit and free tongue. There was in the Countess's demeanour an air of confidence that some were prepared to interpret as arrogance – in particular the confidence she displayed towards the Count her husband, as though – they felt – she were his equal, even (it was suggested) his superior.

There were two such people in particular. One was the Lady Adelaide, wife of Roger de Montrésor, and the other the Count's chaplain, Baudouin. Neither was foolish enough to exhibit their disapproval publicly, of course; at the same time neither of them was capable of disguising it when it came to a glance or the set of a mouth, so strongly did it touch on their deepest feelings. Both the wife of Roger the Devil and Fulk's chaplain were inhabited by a revulsion from all displays of human love that descended from the loftiest sphere of the spiritual. For Baudouin this disgust was rooted in the soil of his church teaching which held that all physical engagements between a man and a woman beyond the kissing of a hand were impure and only necessary – alas! – for the purpose of breeding more souls for God. For the Lady Adelaide it was perhaps more personal – that she did not like it. From both viewpoints there was much horror at how shamelessly, even joyfully, the Countess succumbed to Fulk's attentions, thus wantonly hindering her lord's recovery of strength as well as exhibiting a disgraceful appetite for carnal pleasure – a weakness permissible only in men. Her influence in this respect was nothing less than evil, and the moral impact on certain other ladies of the court was demonstrably lamentable.

'Have you met the Lady Adelaide yet?' said Sebrand with a slight laugh.

He and Rollo were walking back from the cathedral of St Maurice where the Norman had spent the day preparing plans for the reconstruction which had now been occupying him for several weeks. He had seen little of Sebrand in this time. Aware of his friend's grief and of his new high office, he had deliberately kept his own company, taking meals in his rooms and working with a growing absorption on this first task he had been given in his new home. Strangely, he had still not met Count Fulk, though Chancellor Audemand whom he saw almost daily constantly assured him that the Count's recovery would very shortly bring him a summons, and once that happened he would find the days too short for the work Fulk had in mind.

'No, Sebrand, I haven't. And you make it sound as though I'm fortunate.' Rollo smiled. He felt happy to have time again with his friend, strolling in the warm evening. The late sun glistened on the slate tiles of the houses, and dogs sniffed and barked as the two men made their way towards the castle. Sebrand was just as he remembered him from their journey nearly a month ago.

'Well, you'll probably not meet her alone – which is also fortunate. She haunts the Lady Ermengarde, the Treasurer's wife.'

'Who I *have* met ... She was naked.'

Sebrand turned to look at him in astonishment; his eyes widened and then he began to chuckle.

'Naked!' he said rather loudly. People stared as they passed. 'When?'

Rollo started to explain, but by now Sebrand's incredulity had blossomed into pure delight, and laughter began to well up within him until he reeled about grasping Rollo's arm for support.

'Naked!' he called out even more loudly. Again people turned to stare but Sebrand appeared not to notice. 'When, for God's sake?'

Rollo was forced to wait until Sebrand's convulsions showed signs of subsiding. Then he began to recount the incident which had happened soon after his arrival at Angers when he returned with Audemand from his first audience with the bishop. Sebrand's face was now alight with pleasure.

'You mean to say she was just standing there?'

'The door opened.'

'Ah ha! That would have been Adelaide.'

'What do you mean?'

'Because that's exactly the sort of thing she does. Let me explain.'

Sebrand did, and another colourful picture of castle life at Angers began to create itself before Rollo. The Lady Ermengarde he knew about: the Countess had told him about her predilections; indeed he had encountered her on a number of occasions since and had noticed the predatory scan of her dark eyes. But the role of Adelaide was fresh to him and he was more than a little surprised.

According to Sebrand, Ermengarde's tastes were of a rather public nature; and as for Adelaide, her declared disgust for all things amorous did not preclude a fascination for observing what went on in others. He could not swear that she was present *all* the time: perhaps even the Lord Treasurer's wife might draw a line at that. What was certainly true – and it was a joke much enjoyed throughout the castle – was that Adelaide had a wonderfully sensitive nose for acts of infidelity that Ermengarde was about to commit; and being deeply concerned to be her friend's moral guardian, she would invariably contrive to appear in time, as she hoped, to avert them. Ermengarde was actually fond of the righteous lady, she said: Adelaide possessed a warm heart beneath the chilly exterior (and who, after all, could blame her for that with Roger the Devil as a husband?). None the less, her inopportune appearances were inclined to grow exasperating in the extreme, Ermengarde would admit.

Sebrand was by now enjoying his tale hugely. Ermengarde had regaled the Countess, he said, with descriptions of how she would become tired of pious conversations with her visitor when the servant of her fancy was already in attendance with wine and fruits; and as a result she would begin to imbibe heavily. And then ... well! — Sebrand seemed to remember that he was High Constable and lowered his voice — the wine would induce her to remove her clothes for some reason. Sebrand was laughing again. After which, he went on, the servant would be commanded to remove his; whereupon the Lady Adelaide would be goaded into a horrified discourse about hell-fires and the foulness of the flesh (Sebrand could scarcely splutter out his words by this time) and call upon the saints to witness and denounce such horrors. By which time the Lady Ermengarde had grown exceedingly hot with wine, lust and indignation in equal measure, and had been known — he had the Countess's own words for it — to fling open windows and doors in angry refutation of all these accusations, declaring to the wide world that nothing could be lovelier than a human body and all the pleasures attendant upon it, and if the saints disapproved then they must all have been as dried up as the Lady Adelaide and probably got the martyrdom they deserved.

It was, Sebrand assured Rollo, almost certainly at such a moment when he and the Chancellor happened to be passing, instead — Sebrand was almost choking as he said it — instead of the holy saints.

In truth (he went on as the laughter began to subside) he always imagined that one day the two ladies would discover the most blissful communion between themselves, the one as a relief from excess, the other as a relief from abstinence.

'But seriously, Rollo, I malign the Treasurer's wife. She's a vigorous lady, and to be married to Bouchard would be like a prison sentence without water – what's more, to someone with quite a thirst! You know, of course, that Bouchard delights in the same servant. People say – I suspect the Countess actually said it first – that they both have the boy at the same time, he from the north, so to speak, and she from the south.'

Rollo stopped and looked at Sebrand in some amazement, then both men burst out laughing. They had almost reached the gates. Shadows veiled the narrow passageways of the old city, choked with carts and animals. A figure passed them, and beneath the shawl pulled about her face Rollo saw the dark-eyed girl he had noticed so many times as he made his way back to the castle at this evening hour: the same girl he had seen that first evening Audemand had led him to the cathedral. She always looked at him as she passed, and seemed half to smile.

'Who is that girl?' he asked Sebrand when she was out of earshot.

'A strange one, that. Milesende. You've surely met her sister who everyone lusts after – Hersende, the Countess's friend. They're Bretons. They live here because Conan banished their cousin Judicael, the count of Nantes. She's very young.'

The mention of Hersende roused his interest, and Rollo hoped he would say more. But Sebrand's mind already seemed elsewhere. He merely added, 'I suppose they'll return to Nantes now that Conan's dead.'

A flock of Fulk's white doves circled the roof-tops and fluttered over the walls. Rollo's eyes followed the slender figure of the girl as she entered the castle, and he thought the shrouded head half-turned to glance back momentarily before she vanished through the open gateway. The two men made their way slowly in the same direction, talking; and when they looked up again another figure was standing by the open gate. It was Audemand. He waited for them to approach.

'Good evening, sirs.' The Chancellor's deeply lined face crinkled into a smile, and his staff tapped on the stones in the lightest display of ceremony. 'My lord Sebrand, the Count wishes a further word with you . . . He's getting quite exhaustingly better. And tomorrow at noon, my dear Rollo, you are to present yourself – with your plans for the cathedral. He seems impressed that you've moved so fast, but I reminded him that Vikings have never been known to sit about, as his grandfather would have vouched.'

Audemand had a kindly hand on the Norman's shoulder as they made their way through the familiar corridors. Sebrand bade the two of them good-bye and hurried ahead towards the Count's rooms.

'You may find Fulk more occupied with other things, Rollo. Castles. Matters of some urgency. Once the harvest is over we can expect our angry neighbour to come looking for trouble. Sebrand tells me you've already seen what Odo can do.'

Audemand's words recalled to Rollo's mind the scenes of butchery at Durtal, and a tremor of apprehension overcame him. How could he, a builder of churches, protect a nation against such fury? It was as if the Chancellor read his thoughts.

'You'll find the Count knows exactly what he wants. He has nothing but admiration for your skills: everyone tells him about them. But you'll have to work fast . . . Ah, Rollo, I see the door is shut this evening.' The Chancellor's face broke into another smile and he looked sideways at Rollo with a mischievous expression. 'Perhaps you have been rejected . . . or the lady is otherwise occupied.'

He continued to chuckle as they passed down the corridor to the foot of the narrow stairway where they would separate.

'Tomorrow, by the way, there'll be a banquet to mark the Count's recovery. You'll see that we don't always live in private cells here. I hope you have a good head for wine. I can tell you there'll be some who'll lose theirs. At noon, remember, I'll come for you.'

Audemand was still chuckling as he left, and his staff could be heard tapping rhythmically along the corridor. Rollo climbed the stairs towards his rooms and made use of the last hours of daylight to work on his plans for the cathedral. His parchments lay unrolled on the long work-bench, and when the servant came in with candles and dinner Rollo ate quickly, then set the candles along the bench and worked deep into the night. Tomorrow felt like a test of his powers, and he would not go unprepared.

The shape grew on the parchment and in his mind, and in the darkness he filled the cathedral with light. In the silence he filled it with song. Exhilaration rode over tiredness until suddenly Rollo felt his head resting on the work-bench and in his dreams he saw his new cathedral crowded with men and women in bright costumes, the sun flooding the lofty nave. But he recognized none of the congregation until, standing at the far end by the door, he caught sight of Hersende dressed as he first saw her in the colours of summer, fair hair stroking her bare shoulders and a jewel resting in the vale of her breasts. She smiled as she saw him, and extended a hand. Rollo felt a pain of joy within him, and he took the hand in his. It was cool and small. Then a breeze seemed to pass between them: her hand dissolved and her face blurred; it was as though she became a ghost. He gazed around, puzzled, and the church was empty except – he noticed suddenly – for the veiled figure of the young sister turned away from him; she was passing through the open doorway, just as he used to see her returning to the castle

Only now she did not look back. He could hear Hersende's laughter, but now it seemed to mock him and she was no longer there. The cathedral was empty and it was dark. It was the old cathedral, crumbled and open to the night. Rollo woke with a start of fear. From the open window he saw that dawn was breaking. The candles on the workbench were low and flickering in the morning breeze. Rollo gathered his thoughts, trembling: relieved to find the new cathedral still before him on the unrolled parchments he got up and washed his face in the bowl of water on the side-table, then took up his pens as the cocks crowed and the sky turned violet, then green, then rose.

There were others in the castle familiar with these earliest hours. The two sisters, Hersende and Milesende, had been deeply stirred by the events of Conquereuil. For both of them the defeat of Conan offered the prospect of a new life: they were, in short, no longer mere orphans at the court of Anjou, with no future except the passing of the years and no present but the passing of the hours. Hersende had decorated the court with her charms; Milesende had decorated her own thoughts with her dreams. But now... The Countess Elizabeth talked almost daily with her beloved Hersende about the changes that would take place in the two sisters' lives as soon as their cousin, the young Judicael, was reinstated as Count of Nantes. Fulk, she assured the elder sister, intended to ride there before the winter set in and establish the youth under the regency of one of his trustiest viscounts, Giraud Berlay. Then, with Nantes once more securely under the vassalage of the Count of Anjou, the lands and riches of the two sisters would be reconfirmed, and there would be no lord in France who would not compete for their hands. Such beauty would not go unrewarded. A little patience — that was all the Countess urged on her friend.

There was nothing Hersende did not recount to her

younger sister Milesende, embellishing every avenue of their future with the most scented garlands, until neither girl could sleep once the first touches of grey had painted the dawn around their bed. For Hersende each new morning brought her impatiently nearer the day which the Countess promised; and with her mind fixed on that day she saw with an almost unbearable longing the man she loved coming towards her. And with a frankness that the Countess Elizabeth had taught her not to shy from, she would lie there with the most agreeable sensation of sharing her bed, not with her beloved sister, but with her lover Sebrand.

The news of Conquereuil, and the Countess's words, made an impact just as deep on Milesende. But for the younger sister the dawn seemed interminable and grey. She listened to Hersende and watched her blossoming with prettiness, but felt within herself a kind of helplessness, as if her life were suddenly to be taken from her and delivered into the hands of monsters. She walked her favourite fields and river banks in the warm evenings while Hersende was with the Countess, and it was as though her dreams were shrivelling like the summer flowers. Autumn seemed to be encroaching on her young life, and her hopes were dry.

Her friend and accomplice the fat cook remarked on her sadness one evening as she returned to the castle holding a bunch of cornflowers. She led the girl aside and looked at her sternly; then she peeled away Milesende's peasant shawl and shook her head.

'Oh, if I had your beauty ... if I had your youth ... I should be bright as the sun. When you marry you can have any man you want. I had to make do with what I could get. Mind you,' the cook added laughing, with much heaving of flesh, 'I did get a lot ... *and* a child with each of them. Well, perhaps there were a few in between.'

Milesende could not hold back a tear. The cook noticed it and dabbed her face with a cloth and much motherly tut-tutting.

'Come. Come. You're too old to cry like a child and too young to cry for love. So, why does he make you unhappy, this fellow you meet out there in the fields?'

Milesende could only shake her head. But the tears made her feel better, and she smiled at the cook, pressing her bunch of cornflowers into the shining red hands. The cook hugged her to the cushions of her body, then pushed her away, flapping her hands as though she were a hen.

'Off with you, my sleepwalker! Find another one and make him jealous. Soon you'll be a grand lady and they'll all come running.'

The gossamer dreams of Milesende lay roughly torn by the events of the past weeks. Her life had been lonely during the year since she was removed so abruptly to Angers; but this loneliness had been assuaged by a delicate fabric of thoughts she carried about with her — thoughts that were spun from her childhood in Brittany and that supported the only future she could believe in. She inhabited an invisible world, one that echoed to the rapid pulse of feelings and was lit by the most delicious extremes of enchantment and danger. It was a world made up of countless tales which she had listened to day after day in what now seemed an intense and distant past; and yet they held a kind of truth that had no place in the rougher world around her in this castle, so that her isolation from those who lived here became a confirmation that she did not belong to it, and would never need to. Then something she had never experienced invaded that private garden of her mind. There was a man standing there, very tall and beautiful, and he too appeared not to belong to the rude world outside. She would see him daily, by accident at first and then on purpose, as she returned from the fields with flowers in her hand. She wanted to give the flowers to him but did not dare. One day she followed him at a distance into the cathedral and stood in the shadows watching as he gazed about him with an intense expression: finally he turned and she hurried away. Now when she walked by the river bank she sensed that he was with her, and pulled her shawl close around her because she felt cold even though the summer heat was intense. Once it was quite the opposite. She had gone further afield than usual and was so stifled by the heat that she nearly fainted. There was a pool among the trees backed by high rocks, and a waterfall that splashed among the irises and the purple loosestrife. A golden bird darted between the trees and perched invisibly among the foliage, giving out a fluid melody that seemed to echo the sound of falling water. It was a kind of paradise, all of her own, and as she stood gazing at the scene she was overwhelmed by an impulse. She removed her clothes, laying them carefully on a rock, and tiptoed into the cool water. She felt the splash of the cascade on her body: then she stepped into the shock of the falls, her eyes closed, head thrown back, hands clasped over her breasts. It was a sensation almost of burning: she was immersed in the embrace of the water as though she were a part of it and the vibrations were within herself — until a shock of such perfect pleasure ran through her that she felt herself falling and the soft pool held her trembling body as she lay.

She returned rather later than usual, her clothing and hair still wet under her peasant shawl. The world seemed changed as she made her way along the narrow streets. Then she saw Rollo, laughing with Sebrand, and hid within her shawl. But she could not resist glancing at him as she passed, and looking over her shoulder as she entered the castle.

The disturbed thoughts of the young Milesende were churned by the contrast between her own situation and that of her buoyant sister. For Hersende the change of fortunes brought about by the victory at Conquereuil opened up only the most delightful of vistas: as a lady of title and possessions she was now free, she hoped, to place herself winningly before the eyes of Sebrand. Perhaps she would have to work for it by aiming her charms elsewhere, but that in itself could be agreeable. But for Milesende the opposite had happened. While she had been someone of no consequence she was debarred from any match that Count Fulk might consider advantageous to the county of Anjou: accustomed to the solitude of that garden of her own thoughts, she knew that whoever entered there would not be from the world where titles ruled. He would be free — free to choose, to love, to love her. But now ... She wondered what sneering nobleman of Fulk's court might even this minute be nodding in agreement to a match in return for ... whatever might be hers in land or titles, she did not know or care. She did know, however, that the tall figure who had already found his way into her garden might never, never be permitted to claim the prize she could offer him. As a lady of rank she felt doomed to be sold like a slave.

But back in her room high in the castle that evening there was a surprise which rekindled her dreams. She was met by an excited Hersende and her maids; and as she entered the door a man in strange bright clothing, holding a lute, rose and smiled. He was not young and had a worn face, but the finest hands she had ever seen, studded with rings. He was, Hersende said, a minstrel: he was to sing before the banquet tomorrow evening to celebrate Count Fulk's recovery, and today he was playing to the ladies of the court: he had promised her a song of romance, a tale of the art of love which he said he had composed himself and had already sung to the greatest ladies in Paris, and in Burgundy, and in the far south where they spoke the language of Oc. It was the story of a rose.

The two sisters listened spellbound as the minstrel began his song. Hersende kept exclaiming and applauding, interrupting the singer with little bursts of joy. Milesende stayed entirely silent as he sang, lost within the music of the strings and the tale he told. The minstrel sang of a dream — how in the month of May he found his way into an enclosed garden of rare beauty where the God of Love was holding court —

how he saw there a rosebud of exquisite form which he longed to pick, but the God of Love shot an arrow into him — how the pain seemed to enter his very heart, and he found himself surrendering to the most cruel and arduous tasks that were imposed upon him in which he felt all the agonies of love (and here the minstrel recounted the most miraculous adventures with dragons and demons and impenetrable castles) until the dreamer could see before him only the prospect of his own death — and how on the shores of despair there appeared before his eyes the same lovely rose in the garden, and he reached out ... and plucked it.

And so — the minstrel explained when the applause was over — true love is able to surmount all the trials and obstacles the wicked world places in its way, whereas the love which is instantly rewarded may instantly die. Hersende folded her arms across her breast with the deepest of sighs, enraptured by the thought that in the nearest possible future her loved one might be embarking on the most testing of tribulations in the face of giants and dragons which he would of course sweep aside to fall prostrate and only lightly wounded before her tearful self. Milesende found in the minstrel's tale a quiet message of hope.

While romance and minstrelsy fluttered delicately round the upper chambers of the castle, Count Fulk again felt the urge for war. He no longer lay on his sick-bed: he strode, and he ordered. First there were other matters to be disposed of. He summoned Bishop Renaud, his chaplain Baudouin, the Chancellor Audemand, the Treasurer Bouchard, several notaries and scribes; then he dictated this charter: *Count Fulk, in expiation for the massacres at the Battle of Conquereuil, exempts the convent of St Maurice, attendant on the cathedral of St Maurice, from all taxes levied on their estates.* He harried the scribe so fiercely that no document was ever produced more quickly; then he applied his large cross, and commanded those present to witness it in their own fashion.

'Now ... another!'

And he dictated again. *Count Fulk here announces a generous gift to the cathedral of St Maurice at Angers for the help of his sinful soul and to obtain pardon for the massacre of Christians which he had caused on the plain of Conquereuil.*

'This, Chancellor, to be proclaimed on Sunday in the public square. Bishop, the Countess has already spoken to you of this gift. In addition our plans are to rebuild the cathedral according to designs drawn up by our friend from Jumièges, Rollo – with my approval.'

Witnesses to this scene noted that the Bishop's approval was not to be sought. The Bishop himself looked grave, and without a word bowed and departed.

'Audemand, kindly stay a while.'

The others took his meaning and departed in the wake of the Bishop. Fulk's long face still looked gaunt, and his hand on the old Chancellor's shoulder lacked its normal bruising force. But he was his restless self again. He had put behind him his guilt over the slaughter at Conquereuil, and he had disposed of the gift to the cathedral which cleansed his conscience in that direction. Fulk now stood four-square with his back to the window and his vast hands dangling as if preparing to stride forward and shake the future into submission. Audemand knew this mood of Fulk's well, and wondered what audacious project lay behind those ferocious dark eyes.

As if to warm himself up, Fulk began to talk of the Church. Bishop Renaud was a proud man, he announced – a vain man who would never have enough. No gratitude could be expected from such a prelate; and when he, Fulk, rebuilt his cathedral Renaud would then expect more lands, more fiefs, more power – as if he were a lord. Audemand pointed out that the Bishop was indeed a lord, but Fulk cut in on him: the Bishop had given up all such titles and swagger when he accepted the office from his father Geoffrey Greymantle. Fulk himself would not have made such a choice. However, the Count went on in a tone that was ever so slightly relenting, it was better – he supposed – to have a godly man as a bishop than a debauchee like the Archbishop of Reims, Arnulf, who ran a harem and had every brigand in the county of Champagne in his fee; or a pederast like Archbishop Hugh of Tours, who made certain that every priest in every diocese was of his own persuasion, and who had just appointed his own lover and archdeacon a bishop. Audemand volunteered the suggestion that this at least insured against priests being married, which was the more normal state, or sleeping with their slaves and servants and then offering their offspring to the unfortunate monasteries. But Fulk was not in the mood for pleasantries and continued to stand as if blocking the path to all the evils of this world.

Then came the plan of action. Conan was crushed, dead. The lord Giraud Berlay, so valiant at Conquereuil, would hold Nantes as regent for the young Judicael against any revival of Breton ambitions – most unlikely, Fulk thought, since Conan's eldest son Budic was now held in the castle prisons here at Angers, where he would remain until his brothers offered a bond of vassalage to Anjou – equally unlikely, he feared. Meanwhile, those two pretty things, daughters of the late Count of Brittany, must be declared legitimate – which they were certainly not – and married with large dowries to suitable allies.

Fulk now turned to the matter of Odo. Henceforth the full weight of Anjou would lean on the Count of Blois. The city of Tours would be choked by a ring of new castles. Already there was Amboise, held by Sulpice's brother the Lord Archambaud: this cut the road and river between Tours and Blois itself. To the south was Loches and Ste Maure, and to the west Langeais. So Tours was already encircled by Angevin fortresses. Fulk thrust a hand out in front of him and slowly closed his fingers round an imaginary city, expelling air fiercely between his teeth.

'But, Audemand' — and the Count's voice became subdued — 'we know from Durtal that these castles can be brushed aside like *that*'; and he swept a pewter goblet off the table beside him and it catapulted against the wall. 'I know exactly what we need.' And Fulk strode across the room and reached for a roll of parchment near his bed. 'Here' — and he tapped the roll with his forefinger — 'is the answer . . . which is where our Norman comes in. Kindly send for him now.'

The Count waited. And in his rooms high on the east side of the castle, Rollo waited. The meeting planned so elaborately and postponed for so long was at last about to take place: and even if no comet appeared in the sky that morning, and no dog was reported to have given birth to a seven-headed monster, it was none the less a meeting which those who knew about it sensed to be more resonant with meaning than a mere encounter between lord and mastermason. Perhaps the old Chancellor, as he made his stately way between one and the other along the corridors of the castle, was the only man to understand fully that here were two men goaded by an urge to shape the world — one a man of peace, the other of war. Audemand had seen Rollo's plans for the cathedral, and was dumbfounded: never could he have imagined a house of God of such audacity and splendour — it was as though the world he knew were in its mere infancy and here was a man with a vision of its full-grown majesty. As for Fulk, Audemand had served under his father and his grandfather; but the young Count — so terrifying in his resolve and in his anger — was driven by a force he had never before encountered, as if he too possessed a vision of that full-grown world and with his bare hands would mould it that way. It was more than the survival of Anjou; it was more than the crushing of Conan and the Count of Blois: the vision of Fulk seemed to embrace all the lands of the north in one glorious kingdom to outshine the Romans. Perhaps,

Audemand reflected, this was why the Count craved so deeply for the son he did not have. An heir to that vision.

Rollo stood at the door. Before him was a room lined in red and sparkling with gold. In the centre stood a man in a plain grey jerkin. He was tall – almost as tall perhaps as Rollo himself. But it was not just his height that was striking: his breadth was such that his legs were wide apart even where they sprouted from his torso as if to support the remarkable width of the man. There he was – Black Fulk. Not black at all, as Rollo noticed, except for a single feature that held his attention as if by royal command: his eyes. They were as black as midnight, but with the brightness of an invisible flame burning there, held before him like an inquisition. Fulk stared, without moving, without blinking; Rollo waited, the roll of parchment held in one hand. If this were a test, he made up his mind not to flinch. Then unexpectedly Fulk smiled.

'It's true that you have the eyes of a magician. Audemand told me they change colour, and I was waiting to see.'

With that the Count laughed. The next minute he had crossed the room with light steps and embraced the surprised Rollo. Then, as he stepped back, he clasped Rollo by the shoulders before taking the Norman's hands in his own.

'I should have liked to meet you earlier,' he said, releasing Rollo from his grip. The Count's eyes were surveying his open palms as if tracing Rollo's imprint there. He looked again at the Norman.

'You have strong hands like mine. And yet you're a builder and mine were made to kill.'

Fulk seemed immersed in the thought. Then he went on, talking almost to himself. Rollo listened, fascinated: he had not expected this from the Count. Fulk continued to look down at his own hands. They were the guardians of Anjou, he said: they had to fight, destroy, in order to build. Without a defender Anjou would disappear – and he squeezed those huge hands together. It was a small land, but one day it would be great. He knew this. He would make it so. A destroyer needs a creator: this was why he had sent for Rollo ... why he was delighted the Norman was here. They would work together. They would build a nation. And again he embraced Rollo.

'So, show me my cathedral,' he went on, his eyes on the parchment Rollo was holding.

Rollo spread it open with some apprehension across the table, securing the corners with candlesticks which he realized as he picked them up were solid gold. Whether he likes it or not, Rollo thought, at least he will be able to afford it. Fulk peered closely for what seemed an age. From time to time he grunted. A forefinger weighted by a gigantic ring set with a deep red stone traced his line of sight – around windows, doorways and up columns, pausing to take in carved capitals, then following the long curve of a roof vault until it reached the highest point above the nave. The finger paused.

'I don't understand.'

Rollo explained. It was the first time he had put words to an idea that had come to him after his first visit to the wrecked cathedral. He had wanted the place to be filled with light, he explained to Fulk: but how? He had remembered the Count's flowering tree rising towards the sun and crowned with white doves – doves of peace – the Holy Dove. That was how it began, in the little garden. But *how* to do it? Fulk was listening intently, his finger still resting on that highest point of the vault. Then the idea had come to him: supposing the arches, instead of spanning the nave in parallel like the hoops of a barrel, were to cross over one another in pairs! They would support the same weight of stone, but now the spaces of wall between the vaults would be free of weight: so windows could be set there, high up, almost at roof level: light could be let in to flood the roof. And at the very centre, where the Count's finger rested, where the arches crossed, he would place a boss – a block of stone – carved with the Count's doves, one after the other down the entire length of the nave.

There was a pause. The Count slowly removed his finger from the parchment. Rollo could hear him swallowing and drawing breath heavily.

'And you think you could build that?' he said after a few moments.

'Yes.'

There was another lengthy pause.

'Extraordinary!' he said at length, gazing at Rollo with those piercing eyes. 'The holy abbot has sent me a genius.'

Rollo could find nothing to say. He felt stunned and not a little surprised.

'Mind you,' Fulk went on, 'I wonder what our lord bishop will have to say. He is, to say the least, traditional: you may have noticed.'

Rollo knew he had an ally.

'It occurred to me that if *you* liked it that might not matter,' he ventured. He heard Fulk laugh quietly to himself as he continued to gaze at the drawings. The Norman felt elated. This man had eyes, and could see. Rollo knew that he could live and work here.

'But listen, Rollo. More urgent matters.' And Fulk stood up to his full height, his hands on his hips. 'If your cathedral were a fortress I could take it with two knights and a battering-ram in five minutes. You saw what happened at Durtal. Now, what could your genius build that I couldn't take? And mark you, if I couldn't, no one could.'

Rollo felt cornered. In the flush of success he had not expected this swift turn in the argument. But Fulk did not wait for an answer. He reached for another roll of parchment that Rollo had not noticed and laid it over the top of his own. It was a rough design for a fort executed in heavy strokes of the pen and blotched here and there. Whoever had designed it for the Count was certainly no draughtsman: Rollo decided to say nothing on that score. But what could he possibly say on any score? he wondered.

'We have to build in stone. Could you build that?'

The fort was circular and raised on a mound, with the indication of some sort of ditch below. It reminded Rollo of what he had seen at Durtal, except that this was not designed in wood, and it had small slits for windows on several levels. Could he build this?

'I believe so,' he replied. 'Give me a few moments.' The walls would need to be thick, and the masonry sound; but that, Rollo imagined, was about it. He found it hard to understand why in all the county of Anjou there were not masons in plenty who could undertake so straightforward a task. The Count gave one of his grunts, which Rollo had come to understand meant another question was on the way.

'And what do you think of it?' Fulk's voice sounded gruff. Rollo would have to be careful. He felt cornered again. He had no knowledge of military matters, but at least the Count knew that. So what did he expect? Rollo looked hard at the parchment. He thought about the kind of stone needed, and how to lay it to offer the greatest resistance to bombardment, siege-towers, grappling-hooks. So what would happen if a round wall were badly damaged in one place? The entire structure would be weakened. And visibility? From a round tower the back of every defender must be at least half-turned to all action except what was directly in front of him, or Rollo imagined so. The answer seemed simple.

'Why don't you build it square? Or rectangular?'

It was Fulk's turn to look puzzled. He peered down at the parchment, then back at Rollo.

'For what?' he said curtly.

Rollo pointed out the structural weakness of a round wall: he had noticed this when building the apse at Jumièges, he said. A single flaw and the wall was apt to collapse outwards. With a square or rectangular shape each section of wall was structurally independent. Furthermore it could easily be strengthened at key points by buttresses — and he traced what he meant with his finger on the parchment. He had used those at Jumièges too. Then, again, the four corners could be further strengthened, and could support four small towers rising higher than the remainder of the wall: in this way defenders could cover two sections of wall from each tower — in fact each section of wall would be covered from two directions — an attacker would have to face cross-fire.

The Count looked at him. His face was severe and his eyes seemed to bore into Rollo. Then he gave another grunt and, reaching down, tugged the parchment free of the candlesticks and hurriedly rolled it up. He tapped the roll on the table in front of Rollo.

'Do better, then,' was all he said, turning away towards the window.

Rollo caught the eye of Audemand who had been standing quietly all this time. His face was expressionless, but he indicated with a quick tilt of the head that Rollo was to depart. Rollo mumbled some words of thanks and, leaving his own designs for the cathedral unrolled on the table, followed the Chancellor out of that red and golden room. The Count still had his back to them and did not move. When the door was closed behind them Audemand placed a hand affectionately on the Norman's shoulder, and from that single gesture Rollo knew that he had passed a test.

'You'll have noticed,' said the Chancellor quietly as they turned into the corridor, 'the Count fancies himself with the quill. There are some who feel he should stick to the sword.'

A look of horror came over Rollo's face.

'You mean . . .?'

And he turned to look hard at the old Chancellor, who said nothing more but whose familiar quizzical smile told Rollo that he had just called Count Fulk a fool and got away with it.

*

Not since long before midsummer had the castle of Angers been witness to such a banquet. In the encroaching dusk of a late-August evening the great hall flickered with colour and light: the aroma of viands and fruits mingled with the savour of dark wines and the fragrance of rare perfumes, and music filtered through the laughter of many voices. It was an evening in which all the splendour of Anjou was gathered to toast the health of its Count. And what splendour! You would have believed that every outpost of the world had been plundered of their richest treasures so that they might be laid out before Fulk. Gold and precious jewels, ivory and damask, porphyry and amethyst, glass, enamels, embroidered silks, silver goblets and candlesticks, finely wrought brooches and buckles, pins, bracelets: these and countless other devices of the most wonderful artifice glittered on every surface and every skin. And within this glistening sea that swirled about the Black Count, what currents of hope and intrigue you could have detected with a sharp eye among those who drank and danced, whispered and consulted, chose their moment to be seen or not seen. For now all those confidences in dark corridors and dreams in lonely chambers were being swept into the light like a huge public confessional that everyone could half-hear: the castle of Count Fulk was taking stock of itself amid the harmony of wine and music.

Fulk himself drank little, seated at the heart of this great gathering, often lost in thought like a silent emperor. From time to time he tapped his goblet on the arm of his chair, but when a servant hurried over to refill it the Count appeared surprised and waved him away. The most attentive figure around him was the Lady Adelaide, surprisingly: her usual distaste for maleness of any physical kind was quite overcome in the massive presence of the Count, and her rather withered beauty seemed to bloom again as she laid a pale arm across his chair beside him. Fulk looked up and gazed through her as if she were transparent. The Countess

Elizabeth, her small daughter on her knee, noticed the girl-ish unfreezing of Adelaide and her husband's dismissal of her attentions, and smiled. Sebrand, who was among those around her, was confirmed in his view that the Countess was the loveliest creature in Anjou: that sweet radiance and slimness of form were an ideal he feared could never be matched. The world available to him seemed populated only by widows or by buxom creatures like the young Hersende who flaunted her charms too generously for his taste, however pretty she might be, as the Countess never tired of reminding him.

The bubbling Hersende was the object of all other male eyes as she danced so enchantingly, fair hair tossed, torch-light modelling her body as she turned. Her glances, who-ever was dancing with her, were for Rollo, to the delight and confusion of the Norman as he moved as unobtrusively as his height permitted among the crowds of revellers, his eyes following her among the skeins of dancers and his heart giving him a stab of pleasure when he caught her green eyes directed towards him. Every now and again his gaze was distracted. A squat, black-haired man whom he knew to be Roger de Montrésor, swayed towards him between two women each clasped like sheaves of corn in either arm: he belched and grinned a greeting with broken teeth, and swayed on. Then Sulpice, the young Adonis, broke from a knot of female admirers to shake the Norman's hand and wish him well; and as he did so Rollo caught the passing glance of the beautiful child Milesende, Hersende's sister, the girl of the sad eyes and the cascade of black hair that until now he had only glimpsed beneath a grey shawl. She glanced back again just as she had the day before in the dusk outside the castle gates, before seeming to melt into the shadows beyond the torch-light, and disappear.

It grew late. The Count had risen. Rollo searched for Hersende, but the dancing had stopped and he could not find her. He saw the Countess carrying her sleeping child from the hall, Sebrand with her. Suddenly he felt a hand slipped into his and turned sharply. Beside him was a tall, slender creature all in red, with a face whose skin was drawn taut over her bones, which made her mouth thin and vagrant. Her dress revealed much of what he had seen momentarily one evening slumped against an open door, and she wore the same blurred smile. Her eyes were bright and predatory with wine, and her rumpled hair lay black over the skin of her shoulders. The thin hand drew his towards her and squeezed it against the muscles of her thigh. Then she turned away without a word. Rollo looked around him and saw Audemand standing near him, his face not quite swallowing a look of amusement.

'A word with you, Rollo,' he said softly. 'Be prepared to leave tomorrow. It seems the Count can think of nothing but your castles: he's been building them all evening. Most unlike him on occasions like this; usually he'd be dancing and making merry. Now you won't have a moment's peace, I can assure you. And, by the way, he's sent you a token of his esteem. I'll bid you good night.'

The Chancellor gave him a friendly squeeze of the shoulder and departed, his staff parting an avenue between the lingering revellers. The Lady Adelaide was among those who followed him from the hall: Rollo saw her glance to where her husband Roger was holding a goblet to the lips of a girl who was bare to the waist, his other hand clasped over one of her breasts. Several men had passed out on the floor among a litter of goblets, bones, fruit and sweetmeats mixed with articles of clothing and splashes of vomit. Among the men still swaying on their feet Rollo noticed the Count's obese brother Maurice, his mouth hanging open like a wound, his hands reaching uncertainly for whatever female flesh he could reach. It was not a pretty sight, and Rollo, his own head swimming with wine, made his way gratefully along the lamplit corridors to his rooms.

It was suddenly quiet and he began to collect his senses.

Today felt like a journey that spanned half his life. He was caught in rapids that had no ending. Tomorrow . . . Audemand had said . . . not a moment's peace now. But where tomorrow? For how long? With whom? The image of Hersende dancing among the flickering torches drifted before his eyes, and with it a stab of regret that he must leave . . . to return when? The look in those soft green eyes would have faded by then. Or the girl herself would be back in Nantes. He reached his door tired and downcast. It was open and the room shone with light. A man stood waiting, and Rollo recognized Fulk's chamberlain. The man bowed, then addressed him with a studied deference. Gifts, he said, from the Count. He, the chamberlain, would be happy to be in charge of their security should the master-mason wish, before his departure tomorrow with Count Fulk and the lord Sebrand. Then he bowed again, and quietly left.

Rollo gazed incredulously at the brightly lit table, for there on either side rose a pair of candlesticks some two feet in height; they were wrought of twisted silver, and from each stem sprouted the forms of strange beasts, birds and half-human faces that glimmered in the lamplight like figures in a dream. And in the centre of the table, between the two candlesticks, stood an object such as he had seen many times at Jumièges, only this appeared to be of solid gold. It was an altar – quite small, barely half the height of the candlesticks. Rollo remembered the abbot would carry such an altar with him when he travelled to neighbouring priories. It was constructed like a tiny church, only the roof was studded with pearls and bloodstones set within a fret of gold, while along the wall was fixed a plaque of copper enamelled in blue representing the figures of angels and amid them that of a bearded man holding what appeared to be a shrine. Around the border of the plaque Rollo could pick out two lines of lettering. He brought a lamp close and saw that the inscription was in Latin, some of it indistinct, but much of it clear enough to read. He made out the following words — ANGELVS AD CELVM RAPIAT POST DONA DATOREM; NE TAMEN ACCELERET NE (the next words were too faint to distinguish) CVI PAX VEL BELLVM MOTVSVE QVIESVE PER ILLVM. Rollo read the inscription again, pausing to decipher the sense of the words: 'May the angel take the giver to Heaven after his gifts; but not just yet lest ... since on him it depends for peace or war, agitation or rest.'

Rollo sank into a chair, bewildered. The meaning puzzled him. Who was the 'giver'? Fulk? And what depended on him? Anjou? If this was his reward for calling the Count a fool, what might he expect next? Rollo had never acquired worldly riches — or indeed worldly goods of any kind: life at Jumièges had always separated him from any such opportunities or ambitions. It had never occurred to him that they might come his way. Now the sight of those glistening jewels was both disquieting and seductive. He was forced to ask himself again who he was. He felt adrift. And yet ... A vision of the lovely Hersende rose before him again: she was bedecked with pearls and precious stones as she came towards him, and in the lamplight her body glowed naked through pale silks.

He had no idea how long he sat there. Gold and silver swam before his eyes in the gentle movement of the lamplight. Finally he rose, and as he did so Rollo thought he heard a sound beyond the door. He stood still, listening, but could hear no further sound, so he went over and quietly lifted the latch. As he opened it, the door brushed against something at his feet, and looking down he noticed a small package that had been slipped underneath. Rollo picked it up — turned it over — and saw it was sealed, but with no insignia. It was small and light in his hand. Quickly breaking the wax he undid the wrapping. Inside lay a small gold key.

Rollo gazed at it. Then he turned it over in the light of a flame. It was just a key; very small, perfectly made. He was puzzled. Who might conceivably have sent it, and for what purpose? The treasure on the table included no box; and even if it had the chamberlain would hardly have slipped it quietly under the door. Rollo closed his fingers on the key and looked about him in case there might be some clue he had missed. There was nothing.

Then he stepped outside into the passageway and looked left and right, but there was no one, only the long flickering shadows cast by the lamps. Then he caught the sound of laughter, followed by a shriek accompanied by more laughter — men's and women's voices. Maybe there was no connection with the mysterious visitor of the night, and yet Rollo was intrigued. He followed the sounds which seemed to be coming from the floor below him though he could hear them quite distinctly. It was a passageway he had never taken, and it began to curve. As it did so Rollo noticed that the inner wall was lined with woven hangings: the sounds seemed to be coming from behind them but on a lower level. Rollo realized there must be hidden windows opening on to some kind of inner courtyard. There was another shriek, then more laughter and the sound of an object falling — a table? a person? — followed by silence until the same voices could be heard again. This time he thought he recognized one of the voices, that of Roger the Devil. Suddenly there was a yell which made him stop, and at that moment he caught sight of a figure half hidden by one of the wall-hangings. The figure seemed to notice him at the same time and stepped back quickly, tugged a cowl over his head and disappeared, a black form melting into the blackness. But for a split second in the lamplight Rollo had recognized the Count's chaplain, Baudouin.

He retraced his steps to his rooms with the uneasy awareness that in Fulk's castle there were dark things and dark lives he did not understand. Rollo closed the door behind him and looked again at the candlesticks and the golden altar, and at the gold key in the palm of his hand.

FOUR

IN THE PALLID DAWN everyone in the city on Angers knew for certain that Count Fulk was himself again. It was market day, and as the straggle of country people made their way through the main gate of the city into the tangle of narrow streets, they brought with them not only their bundles and their creaking carts, their fruit and poultry, panniers, dogs, goats, pigs; they brought a tale of what had met their eyes as they crossed the bridge in the grey light.

All along the river flank of the city the walls were hung with bodies, they said, like a shrike's larder. There had been terror among the peasants at first, and many of them turned back, until as the day grew brighter they saw that the corpses were draped in clothes that were not of Anjou. And they were the clothes of noblemen; some of the peasants exclaimed that when they had fought at Conquereuil they had seen such noblemen and that they were Breton knights. Soon the city buzzed with talk of the executions, and with every barter and purchase came a fresh tale of sounds heard in the night – the clanging of gates, shuffle of feet, cries, thuds, groans, Hail Maries – until so vivid grew the stories that it was a mystery how several thousand citizens had managed not to know what a spectacle presented itself to the outside world until the peasants had told them with wide eyes.

There must have been thirty or forty bodies dangling there, and already the kites and the crows were making sorties above the river bank, and lean dogs were gazing upwards. And in the midst of this drapery of human flesh there was a man alive in a cage, naked. He was a young man

— that you could see even though his head had been shaved
and his body was hunched by the constriction of the iron
bars; there was a smoothness about his skin and a youthful,
defiant look upon his face even when people threw rotten
fruit and bones at him, and a guard on the wall tipped a
bucket of urine and faeces down on him and laughed. He did
not move a muscle. Who was he? people asked in the
marketplace. There were some who felt sorry for him:
others said he was only a bastard Breton who got what he
deserved. It was a member of the guard on his way from the
executioner's tower who spread the word: the naked man in
the cage was Budic, eldest son of the dead Conan. Roger de
Montrésor had overpowered and captured him at Conquereuil: he would be left there in his cage until duly chas-
tened and then held in prison at the Count's pleasure. As for
the others, all were knights who had conspired with Conan
in the seizure of Nantes after the death of Count Alain. Fulk
had not felt merciful: but then mercy was not a quality
which those buying their provisions in the marketplace
associated with their lord. There was a widespread air of
relief among those prodding the haunches of a fine pig that it
was not one of them being fed to the kites.

Count Fulk was restless to leave. Or at first light he had
been restless to leave, but the same light that beckoned him
to Langeais had bathed the sleeping Elizabeth so sweetly
that now, as a chamberlain knocked cautiously at the door
and urgent whispers filled the corridors, he was still asleep in
her arms while she gazed contentedly at the shifting patterns
of sunlight on the wooden ceiling and hoped the chamberlain would not think a journey of some five hours important
enough to make him enter.

While the Count overslept, other occupants of the castle
of Angers were greeting the day more characteristically. It
would be some hours before the Lady Ermengarde would be
conscious of whether it was day at all, or whether her
favoured manservant had departed from her bed or not. Her

less favoured husband, the Lord Treasurer, was already attending to the gifts which the Count would be bearing with him to the Governor of Langeais and, more particularly, to the abbot of Corméry. The castle treasury was considerably swollen since the defeat of the lord of Rennes, and the Count's generosity would see to it that allegiances were doubly secure among allies who might otherwise be tempted by the largesse of the crafty Odo. Corméry, after all, was a mere canter from the city of Tours itself, and there had been occasions when Archbishop Hugh had made it known to Abbot Gervais that several remunerative vineyards in the neighbourhood might pass into the hands of the monastery in return for favourable blessings on the enterprises of the Count of Blois. The Treasurer was therefore ensuring that any such ungodly temptations would be painlessly resisted – at a cost only to those knights now dangling above the river. They had paid for their treachery with their lives, and with the most gratifying quantity of gold.

The Lady Adelaide was already at her prayers: it was hard to say for whom since she prayed for everyone, but certainly those whose salvation was most earnestly sought included Ermengarde, whom Adelaide had observed the previous evening proffering her charms to the tall Viking; and of course her prayers as usual embraced her own husband, Roger, whose place in her bed had remained – as usual – unoccupied. Roger was greeting the dawn from amid an assortment of other female limbs in that region of the castle where such pleasures could be had. It was variously described. To the Count's chaplain, Baudouin, it was 'that sink of iniquity' – a not inaccurate account of the place since iniquity was certainly its trade, and what is more it was carried out in and around a secluded yard not unlike a sink if viewed from above. To the Countess, who was not supposed to know of its existence, it was simply 'the whorehouse'. But among nearly everyone else it was referred to with surprising gentleness of phrase as 'the dovecot'. Presumably this was in reference to the birds who fluttered round Count Fulk's garden; all the same it was a puzzling reference since the Count had never been known to go near the place, and — what is more — Fulk's doves were virginal white whereas the ladies of the dovecot, though many of them white, were scarcely virgins. However, no one seemed bothered by such thoughts, least of all Fulk himself, who took the view that since all the marriages around him were political arrangements (he had seen to that), gratification of the flesh had to be obtained somewhere, and it was clearly better if illegitimate children had no status rather than having to be found lands and dowries and small titles. Indeed some of his best soldiers had hatched, so to speak, from the dovecot, which reinforced his opinion that male children conceived in lust often possessed more vigour than those seeded in a dutiful bed. It was different for him: his father Geoffrey Greymantle had been shrewd enough to choose him a wife in whom beauty and political advantage dwelt together (only the absence of a male child marred the harmony of their relationship). But for his brother Maurice, married to a timid child, and Roger the Devil, married to a holy reptile ... well! what else could a man do when the loins stirred?

The morning, however, did not discover Maurice asleep in the dovecot. He had not been able to stagger that far the previous night, and had been guided by two menservants to the privacy of his own rooms where now he lay oblivious and sweaty across the body of his child-wife, Adèle, whose cheeks were stained salty with dried tears.

The Lady Adelaide still prayed. There was a fresh customer for the salvation she begged of the Almighty: the young Breton girl Hersende. Adelaide had noticed with mounting concern the blossoming of the fair-haired orphan, and the effect her robust charms were exerting on the men of the court of Angers. She had entertained hopes of a nunnery for the unfortunate creature, and had even spoken to her and to Baudouin of such a vocation – Baudouin had undertaken to press the girl on the matter. Yet last night Hersende's behaviour appeared far from that required of a bride of Christ, indeed her dress seemed more fitted for the 'sink of iniquity' than for the cloister. To reveal so much, to display – flaunt! – so much could only, if allowed to proceed unchecked, lead to the path already trodden by the Lady Ermengarde. Adelaide vowed to keep a sharper eye on the girl, as well as on those two young men most susceptible, Sebrand and the Norman, Rollo. She would be doubly vigilant.

Meanwhile the girl in question, still exhausted by the dance, lay curled within dreams of her lover. She could feel as she slept the strength of his arms carrying her and the weight of his body pressing down on her. She was already the Lady Hersende de Chemillé, and no passion like hers for Sebrand had ever been born. Lying beside her half-awake, Milesende let her eyes follow the shaft of early sunlight out through the window until it seemed to draw her into a garden of sparkling water that cascaded over her body and cast drops of liquid like pearls on to the perfect bud of a rose beside her; and she stood waiting in her nakedness as the pure song of a minstrel told her that the dragons were slain and the demons put to flight by the most beautiful man in the world, who would even now be waiting to reach out and take the rose.

And along the walls beyond the sleepers and the dreamers kites flapped among the bodies of warriors whose blood was already dry.

It was the first time the people of Angers had set eyes on their Count since he had stridden blood-stained through the city gates and collapsed in the shadow of his own castle. Now men, women and children hurried to get a glimpse of him as the party of horsemen emerged from the castle. Their clothing told people this was no battle: the soldiers were armed but Fulk himself had thrown only a thin grey jerkin over his bare chest on this late-summer morning, and his huge bare arms held the reins loosely as he looked around him gravely and acknowledged the hubbub of the crowd with a hand raised in greeting. The crowd recognized the new High Constable behind him, Sebrand de Chemillé, more flamboyantly dressed than his master in a red surcoat that rippled across the flank of the grey stallion he rode. But who, they wondered, was the immensely tall, fair-haired man on the chestnut horse by Sebrand's side? He was dressed as simply as the Count himself, but he wore an air of authority, and when he turned his gaze on those pressing around the gates of the city a murmur rose at the sight of those deep blue eyes. Others were looking at him too from high on the castle walls, among them a slender dark-haired girl with her fingers to her lips and a small bunch of blue cornflowers clasped in her other hand. She remained there long after the others had waved and departed – a small motionless figure whom Rollo never noticed as the party of horsemen broke into a canter and headed for the forest.

The principal highway to Langeais followed the River Loire upstream along its northern bank; but Fulk had decided against this. Midway between the Anjou capital and Langeais, on the farther side of the Loire, lay the castle of Saumur high on its rock; here in the heart of Anjou was one of the most powerful bastions loyal to the Count of Blois. It was a thorn in Fulk's side. The Governor of Saumur was among Odo's fiercest vassals, Gelduin – 'the Demon' everyone called him in Angers – and there were those who whispered that Gelduin was the one man Fulk would avoid meeting in battle if he could. Gelduin – who looked like a vulture and had never been known to smile except at an execution. Fulk had no wish to alert 'the Demon' to his movements, and so he chose the road to the north which followed the little river called the Authion for the first hour, then passed by the castles of Beaufort, Longué and Vernantes before plunging into the dense oak-forest known as the Landes de St Martin. This was the same forest from which, six years earlier, Fulk as a mere youth had swept like a storm along with Roger, Sulpice and Archambaud to seize the town of Langeais before the guards could raise a sword. The same forest and the same black stallion, Moro.

Rollo remembered Sebrand telling him that story as the two of them had ridden side by side through forests just like this one barely two months before. Now he looked ahead at the Count seated erect on Moro, perspiration glistening on his shoulders; silent. Fulk had been buried in thought ever since leaving Angers: even a wild boar that charged across their path in the densest area of forest raised not a sound, though Moro reared and wheeled in alarm. Rollo tried to imagine the Black Count hacking his furious path among the Breton ranks at Conquereuil, his sword red and scything through flesh and iron: nothing seemed further from this huge quiet man in peasant grey.

They met no one. The Count's silence spread over them all – Sebrand, Rollo, the guard of armed soldiers, the baggage-carriers taking up the rear. There were fifteen men in all, and the only sounds were the click of hooves and the whine of summer insects. Sebrand threw Rollo a wineskin. He took a long draught; then, as the Norman returned it, Sebrand raised a hand and said 'Listen!' Rollo could hear nothing at first. 'There again!' Sebrand's head was turned towards a low hill to the right. This time Rollo could hear a faint rumble that died away, then started again louder before trailing into silence again. And as it did so a breath of wind snatched at the branches of the trees above them, and the light appeared sharper suddenly, colours brighter. A flock of rooks rose above the trees, circling raucously, and a doe with two young sprang on to the track ahead, zigzagging in panic before darting back into the forest. Then a flash of lightning threaded the branches, followed in a few seconds by another long mutter of thunder.

'The first rain of the summer,' announced Sebrand, taking another long swig of wine, 'and it's about to fall on us.' He laughed. 'I suppose we should be thankful. The grapes will love it.'

The impending storm broke the silence of the journey. Even the Count began to gaze around him, seeming to acknowledge the presence of the others for the first time. The sky ahead darkened into a bright purple, veined every now and then with forks of lightning; but where they rode the sun still blazed so that the woodland appeared incandescent against that wall of thundercloud. They reached the crest of a rise. Beyond them spread the carpet of forest unrolling towards the distant thread of river: the Loire. And in the far distance a cluster of buildings was just visible. Langeais. Yet even as they surveyed the scene an invisible hand seemed to draw a curtain from right to left across the forest and river, a curtain that ruffled and shimmered before them, blotting out the horizon.

'We'll miss it after all, thank God.' But even as he spoke Sebrand felt the sting of rain on his hands and face. Drops of water made tiny craters in the dry earth, and sand lizards scuttled into the undergrowth. The group of horsemen kept in the open for fear of lightning, while around them the thunder growled. Then, as abruptly as it had begun, the rain stopped and they could see it moving ahead of them in a veil of grey trailing among the trees down towards the distant river. The sky was deep amethyst now, bright and heavy on the land. They watched, wiping the rain from their arms and faces while the horses nibbled hopefully at the wet scrub and stubble.

'Another hour, Rollo.' Sebrand had dismounted and was leading a grey horse towards a bank of grass, brushing the rain off his clothing. Fulk was a short distance away still gazing in the direction of Langeais, hidden beyond tha curtain of thundercloud. Rollo was watching the Count, pondering on his silence: Fulk had not spoken a word since their departure. Then Rollo saw him start, and tug at Moro's reins until the stallion's head was raised and pointing in the direction of his own gaze. The Count lifted one hand to his eyes and promptly wheeled his horse.

'Look!' Fulk's voice was triumphant. 'Look!' he cried again.

The others turned and hurried over to where the mounted figure of the Count stood gesturing dramatically.

'See! A blessing on our journey! There!' The long face was radiant, and his black eyes blazing.

They all looked. A shaft of sunlight had burst through the turbulence of purple clouds: it seemed like a finger extended from the heavens and what it touched – lit as though a fire burned within it – was the tower of a church that seemed to be rising up to greet it. The party of men stood in wonder and gazed on the scene. Some crossed themselves; others laughed with joy. There were tears in Sebrand's eyes. Rollo felt awestruck: it was as if God had given a blessing on his own journey from Normandy, and on the work he was to do here.

After a few moments they returned to their horses and prepared to continue their journey. Suddenly they heard the Count cry out as if in pain. They turned. One hand was raised before his eyes, warding off something they could not see. Rollo looked up alarmed; soldiers reached for their swords; Sebrand hunted around him for the danger but could see nothing. The shaft of sunlight had vanished: the storm was passing eastwards and the sky was lightening. Then to their astonishment they saw Fulk spring from his saddle and throw himself on his knees. He was shaking. His hands were clenched in prayer before his face as he continued to stare and stare into the distance. People gathered round anxiously, but Fulk appeared not to notice. Sounds burbled from his lips, but they could catch only a few words here and there. 'Christ!' he said many times. And 'Mercy' again and again: 'Mercy! Mercy! Oh mercy!' His hands were trembling and the sweat stood out on his brow. Some of the soldiers joined their lord on their knees and were gazing about them in terror not knowing what to pray. Rollo stood some distance apart, perturbed and mystified. Sebrand was close to his master as if wishing to cradle him but fearing to do so. Then Fulk appeared to be reciting some incantation. They were dislocated sentences blurted out so that only a few phrases caught Sebrand's ear — '... angel standing in the sun', he heard, and '... the great day ...', and '... when the thousand years are expired ...'

Then there was silence again, and gradually Fulk seemed to collect himself. The afternoon sun was breaking through. A flock of partridges whirred across the scrub before them and vanished into the bracken. Everything felt normal once more, and yet everyone was shaken as they mounted their horses and resumed their journey down into the last stretch of the forest. Fulk rode ahead as before as if nothing had happened.

Rollo never expected the Count to mention the incident again. The journey continued and Fulk still said not a word. They reached Langeais in the late afternoon: the vineyards that circled the town looked fresh after the rain, and the ruts of the bullock-carts were filled with water. The air felt fresh on the skin. Within a minute of their arrival there was consternation in the small town as the word got about that Count Fulk had arrived, and as he rode up the single street he was erect on his black stallion and his head seemed to toss his dignity towards the gaping crowd. The soldiers advanced to clear a path for him, and presently they found themselves before a large wooden house set apart from the others, raised on a limestone rock above the river. This was the governor's house, and in no time ostlers were leading their horses away and the three men were being escorted across the cobbled courtyard where white hounds were chained and into a fine hall draped with woven hangings

Here the governor, an elderly man with a bald head and a long cheek-scar, advanced and promptly engaged himself with the Count while manservants led Rollo and Sebrand to their rooms. Rollo's limbs were weary from riding and he stretched out across the broad couch draped with bearskin. Another servant brought food and wine and he feasted hungrily before dropping into a heavy sleep.

But the Count did mention the incident again. Rollo woke to the sun still flooding into his room. For a moment he wondered if he had slept through an entire night, until he noticed he was fully dressed and a meal was part-eaten on the table beside the couch where he was lying. Then he realized he was not alone. At first he saw only that the curtain between his room and the courtyard had been pulled back, and that the white hounds were basking in the sun on the cobbles. Mystified, he glanced back round the room, accustoming his eyes to the sunlight. And against the far wall, motionless, stood Fulk.

Rollo rose hurriedly from the couch, but Fulk motioned him impatiently to remain where he was. And as he did so the Count began to pace the room between the window and the open doorway. Sometimes he appeared buried in thoughts that belonged elsewhere: the next moment he turned abruptly and seemed about to speak. Rollo wanted to thank him for his generosity of the previous evening, but felt it wiser to wait for Fulk to break the silence. Was it the castle that was on his mind? Fulk's was a mind, Rollo had come to realize, that was always fermenting, and beneath that intense gaze it was impossible to guess what projects, what turmoils, what dark dreams were turning there.

'Rollo,' he said, surprisingly quietly. There was a further pause as Fulk continued to pace the room. Rollo sat and waited.

'Tell me about Jumièges,' he went on. Then another long pause. Rollo waited for an explanation, some clue. But none came.

'Jumièges?' he replied after several moments. 'It was my life.'

'I know – that's why I want you to tell me about it.' Then he went on, as if something in that enclosed cell had opened: 'It's a place of learning, of wisdom, is it not?' Rollo nodded. 'Then tell me – in Jumièges did they talk of the end of the world?'

Rollo was puzzled. 'Yes,' he said after a short pause. 'Yes, they did – sometimes.'

Fulk threw him a glance almost of hate; but immediately the Count's face softened into a look of deep weariness. 'And when', he went on in a low voice, 'did they say that would be?'

Suddenly the truth began to dawn on Rollo. That vision amid the storm – the sun breaking through and the ray of light striking the church. What was it Fulk had seen then? Sebrand had recounted to him the scattered words and phrases he had overheard from the Count's lips. An 'angel standing in the sun', Fulk had said; and 'mercy', over and over again. Memories flooded back into Rollo's mind. Jumièges. Monks quoting the scriptures. The Vision of St John. Of course! The angel in the sun ... which cried with a loud voice to all creatures that fly to eat the flesh of kings and mighty men ... the angel who held the key to the bottomless pit. And the thousand years – 'when the thousand years are expired,' Fulk had uttered. It was clear now. Fulk believed – he really believed – that the world was about to come to an end. The year, now, was 996. So, four years. That was all that was left before the hills would dance, justice descend and the earth be renewed: the Day of Judgement, when Antichrist would be destroyed. That too. It was becoming still clearer to Rollo. Did Fulk think himself to be the Antichrist? Was it not said that the day of his destruction would be foretold in dreams and strange manifestations? That ray of sunlight, it had turned into a sign of doom before Fulk's eyes, and he was terrified. The realization struck Rollo like a bolt. Fulk believed he would roast in hell. This massive man who feared no one, and was feared by all: he lived in terror of divine punishment. What could he reply? Fulk was still standing there, waiting for Rollo's answer.

'I'm no priest or monk, my lord,' he began. Rollo was uncomfortably aware of the Count's eyes boring into him. 'Certainly the abbot used to talk about these things. But he never talked about them as ... *facts*.' Fulk looked puzzled; and Rollo tried to explain the truth as he understood it. 'The monastery had many books,' he went on, 'and many scholars would come and study there. There was much reading aloud, and discussion. Even Duke Richard himself would sometimes take part. We were all led to believe there was a future – for all. That there was a redemption. Sinners could repent and have nothing to fear. So we built ... to the glory of God, the abbot used to say. You, my lord, you fight, but only so that you may build to that glory. Is that not so?'

Rollo felt surprised hearing himself say these things, and he wondered if there was any truth in them. The Count looked thoughtful and more calm. Then, after a while he said, 'And the thousand years?'

'How long is a year to God, when He created the world in six days?'

Fulk was silent again for a long time.

'Thank you, Rollo,' he said eventually. And quite suddenly, as if a weight were removed from his heart, he began to speak of other things – of his plans for the castle which they would build together to squeeze the life out of the Count of Blois – of his longing to found a great monastery where the world would come and worship – of his hopes for a son, many sons, God willing – of his love and hopes for Anjou, his 'fair land' as he described it. Then he veered back towards the question of damnation as if the fear would not entirely go away. He spoke of what he needed to do to safeguard and build Anjou, and how he sensed sometimes that such actions might lead to eternal damnation – but what else could he do? He tried to make atonement for his acts; he endowed the Church lavishly; he offered relics of the saints to monasteries when such holy possessions came into his hands through conquest or through marriage – Rollo would see one of the greatest of such treasures at Corméry. He could only hope, he said vehemently, that his achievements might outweigh his sins, that he would be judged more a saviour than a tyrant; that what he built Christ might be proud of. And then he said – touchingly, Rollo thought – that the oriole was his personal emblem because he wanted his own glory, and the glory of Anjou, to spread like the bird's golden wings.

Fulk seemed absorbed once again in his own thoughts. He gazed out of the window for a long time. And then abruptly he turned to look at Rollo with an expression almost of triumph on his face.

'There's something else, Rollo,' he said. 'Something they won't have taught you in your monastery ... But I know. There are other powers. This evening I'll show you – when it's night.'

And with that he departed. Rollo watched the Count stride across the courtyard. He saw the governor hurry towards him, and the two men became engaged in discussion as the dogs sniffed around them.

Once again Rollo did not know what to make of Fulk. Those protracted silences. The joy at the ray of sunlight that struck the church. Then the vision of the angel of doom, and Fulk's terror. His appearance unannounced in Rollo's room – waiting there until he awoke. The questioning about Jumièges, searching for reassurance as if to offset some malevolent influence (whose influence? Rollo wondered). The primitive fear of Divine Punishment, like some simple peasant. And now this almost taunting hint at other powers – darker powers? How could Fulk believe so fearfully in God's justice and in these powers too? What could Rollo expect later that evening? And why at night?

Sebrand cast some light on these events. He and Rollo had left the governor's house and were inspecting the crude wooden keep which he was to rebuild in stone. It was a soft evening after the storm, and the birds were singing. They had left Fulk deep in conversation with the governor and the castle guard. Rollo recounted to Sebrand what had occurred that afternoon and asked if he knew what might be in store that night. Sebrand laughed. Yes, he had some idea, he thought. Had Rollo ever heard of the weather-makers? Well, they were men — usually men — who knew how to harness the powers of nature; how to influence the spirits. Did that seem strange to him? Well, they were much perse-cuted by the bishops, naturally, but everybody else pro-tected them and the bishops rarely found out who they were. There were two such men here in Langeais whom everyone respected for good reason. The storm this afternoon was known to have been their doing. The land badly needed rain or the grape harvest would have been ruined. No prayers to God had been known to work such miracles, whatever the Bible said. There would be more rain tomorrow, Sebrand assured Rollo; he had heard as much from several people here, and it would be the work of the weather-makers — the *tempestarii* the church called them. They were elderly men; the ones in Langeais were particularly powerful, and the reason for this was that they worked their power through the medium of a girl. Rollo would see her tonight: Fulk had ordered her to come. It was full moon now, and that was when she could work these things. One never knew what messages she would receive, or from whom. She was possess-ed — the church said it was by the Devil, but it was not the Devil; that was a Christian invention. The priests were just envious. She had the gift of sight, this girl, Sebrand said. People kept the priests from her, he explained, or they would burn her as a witch. But it was nonsense. What was a witch? The farmers did not care about the Church, most of them, but they did care about her. She was the reason, they said, why Langeais produced the best wine along the Loire. And Sebrand laughed again.

'You'll see.'

Fulk was in high spirits. Rollo had never seen him like this. The taciturn, brooding figure had given way to a spirit of bounding joviality. They ate well, Fulk calling for more wine, and then more again, in his tremendous voice that had every servant in the governor's house skipping in attendance, while the old governor exuded pleasure at the mood of his noble guest (and presumably at the gifts he had brought). Any visit from Black Fulk could mean trouble: you never knew. Nor did you ever know when he might appear and what he might expect you to do. This time he was relieved to hear that the Count was bent on rebuilding the castle: in Langeais he felt perilously close to the territories of the lord of Blois, and he had heard of Odo's recent forays into Anjou with some dread. With Gelduin on one side, and Odo on the other, life in Langeais was never something to take for granted, particularly with so small a garrison to defend it. He remembered all too clearly the sight of those barges floating past, laden high with the heads of Fulk's soldiers, and was forever wondering if one day his own head might not be found beached on some sand-bar where the river current had offered it to the gulls and the kites. He gazed at Fulk as the Count tore at large portions of roasted pig with his teeth, and felt reassured.

It was quite dark when the four men gathered in the courtyard. The governor unleashed two of the white hounds who were devouring the remnants of the pig, and dragged them to his side with a cuff of his hand. As he did so two men emerged from the shadows of the building, their heads covered so that their faces were all but invisible. But from their gait it was clear that they were not young. They wore dark clothing and both of them carried sticks. They nodded at the governor and bowed low before Fulk, who gestured to them brusquely to lead the way.

The party emerged from the courtyard and descended into the dark street. At least, it seemed dark to Rollo at first, but as they left the shadow of the buildings a pool of light suddenly flooded the fields ahead of them, and Rollo saw a swollen full moon resting – as it appeared – on a shelf of luminous cloud above the vineyards. The two elderly men walked ahead side by side, stooped silhouettes in the moonlight; and behind them the tall figure of Fulk, a dark cloak thrown over his shoulders and his head bare to the night. The governor with his dogs followed a pace or two behind, with Sebrand and Rollo bringing up the rear. No one spoke. Rollo's head was swimming with wine and it felt unreal, this silent parade through the trees and vines slanted with moonlight and shadow. Unreal and eerie. For what purpose were they here? Why was Fulk so anxious to witness whatever it was? 'There are other powers,' he had said mysteriously. Sebrand had mentioned a girl – a girl possessed – a girl protected from the Church who would otherwise burn her as a witch. He had never heard of such things.

They walked on in silence. Perhaps half an hour passed. The pace was slower now as the path led through a wood: the moon lit only the upper branches and they had to pick their way through a dense blackness around them. Rollo's eyes were fixed on the way ahead, wondering apprehensively where the girl would appear and in what guise; but he could see nothing, only the barely perceptible corridor of grey within the dark stillness of the forest.

But why? he kept asking himself. What did Fulk want? He could not ask Sebrand, walking steadily by his side: every sound would be overheard. They went on and on through the wood. Then it came to him. He recalled Fulk's terror that afternoon – that vision of the angel, as he believed. Terror of damnation. And his questioning of Rollo: the thousand years – when? And what had the monks told him at Jumièges? Now he understood. If the 'thousand years' meant some immeasurable time ahead, or not at all, then that terror was unfounded. He was safe. Rollo remembered how relieved Fulk had been to hear this. But more than that, if the storm were no divine act at all, but the work of human magic – the work of the *tempestarii* – then it can have been no vision. If he had seen an angel in the sun it was ... well, something else, a strange sight but no more. So, what Fulk needed now was proof of that magic power: he had to see the girl who was the fountain of that magic, when the moon was full and her powers were at their most potent.

But what on earth, Rollo wondered a little fearfully, were they to witness? And when?

The forest seemed interminable. Then he noticed the two men ahead had stopped. One of them was whispering to Fulk and the governor. 'We must stay here a moment,' he heard Sebrand say in a low voice. The weather-makers were walking on again and soon disappeared into the night. Some minutes passed. There were no sounds in the forest – not even an owl.

The four men waited, saying nothing. Finally they saw movement in the greyness ahead and one of the weather-makers approached close enough to beckon them forward. They walked slowly, eyes scanning the darkness, until to the left of the path they could pick out a glade within the trees, silver in the moonlight and empty, as it seemed. They could make out the figure of the other weather-maker standing on the verge of the forest, and as they approached he joined them silently, gesturing to them to remain still. The moon had risen higher by now and shone full in their faces. They waited again – the massive figure of Fulk a few paces to the right of the others, his legs planted firmly apart and his arms folded, just as Rollo had first seen him. The moon picked out the long profile of his face and beard, and Rollo could feel his eyes blazing into the empty space before him.

Suddenly, seemingly out of the ground some twenty paces

away, a figure rose. It was the figure of a woman. She must have been crouched in a patch of shadow. Rollo felt a quiver of apprehension run through his body as he watched, scarcely daring to blink an eye. There was sweat on his forehead but he could not bring himself to wipe it, nor turn his head to see what expression might be on the face of Sebrand. The woman was standing in the full light of the moon, sideways to them. He could see her features clearly: she was fairly young — perhaps twenty-five or so; hardly beautiful, but with a powerful heavy face and prominent nose. Her mouth was open and her head bare: at her shoulders her hair was covered by a dark shawl, and below that she was dressed in a loose-fitting garment of some rough material that extended to her knees and seemed frayed and torn here and there. The palms of her hands were held slightly in front of her, turned towards the moon like her face. It was as if the moonlight held her, bathed her, and she made no movement.

For ten minutes perhaps, though it seemed an eternity, she remained like this — mouth open, hands open, eyes staring. And then ... Rollo was not sure at first where the sound came from; a low murmur seemed to spread across the glade. Still the woman did not move, but the sound she made grew louder, rising into a moan, higher and higher until it became a wail — as if pain and pleasure and fear were all together in that voice, and she possessed by them, a mere embodiment of them. And as the sound rose louder and higher she began to sway — forwards and backwards — and her arms to flail about her, slowly at first and then faster and wilder until the wail became a scream and her hands began tearing at her clothing, her head tossing from side to side — her hair freed now and thrashing against her skin as her fingers pulled, wrenched, ripped her dress from her body — still swaying quite naked to the moonlight with her hands clasped to her breasts, legs apart, body bent backwards, head tilted to the sky — and this scream continuing to pierce the night, quaking now like her whole body in a long violent shudder until finally the scream expired into a deep deep groan and then a hiss and her arched torso convulsed as if it were being shaken from within.

At that moment she turned – at least her head turned – and looked at them. And the face ... Oh, the face! What torture lay upon it. For a few seconds the open mouth seemed unable to speak; the jaw worked as if to free itself from something clamped upon it, and her hands began tearing at her skin – her belly, her thighs, her breasts, her throat. Then one hand, shaking helplessly with fingers loose, gradually extended and grew still while the rest of her body continued to convulse as if in a storm; and from that one hand a forefinger jabbed towards the motionless figure of the Count. She was gulping now, and words seemed to be fighting from her mouth as her eyes like coals followed the direction of her extended hand. Then the sound came. One word, again and again, in a yell of such pain that Rollo felt his body tense with horror. One word – hurled at Fulk across the moonlit night: 'Burning! Burning! Burning! Burning! Burning!'

The girl collapsed. Rollo could hear sobs from where she lay. The two weather-makers hurried over to her and lifted her tenderly like a naked child. Rollo and Sebrand turned away, stunned.

Fulk stood motionless, his arms still folded. The others waited. The girl had gone. A fox hurried low across the open glade. Rollo could hear the distant howl of wolves. Then Fulk turned and walked away.

The prospect of meeting the abbot of Cormery filled Rollo with delight. He was anxious to come face to face with the man largely responsible for his change of fortunes. What was more, Abbot Gervais knew his own beloved abbot at Jumièges, and Rollo would be able to talk of many things that had remained buried since his departure from Normandy – things that were dear to him, and grew more dear sometimes as the violent currents of Anjou swept him further and further from the peace of the monastery that had shaped his life.

Rollo felt increasingly torn. Each day attached him more firmly to events that hinged on Count Fulk; yet with every new bond there grew a deeper longing for all he had left behind. He missed the certainty of the monastery life – the clear focus of every day – the simple sense of purpose – the path that led through the forest of this life towards the sweet meadows of the next. And yet ... had he really believed all that? Had not his deeper pleasures lain in more worldly gratification – the church he had built, the acclaim it had won him, the awe he had come to inspire, as well as that other gratification which the monastery had known nothing of? Ebba! Ebba of the forest pool, her slender limbs smooth like eels in the moonlit water. And now ... this new life had raised these worldly pleasures out of the shadows and placed them in the very centre of his path. In the dawn light at Langeais within the sound of the river, Rollo half-waking saw before him images that seemed to make the violence and uncertainty around him worth while. He saw the twin candlesticks twisted with strange beasts, and the golden altar studded with pearls within a fret of gold. He saw the churches, the monasteries, the castles that he would build. And he saw the tiny golden key that he remembered lay even now within his wallet near the window. And as he thought of the key Rollo's heart bounded, and the image of Hersende rose before his eyes: Hersende dancing, Hersende bathed in the laughter of summer, Hersende shooting bright arrows with her eyes.

He had learnt enough of the politics of Fulk's court in two months to realize that the cards fell very much to his advantage in any possible marriage to the Breton girl. It dawned on him that such a thing might even happen. She had no titles, lands, wealth, position, and was therefore ineligible to marry one of Fulk's courtiers or allies. As for Rollo himself, he was in a similar state of political uselessness. How fortunate. If the girl really wanted him as she seemed to, then what could intervene? The prospect filled him with tremors of delight as he gazed out over the stirring town of Langeais in the first light. He now wished he was not going to Cormméry at all, but as rapidly as possible back to Angers in order to pursue the hints and suggestions of the other evening.

It was as well for Rollo's peace of mind that he could not. Had he done so he might have discovered that the Count's orders to the Chancellor were already being implemented. The empty spaces in the ancestry of both Breton sisters were even now being patched by Audemand's emissaries in such a way as to entitle them to estates that would prove irresistible to some of Fulk's more troublesome neighbours — in return of course for sworn loyalty to the Count. There were a number of vassals of the former Count of Rennes, for instance, who would be sure to offer a change of political heart for the promise of so many excellent tithes and vineyards, not to mention two such beauteous pieces of breeding-stock who would accompany them.

But Rollo knew none of this. He enjoyed the delicate taste of being just a little in love.

More surprisingly, Sebrand did not know it either. Perhaps if he too had been in love he would have realized that the defeat of Conan would be bound to alter the status of the two pretty orphans at Fulk's court. But he was not in love, and had not given the matter of the two Breton girls serious thought. The very word 'love' filled him with gloom as he considered the withered widow from Maine toward whom he was being reluctantly dragged. The time he was playing for was running out, and Fulk growing impatient. An unmarried High Constable was a calamitous waste in his view, especially at such times of unrest. He kept mentioning it. If only the lady would die, Sebrand thought. If only t

Countess Elizabeth could come to his aid with . . . well, with a woman precisely like herself. Perhaps Sebrand even admitted to himself that actually the one lady for whom he felt what could be called 'love' was the Countess herself. In his eyes she was, quite simply, perfection. As for Hersende, Sebrand could not help but be aware of the girl's feelings for him. He acknowledged her beauty, that she was a lovely thing, that she was shapely and desirable, that she spread happiness all about her, that for all he knew the whole world might be declaring her perfect for him, that . . . in God's truth he could not detect so much as one grain of imperfection about her. And yet . . . he did not want her.

'Make her yours, then.'

Sebrand had needed no rare gift to detect in Rollo a certain amorous lethargy, and had prised out the reason. They were travelling again. Rain was falling gently. Having crossed the Loire by a barge which the current sucked perilously between the sand-bars, they were now following a winding tributary, the Indre, upstream among leaning alders. The scene reminded Sebrand of their journey through Maine earlier in the summer when Rollo had performed his acrobatics between two similar alder trees, boastfully tying them at the top to create an arch over the river. Looking at the Norman now, riding beside him, he did not think Rollo was in the mood for any such antics today. Here was a man brought low by love, he thought mischievously.

'Make her yours, why not? She'll bring you nothing but her love, but what more do you need? And with your skills, my friend, you can build her a great house with your bare hands, and a great bed to lay her on — with your bare hands of course! Lay her on and lay on her, and then you can prove you're a real Viking, Rollo, as half the ladies in Anjou would like you to do, from what I hear.'

Sebrand's rollicking mood was not entirely to Rollo's taste in his present state of mind, but the Angevin did not appear to care and was laughing so richly at his own invention that the Count, riding some way ahead among his soldiers, turned to see what the jollity was about. It was as well that he did not know the subject or in one or two brisk sentences he might have punctured the Norman's fond dreams as well as Sebrand's rough embellishments. But the Count turned away again and the party continued their journey eastwards along the bank of the river in the soft rain.

Fulk rode darkly. Though several days had passed since the arrival at Langeais the events of that first day hung over him, weighing heavily on his spirit. Out of the sky had come a warning, out of the ground had risen a curse. Perhaps it was only now, in these weeks since he had floated so close to death, that the Count was aware how deep ran certain caverns of fear within him. Ever since childhood he had been pressed towards a seat of power, and through his own strivings Fulk had raised that seat higher and higher. And yet ... the firmer his grip on the reins of power the more there seemed always to be forces more powerful than him — powers that lay beyond that grip and were poised to damn him more menacingly the higher he rose. Proud faces rose before him — Bishop Renaud, Father Baudouin, even Abbot Gervais — gazing and judging, always judging, with an authority he did not have and did not comprehend. He could smash them with his fist, but he could not smash the authority they wielded because it was not given to them by men. And the girl, the witch, he could burn her but he could not burn her hate; he could put out her eyes but he could not put out the dark vision within them. He could not reach, seize, crush, subdue whatever powers these voices spoke for, and he felt helpless in the might of his own powers. He rode on in unease, and in a sickly anger.

The Count quickened the pace of Moro. And as he did so his thoughts withdrew from these shapeless speculations and clutched at the purpose of his present journey. Fulk shook all other matters from his mind like dust and rode ahead. A mere one hour's ride to the north-east could, if he chose, have brought him to the city which was one of Odo's two great bastions – Tours. The other, Blois, was at present beyond Fulk's sights. One day he hoped it would not be. But Tours! He could feel each day the strength returning to his body and stoking his hatred for the man who held it. Odo, Lord of Touraine, Count of Blois. Fulk's father Geoffrey Greymantle had cut off one of Odo's arms. He, Fulk, would have his head. But, first, strangle the neck. He had brought with him, as he believed, the strangler – riding some twenty paces behind him with his High Constable. Through this Norman he would knot the cord round the proud Odo.

When Fulk had listened to Rollo's plans for stone castles he had been astonished – angry at first that his own efforts had been so rapidly disparaged, then drawn from anger to amazement by the perspicacity of the tall Norman. This man who until now had built only for God seemed to grasp in an instant the requirements of military defence though he had never seen a battle or a siege; and not only to grasp them as he, Fulk, grasped them but to hatch from his monastic brain a species of fortress unlike anything he could have imagined. More than this, the Norman had the temerity to be quite confident he could build such things. 'Just a matter of towers and buttresses,' the man had said. Then for three days – three days only – they had worked at Langeais. Rollo had explored the site and immediately had begun to draw up his plans. In twenty-four hours they were ready. Fulk had been astounded. The Norman had nodded that he was ready. The two men were standing in the courtyard of the governor's house. It was a fine evening after another day of rain. The Count had waited expectantly, whereupon the Norman had taken a long stick and drawn the outline of the new castle in the drying mud. First there was to be a new, much larger wooden enclosure, rapidly constructed but providing space within for the garrison and protection for the team of under-masons, stone-workers and general labourers. This was temporary. Rollo proceeded to wipe it away with his feet. Then he drew in the usual mound for the castle itself, and the surrounding ditch: but in addition to these he had provided for a much larger area beyond the ditch (and he swept his stick across the mud in a wide arc). This would be connected by a bridge and would likewise be fortified – by an earth wall and beyond the wall a wooden palisade and more ditches. (By this time most of the courtyard had been encompassed in Rollo's design and Fulk was having to stand back against the wall.) By this means, Rollo explained, the defended area was extended far beyond the castle itself and the space would accommodate peasants, their families and – vitally important, he imagined – food and livestock when the castle came under sustained attack. And a source of water from a deep well.

At this point a sudden downpour began to dissolve the Norman's elaborate plans, and for a moment the Count looked exasperated that his master-mason should have done his work so vulnerably; whereupon Rollo politely indicated that they move inside. Fulk followed him into the Norman's room, and there spread across the table lay a sheet of parchment with a fine drawing of precisely the same design – except that it was all but obliterated by figures and strange signs. 'What are these?' Fulk had asked gruffly. 'Measurements,' Rollo replied, 'also notes about materials, stress, equipment, terrain, the order of doing things, the number of workmen required: that sort of thing. I thought it might be easier if I explained it on the ground.'

Fulk had been lost for words. His eyes took in an assembly of rulers, compasses and curious gadgets he had never seen.

'How many men do you need?' was all the Count said.

'About six under-masons, perhaps thirty men with some skills in stone – including quarriers, and men who can dig the deep well. The rest labourers, as many as possible.'

'The masons and the skilled men you shall have,' Fulk had replied immediately. 'Audemand shall see to that. And after the harvest you shall have everyone who can lift a spade. I want it built within months. And many more of them. Every man in every town will be working for you, Rollo, and every slave we have. You're to oversee the work whenever you're not needed in Angers. You'll have guards to ride with you. And my warrant for anything you require. Nothing shall stand in your way. Nothing.'

Fulk turned on his heel and strode into the courtyard. He could be seen contemplating the sodden ruins of Rollo's drawing in the mud. Then Rollo heard the huge voice bellowing for the governor.

Later, Rollo spoke to Sebrand about the events of the day.

'I never imagined I would be put in charge of every able-bodied man in Anjou,' he said in a bemused tone.

Sebrand gave his usual playful laugh.

'It'll keep your mind off love.'

By midday the sky was swept clear of cloud. A damp warm smell of early autumn rose from the vineyards. The river meandered left and right so that as they followed its bank the sun appeared to swing above them like a censer, guiding them towards Corméry. The great monastery of Charlemagne's tutor Alcuin lay only a few hours upriver, Sebrand explained. But first they would stop at Montbazon. Fulk would build another castle here – another link in the chain around Odo's city. But high on a cliff this time. It would command the main route south into Aquitaine. It was the pilgrim route too, Sebrand went on, from Tours southwards: very profitable to the Church, he added with a slight laugh. Tens of thousands venerated the relics of St Martin in Tours each year, and after that pilgrims travelled south to Poitiers to mutter in front of the relics of St Hilary.

Sebrand could never understand, he said, why the bones of old Roman bishops held such power. It did not end at Poitiers either, he went on. Many of them continued even further south: there were relics all along the way as far as Roncesvalles, if you were not butchered by the Gascons or the Basques before you got there. Perhaps that was why there were so many relics — and Sebrand laughed again. A good many of them went even further than Roncesvalles, to the far end of Spain and the tomb of St James. And there you were almost certain to get murdered because Spain was full of Moors. Infidels. Fanatics. A terrible place. The wolves were as large as oxen, so he was told. There must be easier ways of saving your soul, Sebrand declared. And he threw Rollo a flask of wine with a flourish. As he did so a flash of yellow passed between the trees ahead. An oriole, Fulk's golden bird. Sebrand glanced up knowingly.

'And that'll be on its way south too any day now. A much better chance of survival than the pilgrims.'

They could see Montbazon now — a huddle of houses beneath a high rock. Rollo found himself wondering how anyone was supposed to bore a well up there. Sebrand seemed to read his thoughts.

'There's a spring on the slope behind the cliff,' he said. 'That's why the Count chose the place. But I must tell you something,' he added, lowering his voice.

Montbazon was monastery land, he explained. It actually belonged to Corméry — given by Charlemagne as a token of thanks when Alcuin retired. The present abbot was a man of peace. He would never allow the Count to build a castle there. Unless . . . well! Now perhaps Rollo understood why Fulk was anxious to visit Corméry, Sebrand hinted. He had already showered the place with gifts. Had Rollo not heard of St Foy? Ah! The story was this. St Foy had been a virgin martyr, Sebrand did not know when exactly. Whenever the time for virgin martyrs was. At any rate, the relics of the lady were enshrined in a gold figure with staring eyes. So powerful was its stare that she appeared to people in dreams, instructing them how to free themselves from all manner of disaster – prisons and the like. Her fame spread far and wide, and many pilgrims flocked to her shrine. They offered jewels, and these were set into the golden figure of the saint until she became herself like a jewel, wonderful to behold, her body glittering like her eyes. Then one day she appeared in a terrifying dream to Renaud, Bishop of Angers. You may wonder, Sebrand added with a chuckle, why the reverend bishop should be dreaming of beautiful virgins, particularly since he was one of the very few bishops who had not deflowered a good many himself. However, enter his dreams she did – and with a dire warning! Anjou was in godless hands, she proclaimed, and would be destroyed like the tribes of Antichrist. Well, not long after, lightning struck the Cathedral of St Maurice and half-destroyed it, as Rollo had seen. The Bishop's anger with Count Fulk mounted. It was all his fault, Renaud maintained. And worse would surely follow. Fulk's response was immediate. He sent Roger de Montrésor and several other knights to the city of Agen where the saint's relics were held, and on the pretext of some charter – Sebrand was uncertain if it existed – he had the shrine removed in the dead of night and carried back to Angers. With St Foy securely within his boundaries the Count insisted that Anjou would be safe and blessed. But! ... instead of presenting the holy treasure to the cathedral, to the care of the Bishop, Fulk announced that Renaud was too proud a man for such an honour, and instead awarded it for safe-keeping to – he said – the most devout servant of God within his lands. Abbot Gervais of Cormery.

'You shall see the shrine,' added Sebrand. 'And you'll not forget it, I assure you. You may also come to think, from what I've told you in confidence, that there could just be a connection between the Count's generosity and his plans for Montbazon.'

Rollo expected the customary chuckle, but none came.

Sebrand was gazing intently ahead as the party entered the cluster of wooden houses under the shadow of that mighty cliff. Chickens, pigs and dogs scattered before the advance of the horsemen and in their place figures young and old flocked from doorways and narrow alleys to stare and hold their hands to their mouths. Rollo raised his eyes to that giant rock and imagined his castle poised there against the sapphire sky.

Events in Montbazon were more or less a repetition of those at Langeais — except domestic events. The governor's house was a mean construction of wood, into which all kinds of farmyard creatures wandered at will, day and night. It was little more than a single large room in which the men ate, slept and (in the case of the governor) snored. Between the exhalations of the governor and the dawn chorus of cockerels Rollo found little sleep, and after the first night excused himself and enjoyed a peaceful rest by the river bank. The next evening Sebrand joined him, muttering darkly about the barbarities of the peasants in this region. Not even a pretty girl to soften the straw, he muttered. Only Fulk seemed quite unperturbed: throwing the last chicken bone into the yard he would down a goblet of wine and stretch his huge frame by the dying fire with a contented grunt.

Conditions for working were more arduous for Rollo. The sole table in the governor's house was one used for chopping pigs and vegetables, and many years of this employment had given it the shape more of a cradle than of a table. It was not conducive to drawing. Fortunately his plans for the castle at Langeais needed only a few refinements on account of the rockiness of the terrain: many of the ditches, raised banks and palisades proved quite unnecessary when Rollo, together with Sebrand and the Count, rode up behind the town to the high escarpment. From here, Fulk pointed out gloatingly, you could gaze northwards and actually see in the distance the walls of the city of Tours.

'There!' Fulk announced, spreading his arms wide. 'Odo's lair. We'll starve him out like a fox, Sebrand. And then . . .' Fulk drew his sword and with a surprisingly delicate gesture flicked at the air in front of him as if he were beheading a poppy.

'Make this one strong – impregnable – Rollo! Montbazon will be the thorn in Odo's side he'll never remove. Ha ha!' And the Count stood there already triumphant, like an eagle on the clifftop staring down at its prey. The wind tossed his hair and scuffed his beard, and for a while he continued to stand there saying nothing. Then he turned his back abruptly on Odo's city. Rollo had never seen the Count's face so radiant.

'Tomorrow we leave for Corméry.' And in a quieter voice he added, 'You'll say nothing of this place to the abbot, or anyone.'

Rollo stayed on the hilltop while Sebrand and the Count retraced their steps down the steep track. He watched them becoming smaller and smaller until the two men vanished among the trees. He was about to turn back and begin taking measurements and surveys when something moving caught his eye. He stayed still, partly hidden by a tall boulder. Below him three figures had emerged from behind the wall of cliff below him. They wore leather jerkins and carried short swords in their belts. At first Rollo took them for part of Fulk's guard, perhaps keeping watch on their lord. But no! Their manner was too furtive, and they kept glancing about them as they made their way down the same path towards the wood. Then at the edge of the trees Rollo noticed that they took a different path along the base of the cliff away from the town. He watched them until they passed out of sight before he left the shelter of the boulder and hurried across the open clifftop to see where they might have gone. At first Rollo could pick out nothing; but suddenly he saw three men on horseback emerge on to the path far below him and head towards the river some distance upstream from the town. He continued to watch, and saw them ford the river, ride up on to the farther bank and without a glance left or right canter into the forest northwards. Rollo looked up again and picked out in the distance the long smudge of grey that marked the city of Tours. Odo's fortress. And these, surely, were Odo's men. He thought again of Durtal, and the child's hand resting cold in its own blood.

Last threads of sunlight floated on the river. The horses' hooves broke them as they crossed the ford. The way to the abbey was through a deep shelter of trees, damp underfoot after the recent rain.

If Rollo had expected of Corméry a more hallowed version of Jumièges he would have been disappointed; or perhaps proud that his own vision wore so much more splendour. The ancient abbey seemed to sleep as they approached, hardly rising above the forest that cocooned it, and built — as far as anyone could see — out of the very trees it had replaced so many centuries ago. It offered to those who approached it a presence so humble that it appeared no more than the embodiment of that devotion to study and toil which its inmates pursued.

A single lamp hung in the twilight above the wooden gate. A single bell jangled within, dying slowly away. At length the gate swung open and a lay brother stood there in the entrance looking at them for some seconds until Count Fulk announced himself, and then went on looking at them for some seconds more until Fulk — who had dismounted — brushed past him and the silence was torn by the Count's voice barking for service. Rollo felt a stab of indignation at such peremptory behaviour, but followed the party into the forecourt. The horses were being led away; another lay brother was beckoning the soldiers as he advanced swiftly across the yard, as if determined to remove them from sight as quickly as possible. The Count, Sebrand and Rollo were left alone in the gathering dusk, Fulk's demeanour exhibiting more than a little irritation.

Still no one came. It was as if there *was* no one to come, and the place deserted.

Then as the light drained almost entirely from the courtyard the men could pick out blurs of colour from a row of tiny windows in the dark hump of a church facing them. And as they gazed in that direction they began to hear a soft mutter of voices from within, followed by long pauses and then a faint shuffling of feet. The effect on Fulk was surprising to Rollo: the incendiary anger that had been spurting from him as he waited in the darkness evaporated, and he became calm. The Count began to step quietly towards a broad vestibule at the western end of the church, and as the other two followed him they noticed that a door rested open so that the interior of the church gradually became visible through a semicircular colonnade of stone. Indeed, the church appeared to be the only building of stone within the entire spread of the abbey.

The three men stood at the entrance and watched in silence. Most of the cavernous interior was cloaked in darkness, though high on the square columns on either side was ranged a row of hanging lamps — six and six. Each rested in a curved dish so that the light — the little each gave out — was cast dimly upwards, creating flickering patterns like spiders on the oak-beams of the roof. But below everything remained soaked in a blackness so dense that at first Rollo imagined the body of the church to be entirely empty. Then, as his eyes grew more accustomed, he realized that before him stood a mass of human figures, each robed as darkly as the gloom about them. Their faces were invisible because they were turned in the same direction as his own; and their gaze seemed drawn to a single area of brightness at the far end of the church.

For a while Rollo imagined this pool of coloured light to

be the effect of so many altar candles that were mounted in varying heights upon a brilliant cloth of red, gold and purple in a pattern of gorgeous birds. But as he took in the scene he realized that the candles were lighting hundreds of sparkling points of colour around an object in the very centre of the altar as though it were on fire. Amid this shimmer of light Rollo could now pick out a seated figure entirely in gold: the impassive face was beaten gold, the crown, collar, robe, feet, all of them were gold; while in the robes about the figure were set jewels of every colour – red of garnet and cornelian, green of emerald and jade, blue of sapphire, purple of amethyst, as well as the more elusive shades of opal, agate, pearl, crystal and bloodstone. And from amidst this blaze two golden hands, each bearing a lighted candle, stretched out towards the dark congregation of monks as if to embrace them, while from the blankness of that golden face gazed two huge and staring eyes.

This, Rollo understood, was the Saint Foy who haunted men's dreams. Fulk's gift to the abbey of Cormery.

There was a stir in the congregation as though a spell were broken. A figure moved forward out of the shadows to the right of the high altar. He was robed all in white with a golden chain across his chest from which hung a cross. He was almost bald, but the plump reddish face appeared young, and his small hands held across his body fidgeted as if they were beating a vigorous tune against his stomach. His air of liveliness seemed altogether out of accord with the sombreness of the occasion, and he looked perkily around him in search – apparently – of something hidden in that dark void that might match his mood.

Here, then, was the Abbot Gervais. Rollo's mentor. Friend of his own abbot at Jumièges. The most devout servant of God known to Fulk. In a long line of abbots from the tutor of the Emperor Charlemagne, Alcuin. This small bright man seemed to Rollo to inhabit a world in which the spirit shone gladly, and he felt a joy rise within him.

As the abbot moved below the steps of the high altar there was a stirring in the darkness over to the left of the church, and the creaking of a door being opened. Presently a line of men was to be seen shuffling towards where the abbot stood. They were roughly clad, and hatless. Rollo counted five; then a sixth, who was elderly and lame, joined them. They bowed to the abbot, who looked at them for a moment; then he nodded to the first and, as he approached, the abbot placed his arm lightly on the man's shoulder and steered him gently to where – Rollo noticed – a rope dangled by the side of the church wall, reaching almost to the floor.

The man's gaze was lowered, and Rollo waited with some apprehension. The abbot promptly took the end of the rope and tied it at head height into a noose. Then he beckoned the man to approach and proceeded to place the noose over his head, sliding it tighter at the back of his neck. The man made no movement of protest or struggle; he just stood there awaiting his fate quite passively. But the abbot seemed to have something else in one hand, and with that same hand he reached towards the man and laid certain objects on his head: Rollo thought there were four of them. Still the man did not move. The abbot took a pace backwards and, lowering his head, clasped his hands together in prayer before his mouth and chin, after which he made the sign of the cross. Stepping briskly forward again he then reached out and took the four objects from the man's head and, ascending the altar steps, placed them on the brilliant-coloured cloth at the feet of Saint Foy. Now Rollo could see that they were silver coins. The abbot knelt before the altar and uttered a few words in Latin which Rollo could not grasp, after which he rose and made a signal to the man still waiting motionless with the rope around his neck. Straight away the man lowered his body cautiously until the rope gripped his neck, and then jerked it – once . . . twice . . . three times. And each time he did so a bell tolled high in the church roof with a sharp unmusical sound that reverberated briefly and died away.

A murmur rose from the monks in the body of the church as if in recognition of an important event. Rollo's puzzlement grew, and he glanced inquiringly at Sebrand standing a few paces from him in the dark nave, but he could detect no surprise on his friend's face. Fulk was motionless by his side and Rollo could just pick out the long profile tilted back as if he, not the abbot, were presiding over the ceremony.

Then Rollo saw the abbot reach for the four coins on the altar with a final bow of the head, whereupon he advanced again towards the man, removed the noose from his neck, and pressed the silver into his hands. With that he embraced the man as if he were a child, kissing him on both cheeks, clasping his hands with a swift gesture of affection before ushering him down the steps towards the host of monks below who proceeded to engulf him in embraces, one after the other, so that he was entirely lost from view.

This time Sebrand leaned towards Rollo.

'Have you never seen this? They're becoming serfs of the Church.'

'Why?'

Sebrand hesitated, then leaned closer.

'Protection ... probably.' Then in a whisper that had a note of laughter in it: 'Don't worry, my friend. They're not being sacrificed. They'll get a good vineyard out of it ... as well as the silver.'

The strange ceremony continued. The other men in turn came forward, were noosed, tolled the bell and received four pieces of silver apiece. Rollo realised he was soaked in sweat. The horror at expecting to see a man hanged in church had left him shivering in spite of the warm evening. It was the turn of the last man now. He was old and crippled. The abbot aided him up the steps and slid the noose about his neck as he had the others. But when the moment came for him to toll the bell the man, already bent through age, appeared unable to bend any further. He managed to edge his legs wider and wider apart to lower his body until the bell-rope was taut. A few ineffectual nods of the head followed, but with no sound from the bell. So he tried again. The legs parted wider still. The abbot, seeing the old man's difficulties, drew closer and extended his arms to aid him; but as he did so the broad arch of legs gave way altogether, whereupon the bell gave out the most unholy clanging throughout the church. For a second Rollo imagined that he might after all witness a man hanged in church; but at the crucial moment when the old man's neck might indeed have been snapped by the fall the abbot nimbly caught him, and now held him in his arms, the old man trembling and quaking and the bell continuing to clang as if the Day of Judgement were truly upon them.

A tremor of suppressed laughter ran round the abbey church. Two monks hurried forward and freed the unfortunate creature from the first sufferings of his serfdom, and the silver coins were pressed into his quavering hands. Then his fellow serfs assisted him shakily down the steps and the entire party receded towards the side door from which they had emerged.

The ceremony was over. Fulk, who had stood motionless all this time, now advanced the length of the nave as the monks turned in curiosity towards the tall visitor. Rollo watched him approach the abbot, who turned, looked troubled at first, and then his face broke into a generous smile. But he did not move. He waited for Fulk to come up to him, tower over him and lower himself to his knees. Finally the abbot extended one hand on which a ring glowed crimson, and Fulk kissed it. Having done so, the Count rose and the two men embraced with the warmth of old friendship.

The abbot was a churchman unlike any Rollo had ever met. He had the energy of a boy, and something of the manner of a boy. He moved extravagantly. He laughed a great deal. He joked, and his jokes were like sparks that lit up the gloom of the place as he led his visitors to their quarters across the black courtyard under the stars. He would clap his hands, pat his bald head as if it were pastry skip every now and then, rest his arms affectionately or Sebrand's or Rollo's shoulder – all in emphasis of some stroke of wit that flew from him. It was a wit that invited admiration more than laughter: it illuminated how much lay at the mercy of his mind, what an expanse of the world he could subordinate to his judgement. When the Abbot Gervais joked, he joked of things that others feared, and by joking stressed that he did not fear them at all. Thus, even that first brief evening, Rollo was aware that his arrows had brought down several bishops, some far-flung princes, a flock of popular superstitions relating to magic, as well as the morality of no less a person than the King of France. In a very short time it became clear to Rollo why Count Fulk should hold this man in such reverence, and equally clear to him that the abbot was the last man likely to be taken in by the Count's largesse. What Gervais withheld was a quality usually displayed in great measure by those within Fulk' grasp: awe. And, lacking that, he inspired in the Count an awe of him.

In the morning Sebrand volunteered that Fulk had been engaged since an early hour in discussion with the abbot – on matters relating to tithes, church lands, the sale of produce thereof, and such like. He had not been privy to these discussions, he explained, but he would not be surprised if the Count's discourse were to return more than once to a particular area of church land. Would Rollo not think that likely? Sebrand chuckled as he said it. And would Rollo not think it likely, from his impressions of the worthy abbot, that the Count would make little headway in that direction. Sebrand chuckled again.

'And if that is so?' Rollo asked.

Sebrand looked wistful and drew a long breath.

'I think it may be a question of who underestimates the other more ... Or, perhaps, of who stands to lose most. We shall see.'

'The abbot seems most warmly disposed towards Fulk.'

'Indeed. You must remember that when Fulk was a youth, and the Count his father died, Anjou was bleeding and Fulk came here for guidance — repeatedly. He gained strength from this place. And he learnt much from Gervais, though you might not always think so,' Sebrand added with a smile. 'He's a devout man, Count Fulk ... at heart. Many people don't realize it.'

Rollo thought of his strange conversation with the Count at Langeais, and the Count's fears of Judgement. His need for reassurance. And the *tempestarii* ... and the mad girl. The finger pointing at him, and that terrible cry, 'Burning! Burning!' What had it meant? And what had it meant to Fulk? Rollo did not know; and he decided not to ask Sebrand. Yet he thought he could detect in the Angevin's manner a note of anxiety about Fulk's depths of faith, and where they might lead. Sebrand himself, the more Rollo came to know him, seemed so lightly touched by such things, so quick to brush off the hand of God. A practical man, Sebrand. Not given to dark fears. He wished, Rollo suspected, that the Count were the same, and yet if he felt love for Fulk it was for those depths in which humanity lay as well as faith. It was the aspect of Fulk which responded to the Countess Elizabeth. And Sebrand, Rollo knew, regarded the Countess as the mirror of perfection.

'What the abbot doesn't understand' — Sebrand's words broke into Rollo's thoughts as the two men strolled in the courtyard — 'is that he has his walls around him. Fulk does not. Odo is not going to break in here. There's no sanctity about a kingdom, but there is about an abbey.'

A monk appeared from the direction of the abbot's quarters, signalling to them. The abbot, he announced, was anxious to see the new High Constable and the young master-mason. He was waiting with the Count. Would they kindly follow him? The small bustling figure led the way round the north side of the abbey church. The bell was tolling – more rhythmically than the previous evening – and monks were making their way from the garden and the orchard to attend terce. It was all so familiar to Rollo: he recalled how often he used to watch such a scene from high up on the towers of Jumièges. But how much finer a church than this, he reflected with pride. He would not tell the abbot so, but then the abbot would hardly need to be told since he had visited Jumièges himself. Rollo wondered what the celebrated Gervais might want to say to him.

In his plain monk's habit he looked smaller than Rollo remembered from the previous evening. Smaller and older. The boyish manner was deceptive. Gervais was perhaps forty. He had, after all, been abbot here for fifteen years.

He smiled broadly, and without ceremony stepped forward to embrace the Norman. Then he did the same to Sebrand – a little more coldly, Rollo felt. Fulk was standing nearby, looking grave. Perhaps the discussion had not run smoothly, as Sebrand had predicted. The abbot's manner exuded the confidence of one unequivocally in command.

'So, master-mason.' And the abbot stepped back to look at the tall visitor. 'You've made your mark already in Anjou, I hear ... But why is it' – and as he spoke he half-glanced at Count Fulk – 'that you are building castles? I had you brought here to serve God.'

The question was so direct and unexpected from this smiling, kindly man that Rollo felt lost for words. He glanced at Fulk, who said nothing but in whose face Rollo could detect a flush of irritation.

In the silence of those few seconds Rollo felt caught between two inquisitors. The abbot was a man to whom you felt compelled to tell the truth. But what was the truth? There were things he could not say in front of Count Fulk, and other things he could hardly say in front of the abbot. He decided he would speak about Durtal. He related how he and Sebrand had come across that dreadful place: the murder, the savagery of it; the defencelessness of those peasants;

the helplessness; the horror. He did not tell of his anger with God for having stood by; he told of his anger at such injustice on earth, how he had felt a burning need at that moment to use these hands to build for justice, to protect man against barbarity, to be of service.

He paused. He felt he had spoken enough. The abbot was looking straight at him.

'And if the world *is* barbarous? And if it is the will of God that those people should have died then? Would you put yourself between God and His will?'

The abbot waited. How could Rollo tell an abbot that such a God would be a heartless God in whom he could not believe? To his surprise it was Fulk who answered.

'My lord Abbot' – his voice was unexpectedly calm – 'I cannot believe that resisting a tyrant is to stand in the way of God. Odo is not some puppet dancing on the string of God's will. Rather, he's a boulder aimed at crushing Anjou. If I put up a barrier against that boulder, am I thwarting God's will? Are you suggesting that I lie back and let it roll over me?'

Fulk had taken up his familiar stance – legs wide apart, hands on hips, head thrown back. Gervais half-turned towards him and pointed his finger in a correcting fashion.

'Odo is not a boulder, my lord Count. He's a man. So he makes choices. That's what it is to be a man: to be free to make choices. You too are a man – and must choose. Between good and evil. Turn your face towards God and be bathed in His light; or turn towards evil and live in the darkness of this world. It's for you to decide.'

Fulk seemed to grow more haughty as he watched the abbot's finger stabbing at him.

'I cannot close my eyes to this world, whatever you say. I cannot sit back and see my people suffer.' There was passion rising in Fulk's voice as he gazed down on the abbot. 'There are battles that have to be fought. And it's because people like me fight them that the Church can keep aloof.'

It was Gervais' turn to wear a look of anger. But Fulk continued, and his voice had a hard edge to it.

'The Church has been happy enough in the past to use men's strength to protect it. What if Charlemagne had never drawn a sword – would Alcuin have ended his life peacefully here? Would this place have survived at all had my ancestors not fought for it?'

Rollo could hear a whistling sound as the abbot drew a long breath between closed teeth.

'I must remind you', he said in a voice flat with self-restraint, 'that the Church survived a great many centuries without your strength and that of others like you. Indeed, that strength you boast of was long turned against the Church. And still it survived ... and flourished. Men's battles are for men, Count, not for God.'

Having delivered what he considered to be a conclusive reproach, the abbot walked slowly towards the window and gazed out, as if to shed the burden of his anger on the sunlit courtyard. Then he turned and spoke in a quieter voice.

'You make the mistake, my lord Count, that many of your kind make. You believe that the Church should enter the world and draw its sword. But that is not the lesson of our Saviour; nor is it the obligation laid down by our Rule.'

And he stepped forward and placed his knuckles on the table in the centre of the room, his gaze turning from Fulk to the other two men, and back again.

'This is a place of worship and of study,' he went on. 'We are like bees: we gather nectar far and wide, and we store it here in safety, away from contamination and foulness. Let me recount to you the words of Pope Gregory on Saint Benedict, the beloved founder of our Order. I know them by heart and often repeat them to myself. "Benedict was brought up in Rome," said Gregory, "in the study of humanity, but for as much as he saw many by reason of such learning to fall to a dissolute and lewd life he drew back his foot which he had as it were set forth into the world lest entering too far into acquaintance therewith he likewise might have fallen into that dangerous and godless gulf." '

The abbot continued to look at the three men in turn. His expression had resumed some of its boyish sparkle.

'And Benedict', he continued, 'proceeded to cleanse himself by dwelling as far as possible from man's iniquities — in a cave. And that in a sense is what we do. It is not for us to fight your fights.'

Fulk had not moved all this time. Rollo looked at the Count, standing in a lofty silence, and wondered what he would reply, or if perhaps he would say nothing more. Rollo was aware of having heard Gervais' arguments before — many times. His own abbot had often lent an ear to such views when younger monks — and invariably they were younger monks — expressed them in similar words. And Rollo could hear at this very moment the old abbot's implacable reply. He had lived through times of the utmost barbarity, he would say, such as no one else at Jumièges had witnessed. It was this experience which had taught him that you cannot do nothing in the face of Satan. The Vikings had to be resisted, not merely endured. There were moments for the Church to arm itself and be prepared to fight for what it believed. That was to be a true Christian. Rollo recalled the fire that used to burn in that wizened man as he spoke, and he felt a deeper respect for him than for this hard man with a soft face.

It was Fulk who broke the silence. His voice was calmer now, and his bearing less haughty.

'I understand what you say, my lord Abbot. Yet let me remind you that Christ himself did not turn from the dirt of this world. He entered the house of Levi. He cast the money-changers from the temple. He touched lepers. He walked with sinners. He was *of* this world as well as *in* it. Is that not so?'

This time the abbot gave a little laugh as though he had been listening to a foolish boy.

'My son ... Christ was God. He was blessed. Incorrupt ible. Benedict, though a saint, was a mere man. Therefor vulnerable. Could it be that you are less vulnerable than he Can you touch power, walk with corruption, can you kill and not feel your soul rotting like a leper's body?'

Fulk did not enjoy being laughed at, and he responde stiffly.

'Souls are your business, Abbot. It's bodies I care for bodies I cannot sit by and let suffer. So how can I help bu touch evil?'

The abbot nodded gravely.

'Every man has a choice.'

Fulk shrugged. He looked weary suddenly, as thoug aware that nothing was to be had from this discussion. The were a match for one another, Rollo felt; but one day the would surely hate each other, because neither would eve bend.

'It's a simple choice,' the abbot added. 'Good or evil?'

And he looked hard at Fulk as if demanding an answe Rollo heard the Count draw a long breath.

'My lord Abbot, we live in a twilight world. And in th world, yes! I have choices. But they are not choices betwee good and evil. They are choices *between* evils.'

The abbot gazed at him, an expression almost of sadne on his face.

'Then it seems you must do evil.'

The abbot promptly turned away from the three me adjusted his habit and moved towards the door.

'But try to remember', he added, pausing momentaril 'we are all of us only serfs. Not only the men you sa yesterday. *Servi servorum Dei*. They are merely serfs of t serfs of God ... Go your way.'

And with that quiet affirmation of his authority the abb terminated the audience by walking out into the courtyar leaving the others to follow him. There was scarcely good-bye, and within half an hour the gates of the abb closed behind Fulk's party and they were riding once again along the woodland track towards the river and Angers.

Fulk, as usual, was riding ahead with the soldiers. He had said nothing. Sebrand, who had remained silent throughout, now turned to Rollo with a wry smile.

'You'll have noticed, Rollo, how churchmen love to round off an argument with Latin. I believe they keep a stock of such tags under their habits, and bring them out in times of need. The truth is', Sebrand went on, his tongue loosening as they distanced themselves from the abbey, 'Latin can make anything you want sound God-given. There's one of Odo's viscounts, Landri of Châteaudun, who's invented the right to deflower any girl who gets married on his lands, and he has a Latin phrase for it too. *Ius primae noctis*. If he called it rape there would be an outcry from the Church. As it is they all think it's God's will, while he lives in heaven every night.'

Sebrand gave a snort, then kicked his horse's flank so that he could catch up Fulk who was waiting ahead with his face turned towards them. The tall cliff of Montbazon rose above him. As the two men approached, the Count glanced up at the gaunt rock.

'Build it, Rollo,' he said in a defiant voice. 'And build it strong.'

FIVE

WINTER CURLED AROUND ANGERS, clasping the city in a frozen hand. People wondered if it would ever let go, and how many more of them would die before it did. Peasants with no produce paid their tithes in fuel, then froze to death in their hovels for lack of it. Within the city walls the houses warmed each other a little, huddled like sheep: during the early months of winter the smoke from a thousand fires rose into the windless air, and the most frequent sound to accompany the barking of dogs was the slither of melting snow followed by a thud as it tumbled on to frozen streets. But as the icy months continued the plumes of smoke became fewer, and fewer dogs barked. People sleep longer in winter: now they slept as long as they could, and increasingly they slept never to wake. Those strong enough foraged for food, often returning too weak to forage again. Not a mouse or a rat survived that winter; and hardly a hen. Melted snow with a drop of chicken fat made soup while there was fuel to heat it; after that whatever was eaten was eaten raw. There was talk of cannibalism; but nobody talked much.

In the open spaces around the castle peasants from the countryside gathered with their families in increasing numbers, begging for food. They erected makeshift huts of animal skins draped over poles – and waited. They were more fortunate than many. Being serfs, most of them, their freedom had been sold by their fathers and forefathers in return for protection, and now that sacrifice brought some reward. The lords of Angers – members of the Count's *familia* in that labyrinth of a castle – would be sorely disadvantaged were their serfs to die in great numbers, and so gave them what they could. Each day the massive gates would creak open and a crowd of figures in rags would rush, hobble, limp, crawl, and extend thin hands towards henchmen who would call out names in harsh voices, beating off those not in their masters' service. In this way a surprising number of peasants survived — those at least who were close enough to the city to make the journey. The luckier ones found work within the castle, while those with sisters or daughters were luckiest of all provided that an inspection showed the girls to have their limbs and teeth intact. There were many serving-girls acquired for the castle at a small price during those frozen months, by men bored with the winter or with their wives. Besides, the dovecot or the master's bed was warm.

There were days of crisp sunshine when misery seemed to be covered by the night's fall of snow, and the landscape glowed brightly. The forests were feathered white, dark birds swooped among the cattle and horses steaming in the trodden fields, and even in villages numb with hunger there were frozen pools that rang with the laughter of children playing. Parties of horsemen in colourful clothing would emerge from scattered towns along the river. Soon a barking of dogs echoed from the muffled forests: there was the rush of an arrow and a stain of blood marked the fresh snow. The stumbling footprints of a deer led to a panting carcass, and the sound of merriment rose from the party of huntsmen. There would be a feast in the castle that night. Sometimes as they made their way home in the last of the sun the horsemen came across a gibbet with a corpse frozen to its post; and they knew that a peasant had been caught hunting on his master's land.

Often there were ladies in the party, swathed in their furs and with long slim boots. You could hear their laughter as their horses cantered between the trees, the menfolk in pursuit. Glowing faces were dusted with snow where branches had been shaken as they passed. Eyes glistened with pleasure. Hersende was frequently one of them, her fair hair tied with a scarlet ribbon or else flowing free as she galloped. She rode well – better, many thought, than her male companions, and certainly more prettily. Her attendant was usually young Sebrand, who had little to occupy himself during these long winter months, and who seemed to enjoy the spectacle of himself in hunting clothes just as much as the company of the young lady. But sometimes Hersende had a more soberly dressed companion, so tall he made his horse look no bigger than a donkey: this was the master-mason, Rollo, whose enjoyment was not at all the spectacle of himself, and who rode as close to the lady as the tangled branches, his own ungainly skills, and Hersende's evasive gallopings would permit.

Another figure in the party, riding more quietly and slightly apart from the others, was her younger sister Milesende. The men rarely spoke to her, though many looked at her, admiring the slim grace with which she guided her steed along the narrow tracks, dressed all in black with her black hair glistening as if the sun had polished it. While her sister's laughter rang through the woods, and Rollo ducked and struggled in pursuit, Milesende would find her own path some distance to one side, keeping them sharply in view without appearing to notice them.

One specially cold day Count Fulk accompanied the hunting party, which accordingly was larger than usual, swollen by many members of the court and their ladies who normally preferred the warmth of the castle to such brisk exercise. It was a more colourful occasion than usual, too: by midday dense snowclouds were gathering, and in the purple light of the forest the reds, blues and yellows of the huntsmen shone like torches moving between the trees. And because the Count was among them they took a more remote and wilder route in the hope of sighting a bear

Tracks had been seen. After a while these led down a rough limestone ravine where slender pines sprouted between rocks and leaned across the stony paths half-covered by snow. The party picked its way towards the deep valley below from where the sound of rushing water rose to meet them. The horsemen were scattered here and there, each finding his own way among the boulders. To the right of the main party and somewhat ahead of the others were Hersende and Rollo, the latter testing his horsemanship to the limit to keep up with the fair-haired girl whose mare was prancing nimbly ahead. Sebrand was a considerable distance behind, riding more sedately with the Count. Milesende, as usual, was apart from the others, a lithe figure in black slipping between the trees and rocks far down to the right where an area of flat ground bordered on the stream which they had all heard growing louder as they descended.

Milesende bounded over the stream first, effortlessly, and her horse was picking its way up the farther slope as Hersende, followed by Rollo, splashed through the water a short way upstream. The main party was still negotiating the rough descent, while the archers scrambled from rock to rock, their bows held in readiness for the beast whose tracks they were pursuing.

At that instant snow began to fall heavily: a dense veil passed across the valley with a muffled hiss, blurring the view. Suddenly a cry rose from among the trees on the far side of the stream. Nothing was visible through the curtain of falling snow, but Rollo was nearest to where the sound came from and urged his horse up the rocky slope through the pine-trees. There, on the ground, lay Milesende, her horse standing nearby quite still. Rollo hurriedly dismounted and bent over the girl, who turned her head and moved as if to rise, then stopped. Large flakes were settling on her black hair spread out on the white carpet of snow where she had fallen. Her dark eyes were looking up at him. Rollo reached down and gently, effortlessly, raised her in his arms. She seemed almost weightless. Then he bore her down the slope and picked his way cautiously across the stream towards the flat ground on the other side. As he did so she raised her arms and slid them around his neck for safety and he felt the girl pull her body closer to him as he stepped, stone by stone, across the water tugging at his legs. Snow was floating on to her face and hair, and as Rollo glanced down he was aware of moist dark eyes blinking at the soft flakes as they gazed up at him; and he remembered the look of those same deep eyes turned on him for just a second in the summer dusk by the castle gateway, hooded by a shawl. Somehow the light burden, as it moved very slightly within his arms, felt settled almost as though it belonged there, so that as he stepped on to the bank Rollo found himself strangely reluctant to put it down. He sensed that a part of his brain was being readjusted by his recognition of that look, and something unexpected was breaking the surface of his mind. He was quite unprepared to recognise what that might be, since the lady he loved — and loved solely as he imagined — was close by. And yet . . . what was the sensation that was overcoming him? And what did it mean? It was as if here was somewhere he had never travelled, and only the falling snow registered the passing of time.

As for the young Milesende, she lay in the joy of her dreams; and between gazing at the man she adored she closed her eyes and found no difficulty at all in imagining her prince in disguise bearing her through the most hazardous of wildernesses into the garden of love where a rose of perfect form was waiting to be picked, just as the minstrel had said. She did find more difficulty, however, in acknowledging to herself the deception by which she had brought this about. It was as well, Milesende reflected, that the bear had departed. As it was, she had picked her moment well, when there seemed no chance at all that her rescuer might be Sebrand or the odious Maurice. And how convincing the cry of pain. For all her dreaming and her wandering among flowers, Milesende was beginning to learn the ways of the world.

Perhaps the agent of that learning was despair.

Count Fulk had not been inactive during the months since his return from Corméry. Rollo had been kept busy into the very depth of winter on the Count's castles. Never had so many men been placed in his charge. If he needed more, more were instantly produced. Stone was quarried. Ditches were dug. Wooden towers were constructed on which the masons could work. Seasoned wood was procured for the flooring, iron for the gates. Rollo personally supervised the buttresses and cornices he had meticulously designed, even watching over the sawing of each stone. By the time of the great freeze work was well advanced both at Langeais by the river and at Montbazon high on its cliff. Rollo's regular visits to the latter were accompanied by a heavy guard of soldiers lest Odo should spring an attack. But none came. Nor was there any word from the abbey about the work proceeding on the abbot's lands. Rollo heard to his relief that Gervais had departed for the abbey of Cluny for the swearing-in of Odilo following the death of Abbot Meyeul. In all probability the severity of the winter would delay his return – so Rollo hoped. With good fortune the abbey of Corméry would continue to sleep in its woods until work was completed.

Meanwhile Fulk himself departed for Nantes, as he had promised after the battle of Conquereuil. His main purpose here was to reinstate the boy Judicael as Count, under the regency of the viscount Giraud Berlay who had held the city for Fulk since the death of Conan. Having concluded this ceremony to his satisfaction, and seen loyalty sworn to the young Count by all the lords of the Nantais, Fulk now turned his mind to other matters of security. Fulk's strategy was, as always, to ensure military security first; then to make sure that this was underpinned by more subtle but indestructible foundations – those of marriage.

In other words Judicael, though a mere boy, needed a wife. But first he, and the lady of Fulk's choice, must be provided for. In Nantes, Fulk summoned all the surviving family of the boy's uncle, the dead Count Alain. It was a shrewd move. As Fulk anticipated, a confusing scene shortly took place within the walls of the castle of Nantes. The cause of the confusion was that no one knew for certain who were relatives and who were not, Alain not having concerned himself much during a long life with matters of legitimacy. Many knights and ladies answered the summons of the Count of Anjou, travelling from far and wide, doubtless in expectation of profit. But if the word of each were to be believed, it soon became clear that the estimable Alain had done little with his days and nights but father children; and though in truth this was not far from his reputation, it appeared ever more unlikely to Fulk and his advisers that several *thousand* offspring should have sprung from his noble loins, especially since the eldest of those tottering into the castle would have been conceived when Alain was barely three, while the youngest – a babe in arms – must have lain two years in his mother's womb.

The situation was precisely as Fulk had wished. And he proceeded to deal with it in a manner as conclusive as it was advantageous to himself. He pronounced that, besides Judicael, the number of heirs of the late Count Alain was – twelve. And he uttered the word 'twelve' with the weight of much authority, managing to imply that it had been arrived at on the basis of careful investigation of the facts. There were of course no facts, twelve seeming to Fulk the right number of beneficiaries to ensure a solid caucus of support round the young Count, while allowing to none of them so large a portion of estates as to offer any potential threat. In naming the fortunate twelve Fulk was careful to select those with lands of a bleak and unproductive character, sufficiently widely dispersed one from another to render any concerted rebellion impractical. The rich, wine-growing lands to the south and east of Nantes turned out to be the property of those who found themselves disinherited. But – Fulk now made a public gesture of generosity – those lords who to their misfortune now found themselves to have been wrongful claimants to the noble Alain's estates should not be allowed to suffer undue deprivation, he announced. They would forfeit a mere half of their lands. The rest they would now own by right of law, on the renewed swearing of loyalty to Fulk's vassal Judicael, and of course the usual annual payment of tithes. As to the remaining half (and Fulk was referring to much of the most profitable land in the entire county of Nantes) this would be distributed on the basis of one-half, one-quarter and one-quarter, with Count Judicael the principal beneficiary, the remainder to be divided equally between the late Count Alain's two acknowledged daughters (whom he had never in fact acknowledged), the ladies Hersende and Milesende.

Matters were now concluded – not without some hubbub rapidly subdued by the appearance as prearranged of Fulk's guard. Very old and very young, the disinherited departed. And as the autumn mists gathered over the vine-lands there was talk of an exceptional crop after so fine a summer. Handsome tithes would before long be going to the future Count and Countess of Nantes, who now found themselves miraculously the owners of much of the richest land in western France.

Hersende sobbed inconsolably when she heard the news.

'It can't be! It can't be!'

The Countess Elizabeth offered what comfort she could. However, she was powerless, she said, to change the Count's mind.

'But listen!' she said to the weeping girl, having first

ensured that no one was listening. She waved her chamberlain Garnier away.

'Listen!' And the husky voice was more than usually tender. She placed an arm round the girl's shoulders. 'There are one or two things you should know, Hersende. Judicael is not yet twelve. The Count intends you to marry him after that date: it's not clear to me why, but that is so. Now . . . I have it on authority that the boy is of poor health. Very poor. Even the Count does not know this. If he lives long I shall be most surprised.'

The Countess was wearing a serious look as Hersende turned a tear-stained face towards her. The girl had stopped crying now and was waiting intently for Elizabeth to continue.

'If the boy dies before the marriage takes place, then . . . well! you may shed a polite tear but at least nothing else. If not, and you marry him, he's too young to . . . what shall I say? . . . inconvenience you.' And the Countess gave a wicked laugh. It was Hersende's turn to look serious. 'And since he's most unlikely to survive long, you will then, my beloved, be an extremely wealthy widow. And still, what's more, intact.' She laughed again. 'And who could you not marry then? Do you see?'

Hersende was gazing at her with those wide green eyes, still moist with tears. She threw her arms round the Countess's neck and kissed her. Elizabeth gently pushed her away.

'There is something else. The sister of the Count of Maine' – and with the mention of the widow Hersende sat bolt upright with a fierce expression on her face. 'Well! The Count heard yesterday that she has been taken sick. Gravely so. How gravely nobody knows. But . . . surely I don't need to say more, my pretty one. Be patient.'

Hersende's face was aglow suddenly, and she was wiping away her tears.

'You'd better go now.' The Countess rose to her feet and

seemed to be gazing far away across the winter landscape. 'I was thinking', she added as Hersende was on the point of leaving the room, 'that the Countess of Nantes and the lord of Chemillé would make a fine match, don't you think? What's more, I hear that the lady is rather beautiful, and of a shapeliness second to none.'

Such, then, had been the cause of Hersende's rippling laughter when out hunting in the snowy forests. People marvelled at her good humour and attributed it to her turn of fortune in being now a lady of title shortly to become the mistress of Nantes.

But Fulk's plans had not stopped at arranging for the now-wealthy Count Judicael to marry the now-wealthy Lady Hersende. The remaining quarter of the late Alain's estates were to be settled on Hersende's sister, the young Milesende. Chancellor Audemand's inquiries had not produced a suitable candidate for the girl's hand. Accordingly Fulk had made his own decision. Weighing heavy on his mind since Conquereuil had been the alliance formed against him between the late Count of Rennes and those lords of Vitré and of western Normandy who, it seemed, had been wooed to the cause of Brittany and remained a continued threat to Anjou from the north and north-west. The county of Maine, which lay adjacent both to Anjou and to those lands, was loyal to Fulk, and that loyalty would of course be further strengthened by the marriage of his High Constable, Sebrand, to the Count of Maine's sister (though he did wish the lady were younger in years). But there remained a weakness further to the west. It had been for this very reason that Fulk had summoned Viscount Bernard of Combourg to Angers. The bloody tale of Bernard's wife, raped by her nephew and dying by her own hand, was still fresh in Fulk's mind. All Bernard's family was now dead. He had no heir. Why not secure that region by a further marriage? A marriage, what was more, that would strengthen a bond between Combourg and Fulk's western bastion —

Nantes? In other words, the girl Milesende. Youthful, of growing beauty, and now endowed with rich estates. Bernard, true, was old – but still vigorous. Fulk's emissaries had been assured by the viscount's mistresses that he was entirely lusty, and children were produced for inspection as proof of this fact. Many of them (though these would have to be dispossessed).

The tears of Hersende were nothing compared to those that fell from Milesende. This was the cruellest blow of all. Bernard seemed almost old enough to be her grandfather. Not that it mattered what age he was, or even that it was he who was chosen to be her husband. All that counted was that he was *not* Rollo. It was as if a monster had entered her secret garden, and her prince were locked out. Was there no one – no one at all – to rescue her? And the wedding was to be soon, in the spring, as soon as the roads were passable again. (The viscount had suggested to Fulk that at his age such matters should not be delayed, and that at fourteen the girl was quite old enough for child-bearing. Fulk had agreed.)

It was her sister who tried to comfort her, but there was little comfort to give. They were alone in their room as the first snow was falling.

'If I pray to St Albinus, will it snow for ever, Hersende?' the girl sobbed – with such appealing despair that the elder sister felt her own heart to be in pain.

What could she say to assuage that misery? She had imagined her own plight to be the worst imaginable, but the Countess had shown her the way out. Besides, her own wedding was not to be for almost a year, and in that time . . . as the Countess had said, much could happen and in all probability would. But Milesende. Her own frail, beautiful sister. And so young, so full of dreams wrapped in flowers. She was like a dark rose waiting for the sun, waiting for her prince. And with that thought Hersende remembered the song of the minstrel that summer evening a few months ago – how the lover had been compelled to surrender to the most cruel tasks imposed upon him – the dragons and demons and impenetrable castles – how he could see before him only the prospect of his own death, until finally on the shores of despair there appeared before his eyes a lovely rose in the garden of love – and how he claimed it – how he had earned it by proving that true love could surmount all the obstacles the wicked world set in its path.

'You must make Rollo fall in love with you,' said Hersende suddenly.

Milesende looked up from her bed of tears and gazed at her sister for a moment. Her lovely eyes were red, and strands of hair hung damp over her pale cheeks. Then she began to sob once again – even more painfully, it seemed, with the mention of Rollo's name. But then, quite abruptly, she stopped and gazed again at Hersende.

'Why? What's the use?' she asked almost angrily, but in her eyes was a look of hope.

'Remember the minstrel,' replied her sister. And she reminded her of the song about the lover and the garden, and the obstacles placed in love's way. 'Perhaps this is what he meant.'

Milesende looked thoughtful. She said nothing for a while, but wiped her tears and sat gazing out at the slow flakes of snow that were floating past the window.

'Do you mean ...'

And Hersende nodded.

'... that Rollo, if he loved me ...'

Her sister was smiling now.

'... could still win me?'

Hersende nodded again.

'But how? If I'm to be married ...'

'You must put your trust in love. That's the point of the tale. On the shore of despair you can see no way. Of course, else you wouldn't despair. But ... if Rollo loved you – truly loved – he would find a way. That's what the minstrel said.'

A frown appeared on Milesende's forehead.

'But he doesn't love me. He loves *you*.' She spoke with a sudden bitterness and began to weep again.

Hersende rose and put her arms round her younger sister, who wrenched herself free with an angry twist of her body.

'Milesende, listen to me.'

And Hersende waited until the black-haired girl turned and raised her head towards her. The look was almost pleading as she did so, and tears continued to trickle down her cheeks. Hersende could not help wondering how many tears a human body could produce, and tried not to smile.

As she talked to her sister she began to feel surprisingly old and wise. All those long talks with the Countess Elizabeth had added years to her understanding of such things. She found herself speaking as she imagined the Countess would have spoken, and she wished she could produce the same husky voice to give her words that particular flavour of meaning.

Rollo, she explained, knew her — Hersende — not at all. He was in love with a face. And perhaps, she added with a little laugh, with — and she looked down with some satisfaction at her swelling breasts — other things. She had gazed at him, it was true, with wicked eyes, but that was only to arouse some jealousy in Sebrand. A love so easily planted, she said, could just as easily be transplanted.

'Look at yourself,' Hersende went on. 'How beautiful you are. I wish I could show you your eyes. They would melt any one you cared to look at. And your hair: it's like a dark river. And your face. Your body. Perfect. And you — all of you. You're a jewel, my lovely sister, and I love you. So would any man you chose, if you wanted him to.'

Milesende lowered her gaze. Then she gave a final sob and looked up again.

'Really?' she said.

The two sisters were looking out at the falling snow. At that moment a servant entered and announced Father Baudouin. Before either girl had time to answer the chaplain was standing there, his throat wobbling, eyes bulging eagerly. He looked dusty. Hersende noticed the hairs protruding from his nostrils. He fidgeted with his hands. His voice had slime on it.

'I came to offer some words of guidance on your forthcoming marriages.'

His eyes seemed to take in those portions of the girls' anatomy that would be most affected by such events.

'It is a holy state,' he began. But Hersende, emboldened, interrupted the chaplain.

'Reverend Father, I beg you not now,' she ventured. 'My sister is most unwell.'

Father Baudouin gulped, and small noises issued from his throat. His eyes continued to roam from one sister to the other. His hands stroked his habit.

'Very well. Another time. I have things to say. Things you should know.'

'Indeed, Father! We wait to be instructed. Another time, if you will. Thank you.'

The chaplain lingered a few moments. Hersende noticed his habit to be of an unusual shape below his belly. Milesende had turned away towards the window, hand to her brow in proof of her sister's remarks. Then he had gone.

The two sisters breathed heavily with relief. As the snow continued to fall, and the light faded over the white fields beyond the river, they talked between themselves with an affection neither had ever felt so free to display. Two unwanted marriages. Two schemes for surmounting those obstacles. And as they talked the brightest avenues of hope opened up in the dusk of a winter evening.

'So, I must trust in love to find a way.'

'Yes.'

It was not many days later that Milesende ventured out hunting, with a determination that whatever other prey was brought down she would bring down the man she loved.

*

Suddenly it was spring. The cruel winter departed as swiftly as it had come. Nearly a thousand people had died in Angers — almost one out of every three inhabitants. The city lay weak and exhausted. Many survivors were without the resources to begin again. From the countryside came stories of villages without a living soul: only the howl of wolves. Some had been more fortunate: the freak winter had struck unevenly, and it soon emerged that much of the land to the south and east of Angers had suffered only lightly — round Brissac, Doué, Montreuil (the seat of the noble Giraud Berlay) and further east to Chinon, L'Ile Bouchard (where Fulk's treasurer was the lord), Langeais, Ste Maure and Loches (where the Count's pious cousin Hildegarde was mistress). And since these were the rich vine-lands there was much relief and celebration within the castle at the news. The Lady Ermengarde's only interest in her husband the Treasurer during those long frozen months had been to inquire anxiously whether the famous vines on the Bouchard lands would be safe from the hand of winter. There were many who felt sure that, had she been able to, she would have gone and personally wrapped each plant in her finest woollens, willingly baring herself to the cold rather than risk such an unthinkable tragedy. After all, it was felt, she bared herself so often that she would hardly notice. When reassurance came she was beside herself with joy, and set about hastening the exhaustion of last year's vintage in eager anticipation of the new.

The Lady Adelaide had prayed that it might be otherwise. Provided, in her view, there remained enough wine for the sacrament it would be a blessing — a sign that the holy saints had indeed listened — if the vines should perish and the land be vacated for more useful purposes: a new monastery perhaps. She had imagined the winter to be like the sickle revealed to the apostle John — thrust into the earth and gathering the vines into the great winepress of the wrath of God. She had looked forward to ministering to the Lady

Ermengarde on the lessons of God's anger, and had even prepared a number of helpful speeches to be used when the word came that her husband's vineyards were no more. Alas, her plans were now set at nought, and it was to her mortification that as spring burst out of winter she saw the lady's excesses scale new heights unchecked: as to the Lady Adelaide's protestations of divine retribution, these were swept away like twigs in a river of wine, laughter and lust.

The entire castle stirred itself from a long sleep. The Count himself was like a creature reborn. Even before dawn the clatter of horses' hooves would wake the city, and guards fling open the gates as he rode out in his heavy surcoat to rouse some neighbouring vassal with orders for rebuilding, resettling, replanting – repairing the destruction of winter. He was generous and impatient: stores of grain and fodder that he found unshared were seized by the provosts who accompanied him for distribution among the starving, while those who had hoarded them were either heavily fined, or lost their lands and – if they resisted – their lives too. The lord of Daumeray, who had the temerity to point out that the greatest hoards of food were within the castle of Angers itself, found himself greeting the next dawn from an iron cage – the very same cage in which Conan's son Budic had languished until the Count's mercy found him a darker dungeon.

Often Fulk accompanied Rollo to Langeais and Montbazon to inspect the two castles, now well advanced. The Count said little on these journeys, often returning to Angers the same night. Ten hours on horseback was no burden to him at all, and the next day he would be somewhere else. Sebrand or Audemand would convey to Rollo later that he was pleased.

Rollo was rarely at Angers now. There were scores of workmen to supervise. Never, he imagined, had castles been built so rapidly, and the Count hinted that there would very soon be more – the stone collar round the neck of Odo.

Rollo had only to snap his fingers and whatever he needed seemed to materialize without a word. It was Fulk's command. He began to feel like a lord, and there was a tingle of power about his days. At the same time he was conscious of being swept along on the irresistible current of Fulk's will that was carrying him ever further from the life he felt happiest to lead. There were days when he longed for the peace of Jumièges and the company of holy men. Now there was no time to reflect upon those matters that filled the thoughts of the monks, and which he as their mason had endeavoured to translate into stone. He began to wonder if he would ever again build for God, or build for the human spirit. Those visions of light, of vaulting the heavens – where were they? Of the new cathedral at Angers not a further word had been said since that first meeting with the Count. No one here, it appeared, had time – except for war.

Only riding eastwards towards Langeais on spring mornings did he have the ease and space around him to wonder what he was doing in this new life. He would look down at the bright stars of wood anemones in the young grass that his horse trod, and be aware that they were the only stars he now followed. Those above were obscured by the heavy cloud of Fulk's ambitions. Whatever the Count decreed became Rollo's own future: there was nothing else. And what kind of future was it? Here was he, with no titles, no lands: only the skill of his hands, the skill of his brain. He was a builder, without belonging to anything he built, or anything belonging to him. Fulk needed him to create castles, but he would never allow him to own one. And Rollo laughed out aloud. The soldiers riding with him turned in puzzlement. Even they had lives of their own somewhere, he thought: parents, wives, children.

At Langeais, Rollo stayed at first with the elderly governor, in the room off the courtyard: then a house was found for him, with servants, everything he could need. It had been decreed. The same at Montbazon. The Count provided, for just so long as it suited him. Rollo was a privileged servant. *Servus servorum Dei*. Except that God, like the stars, was obscured.

At Langeais, Rollo grew accustomed to living alone. After the bustle of Angers, it became a relief. His work tied him here: Montbazon was only a short ride along the shaded banks of the Indre, bright with spring now, and he would return in the evening rather than pass the night under the shadow of his own castle rising menacingly on its cliff. Besides, he felt uneasy lying within sight of Odo's watchful eyes. He remembered the three horsemen and imagined them still lurking, reporting back to their master on how the castle was progressing.

Langeais on the other hand was peaceful. In the mornings he could hear the river bubbling past the walls of his house, and in the evenings he would sit by the bank fishing, and a servant would grill what he caught on an open fire. The smell of herbs would fill the warmth of the room as he sat alone, sometimes tracing details of a cornice or a buttress on a slab of limestone or a piece of parchment. He felt at home here. His room became a workshop, and life began to resemble the one he had been accustomed to lead in Normandy when he had known no other life, and wanted none.

Outside the house he had begun to make a garden. Gradually he cleared the undergrowth along the river bank, then carefully levelled, dug and manured the ground, hoeing it until its texture was fine and smooth. He created small square plots between a mesh of paths, each plot raised a little and edged with stones of just the right size and shape. People would stop and watch, and he enjoyed their silent admiration. Sometimes they would ask questions, or look blank: sometimes they would bring him seeds and young plants. At Jumièges, Rollo had often helped the monks cultivating herbs in the physic garden. They had known the properties of each plant, and would impart their knowledge to him. He had found it extraordinary that such tiny growing things should possess such powers. Monkshood for reducing fever and as a bait against wolves. Parsley against baldness. Bittersweet for the skin. Eyebright – with a little white wine – for the eyes. Mistletoe for epilepsy. Chervil for cleansing the blood. Comfrey for broken bones. Pennyroyal for giddiness. Rue and tarragon against snake-bites. Wormwood against the poison of toadstools and hemlock. And so many more.

He had begun to put them to use and found to his surprise that they worked as the monks said. Once a mason had fallen: he had bound the broken arm in comfrey within a splint, and it had mended more rapidly than anyone could believe, with no impairment or deformation. Wounds among quarriers he had treated with lemon balm, and they healed without inflammation or discharge of poisons. People started to come to him as often as they did to the monks, and to look upon him with wonder. And here in Langeais he recognized those same expressions of suspicion, at first, and then curiosity as he went about his work.

Rollo also took to wandering in search of these herbs now that the sun had woven a carpet of green over the meadows crushed and bleached by the winter's snow. He explored the fields and forests, noticing the young violets, primroses and wood sorrel; and these too reminded him of the woods round Jumièges where he would walk with Ebba. Gentle Ebba of the forest. Soon the woodland floor became stained with daffodils, and then bluebells. Rollo noticed the birds returning. The evenings rang with nightingales: there were warblers in the reed-beds by the river, and swallows swooping over the water; hoopoes dipped between the trees, and sometimes formations of white storks trailed across the morning sky, occasionally with blue cranes accompanying them and keeping the same rhythm of their wings. And echoing once again across the water came the flute-call of the oriole – Fulk's golden bird – and Rollo imagined the feasting back at Angers. He remembered Sebrand telling him of the roistering whenever the oriole returned; and he smiled. Rollo imagined the Count enthroned, brooding above the assembled company. Elizabeth sparkling, her red hair flowing among jewels. The stately Audemand quietly amused. The Lady Adelaide fluttering primly. Her husband Roger slumped colossally drunk between two serving-maids being disrobed for their pains. The Lady Ermengarde slithering like a snake with hot eyes. Sulpice, the young Adonis, dancing lightly. Sebrand dancing too – with ... probably the lovely Hersende, eyes darting, breasts rounded in the torchlight. Rollo felt a pang of hunger and of sadness: she had danced for him, as it seemed, and then danced away. Besides, she was the *Lady* Hersende now, and not for him: to be the Countess Hersende, so Sebrand said. And what of her young sister, the child Milesende who had clung so light and so firmly in his arms, snow falling on her face and hair as she melted him with those dark knowing eyes? But what could a mere child mean to him?

He dismissed the thought. Then bitterness rose in him as again he remembered Hersende dancing for him – as it had seemed; her eyes following him, lighting fires in him, hopes, elation. Then to realize that all those burning glances were for the benefit not of him at all, but of Sebrand, in order to light fires of jealousy. And Sebrand did not care. That made it worse. How dare Sebrand not care? How could he not care? Sebrand – who could cheerfully whore his way from inn to inn, pour wine down women's breasts, heave them like sacks to his rumpled bed – how could a man clutch so joyfully at toys and then not grasp a jewel? And how could Hersende cast herself at such a man? Rollo wanted to despise them both. But jealousy is a kind of admiration, and all he could wish was that he were Sebrand, and Hersende his. Rollo's bitterness dissolved into a lonely sadness.

It was evening. He was returning with a reed basket of young herbs. It was a path Rollo had not taken before, which led along a shallow valley he had never noticed among slender birches through which the late sun sparkled, and hoops of young bracken rose brilliant green through the undergrowth. Suddenly he noticed a shawled figure among the trees, standing motionless. Her dress was long and ragged and he could not see her face, but there was something familiar about her: he could not identify what.

Rollo looked more closely, and as he did so she turned her head and pulled back her shawl a little with her fingers. He knew that face. But from where? She was looking at him. Then slowly she turned again and began to walk ahead along the path among the birch-trees, not looking back. She had a heavy body but she moved with surprising gracefulness, never altering her pace as she slipped between the trees and the tangles of woodbine and honeysuckle that protruded across the path. She had bare feet and her step made no sound. He kept his distance, but without her appearing to slow her pace she constantly seemed to be shortening that distance. He walked even more slowly. Rollo wondered if each time trees obscured his view of her she would halt for a few seconds: but how did she know that his view was obscured? When next he saw her she was moving again with the same stately pace, her body swinging slightly as she walked, but her head quite still as if she were accustomed to balancing something – a basket, perhaps, or a water-jar.

The path descended a gully, twisting between limestone rocks. Round a corner suddenly there she was, a few paces away in the track, her back to him. He stopped, uncertain whether to speak or to pass her with a mutter of greeting. Before he could decide the woman extended her right arm as if to clutch at something. Now he could not pass without brushing that arm aside. Then she spoke.

'Let me see what you've gathered.'

The voice was calm and low: sounds floated from her like woodsmoke. The arm was still extended, and her back turned to him. He placed the reed basket in her outstretched hand, and she took it: as she did so she half-turned, but the shawl still covered her face. Rollo noticed the hand was that of a youngish woman, though it had marks — tiny scars — scattered across it.

With her other hand she began to finger very gently the tiny herbs within the basket. With each one she made small noises of recognition before carefully replacing it, and her fingers would delicately pick up another. Finally she held one of the herbs for rather longer, and looked up at him. She had a strong, almost coarse face; weather-beaten but with a fierce beauty about it. She was perhaps his own age. Again he felt sure he knew her. But where?

'So you know about healing . . . a little.'

Rollo nodded. Their eyes met. There was a pause. She gazed at the tiny herb in her left hand. It was rue. Small oval leaves: Rollo had picked the young sprig with the intention of striking it.

'Monks taught you,' she said. That smooth low voice again.

'How do you know?' he answered, puzzled.

'Because . . . monks know a little, though not round here. But then you're not from round here.' She spoke as though stating the obvious. Then, without waiting for a comment, she went on, still looking at the sprig of rue.

'For snake-bites. But also for . . . seeing things.' And she placed a forefinger beneath her left eye, and tapped it several times. 'But the monks wouldn't have taught you that,' she added.

She looked hard at him.

'With your eyes you should be able to see better than you do. Vikings' eyes. Blue like the sea. Sea-caves.'

Again Rollo wanted to question her. But she handed him the basket and went on in a matter-of-fact voice.

'Would you like more herbs for your garden?' There was the suggestion of laughter in that low, calm voice, as if she knew she was teasing him with fragments of her knowledge of him, and her lips gave the tiniest flicker.

She turned without waiting for an answer, and Rollo followed her. They walked on for several minutes in silence, the strange woman a few paces ahead, never turning. He noticed how her broad feet seemed to stroke the ground as she moved, the underside darkened with mud, ankles surprisingly slim, strong. All of a sudden she turned off the track towards a small meadow below them, fringed with trees. Except from this path you would not have known it was there. The sun had sunk behind the hill now, and a cool dampness rose from the grass. Her feet glistened with dew. Rollo caught sight of animals on the far side of the meadow: a cow, several pigs, geese, hens. A ramshackle hut, or several huts, had been built under the trees. From one of these a haze of smoke rose from the thatch, and beside the hut a large dog rose silently from the grass as they approached, and wandered towards them. Rollo looked again. It was not a dog: it was a wolf.

The grey beast took no notice of Rollo, to his relief, but went up to the woman as they approached, and licked her hand. She stroked it, and it lay down again on a patch of bare earth beneath a tree. Only then did Rollo notice that the wolf had cubs. It stretched and curled its legs round the small balls of fur as they scrambled against its belly. The wolf closed its eyes, and Rollo could see its heart pounding.

'Come in.'

The woman had unlatched the door of the largest hut and was lighting a lamp from the embers that glowed in the centre of the single room. She hung the lamp on a low beam and arranged pieces of wood on the fire, which began to spurt flame and cast wavering shadows on the beams that rose to a cluster above the centre of the room. The smoke made Rollo's eyes smart, but soon it began to billow against the thatch above before being drawn out through the reeds. The air around them became clear, and filled with a sweet wood smell.

His eyes began to take in the interior. It was bare of

furniture except for a table to one side, and a bed of straw nearby; but in the gloom Rollo could make out quantities of jars, flagons, cauldrons, bowls, cups – all crowded under the low thatch around the fringe of the hut. Above them, on pegs sunk into the beams, hung sheaves of dried plants: there was not enough light to recognize them, but smells that he could not identify caught his nostrils. As his eyes grew accustomed to the half-dark he could make out other things hanging among the dried plants, and he gave a start. There were bones – many of them, of various shapes and anatomies, some shining as if polished, others brown and crumbling, others almost black. Some were huge, and Rollo found himself wondering what creature they might have belonged to.

He began to feel uneasy: he decided not to stay here. The woman had her back to him by the table. He glanced outside through the open door. The light was beginning to fade. And facing him was the wolf.

Suddenly the woman turned, and in the lamplight he could make out a faint smile on her lips. She was looking at him intently. Then she held out a wooden beaker, and he saw that her other hand was grasping a pitcher which had been resting on the table.

'Wine,' she said in that same matter-of-fact calm voice.

He took it hesitantly.

'I always have good wine,' she added. 'The farmers are my friends.'

Rollo took an uncertain sip. The woman laughed.

'You think I might poison you?'

And she took another beaker from the table, poured it full from the pitcher and took a long draught, gazing at him over the rim as she did so. He responded by draining his own. Then she walked across the room and reached up to one of the wooden beams and unhooked something. As she returned she extended a hand towards Rollo. In it lay a dried, spiky plant.

'I could poison you more easily with this,' she said. 'Hemlock . . . And afterwards, to cure you,' she went on, reaching into Rollo's own basket which he had laid on the rush-mat floor, 'one of your own herbs. Wormwood . . . But I promised you some herbs, didn't I? For the garden you're making. Come! Before it grows too dark.'

And she planted her empty beaker on the table and led Rollo out through the open door. She had powerful hands, and she took one of his in her own as if it were the hand of a child. Again Rollo noticed the minute scars.

Still firmly grasping his hand, she led him round the side of the hut. The wolf stirred, but only to gaze at them. The cubs were sleeping against her body. The light was beginning to fade, and the evening was quite still. No birds sang.

'Here,' she said. And along the verges of the woodland beside the hut were patches of shrub and greenery, and earth that had been lightly hoed. The woman bent over and grasped a wooden fork, then began to uproot plants here and there, and break off shoots. Rollo noticed how lithe and vigorous were her movements, her fingers swift, her bare feet widely spread and firmly pressed on to the soil. Finally she rose and flexed her back, and Rollo was aware of the roundness of her breasts beneath the shawl.

'Take these,' she said. And one by one she picked the small plants and roots from her left hand and passed them to Rollo.

'For when you need courage . . . Float this in a syrup cup. Borage . . . And this you should know. Angelica. After St Michael Archangel. It will flower soon – on his day, May the 8th. Or so your Church says.' And she gave a low laugh. 'For the plague . . . And for breaking the power of spells. Keep it well, Rollo.' It was the first time she had used his name. But who had told her?

'This against lightning. Bay . . . This to hang over doors on Midsummer's Eve. Fennel. And this . . . Judas hanged himself from it. The elder tree. Your Church will tell you what to do . . . And this' — and she picked out a small sprig — 'they call this the holy herb. Vervain. Take it.'

Rollo now had a handful of plants. He watched her, intrigued. She had taken the wooden fork again and was digging energetically. She pulled out a twisted root and held it up, laughing again and looking at him out of the corner of her eye.

'Did you hear anything? . . . It's said to shriek when you dig it up. And if you hear it, you die.' She laughed again and loosened her shawl a little. Rollo caught sight of her bare, deep neck. 'But it's also said to grow only under gallows.' Rollo instinctively found himself looking up, and the woman laughed more loudly. 'Take it. It's powerful. Everything you have in your hand is powerful. Much more than your Church knows.'

She let the fork drop to the ground and began to walk back towards the hut. Rollo saw she had a bunch of herbs still grasped in her hand. He followed her. The wolf stirred and opened its eyes, watching Rollo as he passed. He followed the woman inside. There was only the light of the fire, and the lamp hung on the beam. She refilled his beaker, and her own, then placed the handful of herbs on the earth floor beside the mat.

'And these . . . I'll tell you about these later.'

As she spoke she began to untie her shawl without once taking her eyes off him. In the flickering light Rollo could see her smile — a knowing smile. He was becoming aware of the effect of the wine, and his own eyes seemed to be guided by the movement of her hands. She wound the shawl slowly in front of her as she pulled it free of her head and shoulders. She held it there for a moment, her fingers playing with the threads. Then she let it drop. Rollo felt his stomach give a twinge. Underneath she was wearing a coarsely woven garment — dark brown — draped loosely upon her body and quite open at the front where the lacing had been left untied.

Her breasts were all but bare, and the lamplight from above carved a deep shadow under each.

Then, still holding her gaze, she said:

'Now you know me.'

Rollo stared. For there, across her right breast, lay a dark-red weal. Three weals — close together. A number, repeated twice, had been burnt into the skin. 6 ... 6 ... 6.

Yes, he knew her. He could feel himself trembling. Her eyes seemed to burn into his face like that terrible weal. He could not move. Pictures swirled through his mind. The thunderstorm and Fulk's vision. The weather-makers and that long night path through the forest. The silent clearing in the moonlight. The figure rising from the invisible ground — moaning, swaying, tearing her flesh, gasping, turning to him, then to Fulk. And that cry — shrieking into the night, finger pointed. Oh God! What was it she saw?

She was gazing up at him with a deep, deep smile. Very gently he placed his hands over her naked breasts. She shuddered and closed her eyes. He bent down and kissed the weals, and her head fell forward on to his neck. He placed a hand round her bare shoulders and with the other lifted her into his arms. Her eyes were still closed and she made not a sound. Rollo carried her lightly across the room under the trembling lamp and laid her on the bed of straw. Her garment slipped off easily in his hands, and her body gave off a sweetish fragrance. The skin was so soft to his fingers as she lay there. He removed his own clothes, then knelt down and began to kiss her — her toes, sliding his tongue between each, then her feet and ankles, her calves, the inside of her knees, her thighs. The strong scent of her skin melted with the fragrance of her herbs, and as his lips and tongue moved slowly up her body she began to moan and grasp at him, her head turning on the straw and her mouth wide; and when he took her it was with a frenzy which seemed never to cease.

They lay there — Rollo did not know how long they lay there. He could not imagine the terrors that had gripped him arlier. He stroked her body coiled within his arms and eard her breathing deeply. Gradually their sweat grew old, and she stirred. He realized he was shivering. He could eel that she was awake, and she reached out and drew a lanket over them. A few sounds came from the fire, and the mp was low.

The next time he raised his head it was dawn, and a chill f dew filled the hut. He could hear the stirring of animals. A runting. A flap of wings. A soft thud of hooves on turf. The rag of a chain.

She rose quietly, and he watched her rekindle the fire, our water into a pot and lay it among the sticks, sprinkling some leaves. Soon the scent of mint began to fill the hut nd the first rays of sun stole through the open door. She was aked in the dawn, pale sunlight on her strong body. She urned and gazed at him for some time. Then very slowly she nelt down and took his member in her hands until it stirred. he bent forward and stroked the tip of it with her tongue, er breasts brushing his thighs with slight movements. till holding him, she eased herself forward and down on him and, after a few moments, convulsed into his arms.

The sun was high over the hill. They drank mint from the ot on the fire, saying nothing. Then she lay back naked in he morning sunlight, looking at him. Her face wore that miliar warm smile.

'My Viking!' she said after a while. 'I've been waiting for ou.'

'How did you know of me?'

She laughed and rose on to one elbow, still gazing at him.

'Everybody knows of you. The giant with the strange yes. The castle-builder. Besides, I saw you that first night.'

'But it was dark. And you were in a trance.'

'It's in a trance when you see best,' she answered smiling. nd she stretched out a hand and slipped her fingers rough his fingers. 'I made love to you that night. Didn't ou see?'

199

'Why did you choose me?'

She laughed again, and ran her hand down his bare che
and stomach.

'Because ... you're a Viking.' She gave a low chuckl
Then her voice became serious, far away. 'And because ..
we meet in dreams.' Her fingers were making pattern
across his body. 'I see things – know things – that othe
don't. So do you ... you have your visions.'

She was silent for a moment, gazing down at him. The
she looked intently at his face.

'But remember! The world would call you evil if it knew
She ran her fingers lightly down his face. 'A tool of the Devi
... You've slept with a witch. What would they think abou
that at your monastery? What would Fulk say? You mu
never say a word. Never! Or you'll be in the worst danger.

The sun was warming their bodies through the ope
doorway. She was resting her head on his chest and her ar
round his shoulder. He could feel her strong thigh pressed t
his. They lay there in silence.

There was something Rollo understood now. The Churc
was supposed to be about love: yet it abhorred carnal lov
Gave it to Satan. So – this woman – of course the Churc
had to give her to the Devil. Those tales, Rollo remembere
about witches: how no man could satisfy them; only th
Devil with his gigantic member, always erect, always hu
gry. But how could you separate spiritual and carnal love
This creature lying beside him was both. Rollo's eyes gaze
at the swell of her breast squeezed against his body, and
that terrible weal. Those numbers burnt into the skin. 6 .
6 ... 6. And he rolled over and kissed her with his tongu
He held her breasts and could feel the scar under his fingers.

'Tell me about that,' he asked after a while. 'Who did it
At first she said nothing. Then, without raising her hea
and her eyes still closed, she said:

'Don't you know?'

'No!'

There was another pause.

'Yes, you do,' she said.

A look of horror came over Rollo's face. He half-raised himself and his eyes searched around as though for help. He wanted to vomit. Hatred rose in him. He looked down at her, and she seemed so calm. Sunlight was stroking her body – the body he had loved – the body Fulk had tortured. Black Fulk. How could he have done this? But of course. And Rollo recalled the words they had exchanged on that first evening in Langeais. Fulk's terror at his vision of the angel in the sun. His vision of damnation. Fulk's relief at Rollo's words about the monks at Jumièges and their promise of life. And the Count's joy at the weather-makers – his relief that the storm was their doing and not God's – how he seemed to gloat at their powers, and the powers of this woman through whom they worked. And then! Her trance, her vision, her finger of damnation pointed straight at Fulk. 'Burning. Burning. Burning,' she had said. Of course Fulk had to give those words to the Devil. He had to destroy the Devil's messenger. Fulk had been trapped between one damnation and another. And he struck in order to break free. Fulk's only weapon – to kill!

She saw the distress in Rollo's face and put out a hand to touch his leg. Then she smiled at him.

'It's all right,' she said lightly. 'I was fortunate. He had me passed over to the bishop.' She sat up and her skin glowed in the sunlight. He was aware again of the sweet odour of her body.

'I was to be burnt,' she added quietly.

Rollo felt a twinge of horror.

'And what happened?'

She gave out a deep laugh and turned her head towards him. She looked young and beautiful, her face almost taunting suddenly.

'Do you really want to know?'

Rollo nodded.

'Well! It was the Bishop of Loches. Not your bishop at Angers, luckily. And he was ... prepared to be pleased.' She was smiling. 'Most churchmen are.'

She went on gazing at him with that knowing smile. Then she looked away and arched her back, stroking her hands down her body in the sun.

'Kiss me!' she said.

Rollo smothered her with kisses, and he felt tears in his eyes. Fulk. The monster. The unforgivable monster. To think of it – he, Rollo, had come to Anjou to build for God, and instead he was building castles for an ogre who caused men of God to do this to a young woman because she had visions. Did not St John have visions? How dare they burn his prophecies on this woman's breast because she had them too? Once again his mind went back to that night under the full moon in the forest clearing. And her finger pointing at Fulk. Had she meant that *he* was to burn? Or herself?

'Can you tell me what you saw that night?' Rollo asked fearfully.

The woman shook her head. Then she shivered and reached for her garment.

'You must go,' she said softly. Then as if she regretted what she had said she let it drop, took his hands and laid them on her breasts.

'Rollo,' she went on, 'you must know that because of what I am I cannot love. I can only make love. And make others love.'

He gazed at her, puzzled.

'But when ...?' he began, distraught at having to depart.

She was shaking her head again, not looking at him. Rollo thought he saw tears in her eyes. Then with a sudden movement she rose and picked up the bunch of plants she had never given him. She had promised to tell him about them, she had said.

'You'll never have need of these.' And her voice was light again. Her face wore that taunting look. She reached towards him with a little laugh and stroked his groin. Then she looked up at him, touching her top lip with the point of her tongue. And as she did so she raised the bunch of plants in front of him and dropped them, kicking them to one side with her bare foot.

'But', she added, 'they did save my life. They're love potions.'

She pulled on her garment and began to lace it up to her neck. Then she walked outside. The wolf rose and went to her, and licked her hand. The cubs wriggled blindly in the dust. Rollo could hear the birds singing: it was as if the valley were suddenly open to the sound.

'You must go,' she said without looking at him. 'And quickly. Back to Angers . . . Someone there has a garden for you to walk into, and only you have the key to it.'

Rollo started. The gold key! It was with him always. But whose? And how would he know?

'You'll know because she's the one who loves you,' she went on just as though he had been speaking to her. 'And because I've opened your eyes. You *must* go quickly. I shall do what I can to keep her for you, because . . .'

Her head fell forward, and Rollo saw that her hands were trembling. The wolf stirred uneasily, glaring at him with hostile eyes. He backed away.

Rollo turned his head again to speak. She was not there.

SIX

WHILE ROLLO WAS AT LANGEAIS, tumults of a different nature were disturbing the peace at the castle of Count Fulk. The Count became distracted from his plans for the wedding of Bernard of Combourg to the young Milesende by what he felt to be an infuriating ecclesiastical matter. This affected the cathedral of St Maurice where the marriage was to take place, and in particular the Bishop who was to perform the holy ceremony.

It has to be said that virtually everyone at the castle apart from the Count was privately delighted by these events, there being nothing that members of Fulk's court enjoyed more than a battle between their lord and someone who had the temerity to oppose him. There was perhaps a certain bloodthirstiness in such enjoyment, since the usual outcome was the opponent's mutilated corpse making its appearance on the iron spikes protruding from the castle walls. But on this occasion that seemed an unlikely eventuality since the opponent was none other than the awesome Bishop Renaud – whose bloodied corpse would not improve the Count's standing with the Holy Father in Rome. So the ensuing battle appeared likely to be of a more complex nature, and the occupants of the castle speculated with discreet relish on how the battle-lines would be drawn up, and who would strike first.

No one was more delighted by the storm brewing than Milesende. Having braced herself for marriage with the ageing Viscount of Combourg as soon as spring arrived, she saw these new thunderclouds as a heaven-sent reward for her trust in the power of love, and as proof of the utter truth of the minstrel's story. She prayed, hoped, begged, wept for the delay to be interminable, and in the meanwhile she scanned the horizon from her lofty room for a sight of her beloved Rollo galloping to her rescue transformed from mere stonemason to shining prince.

'He will come! He will come, won't he?' she pleaded to her sister, her eyes moist with tears of hope.

Hersende, with the worldly advantage of being nearly eighteen, privately found it hard to see how Rollo could do anything about it at all, even supposing that he cared. It was not clear to Hersende that her sister's piece of deception out hunting had necessarily brought about the instant capture of the man's heart that Milesende had wished. Lovely though she was — loveliest of all in Hersende's eyes — she was still such a young and dreamy creature, and a man who built castles and cathedrals for the Count of Anjou might well have other things on his mind. Besides, he was not here, but far away in Langeais.

She took Milesende in her arms with an aching heart.

'Something will happen, I know,' she said, wishing for all the world that she could believe it.

Count Fulk, meanwhile, was in a furious mood. Such patience as he had with Bishop Renaud was rooted in the fact that his father Geoffrey Greymantle had appointed him. Fulk had seen it as filial duty that he should concede to the noble bishop certain privileges pertaining to the Church of Anjou. Taxes, tithes, tenure of land, the ownership of serfs, the appointment of priests, rights of vassalage, the exercise of punishment and fines relating to servants of the Church: these and many other benefits Fulk had handed over to the prelate one by one during the past few years. Always there had been that fierce glare in response, the lofty reference to divine authority, the unyielding pride of office. Fulk's own material gifts to the cathedral had been, in the Count's view, beyond generosity. But never a smile of thanks was given back. It was true, as the Countess Elizabeth gently pointed out to him, that the cathedral itself remained in ruins; but his own master-mason, who had drawn up brilliant plans, was now employed on matters of great urgency upon which the very security of the Bishop's diocese depended, Fulk reminded her. Furthermore, when that security had been directly threatened by the late Count of Rennes, what had the proud Bishop done? He had refused, in contravention of all laws of vassalage, to contribute any soldiers to the war against the Breton usurper – a war in which he, the Count, had nearly lost his life and in which one-third of the lords of Anjou had perished while the Bishop endangered his holy self no more than by muttering a few prayers. It was quite clear that Bishop Renaud was determined to establish a lordship over church lands and servants that would vie with his own.

And now this new insult! News had recently reached the Count that the Bishop had delivered an outburst to his cathedral canons against what he claimed to be the malice, dishonesty and theft practised by secular rulers who were in the habit of selling benefices and posts of high office within the Church for 'gains of a non-spiritual kind' – the Bishop's words had been reported back to him. Fulk had not been named personally, but no one present had been in the slightest doubt to whom he was referring.

Count Fulk was stunned by the arrogance of the man. Members of the Count's court who were accustomed to seeing his enemies impaled on hooks for the kites to peck at were not far from envisaging what was in Fulk's mind at that moment. He would have liked to dismember the prelate with his bare hands, and was restrained from doing so forthwith by the reflection not only that Renaud had been his father's appointment, but also that Geoffrey Greymantle's motives had not been entirely without self-interest. The Bishop's father – Viscount Renaud the Thuringian – was the lord of the Mauges, a region to the south-west of Angers which the late Count had considered well worth the acquisition, even perhaps at such a heavy price. So – Fulk stormed – had the Bishop not *bought* his own proud office? And was that not a gain 'of a non-spiritual kind'? How dare the proud cleric now turn that accusation against him.

The Countess was accustomed to such storms, and she was grateful that at least on this occasion it was unlikely to end in bloodshed – though, if the Bishop had been present at this moment, she doubted if her husband's flailing hands could have been restrained from pulping the austere ecclesiastic.

The storm continued for many days and showed little sign of abatement. It was clear to the gentle Countess that Fulk's deepest anger was over being powerless. There was really nothing he could do except denounce Bishop Renaud to the archbishop; but Archbishop Hugh was resident in Tours – Odo's city – where of all places Fulk would be least welcome. Instead, in his impotence he raged, and the court of Angers kept a safe distance.

Then, after a week, Fulk's luck turned. It was towards the evening of a fine spring day. The Count was smouldering more quietly than usual, and the Countess had taken advantage of the relative calm to play with their small daughter – whose nurse had wisely been keeping the child away from her father for some days. Suddenly there was a discreet cough, and the chamberlain, Garnier, advanced a few paces very quietly. The Chancellor Audemand, he announced, wished to see the Count on a matter of some gravity.

Fulk looked up and with an automatic gesture waved the chamberlain to send the Chancellor in. No expression from the Count greeted the old man, but when he bowed to the Countess she smiled in such a way that Audemand understood immediately how grateful the lady was to be sharing her husband's presence. Then he addressed himself to Fulk.

'My lord Count, I have some news that will interest you.'

Fulk looked at the Chancellor without the least display of interest. So Audemand continued.

'Viscount Renaud, the noble Bishop's father, is dead.'

The Count uttered not a word. But his eyes had a gleam that Audemand had not seen for quite a while. Then he slowly rose, strode to the window and turned to face the Chancellor in his customary pose, legs wide apart, hands clasped to his hips, head back.

'And when did this happen?' he asked quietly.

'Some days ago, I believe,' answered Audemand, 'but I have only just heard. I understand that the noble Bishop will leave tomorrow to bury the Viscount and to attend to his father's land and property.'

There was a lengthy silence. The Countess, who had sat her daughter on her knee to keep her quiet, could see from the expression on the Chancellor's face that the old man was reading some very dark thoughts in her husband's mind, and she wondered what these might be. She did not have to wait long.

The Count breathed in loudly through his nostrils. Then he cleared his throat.

'Well!' he said. 'So Renaud is going to see to his inheritance, is he? ... If he finds he has any.'

There was a long pause. No expression crossed the Chancellor's face, or that of Fulk. The two men looked at one another. Countess Elizabeth lowered her eyes to her daughter. Finally Fulk spoke, and his voice had that calm she always associated with her husband's more violent decisions.

'Tell the High Constable to take a hundred men and seize the late Viscount's lands and castle. Tomorrow.' Fulk breathed in again deeply. 'And you, Chancellor, kindly inform the Bishop that his inheritance is forfeit. Remind him that his appointment by my father was on the condition that he renounce it. Tell him that, Audemand. Tell him now!'

His business concluded, Fulk turned his back on the Chancellor. And then, by way of an afterthought, he added — over his shoulder —

'You were my father's Chancellor at the time, Audemand. So you can verify this to him.'

The old man looked as close to being startled as the Countess had ever seen him. It needed no more than a look to inform her that no such condition had ever been made, and that the Chancellor was about to perform one of the most uncomfortable missions of his long career. She also knew that any contradiction offered by Audemand at this moment might terminate that long career rapidly. He would stay silent.

But, as he left the Count and prepared to make his way to the Bishop's residence, Audemand knew he would not verify it. Orders of Fulk he would carry out; but fabricate orders supposedly given by the Count's esteemed father – that he could not do. If the omission was brought to the notice of Fulk, then he would stand the consequences. At the same time, as he tapped his staff along the echoing corridors, he reflected that with his long experience of diplomacy such an event would be less than probable – unless he was losing his touch.

For Fulk the issues were perfectly clear. His father's appointment of Renaud had been for one purpose only – to ensure that the Bishop's father would hold unswerving loyalty to the Counts of Anjou, thereby safeguarding his south-western boundaries against the treacherous Conan and his allies. The security of the Mauges region was vital to the interests of all Anjou, and the appointment had been one of Geoffrey Greymantle's shrewdest political moves. It had nothing to do with God: any number of buffoons could have been found to hold the office of bishop if a few prayers and sermons were all that was required. What irked Fulk was that the appointment had gone to his head, to the extent that he now undertook his godly work with tiresome zeal. More than this, he had set about equipping the Church with all the trappings of power and grandeur against the interests of the house of Anjou which had appointed him. Fulk's nose told him, when he heard of Renaud's imminent departure for the Mauges, that the Bishop was intent on one course alone: he was determined to swell the power of his Church by ceding his father's lands to the diocese and to the attendant monasteries of St Aubin and St Serge.

And in this Count Fulk was perfectly right. Bishop Renaud had been awaiting his father's death with the intention of doing exactly this – and quickly, before any counter-moves could be made by the Count. Only then, the Bishop calculated, would the dignity and independence of the church of Anjou be established, and the word of God echo throughout the land.

These were all his thoughts on that final evening before his departure. He was not in the Bishop's residence where Audemand had expected to find him, but in the cathedral – offering his prayers and seeking divine blessing on his enterprise.

The Chancellor found him on his knees, alone. A few lamps dimly lit the altar steps, and a single candle flickered on the high altar itself. The gaunt bulk of the crumbled cathedral was hunched around him. As he approached, Audemand could pick out a low mumble of words. He stood in silence, waiting.

At length the Bishop rose, bowed his head towards the altar and half-turned, ready to depart into the sacristy. When he saw Audemand he checked. His face was grave and he made no motion of recognition or of welcome. He stood there. The bare stone around echoed the coldness of their meeting. Proud cleric faced proud servant of Fulk.

'What is it, Chancellor?' The Bishop's voice was without inflection or greeting, and his lips scarcely moved.

Audemand told him in one sentence what Fulk had ordered, and said no more.

Not a sound came from the Bishop. He stood quite motionless on the altar steps for a while. Then he reached for a lamp, and the tall stooped figure walked past the

Chancellor down the length of the darkened nave, his lamp guttering in his hand; and as he reached the ruined walls where the cathedral opened into the deepening twilight he halted and turned his head.

'I shall see that heathen excommunicated before I die. This I vow!' was all he said, and his voice was like a cold knife.

He had gone, and the old Chancellor made his way slowly back through the quiet streets, his staff tapping on the cobbles.

In the Countess's garden the tree that spread a canopy above it was in flower, and she would spend hours sitting beneath it playing with her little daughter and telling her stories. The early-summer sunshine filtered down through the blossom, and the murmur of the Count's white doves completed the air of utter peace. Happiness had not been the usual condition of her life at Angers – she still ached sometimes for the gentleness of her father's house at Vendôme – but now she had an extra reason to feel contentment. Her stomach was already swelling slightly and she could begin to feel the tiny, twitching movements of a child in her womb. Fulk's eyes had lit up when she told him, and he had embraced her with unusual tenderness. She hoped a little anxiously that it would be the boy he craved for – perhaps two at once, she wondered at moments when the movements became particularly strong; and the thought made her smile as she imagined the problems of identifying the legal heir, especially if they looked exactly alike. Perhaps she would be the only person close enough to them to tell one from the other – perhaps she could cheat, and she laughed aloud at the idea of such secret confusion at the heart of great decisions of state.

But even if it were not a boy, would it really matter? There might be other children, or Fulk could make his heir a daughter, just as she herself was heiress of Vendôme. Why not? – just because there had always been sons in Fulk's family since Torquat the forester (most of them bandits of one kind or another, the Countess reflected. It was as well, sometimes, that the Count could not read her thoughts).

There was a soft rustle, and the person she was awaiting stood before her shyly. It was the twig of a girl, Adèle, the sad little wife of Fulk's brother Maurice. Only, she was not a twig any more. Her stomach was round as a wineskin, and the girl's eyes were lowered as if in shame. Not that shame was called for, the Countess considered: astonishment, rather, that this should have happened at all – or sadness for the unborn child that it should have such a brute for a father. Poor Adèle! Thirteen years old and carrying the child of a monster: what oceans of tears she must have shed since her uncles Archambaud and Sulpice brought her here from Amboise as an orphan of nine. She seemed hardly any older now – apart from that absurd protuberance. From now on she would breed till she died, and from the sickly look of her the Countess could not imagine that to be too many years ahead. She had felt so sorry for her, and as a sister in motherhood she was determined to extend the girl a little comfort and understanding.

'Come. Sit down, my child, and we can talk of things we share.'

Adèle approached like a frightened bird, her hands shyly on her belly and her eyes still downcast. Elizabeth placed an arm round her shoulders and the girl burst into tears. How little she needs, thought the Countess, and she has never had even that.

Meanwhile, the man who had given her the child, and nothing else, was engaged in a favourite pastime – ogling Hersende. Access to her rooms was less straightforward now that she was a lady of title surrounded by attendants and servants; but Maurice – as the Count's brother – still had his ways of obtaining entry, and nothing had impaired his instinct for when the girl would be most scantily attired. He prided himself on the knowledge that there was now no portion of her anatomy which he had not seen: never all at once, it was true — he still had hopes of that triumphant moment — none the less the parts of the girl fitted together most deliciously in his mind and there was no body in the entire castle, he knew for certain, which offered such delectable prospects of heaven. Whatever would such a body do with a mere boy, Judicael? Not even as much as he had managed with his own child of a bride. In God's name, Maurice said to himself, he must indeed be Zeus to have fathered an heir on so improbable a creature as Adèle. With this one — Hersende — he could have raised a tribe and, oh, what bliss in the begetting! Maurice had not altogether lost hope.

Hersende's maids wore looks of dismay, and the girl herself threw him a look of loathing. But his eyes were not on her face.

'I was considering, my lovely lady' — and Maurice produced what he believed to be a smile — 'since your husband-to-be is a mere child, you might be requiring the services of . . . a man.' He laughed, and with his hands indicated the portion of his anatomy that might offer such services.

'You are revolting,' replied Hersende quietly. She had never answered him in such a way, and for a moment he appeared taken aback. But Maurice was not one to be put off by mere hatred. Rather, he thrived on it.

'I could please you, if you would let me,' he went on, the smile folding into a leer.

Before he could utter another word someone had darted forward and struck him full across the face. Blood poured from his nose and cheek. He gave a cry and clapped his hand to the wound. The assailant struck again, catching him on the fingers and forehead. He turned and fled, bleeding profusely. Standing in the middle of the room, a reddened candlestick in her hand, was Milesende. Then she threw down the weapon and rushed away, sobbing. No one in the room said a word.

Maurice was not seen about the castle for some days. It was put about that he was unwell. Enquiries as to his health produced no further information: even his wife Adèle, resting palely in her room, had no knowledge of him, but then she was so unaccustomed to seeing her husband except when he was too drunk to stagger as far as the dovecot that there was no look of surprise on her face as she shook her head. Adèle was in fact the last person to learn that anything was wrong with him at all.

It was Audemand who cast a little light on the mystery. He was walking with Sebrand, discussing the affair of Bishop Renaud and the lands of the Mauges from where the High Constable had just returned. The conversation turned to lighter matters. What news had the Chancellor to tell him? By 'news' he meant 'gossip', as Audemand understood.

'Only that the Count's brother has suffered a hunting accident,' he replied.

Sebrand looked at Audemand sharply. The month of May was not the season for hunting. So what did he mean? Audemand's face told him that something disreputable had taken place, and that the Chancellor was enjoying himself enormously.

'When I say *hunting*,' Audemand added, 'you have to recollect what the Lord Maurice prefers to hunt.' And his mouth twitched as if attacked by a plague of mosquitoes.

Sebrand checked his step. They were close to the rear gate of the castle, and fine rain was falling. A grin began to spread across the young man's face as he gazed at the old Chancellor.

'Who struck him? Tell me!' he said at length.

Audemand resumed his steady step until they were out of earshot of the castle guards. The street echoed with the cries of a market, and the gentle rain glistened on the cobblestones. The old man raised his cape over his head: only his nose, moustache and beard protruded.

'As I understand, a young lady whom you might not expect would do such a thing.'

Sebrand went through a list in his mind of ladies who certainly *would* do such a thing, given the chance. So, who would not?

'The Lady Adelaide?' he enquired.

The Chancellor shook his head. Sebrand thought again.

'Adèle, the Lord Maurice's wife? But no!' he went on, 'she's in no condition to strike anyone. Mind you, if she'd done so before, she might not be in that condition.' And Sebrand chuckled. He glanced at Audemand: from the movements of his moustache it was clear that he was relishing the game. Sebrand tried again.

'It wasn't the Lady Ermengarde: she would have missed.'

It was the Chancellor's turn to laugh.

'Who else? Hersende?' A note of anxiety had entered Sebrand's voice. 'What did he do to Hersende?'

Audemand registered the new note of interest in the young man's words – but shook his head once more.

'Well then – just tell me, Audemand.'

The old man said nothing for a few seconds, but made exaggerated tapping sounds on the cobbles with his staff.

'Someone who's beginning to surprise the men of Angers in many ways, it seems,' he said at length, glancing sideways at Sebrand. 'Hersende's young sister!'

Sebrand raised his eyebrows in surprise.

'She has quite a spirit, that girl,' Audemand added. 'I think the lord of Combourg will have more on his hands than he realizes.'

The two men walked on. Ahead of them lay the cathedral square. The sight of the plain crumbling church put Sebrand in mind of Bishop Renaud and the postponed wedding of Milesende.

'I hardly imagine the Bishop will be conducting any marriage services on behalf of the Count in his present mood, will he, Audemand?'

'I think not.'

'But the lord of Combourg has been waiting for weeks.'

'And the Lady Milesende crying for weeks.' The Chancellor's voice sounded sadly resigned.

'So, what are Fulk's plans since I've been away?' Sebrand asked.

The Chancellor halted in front of the cathedral.

'I understand the wedding is to take place in Nantes. Very soon! ... And now, if you'll excuse me, I have some diplomatic work to do. The Count has made certain concessions to the Bishop – which will not, I fear, be enough to curb his anger. But I must try.'

With that the old man lowered his cape and walked slowly into the cathedral. Sebrand was left reflecting that these marriage disturbances were at least distracting Count Fulk from arranging his own. He had been relieved to hear, besides, that the Count of Maine's sister was still confined to her bed, which mercifully put off the day when he would have to take her to his own.

Rollo set off from Langeais with an uneasy heart. It was more than a month since he had set foot in Fulk's city; and though his solitary life suited him admirably, and work on the castle of Langeais had proceeded almost to completion, recent events had left him deeply shaken. The encounter with the mysterious woman of the woods – knowledge of Fulk's terrible cruelty – most of all, those strange intimations of love awaiting him in Angers – love ... and the imminent danger of loss of love. These things weighed on Rollo's mind, adding to his sense of isolation from a world that had trapped him, and of being a mere twig in the torrent of Count Fulk's ambitions. Altogether, he had no idea what he might be returning to; he knew only that the woman had said he must return — quickly!

The forests were stained the sharp green of early summer. The distant Loire flashed silver in the sunlight. A party of deer plunged across his path, and a blackcock with a splendid drift of tail-feathers whirred with fierce wing-beats into the silence of the trees. And there — suddenly — was the flute-call of Fulk's bird again, the oriole. Too lovely a bird for such a man, Rollo reflected: he should have chosen a bird of prey with blood on its feathers. Rollo and his guard of three horsemen passed the spot where the Count had seen his vision of the angel in the sun. The landscape looked so gentle now. Perhaps it was a true vision, and damnation *was* Fulk's destiny. Then Rollo thought ruefully how no man of God, no churchman, would even criticize Fulk for what he had done: rather, they would condone it. Was it not a spokesman of Christ who had inflicted those wounds on her, engraved those letters on her breast — having first taken her love potions and her body? Fulk, then, was no more than a servant of such people. Would the abbot of Jumièges, even, have done the same? No, Rollo could not believe it. He had not built his abbey for men of cruelty, or for a cruel God.

His weeks of solitude made him resent the soldiers, whistling and spitting as they rode. Fulk always insisted on a guard whenever Rollo made this journey. If Odo — or Gelduin — knew, he said, that his master-builder was riding through the forests, he would lie in wait. Rollo doubted privately whether a few whistling horsemen would deter the Count of Blois or the lord of Saumur: he would probably be safer on his own, riding in silence and using his wits. But those were Fulk's orders. Perhaps he would be unwise to disobey them ... yet he could bend them. And after several hours, as the distant castle of Angers at last came in sight, he dismissed the soldiers and watched them grow smaller and finally disappear.

It was late afternoon. He was alone. Rollo dismounted

and lay for a while against a bank in the sun. The air was warm, and swallows dipped over the young hayfields. Without thinking, he found himself identifying some of the wild herbs he had transplanted into his garden at Langeais, and it made him sad to have left it. The garden he had so carefully made would be choked with weeds before his return, and he wondered if the woman would pass by and know that he had gone.

Rollo removed his jerkin and enjoyed the warmth of the sun on his chest. His horse was browsing under the oak-tree where he had tethered it on the edge of the hayfield. Anjou spread out below him — small fields, then vineyards, a stream beyond winding between alders. How very far it all felt from the savagery of power, the battles of Fulk, the interminable preparations for war. He should have been a farmer, perhaps, growing all his needs in this lovely place. He would build a house — here — and his children would play in the grass, their laughter flowing over the fields. What rich dreams! And how far away!

It was as if a weight had been lifted from him. At first Rollo did not know what it was; only that his spirits felt lighter. There was an absence of something — of someone. Then he realized what had gone. He was free of Hersende. Quite free. Relieved. For so long she had danced before his eyes, turning in the torchlight, and her body as it turned had twisted a knife in him. Day after day she had returned to torment him while he was alone in Langeais — in the stoneyard, in his garden, on the river bank, a silent unending flow of pain and longing. He had wanted and wanted and wanted — incomplete without her, only alive for her. The dark forest all around. Lying alone at night listening to the far howling of wolves. It had grown to be what he was. He had built loneliness around him like a castle.

Now he was free. Freed of it, perhaps, by the woman at Langeais. Released. It had been a dream. She had opened his eyes, she said.

He remounted and threw his jerkin over the horse's neck in front of him. The track led down towards the stream he had been gazing at from a distance. As he rode gently through the young vineyards perspiration trickled down his naked chest, and the sight of cool water made him turn his horse towards the edge of a nearby copse where rocks and a small waterfall created a pool part-shaded by the alders and flanked by tall yellow irises just coming into flower. The water was clear and dark. Patches of sky shimmered between the trailing weeds. He removed his boots and stepped in; and he winced at the cold of the stream. He felt the mud close round his feet, and the water bubble past his bare calves. Then he bent down and cupped the chill water in his hands, and tipped it over his perspiring body. Rollo gasped. But after three or four times his skin felt taut and his torso strong. He stood there for a while, sunlight wavering across his face through the alders and water trickling down his arms and chest. He closed his eyes and listened to the whisper of the stream. How long he remained there he did not know. But after a while he felt himself shivering and opened his eyes. And standing motionless only some ten paces away was the dark shawled figure of a girl he knew.

In her dream it was always the month of May. She seemed to be forever wandering – far from the castle, by the banks of a secret river, her feet among flowers. Her companion was invariably loneliness and she would hug it to her like a friend. Around her spread a boundless forest, and the trees were dark as night and alive with evil things. But, concealed somewhere there, was a man of surpassing beauty who lived like a wild beast – an outcast in the forest; and he would remain an outcast until she could discover him. Only her love guided her footsteps; only by discovering him would she shed her loneliness; and only by taking him as a lover could she wake from the pain of her dream.

There was something in the look of the girl that Rollo had seen before. She had lowered the shawl from her hair, and her face seemed pained and beautiful. She stood there staring at him — all in black, her hair black, and her eyes. Her mouth was small, and her lips lightly parted. He had noticed that look as he had carried her through the falling snow — those same eyes, questioning, searching, beseeching.

Day after day she had walked along the verges of the forest by the secret river, until one day she saw a creature standing almost naked in the water as though it had come down to drink. And as he looked up and saw her his face became as beautiful as a god and his body as strong as Hercules. She wanted to run towards him but he did not seem to recognize her.

As he looked at her she suddenly seemed no longer to be a child. It was as if he were seeing her for the first time, and that she was waiting for him, that she belonged to him. He forgot the chill of the water and the moisture drying cold on his body. He wanted to take her again in his arms. To carry her away. The words of the woman at Langeais came back to him — 'You'll know because she's the one who loves you, and because I've opened your eyes.' It was as though her voice came from close behind him, directing him.

Then, just as his eyes began to speak to her, a terrible figure all in red rode up and lifted her into his saddle. She tried to cry out, but no sound came. The man laughed, and wheeled his horse. One hand was clasped across her breast. She looked back in despair, but he rode away with her into the forest, and her lover had gone.

Rollo saw that she was crying, and again he heard the voice from behind him — 'You must go. And quickly. I shall do what I can to keep her for you . . .' Then the voice faded. He was standing there, shivering. The girl was still motionless, gazing at him through her tears.

'Milesende!'

Rollo waded to the bank of the stream where she was waiting. She seemed to grow in loveliness as he approached her, and in those seconds he felt all the loneliness of his heart leaving him like a flock of birds dispersing at a clap of hands. She had entered his consciousness almost unseen, and yet was standing there in possession of him as if everything until now had been waiting for this moment without his ever knowing it was so. A hundred fragments of memory fell into place to form a pattern he had never believed to be there, and the pattern was his own life and the direction it would take. It was rounded, complete, strong: the storms battering the world out there could not touch this cell of happiness.

'Milesende!'

She was holding something in her hand. He could see the gleam of gold. It was a small golden heart on a golden chain. She had removed it from her neck. As Rollo drew close he could see that set into it was a tiny key-shaped hole. . . . Now he knew. Rollo held out his arms and the girl sank into them. He could feel the slimness and softness of her body pressed against him — and her stomach heaving from the deepest well of her tears. Rollo very softly, slowly, kissed her lips, and her hair was like black silk to his fingers. He wanted to lie with that body, those lips and that hair all his life.

To hear from Milesende about her marriage was the cruellest shock of Rollo's life. If the two of them had been standing on some high cliff, he knew he could have jumped to his death with her at that moment. The pain felt intolerable, and the girl's tears added to the ocean of his pain. He hardly remembered their journey back to the castle — he leading his horse, she walking by his side, weeping at first, then silent, her hand in his. They parted close to the city gate without a word passing between them; only an exchange of looks so helpless that neither could hold their eyes upon the other. Then they walked away. The fat cook saw Milesende, but even she could not bring herself to comfort the girl, who walked past her without seeing. Rollo made his way to his own rooms and had no recollection of the evening as the darkness crept around him and his servant brought candles and quietly left. He lay there, stunned, and no one else came.

The wedding party left for Nantes early the next morning, and he never saw her. He saw no one. The servant brought him food and wine, but he did not touch it. The only comfort was to realize that neither Fulk nor anyone around him knew that he had returned. Perhaps he could slip away again quietly and ride back to Langeais, and try to mend his life. It did not matter to him if he did not, if he should just fade away. There was nothing more. Perhaps the woman would give him something to bring lasting sleep: she would understand. But then he thought of Milesende and her own sufferings. What right had he to add to these with his death? No, he would have to live: even the knowledge that she was in this world brought him some relief — and the knowledge that she would never love the man who had married her. In spirit she was his, and perhaps in the end that would have to be enough.

After two days a messenger rode breathless into Angers. Rollo did not know it because he was a recluse in his rooms, having eaten nothing and seen nobody.

Count Fulk was engaged in the Mauges on matters concerning the lands confiscated from Bishop Renaud — who was still refusing to talk to him or even to see him. It was Audemand, wearied by his negotiations with the enraged bishop, who received the messenger in the Chancellor's rooms. With the messenger was the chamberlain of Bernard de Combourg: the two men had ridden that morning from Nantes, and they had a single piece of news to tell. Viscount Bernard was dead.

Very soon the castle was aware of what had happened, and as usual even the more inert members of Fulk's court became roused to the most lively interest in the disaster, dividing into several camps according to how they chose to fill in the details. The broad truth offered no space for imaginative efforts: on the night before his wedding to the young Milesende the noble Viscount had suffered a sudden seizure and had passed away within minutes. No one but his bride-to-be had been with him, and his chamberlain had rushed into the room in response to her screams. He had found the lord of Combourg on the point of death – clutching his heart – with the young girl in a state of some hysteria dressed only in a night-robe.

From those raw threads of fact a number of artful speculations promptly began to be woven, each version reflecting much about the gifts of the weaver.

To the less talented imaginations among Fulk's court it appeared a straightforward and sad story: here was a man of advanced years whose lifetime had been spent in brave battle safeguarding his territories and those of Anjou, and whose lease of life had quite simply expired. This considerate view found some opposition on the grounds that it ignored an obvious fact: that his bride-to-be was actually in the room with him, dressed for the customary pre-wedding-night ceremony – as one timid voice put it.

Sebrand, discussing the matter with the Chancellor on the evening the news reached Angers, was inclined to a more radical view. If the young lady had been spirited enough to inflict a 'hunting' wound on the Count's own brother, might it not be probable that she could have done the same to the noble Viscount – who had been quite improperly advancing his cause before he had the legal right to do so? The Chancellor nodded wearily, as if enough troubles had already settled on his aged shoulders without those caused by hot-tempered maidens in defence of something about to be lost anyway.

A more shrill version was proposed by the Lady Adelaide during one of her moral visitations to the Lady Ermengarde. It was clear, she maintained, that all manner of revolting intimacies had taken place between the Viscount and the ambitious young lady – probably they had been taking place for quite a while, for was that not the style of life he had always maintained at the castle of Fougères, so she understood? And she drew breath only to pronounce the more loudly that God's punishment upon those who committed sins of the flesh had justly been meted out, as it undoubtedly would be to all those enjoying foul pleasures – and she left no doubt in Ermengarde's mind as to the fate in store for Adelaide's husband Roger, and for herself.

Ermengarde was more circumspect about the fateful incident. She did not reply to Adelaide, merely lay back with her eyes closed and her right hand clasping a cup of her own husband's most excellent wine. But afterwards, speaking privately with the Countess, she suggested to Elizabeth's willing ear that any woman with experience of men would understand perfectly what must have taken place. Nothing, she suggested, aroused a man to so great a frenzy as the first sight of a beautiful virgin who was about to be his. She could recall the many delectable occasions on which her own virginity had been taken by men in such a condition – alas, it was some years now since her tearful protestations of purity had held much conviction. None the less, she went on, one must imagine the noble Viscount, in the twilight of his prowess, casting his eyes over the beautiful bud of a creature that he was imminently to pluck. Was it surprising that the sight was altogether too much for him? As for the girl, she just had time to slip her night-robe over the sight that had killed him before screaming as any woman should. And here Ermengarde gave an exaggerated sigh, with her eyes raised in the manner of the Lady Adelaide. The Countess laughed and clapped her hands in delight as her friend added:

'And to think that, unlike me, she will be able to do it again – *truthfully*. Oh, my dear Countess, what powers we women have! Mind you,' Ermengarde went on, her expression serious for a moment, 'the young thing would have done better to wait until the night *after* the wedding: she would still have been a virgin, only now she would be the widow of Combourg and twice as rich. No doubt she will learn with practice. I should really have a word with her.

You, Countess, are far too discreet, but I promise to inform you of our conversation.'

Apart from the absent Fulk, Rollo was the last person at the castle to hear of the tragedy. It was Sebrand who discovered through a servant that the Norman had returned from Langeais, and he made his way to his friend's rooms on the day following the incident. The two men had not seen one another for more than a month.

He found Rollo reclining in a pale and dishevelled state, his breakfast uneaten. The Norman gave a start when he saw his visitor, then turned his head away. By now, Rollo knew, the wedding would be over. The wedding night would be over. Rage and jealousy swamped him. He felt utterly lost. Fate had presented him with the most precious of all gifts, only to snatch it away. He thought with some bitterness of the woman at Langeais. Had she not urged him to return he would never have encountered Milesende, would never have known of her love, or his own. 'I shall do what I can to keep her for you,' the woman had said. Then her powers were not so great after all. Those of Fulk were, in the end, greater.

Rollo had no wish to see Sebrand. The High Constable, on the other hand, had no knowledge of his friend's passion for Milesende: he still imagined it to be Hersende whom the Norman cared for. Therefore the news he came to impart he delivered in a light-hearted tone, almost of amusement.

He was barely halfway through telling it when Rollo leapt to his feet and embraced the Angevin like a long-lost brother.

'Is it true? Can it really be true? Where is she? Tell me! Tell me! How did he die? They were never married? Are you sure? Quite sure? Who told you?'

And so on. Sebrand, squeezed to pulp, was so taken aback he could hardly reply.

'Wait a minute. One question at a time. What does all this mean?'

Gradually Rollo grew calmer. Gradually Sebrand pieced together the story. He listened attentively, and as he listened he was touched by the tale. He had always admired Rollo, and now he found himself admiring him more for a passion he never knew to be there in the man. The Norman paused, and began to pace the room. Then he declared a ravenous appetite, and Sebrand called a servant to bring several days' supply of food for the Count's master-mason who had been taken ill on his return from Langeais – let this be put about, he ordered. And when food arrived Rollo ate so that his belly hurt and drank so that his head swam. Within a few minutes he felt too drowsy to keep his eyes open, and Sebrand with a smile of affection left him.

'I'll be back in a few hours,' he said, departing. 'We have much to talk about, Rollo.'

The Norman's last thought before settling into a heavy sleep was that the woman of the woods indeed had the most remarkable powers.

Sebrand's return found Rollo awake and dressed. He noticed a work-table upon which a sheet of parchment had been stretched, and designs drawn upon it. Sebrand glanced at Rollo, then at the drawings. They were of buildings the like of which he had never seen: intricate patterns of arches poised one above the other, each banded like a crown with a curve of tiny figures, and below and between the arches stood ranks of smoothed columns embossed with further clusters of figures. Then, to one side of the parchment, just a sketch that was all soaring lines converging high up in points like stars tethered to the ground, Sebrand thought. Next to it Rollo had drawn the sun, and its rays penetrated the entire building. Sebrand was astonished: the black charcoal on pale parchment seemed to change before his eyes to dazzling light against a dark sky. He looked up at Rollo again with a bemused expression. The Norman laughed.

'Don't worry: it's not one of the Count's castles. Just ideas. I woke up with them in my head.'

Sebrand grunted, then looked again at the tangle of lines and curves.

'I won't ask you how you intend to build it. The last time I did that you climbed a tree – if you remember.'

'I couldn't build it,' replied Rollo, 'but I will one day if I have the chance.'

'Was that the way you built Jumièges?'

'In a way, yes. I saw it in my head ... then I discovered how to do it.'

'Well!' Sebrand turned away from the work-table and stood by the window, gazing out. 'You'd better forget the cathedral for a while.'

And he described to Rollo the battle between Fulk and Bishop Renaud, and Sebrand's own journey to the Mauges to confiscate the lands of the late Viscount. Rollo listened aghast. What might Fulk not do – if there were gain in it? And what of Milesende? He hardly liked to ask Sebrand. His joy at hearing that there was no wedding was already growing clouded by the thought that Fulk would surely find some other nobleman for her hand before long: this was only a stay of execution. And what could he do about it?

As so often, the young Angevin seemed to read his thoughts. He surprised Rollo by crossing the room and embracing him.

'You know, my friend, if it weren't so painful I should laugh. In your monastery you could never have married without leaving it. Now you're free to marry you find yourself in another trap.'

He looked thoughtfully at Rollo.

'Nothing is more private than marriage,' he went on, 'yet in our world it's public property, isn't it? Our beds are bought and sold like goats. Our love-making is about dynasties.' He picked up a piece of charcoal and crumbled it in his fingers. 'I suppose the best way would be not to care, wouldn't it? To love success, love power, and use women to breed. But what sort of man would you be then? Or me?'

Rollo had never heard Sebrand talk like this.

'You're right,' he said. Rollo looked down at his own hands – hands which until a few moments ago, he reflected, had been drawing buildings in which the human spirit could live and rise. That was why he drew them. 'I'm here on this earth with one gift,' he went on. 'I can build. I know how to create places where people may feel more proud, or more rich, or safe, or noble. Where they can live not so meanly as they do: less like animals, and more like men. And yet' – he looked at Sebrand and smiled wryly – 'there are only two places where I can use that gift, and both of them deny me the right to be a man.'

And when Sebrand said nothing, Rollo added:

'A man is someone who can love his fellow creatures .. isn't that so?'

Sebrand nodded, and still said nothing. There was so much truth – sad truth – in Rollo's words: they made him realize how unquestioningly he accepted that it was like this – that the price of his own high position was that very right to be a man, as Rollo put it. In other words to be able to love and live with someone you love. These things were not permitted to him either. A thought came to him: all the tales the minstrels told, and the songs the court so clamoured to hear on feast-days, they were always about true love and the struggle to find it. And yet who in the court of Count Fulk had ever looked for true love or had made any struggle to find it? Except ... and he realized that this was where Rollo and Milesende were different. He would have liked to be able to include himself.

Sebrand returned to Rollo a third time that day, just as the day was fading. He found the Norman still at his work-table. Two lamps were lighting up the arches that were soaring even higher on the parchment than a few hours earlier.

'Still building for God, I see!' Sebrand had retrieved his good humour, and he rested an arm on Rollo's shoulder as he sat crouched over the outspread parchment. 'Well! You'

228

better lower your eyes a little, Rollo. The Count has returned, and commands to see you. Now.'

Rollo looked up.

'You don't seem pleased,' Sebrand added with a laugh. 'So, let me tell you. Things are about to happen. Fulk has his new lands; his new vassals. And he's like a dog on a leash, I can tell you. He's going to attack the Count of Blois. He's going to storm Tours. And this time I shall be there.'

Sebrand's face looked flushed at the thought. Rollo stood up. At first he could not grasp why Fulk should want to see him.

'Oh, Rollo, come down from heaven,' said Sebrand raising his eyes and hands in mock piety. 'Don't you see, it's your castles he wants to know about?'

Rollo moved quietly towards the work-table and blew out the lamps. Then with a solemn look at Sebrand he walked towards the door. As he did so there was a sound of heavy feet outside and the door was flung open. It was Fulk. He stood there bare-chested (Rollo noticed the jagged scars on his body) and he glared at Rollo with those dark eyes.

It was like looking at a monster, Rollo felt. His astonishment at seeing Fulk here in his rooms could not prevent a sense of loathing rise within him. The Count continued to glare for what seemed an age. Then, without any change of expression, he said –

'Langeais! How is it?' His words sounded cold and grim, as if expecting an excuse.

Rollo looked at him hard.

'Ready, my lord,' he said.

Rollo watched as Fulk's face changed. His mouth opened. His eyes widened. He glanced at Sebrand, then back at Rollo.

'Ready?' he repeated incredulously.

'Ready ... enough.' Rollo kept his gaze on the Count. 'There are things still to be finished, my lord, but it's ... built. Montbazon too, nearly so.'

229

There was a moment of silence as the two men faced one another. Then suddenly Fulk took two rapid steps forward and seized the Norman in a bear hug. He kissed him on both cheeks, and grasped his hands. Rollo sensed the irresistible dominance of this man: it was like being caught in a flood. Yet he felt his own hands matching the strength of Fulk's.

'You, Rollo,' he said in a voice that croaked with joy, 'you shall have everything if I destroy Odo. Anything you want.'

Rollo felt a chill pass through him at the Count's terrible glee. And he felt a helpless dread lest what he had built should fail. But along with these sensations a small dream floated before his eyes of what he might ask of Fulk if all went well.

The Count strode briskly from the room, Sebrand in his wake. A momentary glance from his friend told Rollo that his own future was either to be glorious, or doomed. There could be nothing in between.

Fulk's army moved like ants through the forest. Rollo had imagined armies to proceed with a clang and clamour, amid flags and brave shouting. Far from it. Only a soft rustle disturbed the silence of the woods. With eyes closed, you might have thought small creatures were browsing among the leaves. When you opened them, at first only a few figures seemed to be passing between the trees; but then, as you looked, there were more and more of them and the trees were like screens, each hiding a man. There might be one, two, five thousand men proceeding scarcely noticed through that quiet forest. Only when they came to a river was their passage visible as figures converged upon fords; then for a brief space between the canopy of foliage a band of open water became darkened by teeming forms that emerged from the forest and disappeared into it on the far side. With the eye of a bird you could have followed the progress of that army as, further and further east, those threads of water became broken by a seething transit of figures drawing ever closer to Tours.

Fulk's plan was precise and careful. His soldiers were gathering from every region of Anjou, and from the Mauges, from Maine, from Nantes, Combourg and Fougères: the parties of men grew larger, and larger again, as groups met and joined until the forests grew thicker and thicker with men. But there was to be a delay. The progress of these forty or fifty parties making up the main army was held back – on the Count's orders – until his own personal force had gone ahead with two primary objectives. These were the garrisoning of the two stone castles of Langeais and Montbazon which lay within a short distance of Tours, one to the west, the other directly to the south. No castles had ever been built which could hold so many men.

Fulk led this force himself, travelling by night. With him were many of his bravest nobles, among them Roger de Montrésor, the brothers Sulpice de Buzançais and Archambaud d'Amboise, and three of the sons of the Chancellor Audemand, as well as the lords of Baugé, Loudun, Passavant and Ste Maure. Also with the party travelled the Count's master-mason, Rollo, who was to supervise the final details of the two castles that he had built.

They came within view of Langeais at first light: some five hundred men – knights, foot-soldiers, servants. Fulk kept them concealed within the forest until late in the day in order to lessen the chance that word would reach Odo of their presence. Then the force moved in on the town and proceeded to take possession of the castle. Many of the men had to be encamped in the large fortified area which the Norman had created below the castle mound: these were the soldiers who at dawn next day would cross the Loire on barges and follow the course of the Indre to Montbazon where they would form the garrison there. From these two manned fortresses Fulk would then have twin bases, fortified and equipped, from which to launch his assault on the city of Tours. Leaving each castle in charge of a governor, Fulk himself and his senior nobles were then to depart and establish contact with the units of his main army still widely dispersed an hour's ride westwards under the overall command of the High Constable, Sebrand de Chemillé.

Such was Fulk's plan. Odo, he knew, would need time to assemble a force to oppose him – though he was aware, too, that the numbers available to the Count of Blois greatly exceeded his own. It was the more vital, then, that the twin castles be occupied, and securely garrisoned with stores and arms, before the Angevin army made its strike on Odo's city. By Fulk's calculations his force should be able to hurl itself upon Tours with only the normal garrison to overcome. And with any luck Odo himself would be caught – trapped in his own lair. He would have the one-armed lord at his mercy.

Why Fulk had chosen to attack before his collar of stone castles around Tours was complete he confided to no one. It had been the Count's intention to spend the next year constructing further fortresses at Montrichard, to the east of Tours, at Montrésor further south (where Roger was lord), at Amboise (Archambaud's seat), at Renault to the north, and even at Montboyau just across the river from Tours to the north-west – the most daring of them all.

Perhaps – his nobles considered – he knew of a special weakness of Odo at this time. Or perhaps it was the renewed alliance with the king, Hugh Capet, whose cause Fulk's father Geoffrey Greymantle had so stoutly upheld. But perhaps it was quite simply impatience: Fulk had an old score to pay; there was no one he hated more bitterly in the world than Odo; and flushed with his new support from Nantes and from the Mauges he felt now to be the moment.

As the light faded a crowd of waggons, carts, barrows, loads carried on mules, on poles, on shoulders, on heads, was still pressing forward across the causeway and into the vast store-rooms of the castle that lay beneath the spacious hall where Fulk and his nobles had gathered and were drinking wine. The rumble of wheels and the sounds of animals filled the air of an early-summer evening, mingling with the voices of soldiers and the scrape of weapons. Beyond the walls of the castle, spread out across the open space within the outer ditch and palisades, hundreds of men sprawled among open fires that studded the darkness of the night.

Rollo felt stunned to see his handiwork in use. Until the last of the light there were still masons perched like birds high on the walls finishing the stone-work, and the sound of carpenters' hammers continued to echo round the building as the call for more wine sent servants scurrying for barrels still being rolled across the causeway. Shouts and curses filled the night, soon mellowing into bursts of song and unsteady laughter. Rollo observed the scene with bewilderment.

There was the tap of a hand on his elbow as he stood somewhat apart from the crowd of nobles in the hall. In the lamplight he saw the servant who had accompanied him from Angers. There was a messenger at the entrance, he said. An urgent matter, the guard had been told. The messenger was from Montbazon: the stone causeway across the ravine in the cliff had partly fallen. Could the master-mason ride urgently to Montbazon and have it rebuilt before Fulk's soldiers arrived? This was serious. Rollo hurried over to the Count and explained the emergency. He would like to leave immediately, he said. Fulk nodded, and waved him away. Rollo dispatched the servant to saddle his horse and tell the messenger to wait for him by the castle gate.

Perturbed by the news, Rollo hurried after the servant down the stone stairway of the tower that led to the entrance. He spoke to the guard, who confirmed the story and pointed to a figure just visible beyond the aura of the lantern. A man was standing with his back to the castle, a broad

233

cowl covering his head and shoulders. He was holding th
bridle of his horse in one hand. Then Rollo saw his servar
leading his own horse towards the man, but still the me
senger made no move or gesture. He continued to stan
there in the darkness.

Rollo approached the man.

'It's you who brought the message from Montbazon?' h
asked.

The man nodded, and grunted.

'The governor sent me,' he said in a soft voice. 'They nee
you. Follow me. I know the way in the dark. We can be the
in three hours.'

Still the man did not raise his head to look at Rollo. He fe
suspicious, but there was nothing he could do but go. Th
causeway needed his skills: with any luck the damage wou
not be so grave that it could not be repaired quickly. H
could rouse the under-masons and begin at dawn.

'How shall we cross the river at night?' he asked.

'There's a barge. And boatmen ... waiting.' The same so
voice, barely more than a whisper.

'You'd better come too,' Rollo called to the servan
'Armed.' He glanced at the messenger to see the man
reaction, but he merely turned his horse and leapt lightly
its back. Before Rollo himself had mounted, the man w
already some distance down the path, hardly visible. Rol
could hear the clip of his horse's hooves. The two m
followed the sound, and in a few moments the grey sheen
the river came into sight. Ahead of them lay the bla
outline of a barge, and as they approached two figures ro
from it out of the darkness and called a greeting in gru
voices.

The night journey was calm. The servant and Rollo fo
lowed the messenger, who rarely spoke, and who turn
towards them only to warn of hazards in the path. Th
moon was too pale to see his features: his cowl was so f
it was as if he had no face. They followed the same pa

along the Indre that Rollo had taken with Fulk and Sebrand, and which he had taken so many times since that day. He could easily have done the journey alone, so that at times he forgot he had company and rode within his own thoughts in the whispering night. Around him was a continual scuffle of tiny sounds which he set himself to identify, and realized that he could not. Only the screech of an owl was familiar, and once or twice the dark furrow of a water-vole cutting across the moonlit river. Everywhere there seemed such tranquillity, and silence. He would have loved to have been riding with Milesende on such a night: they could have drawn their horses abreast and followed the river each held in the other's eye; then tethered their horses and bathed in the chill river, her body hidden within the dark water, hair spread, a leg, a shoulder, a breast catching the moon for an instant. Where was she? He had not seen her since that day by another river. He ached for her, and she seemed so alone and so far away.

The silhouette of the castle stood against the night sky. Three hours must have passed. Below, hidden in blackness ahead of them, lay the sleeping town. Montbazon. Rollo was plucked out of his thoughts by the sight of the messenger's horse motionless ahead of him.

'You know your way now,' came the soft voice.

And with no further word the messenger turned his horse and Rollo heard the plod of hooves long after he could see nothing along the path they had taken. He waited a moment, surprised by the man's sudden departure, then rode on through the silent town towards the castle. At dawn, only a few hours away, he would have to rouse himself. He felt tired.

As dawn broke over Langeais, the encircling forests where Rollo had ridden a few hours before were alive with eyes. Well-disciplined shadows slid forward without a sound until all those eyes could see before them the castle where soldiers were still sleeping heavy with wine. There was a noose around Fulk, and time would pull it tight. Odo was about to strike.

Rollo did not yet know that he had been rescued.

SEVEN

MILESENDE'S FATE of alternate misery and joy delivered her another thrust into darkness on her return to Angers. Longing to see her lover, and fall into his arms, she learnt that he had departed with Fulk's army which had been surprised and besieged by the Count of Blois in the castle of Langeais. She might never see him again.

It was her fifteenth birthday: a year had passed since she had first set eyes on the fair Norman as he made his way with Sebrand across the water-meadows on the day of his arrival, and she had hidden behind a willow tree by the river bank as they rode past. It had felt exactly like the tales her nurse used to tell her back in Brittany, of a knight in disguise riding from the far forests to the castle to rescue her. They were tales she had listened to over and over again until the bright world they painted before her eyes had grown more real and more lovely than the world she walked in.

'He'll be safe,' Hersende tried to reassure her sister, her voice reflecting the relief that Sebrand at least was safe. Rollo, she could not help thinking, was actually far from safe. A man who built castles to threaten the safety of Odo's city did not seem likely to be set free with a kiss when Odo caught him.

But Milesende's pleading eyes made her swallow her dark thoughts. She was about to say, 'Put your trust in love, my beautiful sister,' but then she recollected that such trust had already been stretched far beyond the limit, and it was improbable that the power of love could be relied on to perform any more unlikely deeds. Instead, she said rather feebly, 'It's your birthday, beloved. Try to be happy!'

— at which her sister awarded her the look she deserved.

Milesende's birthday was the pretext for numerous visitations from people burning to know how Viscount Bernard had died. Not even the siege at Langeais had managed to replace it as the favourite topic for speculation and embellishment: this was not perhaps surprising, since however anxious people were about the siege it was hard to be prurient about it, and prurience was the favourite diet of Fulk's court.

The Lady Ermengarde arrived to bestow good wishes and a fond embrace. But hardly were these formalities over before the Treasurer's wife was examining Milesende with the most knowing of eyes.

'Yes, quite lovely, my dear,' she said approvingly. 'No wonder!' she added with a nod, leaving Milesende puzzled, but herself reassured that the impact of the girl would indeed have been deadly. Let us hope, she thought, that next time the man has a stronger constitution because the girl is growing prettier every day. And she departed with a sigh.

The Lady Adelaide had of course been shadowing her, not entirely convinced that her destination was Milesende's room and rather disappointed to find it was. She was standing behind Ermengarde, and stayed only long enough to suggest that mourning might be a more appropriate form of dress for a young lady in her situation. When Hersende pointed out that her sister still remained unmarried, Roger's wife put on an expression of knowing disgust before retreating hurriedly in pursuit of her quarry.

'I feel like some nasty curiosity,' commented Milesende. 'I'm unhappy enough without these crones. Why can't they leave me alone?'

'Because they're envious,' replied Hersende rather wearily, her mind already drifting towards Sebrand who was somewhere out there with the army in those forests she was gazing at. What dangers was he facing? Then her eyes returned to her sister, standing so sadly, gazing nowhere.

'Now we're rich they can no longer ignore us,' she added.

'I wish I was as poor as a peasant,' said Milesende vehemently. 'Then I would never have had to go through all this.'

'And you would never have met Rollo,' Hersende commented unhelpfully.

Milesende ignored her sister.

'What a dreadful, dreadful birthday!'

But the birthday worsened with the arrival of Father Baudouin. Hersende would have liked to retreat to the neighbouring room and become heavily involved in her embroidery, but she could not abandon her sister to the gobbling prelate. Baudouin had been prevented by the urgent needs of Adèle from delivering the moral sermon he had prepared for Milesende before her departure for Nantes. It had all happened too quickly. He felt sure that such moral deprivation had been in some way responsible for the subsequent tragic events, and he had listened with rising horror to accounts of the chaste girl being almost naked – it was said by the Lady Adelaide – in the late viscount's presence. He must know – indeed he owed it to his calling to know – every detail of that wanton occasion, however distastefully it might assault his ear.

Father Baudouin prepared himself for the worst, his eyes bulging with duty. Hersende thought her sister looked unusually fierce, like a cat trapped by a hound.

After a few preliminary gulps the priest began on a general note, anxious to prepare the girl before inviting her to deliver a precise account of what took place. He offered some gentle and holy words about the supremacy of the human spirit rising to God, and the irrelevance – nay, the baseness – of the life of the flesh. Having established such a division of priorities Father Baudouin felt compelled to dwell upon those irrelevant and base matters of the flesh, leaving matters of the spirit to look after themselves. It was, he reminded Milesende, her birthday – a holy occasion that reminded all Christians of the day Our Lord was born of the

Virgin Mary. She should remember that. But she, Milesende, had not been born of a virgin, she should understand, but of a woman impregnated by a man who was her mother's wedded husband. (Hersende felt herself blushing at this singular inaccuracy.) Had God wished it to be otherwise He would of course have arranged it so: however, it was part of His great plan that women should be compelled to perform an act that would forever remind them of Eve's sin in tempting Adam. For, without that act, no child could be born unto woman and mankind would pass into extinction. It was man's punishment that he too must conjoin in this base act, and the young lady should know that the burden of this punishment for a man was that he must carry with him till the day he died the tool of his own shame. (Hersende's eyes were growing round with amazement as she watched the Chaplain becoming visibly excited by his own sermon.) She should not think – he assured her – that the Almighty had spared even his own priests from carrying such a burden, though they were spared the act. (Hersende saw the Chaplain become agitated and begin to finger his clothing.) It was as well, therefore, that she should be acquainted with this knowledge without risk of temptation.

At this moment the priest leaned forward to raise his habit, but as it reached his knees and he looked intently at the girl his face met a stream of spit directed with perfect accuracy from the mouth of Milesende. He let the garment fall and gazed at her in horror: but only for a second, because a scream of such intensity burst from the girl that he started back with his hands raised as if to ward off the sound. Then, wiping the saliva from his face with his sleeve, he glared at Milesende while his throat wobbled in search of speech. A few sounds bubbled from his lips, his hands clenched and unclenched, and the stray hairs on his pate floated on a sea of perspiration.

'You!' he managed to utter at length, between gulps. 'You! You dare to strike a servant of the Lord! So plunged in sin are you' — and he waved a pale finger towards Milesende — 'that you cannot hear the voice of virtue. You see even my humility as sin. You are damned! Damned! Whore of Babylon! You ...'

But another scream tore his words away. And suddenly he was gone in a swirl of black robes.

Whether or not anyone in the rest of the castle heard Milesende's screams her sister never knew. If they did, it was not altogether unexpected that they should take little notice: a scream was no unusual occurrence at the court of Fulk.

The poor girl was by now in a state of hysterical collapse. Hersende did what she could to comfort her. With her arms tightly embracing her sister, and her face pressed to her moist cheek, she heard over and over again the same stuttering cry of despair — 'I want to die! I want to die!'

It was a merciful release from this vale of misery when the Countess's chamberlain, Garnier, arrived to announce a summons from the lady of the castle. The Countess Elizabeth wished to see the two sisters and to greet Milesende on her birthday. It was some moments before the younger girl was able to collect herself sufficiently to rise, dry her face and hands, and prepare herself to follow Garnier to the large sunny room hung with tapestries.

The Countess was with the Chancellor, Audemand. She looked paler than usual, and more drawn, so that her red hair set with pearls seemed almost too heavy for that fragile countenance. She greeted the sisters quietly, planting an extra kiss on Milesende's cheek, and noticed it to be flushed and moist. Knowing nothing of the encounter with the Chaplain she attributed this entirely to the stress caused by the sad business in Nantes, for it was the first time the Countess had seen Milesende since her return.

Audemand, too, was unusually withdrawn. The conversation was polite and rather hollow. The prospect of the forests and the vineyards from the open window seemed unduly bright for such a subdued occasion. But the tone of the conversation had a restorative effect on the two sisters. Gradually the dramas and heartaches of their own lives began to be seen within the setting of others' pain. Audemand had three beloved sons caught in that siege at Langeais, and the Countess her own husband and father of the child within her. Supposing none of them returned! The sisters became aware that fear and grief dwelt in the faces of the Countess and the old Chancellor. They departed feeling a troubled reassurance in the fact that theirs was not the only burden of the heart to carry.

A siege is silent. Within and without, people wait. Eyes meet eyes. Time passes slowly. The real enemies are always invisible, and the fiercest battle is between nerves: he who wins is the one with the toughest armour inside him. The weeks pass and concentration shifts. The wall, the palisades, the ditches, the ranks of archers, the watchful eyes — these take on the unimportance of permanent things. It is the new and unexpected that occupy the mind — the yell of a neighbour's dream, the eagle that appeared and circled for one whole day, the woman passed from man to man like a flask for the thirsty. And of course the rain. There is never anywhere to get out of the rain.

In the first days Odo led attack after attack against the ditch, the earth-wall and the palisades. The one-armed Count, squat and powerful, yelled from his stallion for his soldiers to press forward and breach the barriers. But the ditches were steep, the walls and palisades sound. Arrows picked off Odo's men like rabbits until they lay bleeding in gross heaps around the perimeter, slowly devoured by flies and ants. Furious, Odo rode forward with head lowered, and his horse was shot from under him. His men tried hurling fire, but there was ample water within the castle to extinguish it — drawn at Fulk's command from the deep well and stored in huge caulked cisterns laid across the open ground. He tried siege engines, but the causeway was steep-sided and they lurched into the ditch. He tried a direct assault on the main gate, but it was sounder than any gate Odo had encountered, while above it and on either side were cleverly concealed slits between the stones from which the Angevin archers massacred the assailants, their arrows shot from such close range that they flung the victims back against those behind them, and as they lay dead on the causeway the arrowheads could be seen protruding from their backs.

After a while Odo cursed, and decided to wait. He watched, and the weeks passed.

From high in the castle, through the narrow windows, Fulk watched him.

And thus began a game of hunter against hunter. It was a hunt mostly in the mind – each weighing the chances he could take, the moves he could make, the weaknesses of the other that he could afford to exploit, his own weaknesses that he must protect. One man gazed day after day at a stone castle, the other at the forest. And they waited.

It was a game of waiting, but it was also a game of secrets. Fulk, as the green of the spring forest turned deeper with the advance of summer, was still waiting for the High Constable and the army he knew was quietly converging on Langeais. Any day Odo's force would be routed from the rear and his own garrison emerge and complete the slaughter. And for that moment he watched.

What Fulk did not know was that every road and track, every bridge and ford, to the west of Langeais was already manned by Odo's men. His spies were well paid. They had kept him accurately informed of Fulk's movements and Fulk's plans, and he had splintered his own army in such a way that they could be re-formed to engage Sebrand wherever he chose to attack; meanwhile Gelduin de Saumur, the Demon, was in readiness to surprise the Angevin army from the rear. Odo had watched the building of Fulk's castles, knowing that sooner or later the Count of Anjou would be drawn to his own downfall. Now he had Fulk locked in his own castle, while his army, separated from its leader and its most powerful knights, was about to be squeezed. It would be the end of Anjou, and he would add the fair city of Angers to his realm.

Odo waited with patient eagerness. His men had already found Montbazon ungarrisoned except for a handful of men: the rest were stonemasons and they had fled. The castle had fallen without a fight. As for Langeais, it mattered little that the early assaults had failed. The Angevins would soon starve, or die of thirst, or both. The thought contented him: Fulk would emerge gaunt and defeated. With his one hand Odo would tear out the man's eyes and send him stumbling into the forest for the wolves. He laughed, and his sons with him laughed.

What Odo did not know was that the castle of Langeais had a well so deep that an army could drink from it for a year. Not only a well: the store-rooms were of a size and a temperature planned to feed a garrison for many months – more months than Odo could possibly keep his soldiers from returning to the land. The lords of Touraine were bound by the laws of vassalage to marshal their serfs and freemen at the command of their count when he needed an army – but not indefinitely. No one knew better than Fulk that loyalty had its price. Once the prospect of reward (either loot or lands) receded, and meanwhile their own crops suffered for lack of tending, then discontent grew and loyalty crumbled away. Armies could soon disperse like a bored crowd. The huge force of men whom Fulk could see idling their days around the forest verges would not be likely to remain so eager and expectant once June became July, August, September. Odo, standing there so proud among his thousands, would become nakedly alone before the harvest was to be reaped.

Fulk was happy to wait. And when the moment came, and

Odo's numbers dwindled, he would have a surprise for the Count of Blois, and for this he blessed his resourceful master-mason during those long weeks when he paced the hall and nothing happened. The game of secrets was being played at the slowest pace.

Count Fulk was a lucky man. Those who loved him, or feared or hated him, acknowledged that an angel seemed to ride on his shoulder at the worst moments. His enemies believed him to be in league with the Devil, or to be the Devil himself. His allies saw some divine protection around his brow, though they could not always comprehend why the Almighty should have put it there.

Never was Fulk's luck of greater service to him than at this moment. For while he and his closest lords were trapped within the castle of Langeais quite ignorant of Odo's strategy, an act of fate — as it seemed — spared his army within hours of being annihilated.

Three days after Odo's ambush at Langeais two messengers reached Fulk's High Constable, Sebrand de Chemillé, as the Angevin army gathered in the plain of Vernantes. Through the previous day parties of soldiers had been emerging from the forests to the west and the north until all were collected here, and that night Sebrand planned to move eastwards to reach Langeais before dawn, and then on to Tours with Count Fulk and his vanguard as planned. Everything had been stealth until now: hereafter the army would move quickly and strike at Odo's city before the Count of Blois could assemble a force to resist the Angevins. The great day was almost upon them.

But in the evening a man arrived breathless. With some surprise Sebrand recognized him to be a servant of Rollo. The news he brought stunned the High Constable. He described how he and his master had been called to Montbazon by a mysterious messenger. How they had ridden through the night. How on arrival they had realized it was a ruse to lure them from Langeais. How the next morning they had hastened to return, only to encounter a small force of Odo's men making for Montbazon. Rollo and the servant had fled into the forest. A peasant they encountered then told them of the ambush — how the castle was surrounded by more than a thousand men, and Fulk trapped. How Rollo had ordered the servant to cross the river further to the west and seek out Sebrand with the news: meanwhile Rollo himself would make his way south and west, avoiding Saumur, and hasten with the news to Angers.

Sebrand listened gravely to the messenger's story; then he called his lords around him and commanded them to prepare instantly to move east and mount a rescue.

The Angevin soldiers gathered their arms. Oxen were harnessed to their carts. The knights mounted. Sebrand wheeled his stallion and gave the signal to follow him. The entire plain seemed to move.

Barely an hour's journey away Odo had set his trap. Gelduin's force from Saumur was already waiting in a hidden valley just to the south of the route the Angevin army were to take. Odo's main force, led by the High Constable of Touraine, Geoffrey de St Aignan, was assembled a little to the north. Sebrand was about to ride straight between them, and the trap would close around them. Sebrand's soldiers were outnumbered two to one.

But at that moment a second messenger arrived. He rode from the west, exhausted, and he brought news even more dire than the first. The Bretons had risen again in Fulk's absence and had marched on Nantes. Sebrand now had no choice. Count Fulk had given orders, on his departure, that should there be any threat to Angers during his absence the Angevin army must protect the capital above all, leaving Fulk with his advance force to look after itself. He would be safe at Langeais and at Montbazon, Fulk had assured him, whatever might happen.

And so, at the final hour, Sebrand turned his army to the west and bid them head for Nantes. He mounted his horse and with his sword raised directed his lords to follow him. The foot-soldiers would march at high speed, and within two days — God willing — they would command the road between Angers and Nantes and block any force attempting to surprise the Angevin capital from the west. Then, if Nantes itself had fallen, they would mount a siege and try to retake it.

The sun was low and the Angevin army followed it as it sank into the horizon of forest. And with every step they moved further and further from Odo's trap. The armies of Gelduin and Odo waited for their moment of triumph, but the plain that lay between the two of them remained deserted as the sun went down, and during the night only the howling of wolves broke the silence of the forest. At dawn it began to rain, and several thousands of armed men gazed disconsolately at the empty plain. Sebrand had escaped.

But the messenger from Brittany had brought only half the news. While the Angevin army was hastening westwards, in the castle of Angers an exhausted man was describing to Chancellor Audemand and to the lords in charge of the castle garrison what exactly had taken place. He was Giraud Berlay, the brave Viscount of Montreuil whom Fulk had appointed regent in Nantes for the young Count Judicael. Berlay was wounded; and with his arm bound and his forehead still clotted with blood he spoke — between lengthy pauses — of what had occurred. The men assembled round him listened with grim faces to his tale.

It was a story that left those who heard it silent and stunned.

'From nowhere, it seemed,' began Giraud Berlay, 'the Breton army appeared in the dawn.' He paused, and his pale eyes looked lost for where to fix their gaze.

'They were through the gates without a blow struck,' he went on, and his face wore an expression of bitterness. 'The city guards had been bribed. The gates were flung open. I rushed down, and around me everywhere there were bodies. The castle guards had been murdered – every man!'

He shook his head, and again his eyes wandered for a place to rest. Two attendants carefully placed a pillow at his back, and the viscount's head lay back gratefully. His eyes closed for a moment, and anxious faces around him expressed the fear that he might be dead. But he opened them again, and this time there was a wildness in that gaze.

'There was blood . . . blood everywhere. And from somewhere terrible laughter! . . . I looked around. I saw a man – in armour. White armour! And white hair! White face! Oh God!' Berlay was shaking, still with that wild look in his eyes. He went on, his voice scarcely more than a whisper. 'I swear it was a ghost!'

A murmur passed through the small crowd of men around Giraud Berlay.

'How . . . ? But how did you know?' one man asked; and his own voice too was no more than a whisper.

Berlay looked at him with terror in his eyes.

'Because he was . . . Conan! And Conan is dead!'

The murmur swelled into sounds of astonishment and horror. Only the voice of Audemand remained calm.

'Tell us what happened, Giraud . . . if you can,' the Chancellor said. He was standing erect and grave in the centre of the room. Berlay breathed heavily for a few moments, and then continued. His voice was more composed.

'I ran, shouting for my own guard. I could see Breton soldiers everywhere. No one came. I knew a place to hide. How long I stayed there I have no idea. But then I heard screams, and the sound of a struggle. And laughter again. And I saw' – tears came to Giraud Berlay's eyes – 'women being led off. They were struggling. Some were dragged by the hair. One had her clothes half-torn from her. I leapt from my hiding-place and struck down three men with my sword before the others could turn on me. I saw four of the women flee through the gates: then I fled too. There was a crowd, and I lost myself in it. No one knew me. I watched, not knowing what to do next.'

Berlay had raised himself on one elbow and was looking at the faces around him, each in turn, as if for reassurance that they were friends he knew.

'Then I saw the worst,' he went on, his face set hard beneath that crown of blood on his forehead. 'A cheer went up. The soldiers were coming out of the castle. And they were dragging ... the young Count, Judicael! Just a boy. He had a look of such terror: I shall never forget that look. The soldiers thrust him forward and he seemed to sway. And then ... the dead man appeared. The ghost. I swear! He caught the boy by the shoulder and swung him round to face him. Judicael had his hands raised in front of him. "Imposter!" I heard the man cry, and the crowd cheered. The man swung his sword and killed the boy with a single stroke. His blood was like a spring bubbling from the ground.'

No one spoke a word in that room. Men looked at the floor, then from face to face.

'I found a horse. Soldiers attacked me but I broke away and rode here. Nantes is gone. Judicael gone.' And Giraud Berlay slumped back and closed his eyes.

So it was that the news of Conan's escape reached Angers.

'I fear it was no ghost,' said Audemand later to the Countess Elizabeth. 'The old fox must have slipped away at Conquereuil unseen. He's been lying low waiting for the moment to strike.'

For almost a year Conan had indeed been waiting. Every thought of Fulk had been a knife in his heart and a knife in his pride. Defeat by Geoffrey Greymantle, then defeat by Fulk, and his own eldest son Budic a captive. Breton soldiers had seen Budic being led off after the battle of Conquereuil, and when they told their Count he wept – with love, with shame, and with a fury so wild that his courtiers feared for their own safety. He became ill. He saw no one. A wild figure dressed in rags was sometimes espied at a window. People said that their Count was mad. Months passed. Then one day his voice was heard within the castle at Rennes. His younger sons hurried to greet him, and they saw a man whose skin clung to his bones like dry leaves. His hair was entirely white. He summoned them, and in his room they saw only a wooden board on which he slept, and a pitcher of water and some dry bread. Then he called for his finest robes, and his sons dressed him. They trimmed his white hair and beard, and fed him. He rested his arms across their shoulders and they were like twigs. But his eyes looked as hard as iron. And he sat them down and planned what they were to do.

Brittany was too weakened, he explained, to fight battles. It was weakened like himself. Their strength from now on must be invisible. No people were more clever than the Bretons. The Angevins were strong, but they were stupid. They must be defeated by stealth. And Conan explained to his sons how this was to be achieved.

Everywhere there would be spies. In Nantes, and in Angers itself. It could be done. Nantes was easy because it was a Breton city, and the people there hated Fulk. Fortunately other men hated Fulk too, and with a thin laugh he mentioned the Count of Blois. Sooner or later Odo would engage the Count of Anjou. When this happened, and Fulk was drawn far to the east, Nantes would become his prey. He would grab it. And Conan made a swift plucking gesture with a hand that was all bones: it was like a beak striking a mouse.

But to know when Fulk and his army were to head east towards Tours — that was the vital necessity. There must be spies within the castle of Angers. Fulk's servants! The Count of Anjou would have many of them in that bloated court. He, Conan, would see to it that one of them would soon be a Breton . . . but who spoke French like a native. Then there were the guards. They were usually drunk. All Angevins were usually drunk. One of them must be ... replaced! ... and the body never found. And with two men planted within Fulk's castle it should not be hard to insert another, perhaps in the kitchens where he could have access to Budic – taking him food in the dungeons. Budic must know that he was not abandoned, and know that the day would come when the door of his cell would swing open and he be handed a sword by his brothers. He, the Count of Rennes, might not be alive by that day – who knew? – but if he were not alive then he would be rejoicing in heaven, and the sound would be as if the skies were singing. This he promised them. This was their destiny.

And Conan laughed, the iron of his eyes bright as a sword. He proceeded to embrace his five sons and raised a toast to each of them, then finally to the one who was missing – in whose cell Conan vowed that Count Fulk should starve out his last days.

Fulk was right. The day came when Odo urged his men forward to attack the castle again, and from this Fulk knew that Odo's time was running out.

From the slender window high in the castle Fulk could see the movements and gestures of the enemy soldiers. He noticed, too, that they were no longer dragging away their dead. Clearly, they were not thinking of staying long. He saw the almost contemptuous arrogance of his own men as the archers spitted the soldiers who tried to scramble up the steep ditches, still holding burning torches in one hand as the other was raised in agony when an arrow bit their shoulder. He saw the whips as they were forced to go forward. And he saw Odo's own anxiety in the way he paced the worn ground between the forest and the castle. There were more kites about than ever, swooping over the fields like black wings of death.

After three days of these renewed attacks by the soldiers

of Touraine, Fulk saw that they were fewer in number. And each day there were fewer still. Finally, Fulk gathered Roger de Montrésor, Sulpice de Buzançais and Archambaud d'Amboise, and the four of them planned what they would do. It was time to act. Here were three men whom Fulk trusted as he trusted few men. There was Roger – wild like a dark storm, with the insane bravery of the loyal. There was Sulpice – with the air of being above battles, but who fought them with a beautiful deadliness. And Archambaud – the calm elder brother, easy to overlook, but always present to cover the rash mistake. With these three Fulk could destroy Odo in the solitude of his vanity. The Count of Anjou was a man who knew what people could do, and what they would do for him.

The four lords stood in an upper room of the castle. Fulk produced a cask of wine. It was the last, he said gravely, but he assured them with a laugh that they would not be needing any more. The other three looked at him intently. They knew Fulk well enough to recognize when he possessed a secret he was about to reveal.

But before he did so there were calculations to make. First – Fulk asked – what of Sebrand, the High Constable? Why had he never arrived with the Angevin army? There could be only two reasons – either or both might be true: an uprising had diverted him elsewhere, or Odo (who had clearly known their movements) had sent an army against him. If the latter, then there could have been no engagement – Fulk insisted – since the High Constable had with him several men whose task it was to warn the garrison here at Langeais by lighting a beacon on that low hill. And Fulk pointed to where a distant outcrop of limestone broke the line of trees to the west. The castle guard had been instructed to watch for it, but no beacon had been lit. This left an uprising as the most probable event. Since Odo had known their movements, he could have warned others of Fulk's departure. And who was most likely to rise up? The others did not need to be told. The lords of Brittany! The allies of the late Count Conan, burning for revenge! Yes, Sebrand must have taken the Angevin army westwards to engage them. Fulk prayed that he had succeeded. But in that case why had Sebrand not returned? Because there was a continued threat to Angers, and he had no means of sending word. Yes, that was it!

Fulk looked at the other three. They agreed that the Count was right: Sebrand was somewhere in Brittany protecting the western lands of Anjou with a small force — the bulk of the Angevin army having dispersed to return to the land just as Odo's forces here were dispersing before their eyes. The High Constable would be waiting in the hope that the Count would break out of the siege and return.

'And break out we shall — tonight!'

Roger de Montrésor looked at him darkly. Sulpice and Archambaud wore expressions of astonishment. Fulk was enjoying their confusion.

'There's something you don't know,' Fulk continued. 'Come with me.'

And he led them down through the castle — through the great hall where the Angevin knights were playing dice or sleeping or lolling in bored groups — down through the echoing store-rooms still laden with sacks of millet and buckwheat — and down still further where only a single lamp shimmered on the damp stone. Then Fulk stopped. He took the lamp from the wall and led them to where the small room turned into a recess and ended in a low door. A man would have to bend to enter whatever led beyond. He stopped again. By the light of the lamp they could see that he was searching in his tunic, from which he produced a large key — intricately cut. Very carefully Fulk turned the lock. The door gave with a creak. Ahead of them all was black.

'Listen.'

The long, stern profile of the Count seemed to wear a smile in the flicker of the lamp. The others leant forward

253

into the darkness. A very faint rushing sound came to them, and they realized it must be the river.

'I'll explain.' Fulk's voice was hardly above a whisper. 'This is the master-stroke of our Norman. He showed it to me that first evening just before he was called away. I wonder where he is now. But' — and again Fulk's face put on that slight smile — 'even if they caught him, tortured him, even if he told them there was a passage, it would be no use to them because — and this is the master-stroke — the passage isn't finished! There's no end to find!'

Placing the lamp on the ground, Fulk described the plan for that night. Odo's men were now reduced to almost the same numbers as his own. They were tired. They were bored. They would probably be drunk. The passage led several hundred paces almost to the river — and stopped. Rollo had calculated that two men with spades, digging a diagonal ramp upwards, in exactly the same line as the passage, could break through to the surface in under two hours. And the place where they would emerge was on the far side of a copse beyond the besieging ring of soldiers and close to the river. There was no danger of water rushing in because the river bank was of heavy clay bounded by boulders; this was why Rollo had chosen the place. But it was close enough to the water for the bank and the dense weeds to provide cover for the men as they emerged. Fulk himself had calculated that once the tunnel was complete virtually the entire garrison of the castle could be outside within a further hour. Enough guards would be left behind to protect the palisades and to avert suspicion. And of course the horses. Fulk knew precisely the layout of Odo's camp, and where Odo, his knights and his sons slept. The Angevins would attack at the first break of dawn. There would be a massacre.

'We'll start digging one hour after midnight. In relays.'

They had been two months shut into the castle of Langeais. It had been hard to bear. The silence. The boredom. The same sky and woods. The same stretch of river – even a piece of driftwood seemed new – or a gull on a sandbank. Fulk's golden bird, calling from the alders across the water, had a mocking sound to those imprisoned within. Behind the palisades it was so crowded that two paces tripped a man over his neighbour. Soldiers begged for guard duty: from high up on the castle at least you could see a patch of the outer world. And you could see the enemy waiting to slaughter you. Within the castle tensions rose. Men killed each other over dice, and were killed to deter others. Some went mad, and were killed too. Fulk himself walked among his men with a hand for all. He listened to every complaint. He promised them they would survive. And he promised every man an extra strip of land, and a dowry for their children. They hated him and they loved him: they were in his power. He felt he loved them. Black Fulk.

And in the black of night he led them out of the castle.

Odo's dwindled force lay in a mindless sleep. If there were guards awake, none was apparent. A sliver of a moon picked out the forms of the besieging soldiers. Here and there a body would move, but only to shift its discomfort on the hard ground. Fulk's men fanned outwards beyond the curtain of trees with the silence of hunters: others filed along the shallows of the river under the cover of the high bank. The occasional clink of a sword mingled with the ripple of water and the squawk of reed-birds. Gradually, quietly, the net of soldiers was drawn around the sleeping army: besiegers were becoming besieged. Wolves howled to one another within the night forests, and from somewhere came the cracking of undergrowth as a boar hurried away.

The faintest diluting of the night appeared above the horizon of trees eastwards. Fulk watched, hand on his sword, tense. His lords were positioned around the cordon of men, and he awaited an owl-call from Archambaud there, from Roger there, and from Sulpice near the river. Each would answer back when ready. At that moment, to Fulk's consternation, the dawn chorus broke as every blackbird, thrush and warbler in Langeais burst into song to salute the dawn. Amid all his careful calculations this was one thing he had never thought of. Would he ever hear a human owl-call through such a torrent of bird-song?

But Fulk's dismay was unfounded. When it came there was no mistaking that rehearsed call, nor its answer from the others. Fulk's own call gave the three lords the signal to attack. It was just light enough: a man could see where to plant his sword – he could see the blood flow black, the terrified faces, the helpless raising of hands, the swift passage from sleep to death. Odo's army was murdered in its dreams.

Fulk saw the Count of Blois stumbling to his feet. His one arm grabbed his sword as he turned towards the lord of Angers. His hair was still rumpled by the night, and his armour lay around his feet. There was a second when Fulk rehearsed the moment all his manhood had been waiting for; and in that moment before he hurled himself on the Count of Blois the contest was already over. Odo's sword fell from his hand. His face wore a look of agony and he collapsed without a blow struck. Death had struck him from within. Fulk's own sword was unbloodied in his hand.

It was over. Those of Odo's men still living buried their own dead. A few managed to flee into the forest and no one troubled to pursue them. And the birds were still singing their chorus to the dawn.

Odo was dead. There he lay by Fulk's feet, unharmed, his eyes wide with the shock of pain.

Fulk looked on the face of the man he loathed. Here was the man who had killed his own father, had massacred his own people, had sworn to destroy Fulk and his state. And yet now, gazing down at the lifeless figure, Fulk was aware that he felt something like pity. He leaned over and with his fingers closed the Count's eyes.

'Tell the prisoners to bring a cart, and to take his body to Tours. He deserves some honour.'

Then Fulk took up Odo's armour and sword, and passed them to Roger. His expression grew hard.

'Take these, Roger. Put them on a scarecrow and go with your men to Montbazon. I think you'll find that the courage of Odo's soldiers will melt at the sight of it. Then leave the garrison there, and return. We'll put this place in order and wait ... You won't be long.'

And, again, Fulk was right.

The news of the death of Odo reached Angers on the sound of bells. Each town through which the messenger rode sent a joyful chime out over the fields ahead of him, and every town that heard it set their own bell chiming from its wooden belfry until the message of great news – people did not know what – echoed across the breadth of Anjou to the borders of Maine, Brittany and Poitou. At the city of Angers they heard it drifting across the forests from Beaufort and Baugé, and borne along the flow of the Loire from Gennes and St Mathurin. And though the messenger was still some leagues away, there was hope beyond all other hopes that the sound told of the downfall of the Count of Blois.

It was as though Angers itself were relieved of a long siege. For two months their lord had been trapped at Langeais to the east; to the west Nantes had again fallen to the Bretons, and the High Constable with his small force was blocking the path of the Breton army should the reborn Conan strike into Anjou. For two months the people of Angers had felt naked and frightened: every morning the castle guard scanned the forests for the smoke of plunder and the glint of iron. Peasants had gathered closer to the city walls out of fear. Terror of Odo, terror of Conan: from east and west had come the threat of death.

Now, from across the vineyards and the forests came the sound of bells. It was like a blessing on the land.

The news, when it reached Angers, confirmed what everyone had hoped and had not dared to believe. Odo was dead. Fulk and his lords were alive; were returning.

In the midst of the excitement an event to which no one except the Countess Elizabeth had given much thought took place amid screams in a lofty room of the castle. Adèle gave birth to a boy. Her husband Maurice, whom she had scarcely seen during her pregnancy, appeared hurriedly by her bedside as soon as he heard that he had a son and heir. Adèle was too exhausted to pay attention to his arrival: indeed he might not have noticed if she had, so fixed was his gaze on the crumpled infant. He boasted of its titles and lands to come, and of the lineage which would extend gloriously across future ages: finally he glanced at his young wife to see if she looked likely to survive. Having satisfied himself that death was not imminent, Maurice touched her hand and departed. There was much celebration that evening in the dovecot.

The Countess Elizabeth's own labour was thought to be not long hence. She spent much time with her daughter, telling her with pride of the feats of the girl's father and how he would soon return to them, and how she would soon have a brother or sister to play with. The child listened with eyes wide, and a look of puzzlement on her face.

'Mamma, will he be bigger than me?' she asked.

The Countess, as usual, saw much of Hersende. It was a hot summer, and the two of them would sit in the shaded garden during the afternoon. They had much to talk about since the news of the death of Judicael. Hersende's horror at the story of the boy's murder was greatly sweetened by the relief that there would now be no marriage. Yet that feeling of relief was in turn disturbed by the thought that, though she was still the Lady Hersende, she once more had no lands or wealth. Might Sebrand again be out of her reach?

She looked prettier than ever, the Countess thought, in her bright clothes of summer. The girl wore a red rose between her breasts: Elizabeth did not need to ask for whom it was picked. Each day since Sebrand's departure a fresh bloom rested there, and sometimes minute beads of dew in the neck of the flower seemed to mimic the tiny freckles that ran into the vale of her breasts. What man, she thought, would not dream of placing his lips where that rose lay? It was to her relief that in the weeks before his departure she had at last noticed the young Sebrand's eyes lingering there. How could they not, unless Sebrand was more stupid than she believed?

Fulk's doves were settled in a crown of white feathers in the tree above their heads. Hersende was gazing upwards, streaks of sunlight playing on her hair and on her skin. If Fulk were here now, the Countess thought, he could not but wish this creature married into his court. How Angers would dance, with her in the heart of it.

'Remember,' she said to Hersende softly, 'with Odo dead, and his sons too young to take his place, the Count's eyes will turn towards Nantes again. Conan won't hold it for ever.' Then she added, taking Hersende's hand, 'And what if Sebrand takes the city? He could be your saviour and your lover, could he not?'

Hersende gave Elizabeth a look of such longing that tears came to the Countess's eyes, and she rose and embraced the girl as closely as her condition would allow. Hersende departed all laughter and roses.

The Lady Ermengarde had quite other matters on her mind. She chose one of Adelaide's hours of prayer to visit the Countess, knowing that their conversation would remain uninterrupted for some time — Adelaide's prayers not being known for their brevity. She wished to report her acquisition of a new manservant who — Ermengarde had reason to hope — might perform his tasks more vigorously than her present lover, of whom, she admitted, she was beginning to tire. The incumbent, she explained to the patient Elizabeth, was from Vendôme. The Countess, since she came from that city, would surely know the reputation of the young men of that region.

'My dear Ermengarde, how on earth would I know?' said Elizabeth with a laugh. 'Do you imagine my father, Bouchard the Venerable, discussed such matters at his court?'

'Well! I imagine he might have had more to say on the matter than my own husband of the same name,' the Lady Ermengarde replied a little waspishly. 'There's certainly nothing venerable about *him*, I assure you. Venal, rather. He thinks only of his gold . . . and his boys.'

'Very appropriate for a Treasurer. He knows about precious things and where they are kept.' Elizabeth gave another husky laugh. She felt in the mood for teasing Ermengarde. 'You should be grateful at least that he doesn't dip into your treasure-chest.'

Her visitor threw her a glance of irritation. She had not come here to discuss her husband's habits. But the Countess was still smiling wickedly.

'You know, you should take care your new manservant doesn't drop dead at the first sight of you,' Elizabeth added, greatly enjoying herself. 'Unless, of course, he doesn't believe you to be a virgin. The men of Vendôme, I have to tell you, are very wise.'

The Lady Ermengarde had hoped for salacious gossip, and instead found herself taunted. She was in no mood for it, and put the Countess's humour down to her condition. The white doves continued to make stupid sounds in the tree above them. Elizabeth, on the other hand, enjoyed nothing so much as parrying words with the Lord Treasurer's wife, and now that Fulk was safe she took a renewed pleasure in exchanging barbs with her.

'You'll have heard, Ermengarde,' she went on, affecting

an earnest expression, 'that the Count of Blois seems to have died of heart-failure at the sight of my lord Fulk. Tell me, how does this affect your theory about virgins?'

Ermengarde glared as the Countess reminded her of the verdict she had passed on Milesende and the unfortunate Bernard of Combourg. And then Ermengarde's ill-temper seemed to pass as suddenly as it had arrived, and she looked at Elizabeth with a half-smile.

'I never suggested, Countess, that every man who drops dead has just set eyes on a lovely creature. Not even you, I think, would call Count Fulk that! As for Odo, no one ever accused him of having the tastes of my husband.'

The two of them laughed, and the Lady Ermengarde bestowed on the Countess an affectionate kiss.

'My new manservant', she added confidentially, 'is very large.'

Elizabeth raised her eyebrows.

'And how do you know?'

'Because I have inspected him,' Ermengarde replied firmly. 'Very promising!'

And with a final nod of reassurance the Lady Ermengarde took her leave.

Alone, Elizabeth longed for Count Fulk to return. The child, she calculated, would be born within a week or so. Fears that it would be a girl still rose within her. She tried to stifle them by appealing to her certainty that Fulk loved her, and that his disappointment would only be temporary. At the same time there were depths of grimness within the Count that she could never come to terms with. The wild beast in him was something she could never love, though there were moments when she felt that she had tamed it. She looked down at her swollen belly, and as she did so she felt the child kick so hard that it took her breath away.

Elsewhere in the castle talk turned on the imminent return of Fulk. The Chancellor, Audemand, had much to report on the continued rage of Bishop Renaud. Messengers from the

High Constable, Sebrand, expressed his joy at the defeat and death of Odo, as well as his desire to return to Angers as soon as the Count might appoint a commander of the force opposing the Bretons who were occupying Nantes. There was little danger, he felt sure, of Conan marching on Angers: his force was small and – so it seemed – ill-equipped. But the people of Nantes had betrayed Anjou, and a siege would certainly be required to retake the city.

Less military matters occupied the sisters, Hersende and Milesende. Their positions were now reversed. The elder sister lamented that events in Nantes might now make her too lowly for Sebrand, even supposing that the sickly widow from Maine ceased to be the Count's choice as his wife. Milesende, on the other hand, rejoiced in the miraculous return of Conan and his theft of her unwanted lands and wealth. Now she was free to marry Rollo. It had been the most joyful of days when her lover had ridden into the city alone, after she and everyone at the castle believed him to be trapped in Langeais. Since then she had spent much of her time with him, and their happiness was without blemish. He would join her whenever she slipped from the castle to walk the fields and the river bank. The fat cook would notice them and smile. The place where Rollo and Milesende had met now became sacred to them, and in the heat of summer afternoons they would sit by the waterfall, or he would carry her laughing and barefoot to the farther bank where they would talk and touch and gaze at one another in the shared joy of a dream.

'When will you ask?' Milesende would say each afternoon, for the pleasure of hearing Rollo's reply.

'As soon as Count Fulk returns. As soon as I have a chance to see him.'

And they talked of how, as soon as Fulk agreed that they should marry, they would make love here – in the cool water – among the flowers – under the sun – under the stars. And he told her everything; about Jumièges, about the utter blankness of his own childhood, about the Duke of Normandy giving him a name. Even about Ebba of the forest, and the Arab girl at Malicorne. And she held him jealously with a fierce beauty in her face.

At least, he told her almost everything. He never spoke of the woman at Langeais — nor of his certainty that it was she who had rescued him from the castle on the night before the siege. 'I shall do what I can,' the woman had said. But what did she know? How could she have known? And what more did she know?

From far away the sound of a hunting-horn told the people of Angers that Count Fulk was near. Men, women, children, all who could walk or run swarmed from the city gates in a tumult of shouting to welcome him. They could remember his last return, in that anxious dawn more than a year ago when the creaking of carts broke into the silence of the morning — carts with their cargo of the dead and dying, the moaning, the lolling of heads, the blood leaking on to the bare earth, the horses without riders, the riders without limbs carried gasping on those bare carts. And Fulk himself — a stiff figure faltering towards the gates, raising his sword which only those closest to him could see was shaking, then collapsing in the dust and his own blood.

Now Odo was dead. Bright banners could be seen moving among the trees as the sound of the hunting-horn grew closer. The sun caught the glint of harness and the polish of helmets. Then the knights rode quietly out of the forest and cries of welcome swept across the fields towards them. There was Roger de Montrésor, beard like a black thicket. There was Sulpice, graceful and slender, smile already visible from afar. There was his brother the grave Archambaud, riding alongside the lords of Ste Maure and Baugé; then the sons of Audemand with the lords of Loudun and Passavant. And there, lofty in their midst, rode Fulk on the black stallion, Moro. He was the only man not in armour. A jerkin hung loosely from his shoulders and his chest was bare to the sun. His reins hung loose in one hand, and from the other trailed the same bejewelled sword that had cut its way through the ranks of Breton knights at Conquereuil. There was a casualness in the way he rode; yet there was no one watching who did not sense a majesty about him, as though he alone in that company required no more than one good hand and one good sword to beat off the envy of the world. The group of horsemen drew closer, and as a thousand figures hastened across the fields towards them the knot of riders loosened to let Fulk pace out in front of them: then as they engulfed him with hands raised in greeting Fulk drew himself erect on that black steed and lifted his great sword on high. Wave upon wave of cheering echoed across the vineyards and the forests. It was as if a god were returning to Angers.

The reunion of Fulk and his Countess moved all who witnessed it. She would have flown to him had her condition allowed: instead her eyes flew to him. Her fingers dabbled in his beard, reacquainting themselves with a long-lost face. Then her hands entwined around his neck and she pulled him down to her in order to kiss him. She touched his eyes, and when she saw tears gathering there she pulled him towards her again so that she might add the moisture of her lips to them. A long sigh, almost a groan, came from the Count as his arms very gently enfolded her, and she allowed herself to be cradled by him as though she were the child that she was bearing. So intimate was the scene that Audemand and others who were anxious to speak with the Count left them quietly and went their own way. No one disturbed them until the following day.

Celebrations began of an excess few people could recall even in the castle of Angers. For three days the eating, drinking and dancing rarely stopped, and there was no hour when music could not be heard rising from the great hall. Men slept where they fell, women where they were carried: a few sober voices were to be heard vowing that an unusually large number of offspring would be born the following spring, and that it would be surprising if many of them grew up knowing who their fathers were.

The Lady Adelaide absented herself except when Fulk himself was present at the feasting, and then only until the occasion when her husband Roger, in some disarray, presented her with a large wrapped gift. She gazed at it with some astonishment before kneeling down to remove the cloth from so unexpected a present from her lord. The court gathered round in curiosity. The wrapping was elaborate and Adelaide's methodical fingers pulled back layer after layer of material. Suddenly she gave out a horrified shriek, and everyone present found themselves gazing down at a gargantuan carved phallus. The lady fled amid further shrieks, and two servants solemnly bore the object after her. In the astonished silence those close to the Lady Ermengarde heard her compare the instrument unfavourably with the one possessed by her new manservant. There were some blushes among the ladies over the whole incident, as well as some notably absent blushes. The Countess Elizabeth, who had put in an appearance only a few minutes earlier, was evidently delighted and exchanged the most public of glances with Ermengarde.

On another occasion Maurice appeared holding his baby son aloft for all to see, attended by two nursemaids wearing expressions of the gravest anxiety lest in his stumbling state he drop the child.

'My son! Look! My son!' Maurice shouted. 'A toast to him!'

Count Fulk was seen to lay his goblet on the table and award his brother a look which others were glad was not directed at them.

This momentary chill was dispersed by the arrival of the High Constable, Sebrand. Fulk had dispatched the lord of Loudun to take his place outside Nantes, and had ordered his instant return to Angers. The Count hailed him with a shout of delight, and the court gathered round the young man, embracing him and clasping him by the hand. There was no more welcome figure at the feasting, and from the fringe of the gathering the large pale eyes of Hersende were fixed with a beautiful sadness on the face of the newcomer.

He in turn glanced towards her, and suddenly it was as if his eyes had never hungered for a woman before. His gaze rested on the red rose set within the swell of her breasts, and he longed at that instant to lay his hands on that lovely body and carry her to his bed. And as he looked at her, something in her eyes and in the movement of her lips told him with a shock that the thought was hers too. He felt a shiver pass through him, and the voices around him became no more important than if they had been the buffeting of the wind.

The arrival of Sebrand prompted Count Fulk to address the company. He clapped his hands, and the voices and the music subsided. Fulk raised his goblet and gazed at the faces around him.

'To the lords – and ladies – of Anjou,' he called out. 'To you all! Good health and good fortune!' And amid cheers and shouting Fulk drained the goblet.

Then he held up his hand for silence. Sebrand had by now made his way across the great hall and was standing next to Hersende. The girl felt his fingers touch hers, and everything in the room vanished before her eyes. Nearby, Rollo was holding the hand of Milesende: he saw the brushing of fingers and smiled with pleasure.

Fulk was speaking. Odo was dead, he proclaimed; and tumult broke out around him. Though everyone in the hall knew of the death of the Count of Blois, to hear it from the mouth of their lord was like hearing it for the first time.

Again Fulk held up his hand for silence. There was a man,

he said, he wished to honour — a man who had come to Anjou from Normandy as a mere master-mason. (Eyes sought out the tall figure of the Norman standing on the edge of the circle of knights and ladies next to the dark Breton girl. Rollo gave a start and let go of the girl's hand.) This Norman, Fulk went on, had built a great abbey for the Duke of Normandy, and soon would build an even greater one here in Anjou, though he did not know this yet. (Rollo's astonishment was apparent to all.) But meanwhile, said the Count, he had become a builder of castles the like of which no one had ever seen. (Milesende gazed up at Rollo with loving tears in her eyes.) It was due to this man that Odo had been unable to take Langeais, and had died of the horror of knowing he had been outwitted. Everyone here in this hall, Fulk added, owed their safety and their very lives to this man.

'Rollo, my friend, come forward!'

The figure of the tall Norman advanced through the crowd of Angevins until he stood before Fulk. The Count embraced him, and cries of acclaim echoed round the great hall.

'I promised you everything you might wish,' said Fulk, 'and I shall be true to my word. From now onwards, Rollo, you are one of us. You are a member of this court.'

Rollo was too bewildered to do more than bow and back away.

'There's more I shall offer you,' the Count added. 'Audemand will arrange everything. We'll talk tomorrow. Meanwhile, we'll drink to a nobleman of Anjou.'

And the wine flowed even more freely than before. The Countess Elizabeth departed to rest, giving Fulk the softest of kisses on the lips to the applause of the company. Merriment filled the great hall, and under the blaze of torches a roasted boar was carried in and set on a table before the Count. The feasting began again.

But there were troubled figures who departed from the

celebrations. Both Milesende and Rollo sensed that the meeting with Fulk and Audemand the next day might bring them disquiet, though neither knew precisely why they felt it. Milesende was aware of a familiar loneliness creeping up on her. Rollo became determined to ask for the thing he wanted most in the world. Whatever was in the wind, had Fulk not promised that? And would he not be true to his word?

Neither Rollo nor Milesende spoke of what secretly they began to fear most. If he was to be ennobled, what was the price Fulk might exact? A shadow of dread hung over them by the time they parted later that evening. As Rollo made his way towards his rooms along the lamplit corridor he could hear the familiar sounds of roistering from the dovecot, and the voices of Roger and of Maurice rose from the inner courtyard, interspersed with raucous laughter and female cries. He passed the shadowy figure of the Count's Chaplain, Baudouin, accompanied by the sinister nun he remembered passing on the stairway once before. The two of them were hastening the other way into the darkness of the passage.

Rollo spent a troubled night. A gale had risen, and he lay listening to the rain as it beat on the roof-tiles. Eventually the wind dropped, and all was silence over the sleeping city. Rollo did not know if he had slept, or whether his dreams had been his waking thoughts. The night seemed full of bad omens, and the dawn when it came was angry like a distant fire.

'The Count will see you,' announced a servant.

Rollo had no idea of the hour, or how long he had been staring at the wakening day. He followed the servant down the familiar corridors and was ushered into the Count's rooms. To his surprise the only figure to greet him was Audemand. He looked weary and grave.

'The Count is with Sebrand for a while,' the Chancellor explained.

There was none of the customary sparkle in the old man's face: his mouth, instead of showing the familiar twitch of a smile, was taut and thin. Rollo wondered what he knew, what he had to tell him, and feared it was as grim as the Chancellor's face.

'News has reached us', Audemand went on in the same flat voice, 'that the king, Hugh Capet, is dead.'

Audemand paused and let out a deep breath. Then he continued, not looking at Rollo.

'As you know, the king was an ally. Fulk's father did him great service. His *fidelissimus*, Hugh called him. But now things have changed.'

The Chancellor crossed the room towards the window and turned to face Rollo, his hands folded across his staff.

'Odo's widow has fled to Paris,' he went on. 'She has sought from Hugh Capet's son, Robert – King Robert as he is now – protection for herself and her children.'

Rollo could see no personal significance in all this, and wondered why Audemand was telling him. The Chancellor continued, still looking at him over the top of his staff.

'Odo's widow, Berthe, is a lady of remarkable qualities. Intelligence and great beauty. It's said that already she is the mistress of the young king. And that he's entirely enamoured of her.' A flicker of the old smile crossed Audemand's face, only to vanish. 'What this means, Rollo, is that Fulk fears royal support will pass from Anjou to Touraine. They may have lost a count, and gained a king. You see!'

Rollo nodded, still mystified about the relevance to himself.

'So Fulk has plans,' went on the Chancellor, beginning to pace the room very slowly, head lowered. 'He wishes to seal his grip on Touraine while Odo's sons are away, and they are still youths. He needs to secure two allies, to the north-west of Tours and the north-east. Maine and Châteaudun. The Count of Maine is not a man entirely to trust. As for the Viscount of Châteaudun, he is an enemy of Anjou, but' — Audemand's bushy eyebrows rose — 'Roger seized him at Montbazon. He's locked in the dungeons at Montrésor.'

Audemand stopped pacing the room and looked hard at Rollo.

'Now, you know how Fulk likes to acquire allies.' There was a pause. The Chancellor's face remained set. 'Marriages, my friend! Marriages!'

Rollo at last began to understand why he might be here, and he felt a hollow sensation within his stomach. Audemand took another deep breath.

'This place is full of marriages that are about everything except marriage, as you will have noticed. That is Fulk's way.'

'And what's all this to do with me?' Rollo asked, vainly hoping the answer might be 'Nothing at all!'

'A lot!' came the reply. 'I can tell you. Fulk is to make you the lord of Combourg. Everything that belonged to the late Viscount Bernard is to be yours. Titles. Lands. Wealth. Fulk values you. He even loves you. But he also needs you.'

To Rollo it seemed as though the world were collapsing and reshaping before his eyes. He did not know whether to panic or to rejoice. He found it impossible to absorb what this extraordinary transition might mean. It was only a moment before he discovered.

'He has a wife for you, Rollo,' Audemand went on without looking at the Norman. 'Landri, the Viscount of Châteaudun, has a daughter. His only child. I cannot tell you anything else about her. But Fulk will free Landri only on the condition that he renounce his lands in favour of her, and that she marry a vassal of Anjou and so become herself a vassal of Anjou. Sebrand, meanwhile, will marry — as you know — the sister of the Count of Maine: it seems she has

270

recovered from her indisposition. So! Two marriages. Two allies. And Touraine in the Count's grip.'

At that very moment Count Fulk entered, together with Sebrand. The latter looked grim. Rollo was too shaken and appalled even to greet the Count or his friend. But Fulk did not appear to notice. He was in a brisk mood.

'Audemand, you've told our friend the news from Paris, and our plans?'

The Chancellor nodded. Sebrand was looking at Rollo questioningly. Fulk turned to the Norman, adopting his customary stance with his hands on his hips and his head held back.

'And how does it feel, Rollo, to be Viscount of Combourg?' he asked breezily.

Rollo looked at the Count, unsure whether he loathed him, pitied him, or was frightened of him.

'It feels an honour... a great honour, my lord,' he replied. His voice was flat, restrained, and Fulk's eyes seemed to be searching his face for signs of emotion.

'I'm glad,' he said after a brief pause. And then, 'Very glad!', as if to fill an unexpected space. 'You deserve it all, Rollo... I owe, very possibly, my life to you.'

Rollo nodded, waiting.

'From now on,' Fulk continued, 'the lands of Combourg and Fougères are yours. Castles. Vassals. Servants. Serfs. Slaves. Tithes. All yours. I've never made a man such a gift – least of all a Norman!' Fulk laughed, and clapped Rollo on the shoulder.

Audemand and Sebrand were regarding one another gravely.

'And on top of all that, my noble friend, I am contracting you a wife. An heiress. She's rich. She has no brothers. And ... quite possibly' – Fulk laughed again – 'no father! What do you say, Rollo?'

Rollo sensed within him not anger – how could he feel anger at such generosity? – but a huge, empty sadness. He had never in his life felt so far away from a man so close to him.

'Well, what d'you say?' Fulk repeated the question, more emphatically.

'I say no, my lord! Thank you, but no!' Rollo's voice was quiet.

A silence of incredulity fell upon the room. Rollo wondered if the Count might strike him, but there was no fury in his face; only astonishment. Rollo looked at him.

'I love a lady already, my lord. I was about to ask you for your permission to marry her, and for your blessing on us both. The Lady Milesende.'

There was another silence. Fulk gazed at the Norman, and his face had a surprisingly gentle look.

'The Lady Milesende,' he repeated. Nothing in the Count's voice told Rollo anything. 'But she has nothing to offer you,' he went on. 'No lands. No wealth. Nothing!'

'She has everything to offer me, my lord. . . . Her love.'

The Count's eyes widened. Neither Sebrand nor Audemand moved a muscle.

'Her love!' Again Fulk repeated Rollo's words. 'And she has yours?'

Rollo nodded. The Count played with his beard, then looked at Audemand, at Sebrand, and back again at the Norman.

'I'm not asking you to give your love to the lady you will marry. You may do with your love what you please. Isn't that so, Audemand?'

The Chancellor gave the suggestion of a nod, and lowered his eyes. The Count stared hard at Rollo, who met his gaze.

'If I may do with my love what I please,' he answered, 'then it pleases me to give it to the lady I marry.'

A flicker of irritation passed over Fulk's face.

'And what if I refuse you the lady you choose?'

Rollo still held his gaze on the Count's dark eyes.

'That is your privilege, my lord,' he answered softly. 'But

if it's true, as you've said, that you owe your life to me, then I can only hope that you may repay me with what I desire more than anything in the world.'

'More than anything?' The look of astonishment had returned.

'More than all the gifts you've laden on me. I would willingly return them all to you. Titles. Castles. Lands. Nobility.' Rollo felt a surge of courage within him. 'If you refuse me, my lord, I too will refuse. That is *my* privilege. I will never marry anyone but Milesende. You may do as you like with me, but you cannot make me marry another lady.'

Rollo saw Audemand close his eyes. Sebrand was looking everywhere except at the Count. Rollo wondered when the blow would fall.

But it never came. Instead, Fulk took a few paces forward and placed a hand gently on Rollo's arm.

'Very well,' he said after a moment. 'Let it be as you wish.'

Rollo waited for the Count to say more. But he had turned away. Rollo thanked him with all his heart. Then he took his leave — too stunned to be overjoyed. A short distance from the Count's rooms he heard the tap of a stick behind him, and turned to see Audemand. He waited for the old man, and they walked together slowly. The Chancellor's face wore an expression of puzzlement, and he took Rollo's hand.

'I hope . . .,' he began. Then he stopped, and Rollo saw his eyes crinkle and his mouth resume the half-smile he knew so well. 'Rollo,' he went on, 'you're a very brave man.'

They parted at the stairway, and Audemand gave him a final squeeze of the hand. The tap of the old man's staff grew fainter and fainter until Rollo was left alone. Only then did joy overtake him, and he rushed to find the woman he loved.

But before he had a chance to reach her room he saw a familiar figure in red hurrying towards him. He saw that there were tears on Ermengarde's face.

'Rollo, have you heard?' she said in a voice that was full of grief. 'The Countess has given birth . . . and the child is dead. It was a son.'

And she burst into further tears and hurried past. Rollo was left standing in the empty corridor.

EIGHT

THE CASTLE OF ANGERS was built to keep people out, and to keep people in.

The city huddled round it for protection, and those who dwelt in its labyrinth of grimy streets were accustomed to that forbidding wall which blotted out the sun, yet diverted the rain upon their heads along a hundred gutters that spat and spewed whenever the heavens opened.

Few people in the city of Angers were aware of anything that took place within those massive flintstone walls unless one day the gates might suddenly open and a troop of knights ride out in armour or in hunting clothes; or the Count himself might appear, triumphant on his black stallion; or sounds of merriment carry on a breeze. Or, sometimes, a guard might whisper a message, or a girl say what she had sworn not to say, and news of death or a marriage or an intrigue would spread across the city.

But on that hot summer evening there were no messages, no one rode by, and there were no sounds of merriment. Since Fulk's return there had been so many nights when the castle rang with music and rousing voices that it seemed natural for sleep to have overcome at last. The castle gates looked as though they had been sealed for ever.

In fact the stillness within the castle was the silence of shock. Count Fulk heard the news of his stillborn son only a minute or two after the departure of Rollo. It was brought to him by the Chaplain, Father Baudouin, who had been summoned by the maids attending the Countess Elizabeth. The birth had been sudden and unexpected. The child, it seemed, had been born feet first, and when it finally emerged the cord was twisted round its neck. It never breathed, the maids said through their tears.

It was a blow so severe that Fulk could barely stand. He murmured something to the Chaplain and put out his arm for support. There was a strange expression on Baudouin's face as the Count swayed against him. If anyone else had been present — somebody who knew nothing of the Chaplain or of the news he brought — that expression might have struck him as one of fierce anticipation, almost of glee.

'Take me to her.' Fulk's voice was weak with pain. He looked up at the Chaplain.

'Is she well?' he added. 'Will she live?'

'She's sleeping, my lord. She's as well as can be expected . . . I believe,' the Chaplain replied.

Head bowed, and one arm resting on Baudouin's shoulder, Fulk walked slowly from that room which glistened with gold and was hung high with tapestries. All his riches at that moment he would have given away for his son to be alive.

'You have to prepare yourself for something else,' came the voice of Baudouin at his shoulder. The voice had a dark note.

Fulk checked his step, and looked anxiously at the Chaplain.

'Tell me, Father.' His face took on a haunted look.

Baudouin's large, moist eyes made a circuit of the Count as if unwilling to meet his stare. He gulped several times, and the apple in his throat rose and fell.

'The child', he said eventually, his eyes still avoiding the Count's, '. . . was deformed.'

Passions Fulk could not grasp or understand churned with his grief as he heard the Chaplain's words. Deformed! His son deformed! How could it be? Suddenly within his mind fearful visions rose unsummoned — beasts with many heads and tongues of flame — horned creatures from whose mouths crawled toads and serpents — a mountain that

opened wide its jaws to swallow him into its black throat —
then a fair woman arrayed in silks and gold who held a
comb in one hand and a mirror in the other, into which she
was gazing with a smile.

'Deformed, Father?' he said in a voice no louder than a
whisper. 'How?'

'You shall see.'

And the Chaplain guided him from the room, and the two
men made their way along the lamplit passage.

Ladies of the court were gathered round the Countess's
bed. She slept, her face drawn with exhaustion. How inno-
cently she sleeps, thought Ermengarde. She knows nothing;
after so much pain, would that she did not have to endure
still more; would that she might never wake. Ermengarde
looked up as the Count entered: terror and grief had torn at
his face, and there was a wildness in his features. Then her
eyes took in the face of Father Baudouin, and she shuddered.
No good will come of this, she thought.

The Lady Adelaide was kneeling in prayer at the foot of
the Countess's bed, her head bowed deep in her hands.
Among the other ladies around the bed was the young
Adèle, her face white with fear, wet with tears. And there
was Hersende, her fingers pressed against her cheeks and a
lost look in her eyes.

The Chaplain glanced at the sleeping Countess, then
without a word he beckoned the Count to a corner of the
room. There was a silence of such intensity around the two
figures that even the movement of an eye would have seemed
to disturb it. Father Baudouin leaned over to where a bundle
of shawls lay on a low table. He unfolded them. Inside lay
the dead child.

For a moment there was not a sound. Then a long hiss
came from the Count, followed by the voice of Baudouin.

'You see!'

That was all he said.

No one had ever heard the Count cry out as he did then.

277

He was down on the floor, head buried in his knees. His body shook. Suddenly he looked like a frightened child. The Chaplain laid a pale hand on his shoulder and murmured something no one could detect. The ladies drew back to the farther side of the room, from where there came only the low sound of sobbing.

Then, unsteadily, Fulk rose. He gave a swift agonized look towards the sleeping Countess before turning his back on the company and making for the door. The Chaplain followed without a backward glance.

Celebrations within the castle had been snuffed out as if a dark hand had passed by. Some of Fulk's lords were in no state to perceive the change with any sharpness of mind: but even a blurred perception of things was enough to inform them that a disaster had befallen the court of Angers. People knew – because they had witnessed such occasions before – that forces were at work which lay deeper than those normally governing the events of daily life and death. No one in that place, behind the screen of those impenetrable walls, was in any doubt that something had occurred which would resound like thunder in the underground caverns of Count Fulk's mind. They knew that mind, and the depths that glowed darkly within. They knew, too, that whatever shadows flickered there, they would seek substance and form until who could say what chimeras might be born? Count Fulk was a man on whom religious faith sometimes feasted like a leech, drawing the blood of the living soul. And there were men of the Church who knew exactly where to place those creatures so that the blood was richest. Father Baudouin was one of them. To Roger de Montrésor, to Sulpice, to Sebrand, to Giraud Berlay, to Archambaud, and to many other lords of Fulk's court, the Count's Chaplain was a disease pustulating within the walls of Angers: and they were aware as the days passed that Fulk had seen no one, as it appeared, except the lugubrious Father. Not even his wife. The Countess, frail and distraught, lay on her bed of labour with the sun curtained from her eyes, suffering alone the grief and sadness of her fortune.

The Countess wept a great deal. Hersende held her hand. She buried her head in the Countess's shoulder and wished, prayed, that it could be otherwise. A child stillborn was enough for a woman to endure: a child strangled by his mother's own cord of life. But for a child to be born with a scarlet mark like that across the face and head, as if some cruel iron had burnt it in the womb; this was a punishment of hell that no one, no murderer, no sinner on the Devil's prong, could have deserved. And she suffered it alone, waking to the hope of a small thing at her breast after that ocean of pain – to find... nothing... only the looks of helplessness and dismay. The child gone, dead. And no man to comfort her. Why had death chosen her son, but deserted her?

Father Baudouin did not leave his lord's side. There were days when the Count said nothing, but would gaze blankly on the summer fields spread like a far paradise, mocking the pain and terror in his own mind. The Chaplain fed him, brought him fruits, held him, reassured him. Never had a sense of mission been more sharply awakened with Baudouin. Never had he felt the power of God move so urgently through him.

Baudouin knew the day would come when Fulk would ask the questions that were torturing the Count's mind. He knew what those questions would be, and he knew the answers he would give. Father Baudouin was a man who felt himself to be in possession of the cup of destiny, and he held it before him like a chalice.

'Baudouin!'

Fulk's voice sounded far away. His eyes looked tired from lack of sleep, and he turned his head slowly towards the Chaplain.

'I have such terrible dreams. Fears haunt me,' he went on.

'Speak them, my lord. As your confessor I am here to free you of fears.' Father Baudouin's throat rose and fell, and his eyes were fixed on the Count.

'What does it mean – a head deformed like that?' There was a tremor in Fulk's voice, and his eyes avoided the Chaplain's.

Baudouin said nothing for a moment. It was as if he hesitated out of fear – his own fears matching those of the Count.

'Tell me! ... I must know!' Fulk's voice was more strident now. He rose and looked menacingly at the Chaplain, who hung his head and raised his hands before him as if to ward off a blow. Then he lifted his eyes towards the Count.

'*Maleficia!*' he said in a soft voice. And he gulped a few times. '*Maleficia!*' he repeated. 'The products of magic!'

The Count stared in horror.

'What ... what do you mean?' he stuttered.

Baudouin breathed in heavily.

'A scarlet mark', he said hesitantly, 'is the burn of the Devil, my lord. The mark of Satan.' His voice had dropped to a whisper, and he waited for Fulk's response.

'Tell me more,' was all Fulk said. The Count was standing in the middle of the room, jaw drooping, hands clasped together. Baudouin breathed deeply again.

'It is known, my lord, that the Countess wished this child more than anything in the world. Is that not so?'

Fulk nodded, and Baudouin continued.

'She had a daughter ... after which there was no child for many years. Women are known to seek aid ... There are potions. *Maleficia*. Magic. I should prefer not to tell you what they are. But potions.'

'How do you know?' Fulk's voice was hoarse, and his eyes bright with anger. 'How do you know all this?'

There was another silence. The Count gazed at the Chaplain with fury in his face.

'Tell me ... instantly!'

Baudouin's eyes were lowered again, and his hands fidgeted with the folds of his habit.

'The Lady Adèle', he went on, speaking softly, 'used such potions. And she had them from Countess Elizabeth. This I know.'

Fulk's mouth opened, but no words came. When finally he spoke his voice was choked in self-restraint.

'Potions!' he said in a tone of disbelief. 'She gave potions to Adèle? To produce a son?'

Suddenly the Count's voice was challenging.

'Then why is Adèle's son alive and perfect, and mine is not? Answer me that!'

The Chaplain's eyes were blinking moistly, and he gulped again.

'Because the Devil chooses where to leave his mark.'

'And why did he not choose Adèle?'

'Because' – and Baudouin half-turned from the Count with his hands clasped to his chest – 'Adèle is *innocent*.'

The Chaplain spoke the word 'innocent' with an emphasis that wrapped the word in many meanings, leaving the Count to unwrap them one by one. And in the silence that lay between the two men in that sun-filled room, the passing of seconds measured the impact of that single word on Fulk. The wound was deeper than any he had experienced in battle, and the pain greater. Over and over again everything that Baudouin had said would recede into a blur without form or meaning, and he would wait for this nightmare to dissolve into a reality of sunlight and happiness: but in the next moment the stab worked its way deeper still and he wanted to cry out in agony.

'You mean', he said hoarsely after a while, 'the Countess has ... betrayed me.'

Baudouin nodded his head very slightly, and looked away.

The Count's hands shook. His eyes searched the room for

somewhere to hold his gaze. His throat was dry. Then from that parched mouth came a yell, and as the sound rang down the passageways of the castle Fulk's hands closed round the Chaplain's neck.

'Lies! Lies! Lies!' he roared into Baudouin's face. And, letting go of the Chaplain's throat, he thrust the perspiring cleric from him.

Father Baudouin regained his balance just as Fulk's chamberlain rushed into the room; but the Count waved him away. The Chaplain gathered his dignity about him.

'If I lie, you can indeed kill me,' he said calmly. 'But I do not lie.'

Fulk was breathing deeply. He was looking around like a creature trapped. Finally his eyes met Baudouin's.

'Go on! Tell me. And whoever it is, bring him here and I shall crush him with these hands.'

The Chaplain felt his own neck, aware of how close he had come to such a fate. Then he folded his hands over his habit.

'That's impossible, my lord. He's already dead.'

Surprise spread across Fulk's tortured features.

'Who?' he said.

Baudouin answered him straight away. 'Bernard, the lord of Combourg!'

Fulk turned towards the window, and his long aggrieved face suddenly wore a look of the deepest tiredness. It was a face from which all hope of happiness had fled.

In all probability, if the meeting between the Chaplain and Count Fulk had been overheard, the tale planted in the Count's mind could have been removed before it rooted there.

Father Baudouin, to his credit (and there was not much that resounded to his credit), actually believed everything that he had told the Count. He was *not* lying – though there were many of Fulk's court who would have sworn that if this constituted 'truth', then truth was surely the eighth deadly sin. It was a dark god who inhabited Baudouin's paradise: perhaps the only way he knew it to be paradise was that it shut out the light and everything that grew in the light. To Baudouin all human passions had ugly faces, and their grins haunted him like rejected lovers. Man's role on earth was to be punished; but in order to be truly punished it was necessary to be a sinner, and Father Baudouin knew a lot about sin.

In the years since the arrival from Vendôme of Fulk's red-headed bride, the Count's Chaplain had watched the young Countess with the sunlight about her, and had known that she had no place in the turgid paradise where his own faith dwelt. She smiled where he would frown; she joked where he would wag a finger; she talked openly where disapproval would clamp his tongue.

'Oh, Chaplain, would you have us all ruled by your frown?' she would say with laughter in her eyes.

Worse, the grim texts and sermons to which his own beliefs clung like ivy she would counter with quotations from the Roman poets and Greek philosophers whose wisdom lay far outside the shadows of his own learning. Those who witnessed these jousts were heard to liken them to a contest between a cat and a slug.

The texts with which the Chaplain was most intimately familiar were those dwelling on the sins of the flesh. No passion wore an uglier face to Baudouin's eyes than that aroused in men by women. He was haunted by the spectacle of Adam beckoned by a naked Eve in the Garden of Eden. The fruit of the Tree of Knowledge meant only one thing in the Chaplain's mind, and in the world around him he saw Eves everywhere — wanton, flagrant and shameless.

'He believes we're all lusting to have him between our legs,' Ermengarde confided to the Countess. 'And wouldn't he love it!'

The two of them used to laugh at the thought, and the Treasurer's wife would offer colourful speculations about the clerical penis.

'I don't think my husband would fancy the other end,' Ermengarde added. And they laughed again.

Baudouin's obsession with the daughters of Eve guided his pastoral rounds of Fulk's court. Some, like the Lady Ermengarde, were already damned beyond redemption in his eyes. Others had sought the better life in spite of marriage, like the Lady Adelaide. Others still, in particular the young Breton sisters, were on the most dangerous brink of ensnaring their men with their loathsome charms.

But it was the Countess Elizabeth who appalled the Chaplain most deeply. That she was the wife of his own lord made her behaviour a good deal worse. She was Fulk's consort, and she was the first lady of the court. She should have set the example of a Mother Superior. Instead Father Baudouin had been haunted by the spectacle of her free ways and her free speech.

'Chaplain, do please read me the words of Our Lord Jesus forbidding you to have knowledge of a woman. I'm sure we could have an interesting debate about it.'

And the Countess would laugh. That intolerable laugh. Her manner, her levity, humiliated him. He writhed with a helpless vulnerability to her wit and her mockery. He had no armour against her barbs except a seething hatred, and it was this which led Baudouin to store and cultivate in his mind every grain of evidence against her good character that he could glean from the whispers and corridors of the castle.

There had been one occasion more hateful than any other. The Chaplain had been emphasizing to the Count the gravity of danger to the young men of the court posed by the two Breton sisters, Hersende and Milesende. He had laid his arguments most carefully before Fulk, supporting his case with cogent references to St Anthony Abbot and St Augustine of Hippo. The Count had appeared less concerned than

284

he had hoped, and eventually had turned to the Countess.

'And what do *you* think?' he had asked her.

The Countess's reply had been brief.

'I think, my lord, that any man who complains of temptation so loudly must be very sorely tempted himself.'

Confusion and horror had filled the Chaplain to such a degree that he was unable to remain longer in the room. As he left in some haste he could hear the Countess laugh once again.

That had been the day when hatred bred an urge for revenge. Not that Father Baudouin acknowledged it to be revenge. The spiritual nature of his calling supplied him with an impregnable sense of moral duty. An evil woman was an evil woman. Her sins must be rigorously identified, her behaviour closely observed, her transgressions pieced together until the day would come when the case against her would be presented with God as his witness. And only God would know when that day might come.

It all seemed entirely clear to Father Baudouin. God had chosen this moment to reveal the Countess for what she was. It was now his duty, as God's servant, to explain to those in ignorance the circumstances of the lady's evil-doing as he had observed them for so long.

The news that the Countess Elizabeth was accused of witchcraft and adultery was received with stunned disbelief. People wept openly. All feasting ceased. Even the dovecot was silent. Deputations were sent to the Count, but he refused to see them. He saw no one. Access to the Countess herself was forbidden to all except a maid who brought her food and saw to her clothes once she was well enough to leave her bed. It was said that when she heard of the charges, and that she would be tried, she fainted away, and had not spoken since. The maid offered the view that she might starve to death.

Even the Lady Adelaide, no friend of the Countess, could not believe what she had heard. She prayed for justice, and for Elizabeth's soul. She believed the Count had gone mad.

'Deluded, rather,' added the Lady Ermengarde, her face red with weeping. 'That accursed priest!' Her hands looked as if they could have torn the Chaplain into pieces.

'Adultery!' she went on, her voice little more than a hiss of rage. Then, 'My God,' she shouted, 'if the crime is adultery the only married women in Angers who are innocent apart from the child Adèle are the Countess ... and, I suppose, you!' she added, looking fiercely at Adelaide. 'As for me, I should have been brought to trial every day of my adult life, and I was married at twelve.'

And she burst into tears.

Ermengarde resolved to visit the Countess at all costs. With no regard to the Count's orders she brushed past a guard stationed outside Elizabeth's rooms, proffering an unladylike jab when he tried to place himself in her way. Then she thrust herself at the closed door, only to be seized by two further guards. Within a minute her husband Bouchard appeared, and the lady was led away with a struggle. On Bouchard's orders she was locked in her own rooms.

'Grovelling pederast!' she screamed through the door and sank on the bed in despair and misery.

Sebrand was the only one to break through the cordon and see the Countess. He simply commanded the guard to let him pass, and the fury of the High Constable wilted their resolve. Sebrand was distraught. He flung himself before Elizabeth, speechless. She touched his hair with a thin hand. But before they could exchange a word Fulk himself appeared. He was enraged, and it seemed for an instant that they would fight; but Fulk controlled his fury and with a ferocious glare ordered Sebrand to leave on pain of death.

'You're mad, my lord,' was all Sebrand said.

Fulk threw him an icy look and turned on his heel. Serand hesitated, glanced hopelessly at the Countess, and departed.

The other lords of Fulk's court were mostly silent. Roger de Montrésor. Giraud Berlay. Sulpice de Buzançais. Archambaud d'Amboise. Maurice. The sons of Audemand. They sipped wine, pulled at small pieces of food, and looked at each other in bewilderment. They shared a feeling of helplessness. All attempts to approach the Count had failed. The Chancellor, Audemand, joined them in the great hall: he looked sick and old, his eyes were small and sunken, his flesh sallow. He leaned more than ever on his staff.

'A mark,' muttered Sulpice. 'A red mark on its face. That's all! Audemand, one of your sons has a mark like that: no one has ever said it was the work of the Devil.'

'And strangled at birth,' added Archambaud. 'It can happen. I lost a daughter like that. We should grieve, not blame.'

The others nodded.

'Baudouin has poisoned the Count's mind,' growled Roger. 'May he roast in hell for it.'

There was a silence throughout the castle. Everyone walked with head lowered.

In the empty garden the white doves fluttered on the single tree.

At a high window Hersende gazed at the summer evening, seeing nothing.

Her sister, Milesende, walked with Rollo beneath the alders by the river. They spoke little. She turned to gaze at him with those moist black eyes.

'Take me from here, Rollo,' she said.

'Yes, I shall take you away.'

'Where?'

'To Normandy. Where I belong. There's peace there.'

'Tomorrow?'

'Very soon.'

Rollo knew that if he fled, the Count in his present madness would treat him as a traitor. They would be pursued and brought back. That would be the end of them. If he could reach Normandy he would be safe: but how to reach Normandy? Sebrand would not dare to help, or that would be the end for him too. He thought of Langeais. The woman. But could she help? Was she still there? Had Odo's men found her, perhaps? Killed her? He would go to Langeais on the excuse of work on the castle, but he would have to leave Milesende behind or the Count would grow suspicious and they would be followed.

'I shall find a way. Be patient, Milesende. Trust me.'

The girl pressed her body within his arms, and he kissed her by the riverside. The water ran so gently by. A kingfisher darted upriver; then an oriole swooped between the alders. All the brightest plumage of nature seemed on show. What a mockery! Nature, thought Rollo, should be in mourning on this day.

The Chaplain left the Count alone now. He had done his work. Fulk's thoughts would do the rest.

The Count's storm of jealousy and anger had subsided into a state of calm in which the details of the Countess's life showed up sharp and bright in his mind. The figure of Bernard of Combourg haunted him. He saw him still inhabiting the castle. Fulk remembered those many months when the Viscount had lived here at Angers, and how many times he had found the man in the Countess's company – the two of them alone. They seemed always to be talking quietly together, about what he never knew. And when he, Fulk, was away – in battle, or at Cormery, in the Mauges, no matter where – Bernard was always here. Elizabeth so often spoke of him; spoke of the sadness of the man's existence, the rape of his wife, her death, his loneliness. And she had spoken of his loyalty. To think of it – loyalty! She spoke of his bravery at arms. Of his courage. She had even spoke laughingly of his prowess with women – Fulk recalled those words now with a twinge of pain – and of what a fine lover he would make for some lady if such a lady could be found. Not that he needed any help, she had said so lightly. Of course he needed no help: the Countess provided it all. How plain it was. How brazen the Countess had been, as if to mock him. All that time – while he was away risking his life – she was lying with him. A fine lover! Indeed! How they must have loved!

And then – had she not argued persuasively against the Viscount's marriage with the girl Milesende? So much so that Fulk had almost bent to her will. Almost! Would that he had: then Bernard would still be alive, and he could hang the man with these hands, himself place the rope around his neck and as Bernard stood gasping on tiptoe he would hack those treacherous limbs from him and hurl them to his hounds, as Bernard had done to his own nephew. But he had robbed himself of that pleasure. Yes, of course she had argued against the marriage with Milesende. Was she not jealous? A beautiful girl about to be offered to her own lover: that was too great a sacrifice for the Countess. And meanwhile she was already bearing Bernard's child, conceived as a result of all those potions. With what intoxication they must have loved and revelled! What sweet nights!

And then – Bernard's death. So sudden. Why so sudden? And why at that precise moment before the nuptials, before he had had a chance to take her? A fresh landscape of doubt and suspicion opened out before Fulk's eyes, and as the days passed he explored every path and every hidden hollow in that landscape, linking them together like a map of accusation.

Potions! The Countess was known to use potions. Perhaps they were not only for love, but also for death. Magic had many purposes, and if she knew about one then why not about others? Poisons, for instance! Nobody had established how the Viscount actually died: he had been seen clutching himself in agony, and that was all. Only one person had been with him up to that moment – Milesende. They must have dined together, just the two of them, the lustful Viscount unable to wait until his wedding night before taking the girl to his bed. She would have understood the preliminary nature of that intimate dinner, and what would follow. And so she dropped poison in his wine – poison which the Countess had given her. But it only just worked in time: the girl had hesitated, had insisted she undress in private, had put on her nightgown, had no doubt played timid. And then the poison had bitten, and the girl had screamed for help. She put it about that the Viscount's heart had failed, and her tears had covered any suspicions that others might have had. Such a pure creature with her mind full of flowers – how could she be lying? Naturally, everyone was sorry for her when she came back in tears to Angers.

The map of accusation became starkly clear to Fulk. The Countess, having failed in her efforts to stop the marriage between Milesende and her lover, determined to kill Bernard rather than be ousted from his bed by another. The girl was a willing accomplice since she loved Rollo and dreaded the marriage. The Countess's plan suited both of them admirably.

The Count told no one of what was in his mind. He would tell only the judges – three of them. He had selected them already, and they were men he could trust, men who were his vassals. There was Hubert, brother of the Count of Maine, whose lands would be most vulnerable to the lords of Brittany without Fulk's protection. There was Odilo de Manthelan, who had been earnestly pursuing the Count for the hand of Fulk's cousin Hildegarde. And there was Geoffrey de Chalonnes, a cleric of some shrewdness and little wealth to whom Fulk had made it known that he might expect to receive the governorship of those lands of the Mauges formerly belonging to the late Viscount Renaud.

Here, in short, were three able men who could be relied upon to apply the law in accordance with the incontrovertible evidence Fulk proposed to lay before them.

But the map extended wider. From where, Fulk pondered, did the Countess obtain her potions, and the knowledge of how to use them? It was unlikely that she had brought such knowledge with her from the court of her father, Bouchard the Venerable. So from whom?

Pursuing this fresh path, Fulk determined to speak to the servants who had attended his brother's wife, Adèle, during her confinement. They were sent for. What, he asked, were the potions the Countess had administered to Adèle? They were to relax the girl, came the reply: she was very young and small. And that was all? he inquired. All that the Countess herself administered, yes! Was someone else with the Countess, then? Sometimes, came the reply: another woman had come occasionally with the Countess Elizabeth bearing a bag of medicines. And who was this woman? The servants did not know. What did she look like? It was hard to tell: her face was mostly covered; but she seemed young. Did the Countess speak with her? Yes! And so, once, did the Lady Adelaide, the servants recalled.

Fulk sent for the Lady Adelaide. She confirmed that she used to visit Adèle regularly to pray with her during the first days of the girl's confinement: after that the Countess would permit only one person other than herself to be in the room. This woman remained there right until the birth of Adèle's son. She delivered him, it was thought.

Did the Lady Adelaide know who this woman might be? Fulk noticed an uneasy look pass over the lady's pale face. According to the Countess, she said in a hesitant voice, the woman was a nurse; and she was sure that this was true. None the less – and Adelaide hesitated again – none the less, she remembered saying to the Lady Ermengarde that there was something not altogether normal about the woman; she could not explain why, but it was so: in a strange way it was almost as if she might have been a witch. All the same, the Lady Adelaide went on, she was perfectly sure this could not possibly have been so.

She did not add — not wishing to make herself appear foolish in front of the Count — that Ermengarde's retort had been abrupt. Superstitious idiot, had been the response. Did Adelaide suppose that everyone not forever raising her eyes to heaven was either a whore or a witch? And did she imagine the Countess Elizabeth would engage such a person to deliver a child? Was it not possible that a midwife, seeing the distress the young Adèle was suffering, might have more urgent matters on her mind than to join Adelaide in genuflection? If she, Adelaide, had spent more of her time on her back and less on her knees, Ermengarde had continued fiercely, she might understand what the poor child Adèle needed at that hour.

But Ermengarde was not present, nor was she invited to be. Neither was the Countess herself questioned on the matter. The Lady Adelaide's coy little fancy, designed more to ingratiate herself with the Count than to damage the Countess, made its black mark on Fulk's map of accusation; whereupon she was asked to take her leave. It was a troubled Adelaide who said her prayers for the Countess Elizabeth that evening, and no mention was made to Ermengarde or to anyone else of what had passed.

A few more inquiries, and Fulk's testimony would be complete. His mind admitted no lingering doubts any longer about the sinful and treacherous behaviour of the Countess. Adultery and witchcraft: the evidence was becoming conclusive.

He sent a trusted messenger to Loches. He wished to be assured that the woman from Langeais whom he had delivered to the bishop as a witch almost a year earlier had indeed been put to death. Some instinct told him that somehow she might have escaped. Later that same day the messenger rode back to Angers and was ushered into the

Count's rooms. No, she had not been burnt: merely branded. The bishop had taken pity on her, it seemed. A servant had related confidentially to the messenger how the woman had wept in front of the bishop most pleasingly, had bared herself to him in a contrite fashion begging to be whipped, whereupon his lordship had requested that they be left alone in order that he might hear her confession. She had been branded the following morning and dismissed.

On hearing this, Fulk paced the room in a state of agitation. Fresh conjectures were forming in his mind. Supposing the woman who had accompanied the Countess in attendance on Adèle were indeed the witch from Langeais, then how had contact been maintained between the two of them at such a distance? It was with a shock of alarm and dismay that he realized the only man who had regularly travelled to and from Langeais during that period of time was his own trusted master-mason, Rollo.

Was it possible that Rollo, during his months spent at Langeais, had been in contact with the woman — whom after all he had seen on that fateful night under the full moon? What had passed between them? What messages, what potions had the Normans brought to the Countess, and what summons had he delivered back to Langeais on his return?

A second messenger was dispatched to make discreet inquiries. Several more days passed; then the man returned with a strange story to tell. Fulk listened without saying a word as the messenger recounted how the Norman, during the spring, had apparently spent much time cultivating a garden of the most singular shape, with small plots of earth in each of which he had planted and tended various sprigs that no man could possibly eat: indeed he never ate them himself, but had been known to make pastes and broths of them which sometimes he gave to the villagers who came to him. And he would disappear for whole days and nights into the forest, and re-emerge with bundles of these growing things which, it was said, had magical properties. The Norman had often been seen, at night, seated by a fire on which these plants were stewing, while he himself made signs and marks on parchment by the light of a lamp.

All was complete in the Count's mind. He knew for certain what he must do. He summoned further messengers and issued urgent instructions. Then he sent word to Hubert de Maine, Odilo de Manthelan and Geoffrey de Chalonnes to assemble at Angers immediately for the trial.

And in the night, as he waited, he remembered that other night under the forest moon when the witch had stabbed her finger towards him with that terrible scream – 'Burning! Burning! Burning! Burning! Burning!'

The Count was unapproachable. Only those he specially commanded to see had been given access to him since the birth of his stillborn son. After debating what he should do, Rollo made up his mind to return to Langeais under the pretext of inspecting the castle after so long a siege and making necessary repairs to the stonework and the palisades. He left word with Sebrand of his departure: not even to his friend did he reveal the true purpose of his journey.

He departed on horseback early one morning without a guard, accompanied only by the faithful manservant who had shared with him that night journey to Montbazon some months earlier. The two men passed through the gates just as peasants with their provisions and their donkeys were beginning to make their way into the city for the weekly market. What Rollo did not know was that eyes were following him as he made his way across the fields towards the river; and ten minutes later another horseman rode through the city gates – a figure in a brown cloak with a hood pulled low. A few passers-by seemed to recognize him and looked the other way.

It was September now. The vines were flecked with red and gold, their fruits hanging dark beneath the foliage. Oxen dragging ploughs across stubbled fields, and children playing and laughing in the wake of the ploughmen. It was a scene of such peacefulness: Rollo's heavy heart felt quite out of place as he rode along those familiar tracks towards the enormous forest. Only once did he glance behind him: he could just make out the high window where the woman he loved would be watching him go. Already it was too far for Rollo to see anyone standing there, but he raised his hand in a sad greeting. How he longed for Milesende to be with him now, riding together far from that hated city — for ever! Would that it were so. But he could never have risked that: her departure with him would have aroused instant suspicion, and the Count at the moment seemed to find suspicion in everything.

His manservant said nothing, riding just a few paces behind, his hat pulled low against the early sun. Though Rollo trusted the man entirely, and he was devoted, there was always the risk that something might go wrong and the man be caught: better that he believe this to be just another visit by the master-mason to the castle of Langeais. There would be no secrets to be extracted by torture. Rollo was aware that he had learned a few things at Angers: he did not like them much.

Then, as the forest closed around them, tranquillity began to settle on him. The whispering trees reminded him longingly of Normandy and Jumièges — of his homeland. More than a year had passed: much more. Sometimes he sensed he had lost the part of himself which belonged only to that place. Now he felt it revive the further he distanced himself from Fulk's city. With Milesende, his life would turn inwards again. At Jumièges there would be enough day by day for them both: there would be a house close to the abbey walls; there would be friends; there would be peace. What did it matter if he never built those dreams of light? Jumièges was his: he had built it, and it was enough. The quiet and humble life was full of riches: he had no need of the Count's gold and titles. If only he could manage to slip away unnoticed. How did he expect the woman at Langeais to help? Rollo did not know; except that she knew so much.

The forest had never looked more beautiful. A deep summer green spread as far as the horizon under the September sun, burnished here and there by the dull gold of early autumn. And there, far away, ran the silver thread of the Loire.

Rollo halted at the place where Fulk had seen his vision of the angel in the sun. Maybe judgement had indeed pointed its finger towards him that day, and he had been right to quake. Rollo dismounted and let his horse graze for a while. He refreshed himself with water from his flask. It was mid-morning now, and the sun was hot upon his face.

It was time to ride on. He mounted again and glanced back at his manservant. As he did so he thought for a moment that a figure moved among the trees; but then a doe bolted across the open space nearby and he imagined that his eyes had misled him.

And now – there was Langeais. It had been spring when he was last here. Since then there had been that bitter siege, and so many dead. Rollo was fearful at what he might find. A town in ruins. A graveyard. But no! It was unchanged. The cluster of buildings fringed by vineyards within the belt of forest – the familiar street – the wooden houses – hens scratching in the shadows – the church belfry rising above the trees – old men seated in doorways – the same children playing. Even his house looked unchanged. The garden was overgrown, and rabbits had burrowed among the square plots he had so carefully laid out. Stones lay scattered across the paths. But there were flowers now among the tall grass – clumps of comfrey, tufts of yellow tansy, spurs of fennel. A flock of goldfinches rose noisily from the thistles already in seed along the river bank.

The door was closed only by a sliding wooden bar, just as he had left it. It creaked open, and a mouse scuttled away. In the dim interior everything seemed miraculously as it had been. The few pieces of furniture were still in place – the table by the fire, the wooden bed, the chairs, even the lamp hanging on the wall. He noticed that the earth floor had been swept: he could pick out the mark of a broom in the dust. But no broom was there. The blankets on the bed were folded neatly, and seemed freshly piled. Then he noticed a small pot of flowers, newly picked, by the window. Wild flowers. He was puzzled. Not a soul had known that he was coming.

The manservant was gathering sticks for the fire, and humming to himself. All felt exactly as it always was.

Still perplexed by the unseen visitor, Rollo made his way to the castle in the afternoon. The guard recognized him and shook his hand warmly. Soon a crowd of soldiers gathered round him: they were clapping him on the back, squeezing his hand, leading him into the familiar hall where a servant produced a pitcher of wine and some goblets. He felt welcomed, warmed. They told him about the siege, and about the toasts they had raised to him after it was all over, while Odo's army still lay slaughtered around the palisades. He had saved their lives, they assured him; and they toasted him again. The young governor came to greet him, dressed in handsome buckskin. He was the son of the old governor, he said, who had died during the siege. Count Fulk had appointed him in charge of the new garrison. But there had been no trouble since. Odo's men had buried their dead out there, beyond the town; after that they had been led away. No one had returned. Peace had settled. In a few weeks it would be the grape harvest.

Rollo climbed up to the walls and gazed out towards the silent river. The water was low now after the long summer, and broad sandbars broke up the flow of the current. There were men fishing, and a dog was barking at water-voles.

Then, with the young governor, he made a careful inspection of the stonework and palisades. There was indeed much work to be done — some that had never been completed before the siege — and the governor sent for six of the workmen who had been employed here before. They would not be needed on the land until the harvest, he explained. Then he dispatched a horseman to Loches to summon two of the stonemasons whom Rollo had used. They would arrive within two days, the young man assured him. Meanwhile, Rollo must stay and they would feast together.

It was strange and satisfying to be working with his hands again: they felt soft and tender after so many months of idleness. He enjoyed the touch of stone and chisels beneath his fingers, the tap of the hammer, the dust, the smell. He worked just as he remembered doing as a youth in the monastery yard, coaxing the stone, knowing its strength and its softness through the vibration of the chisel, feeling it yield to the rhythms of his arms and shoulders. He remained there for hours at a time without looking up except to wipe the powder off his eyelashes, only half-aware of the soldiers and the governor standing around him, drawn by his concentration.

Days passed. Then a week. Still there was no sign of the masons from Loches. Rollo had promised to remain in charge of the work until they arrived. He became aware that he was happy to put off his search for the woman — that he dreaded what he might have to accomplish in order to return to Normandy with Milesende undetected. He even contemplated sending his manservant back to Angers secretly with instructions to bring her: then he thought of how much could go wrong. So he went on working, hiding his uncertainties in the familiar calm of the stoneyard and the quarry. He was seldom alone: the young governor was good company, and life drifted by easily.

Finally the masons did ride in from Loches. Their arrival jolted Rollo into action. He handed over to them the work of repairs to the wall, and promptly set out in search of the woman.

On his way through the town he turned down towards the river and his own house in order to leave his jerkin, which was coated with stone-dust; and as he emerged from the trees he noticed a man standing close to the door as if about to enter the house. The man saw him and hurried away. He was too far for Rollo to run after him. Perhaps, he thought, it was some villager curious to see the house inhabited again, and embarrassed at being surprised.

It was a good hour's walk through the forest to the hidden valley where the woman lived, and Rollo increased his pace so as to be there before dusk fell. The sky was clear, and the moon would be bright for his return.

Scarcely a sound or a murmur of breeze broke the hollow silence of the forest. With every step he rehearsed what he might say, what he might ask: he still did not know what the woman might possibly be able to do to help, but some instinct told him that he had to see her, and that she would know something which would guide him. 'I shall do what I can': the woman's words filled his ears. He began to feel certain that it was she who had been in the house just before his return. How did she know? But how had she known about Milesende, and about his need to hurry back to Angers? And how had she known about Odo? Had she seen his soldiers filtering through the woods, and come dressed as a messenger to warn him? Or had she just known because she had powers? That scream in the night — 'Burning! Burning!' — with her finger pointing at Fulk: what had that meant? Rollo felt a chill pass through him as he remembered that moment, and the woman distraught and naked in the moonlight.

Rollo clambered down between the rocks and the twisted trees towards the stream that he knew ran past the meadow where the woman's house lay. He felt his heart beating fast as he knew that any minute it would come into view, and he wondered what he would find. With relief he saw the cottage there just as before — the animals, the hens, the stream flowing past. Only the wolf was absent, and no smoke from a fire rose through the thatch.

He approached cautiously. There was no movement or sound. A cow raised its head and went on chewing. Hens scuttled away as he drew close. The door was open, and the interior was precisely as he remembered: the plants drying against the beams, the straw bed, the table, even a pitcher and a wooden beaker standing by it. But the room was empty.

Rollo waited. He wandered outside, but there was no sign of her. It began to grow dark, and as the light faded an enormous moon rose between the trees, stretching frail shadows over the silver grass. The sky turned indigo, then gradually deepened into the black of a raven's wing.

As the very last of the day drained from the sky Rollo looked up at that dazzling moon, clear now of the trees. And as he did so a thought gripped him. The full moon! He remembered. Oh God! Would she be there in the clearing? Could he find it? Could he bring himself to witness that scene again?

Something at that moment caught his eye: a glint of metal in the moonlight. He turned; and as he turned Rollo involuntarily thrust out his arm. He felt a sting of pain as the knife cut into his flesh, and in that second before the knife struck again he saw a man's face right before him. Rollo knew he was going to die; but in that second some instinct made him twist his body and flail his arm behind him as he did so. He felt his elbow catch the man's hand as he lunged forward, and he knew that by some miracle he had diverted the blow. Rollo spun round and ducked, and in the same movement he hurled his weight against the man's knees. He could feel them falling together to the ground. Suddenly Rollo knew he had a chance. He was unarmed, but he could trust his own physical strength if only he could pin the man's knife-hand. Rollo clutched him close and they turned over and over: he must not give the man even a split-second pause to use the knife. He pulled, jerked, twisted the man, using the power of his arms and shoulders like levers. Fury rose within him. He would not die. He would kill this man. With one hand he managed to seize him by the hair, forcing his head back and down on to the ground, while his own body heaved his weight on top of him. Rollo pinned the attacker's knife-arm under his: his free hand reached for the man's throat and tightened round it. He could feel the man's strength straining against him with every muscle, and he could feel his own strength holding him down. How long could he hold him? how long? He could hear himself counting. His own body began to go numb. He must not let go. The man's throat was still twisting against the ground, struggling, struggling ... and then still.

Very slowly Rollo rose. There was a dead man at his feet, a white face. Not a sound broke the stillness of the valley under the huge eye of the moon. He had killed a man. As he stood there Rollo felt nothing except astonishment that in all likelihood it would have been he lying there dead. He had always imagined there would be horror and grief at killing a man, but he could feel neither. Only surprise and relief.

He left the knife, and the man lying there. Rollo wondered why someone should have wanted to kill him. He remembered the man in the garden who had hurried away, and the figure in the forest. He had been followed. But why? Again he felt only profound relief that it was over. The night was quiet and sweet, and he made his way back the way he had come, guided by the moonlight. Every rock and tree was sharp and colourless, and still not a sound broke the sleep of the forest.

Gradually Rollo's mind cleared, and as the shock at what had happened began to wear off he could feel his whole body shaking uncontrollably. He rested against a tree and wiped the perspiration from his face. His hands were trembling as he did so, and for the first time he noticed that his left arm was soaked in blood, black in the moonlight. He tore off a piece of his shirt and bound it as best he could with the other hand. The arm throbbed and ached. But he had stopped shaking now, and began to walk forward again — slowly at first, feeling weak, then steadily his strength began to return and with his wounded arm held against his chest he followed the moonlit path along the edge of the forest.

Rollo did not know how long he had been walking. A tired numbness had overtaken him so that he moved automatically, scarcely conscious of where he was. He wanted to sleep. Only the throbbing arm kept him moving. And then, from some distance within the forest he heard a sound, and stopped. At first he thought it was the far howl of a wolf; but the sound rose into a long, terrible cry. It was a cry of pain. There it was again, louder, higher, a scream: the most awful of cries in the stillness of the forest. His body froze. Suddenly the sound ended, abruptly, and around him there was only the moon and the night.

Rollo knew now what that cry was; and even if he had known where it came from he would not have dared to go.

The town was dark. Not even a dog barked. Rollo unlatched the door and without lighting a lamp he felt his way towards his bed and remembered nothing more.

In his sleep the throb of his arm seemed to be turning him over and over. He wanted to rest and could not. He was twisting on the blade of a knife: he could not ward it off.

It felt as though it was the easing of pain that woke him. Or *was* he awake? For a moment he did not know. It was night still, and through the window the moon was lighting the interior of the room. The pain in his arm was less, and his body felt comfortable at last. The throbbing had stopped. Rollo became aware that there was something on his arm; it was cool, soft, moist. Then there was a slight movement — very close to him. Someone was there, gazing at him. She was holding his arm, and the arm was bare except for that cool bandage. He noticed a sweet smell in the room, and he remembered the scent of the woman's body. In the shadows he could see her now, and as she leaned forward the moonlight painted the outline of her and he saw that she was naked to the waist. He could make out the dark scar on her breast. Rollo reached up and touched it with his fingers, and she placed her hand over his.

'Listen,' she said softly.

Rollo opened his mouth to speak, but she laid her fingers over his lips, and as she leaned forward her hair fell over her naked breast and Rollo felt it brush his hand.

'Listen to me.'

Rollo remembered that calm voice, as soft as her skin. She leaned away again from him, and in the moonlight he saw her body rise and fall ever so slightly as she breathed.

'I know why you've come,' she went on. 'But you must go. Believe me, you must go. Dreadful things have happened in Angers since you left. The Countess is dead.'

Rollo gave a start of horror and began to rise from the bed, but the woman placed her hands on his shoulders.

'Wait,' she said in that same calm voice. 'You must know everything – everything that I saw tonight you shall know. It was more horrible than you could ever believe. I felt her pain. They burnt her, burnt her alive. Fulk! I knew this would happen – you heard me.'

Rollo could feel her shiver. She let go of his shoulders and covered her eyes with her hands.

'They built a pyre in the public square – outside the cathedral,' she went on, her voice low as a whisper now. 'The executioner led her out. He bound her. Faggots were laid around. Then a man dashed forward with a sword and tried to cut her free. He was young. The guard seized him but he fought them off. I heard people cry out "Sebrand! Sebrand!" But more soldiers converged on him and overwhelmed him. He was cursing Fulk as they led him away. Then the executioner lit the fire. And all the time she said nothing – nothing at all. Only as the flames enveloped her did she call out.'

The woman was sobbing, her body heaving. Rollo rested his own hands on her shoulders.

'She cried out the name of her daughter over and over again, until ... there was silence except for the roar of the flames.'

Anger. Disbelief. Horror. Bewilderment. Rollo was beset with such a storm of emotions he scarcely knew what to do. The woman was convulsed in the tears of her own pain, and he held her to him tightly. He did not know how long they remained like this: he could see nothing before his eyes but the flames rising, and he could hear nothing but the cry of Elizabeth which was like the cry of the woman in the forest.

He became aware that the woman was resting still within his arms. She was breathing deeply as if she was asleep. Then quietly she raised her head: she touched his cheeks with her fingers and pulled away from him.

'You must go back,' she said, and her voice was low as if drained empty of feeling. She took his hand.

'Fulk is mad. It was he who sent that man to kill you. But you must go back.'

Rollo was stunned.

'Fulk! Kill me!' he said incredulously. 'Why? Tell me why!'

The woman gripped his hand firmly.

'Don't ask too much. I can only tell you what I saw. But listen ...!'

Rollo had risen and crossed the room. Agitation was rising within him. Through the window he could see the dawn beginning to break.

'Rollo, you must go back and find Milesende. Find her, and take her away.'

'Find her?' A terrible fear was throttling him. 'Why? Where has she gone?'

He was kneeling down in front of the woman, grasping her hands. She was weeping.

'I don't know,' she said in a low whisper. 'But you must find her!'

And she rose and pulled a shawl round her body. Then without another word she was gone. A crowd of questions swarmed in Rollo's head, and he had no chance to ask them. He went to the door after her. A light breeze had risen with the dawn. There was already no sign of her, but from the forest he heard the long howl of a wolf.

Rollo made the return journey with dread. He was aware of almost nothing along the way: the river, the vineyards, the woods, all passed him by like shadows. Even the hours melted away. What had the woman meant? 'Find her!' But where was she? What would he find? There was a fearful pain within him as he rode, and his mind wandered through a forest of dangers. Fulk had sent a man to kill him: he had no idea why — unless . . . it was to keep him from Milesende. Was that possible? To be killed for that? But if Fulk could put his own wife to death — that sweet lovely lady — good God, if he could do that then he could kill anyone. Black Fulk! The woman had said he was mad. And she had known this would happen: Rollo had seen her in her trance pointing that accusing finger at Fulk. 'Burning! Burning!' she had cried out. And last night she had witnessed it take place: she had felt the agony of death by fire; she had heard the Countess's voice crying out the name of her child.

There were tears on Rollo's face as he rode. The death of the Countess . . . and after that? Rollo grew convinced with every step that he was riding to his own death. He was being drawn inexorably back to the place chosen for him to prosper in and die, drawn there by the irresistible will of the man he hated most in this world, and who ruled his world.

But if he survived, he would leave it for ever. 'Find her,

305

and take her away.' He would risk all for that – this day.

Rollo gazed ahead. He steeled himself for whatever was to come. Over the next low hill he would see the place where he had encountered Milesende by the river, and had waded through the water to hold her in his arms. A momentary hope rose in him that by some miracle she might be there again, and he would hoist her on to his saddle and they would ride away northwards. Nothing would matter then.

But what he saw from the crest of that hill was not Milesende. Before him, in the distance, lay what at first he could not believe to be Angers. The horizon rose up in flames. The city was on fire. And there, engulfed in that inferno as if it were Elizabeth herself, stood the black castle of Black Fulk – burning, burning, burning, burning, burning.

NINE

FOR FIVE DAYS the castle stood besieged by fire. From time to time the flames died down as if exhausted at striking against those tall black walls. But then another house would collapse in on itself, sparks would scatter like hot grain across the deserted streets, and fresh plumes of fire flicker on the wind between roof and roof. From the outset people had taken to the open fields. There they waited and watched hopelessly amid huddles of possessions where they slept like so many families of mice. They ate roots, nuts, unripe grapes, whatever they could forage or steal. Then, after three days, fights began to break out between people who until the fire had lived contentedly as neighbours. Peasants guarded their strips of land with pikes, dogs, fists, knives: some who resisted most fiercely were killed by townsmen who had been buying produce from them in the marketplace every week of their lives. And everywhere across those crowded fields the word was shared that it was a curse on Fulk's city for the murder of the Countess Elizabeth. Fire in punishment for fire. Death for death.

Within that siege by fire the court of Count Fulk haunted the castle as silently as ghosts. Few people had witnessed the death of the Countess Elizabeth: horror had overtaken the place as soon as the sentence was announced, and in dismay and misery they retreated from each other like wounded animals. Word reached them that Sebrand had made his daring bid to free her, and was now locked in the dungeons for his courage: this added stroke of felony merely deepened the loathing that even those closest to Fulk now felt for the Count.

As for Fulk himself, jealousy had borne him on a dark tide carrying all before it. Now that tide receded, leaving him alone amid the debris. Never had he felt so alone. Beyond his window flames were devouring his city, as they had devoured his wife. He told himself there could be no connection; and yet every minute of the day and night, as the sun rose and sank and rose again, those flames thrust before his eyes the image of Elizabeth's death, until they began to burn into his heart and brand his very soul.

At first his resolution held. He rehearsed daily – many times daily – the arguments that had led him to offer to the Countess's judges such overwhelming evidence of her guilt. He itemized those guilts. He named her accomplices. He listened to his own voice as he paced his room and heard it as the voice of justice. He had done what he had to do – what was right.

But, outside, the fire raged and the houses crashed.

Then loneliness set in. He found himself wishing, longing, that somehow it could have been otherwise. If only the child had been normal he might never have known, and not to know ... his heart reached for that small raft of dreams. Elizabeth! His eyes began to fill with tears. Too late!

And beyond the window, out there, his world was burning.

Self-pity sweetened the pain, but it ate into that grim resolve. Those same arguments he had rehearsed over and again now sent back echoes as he spoke them in that lonely room; and they were no longer echoes of his own voice. They were voices of doubt. He shouted them away, but his orders passed through them like smoke and he heard the voices again just as before. There was the voice of Audemand – 'I have a son who is marked like yours, Count, and he fought with you at Conquereuil.' The words were like a knife within him. Then Archambaud – 'I had a child born dead like yours: we wept for her.' And other voices, jostling upon each other in his ears, and each one was a dagger of fire. There was no way out of the fire – he was all pain.

Below him a roof crumbled, and the beams rose like a flaming cross. Fulk's yell was the first sound anyone had heard from him in the castle. And across the starving fields they cursed his name.

Where was she?

'They took her away! Carried her!' Hersende was weeping into her hands. Her face when she raised it towards Rollo was swollen with so much crying, and her hair and clothes dishevelled.

'Oh, Rollo! Rollo! They led Sebrand away. Then they came for Milesende. Brutes! She was struggling, screaming. They dragged her.'

Where was she?

Rollo was frantic. She was not in the dungeons. A guard he knew well assured him of that – and agreed to take a message to Sebrand telling him that Rollo had returned. Another of the guards swore that a young lady with loose black hair had been carried away on horseback out of the city gates on the very day the Countess was burnt at the stake. Her hands were bound, he said, and a man he did not recognize held her in front of him as he rode. Rollo enquired of anyone who might have seen her go. But the streets had been empty: people had stayed behind closed doors in horror at what had happened that morning. There had been hardly a sound throughout the city until late in the night when the fire broke out. There were several fires, it was thought. No one knew how they had started. It was God's judgement, they said. By dawn much of the city was ablaze, and the population was fleeing. Why had the castle itself not burnt too? they asked. It was the Devil guarding the Count, they agreed.

Rollo had entered the city as the gates were burning

around him. Houses on either side were on fire as he rode by. He had expected the castle guards to seize him, but they were too frightened by the flames drawing closer and closer. He rode past into the castle. No one stopped him. There was an uncanny silence everywhere. People moved as if in a dream. His own servants had vanished.

Where was she?

No one knew.

Fulk reached out to grasp those who had supported him.

'Father! Tell me it was no terrible thing.' His voice was weary and pleading.

Father Baudouin placed a cold hand on the Count's shoulder. His eyes looked anxious.

'You acted justly, my lord!'

But Fulk turned away from the Chaplain, his face drawn with pain.

'What kind of justice?' he said in a soft voice.

'The justice of God.'

The Count was silent. He stared across the room, and the sounds of the burning city filled his ears. Suddenly he plunged his head in his hands, and the Chaplain could hear a long agonized moan.

'Be steadfast, my lord. To feel grief is natural – even grief for a sinner.'

The look that Fulk threw him made Father Baudouin blanch.

'I loved her,' was all the Count said. It was as if he was speaking to himself, and the pain too great to speak more.

He moved away from the Chaplain, who waited a long while to offer further comfort, but when finally the Count turned towards him again it was with a look of surprise that Baudouin was still there. Without a word he dismissed him with a small gesture of the hand.

Later in the day he sent for the Lady Adelaide.

She invariably quaked in the presence of the Count. Now she trembled like a reed. Her skin seemed more than usually drawn across her cheekbones and her twig-like hands made twitching movements as she entered.

'My lord.'

Her voice quavered. Her face, which normally affected a girlishness towards the Count, was suffused with unease. Her eyes met Fulk's and immediately fell. She waited.

The Count's speech was so weary that she had to strain to hear his words. He spoke almost as if she were not there, with lengthy pauses while his eyes shifted around the room. He rambled. He talked of the burden of rule – of the helplessness he felt as his own city was being destroyed around him – of the pain of being betrayed – of the intransigence of divine justice. And so much more. Adelaide was bewildered to hear him speak like this. His words seemed to be reaching out for comfort, and finding none. Pity for him filled her shrunken little heart – pity and a pitiful tremor of love. If she had dared to move, she would have put out a hand to him. If she had dared to hope, she would have wanted him to touch her.

Then the Count paused, and he looked at her so intensely that she shivered.

'Do they believe Father Baudouin was right?' he asked.

Fear choked her. She froze. His gaze seemed to pierce her. Trembling, she shook her head.

Fulk walked very slowly across the room, stared out at the fire and said nothing for several moments. Finally he looked back at Adelaide and his eyes were half-closed as if he was falling asleep.

'Do they believe Elizabeth was guilty?' he said in a voice so soft that Adelaide could barely hear his words.

As no sound came from Adelaide, Fulk's eyes widened and she saw to her dismay that they were washed by tears.

'They believe I'm guilty, don't they? . . . You don't need to say anything.'

She put out her hand. Fulk gazed at her blankly for a few seconds, then turned away.

The fire burned around him. The sound filled his ears. He could see and hear nothing but fire. There was no way out of the flames.

The Count was mad.

At first it was spoken half-seriously, more in horror at what he had done than as an observation of fact. But before long it was said to be true. Only his chamberlain and a few servants saw him, and from their reticence on the subject, and the look on their faces, it soon became clear that their lord's mind had broken apart.

Strangely, from loathing him people began to speak of Fulk with pity, almost with fondness. The ship of state was damaged and in need of protection. His lords shook off their own weariness and began to form a knot around their injured count. The court of Angers had to hold together at times like this.

But first there were wounds to be healed. It was the Chancellor, Audemand, whose quiet voice assumed the authority of his many years: the tapping of his staff down the echoing corridors gave out a kind of reassurance. He had been here guiding the affairs of Anjou for longer than most of the others had lived: he had presided over calamities graver than this, and had seen to it that the ship did not sink. Counts had come and gone, but Audemand was the mast that always remained standing.

'My lord Roger.' The Viscount of Montrésor looked up at the Chancellor under those dark eyebrows, and the expression on his face was one of respect and of hope.

'I have given the order to free the lord Sebrand,' Audemand went on.

It seemed natural to Roger that the Chancellor should have taken it upon himself to issue such an order, and he was relieved. He would never have acted as Sebrand had done, in open defiance of Count Fulk; but increasingly he felt certain that the only man who had behaved with honour and true courage in this tragic business had been the young High Constable.

'I have also given orders that every able-bodied man in the castle help in the rebuilding of the city, and that every vassal of Count Fulk throughout Anjou send men and timber and supplies. Messengers have already departed with those orders under the seal of Anjou. We must build before the winter: we have two or three months – that's all!'

Roger nodded. Then he clasped the old Chancellor by the shoulders. He could feel energy pour back into him.

Within the hour the castle of Angers was alive. Voices rang. Footsteps quickened. The gates were ever open for horsemen riding through. Later that day the roads leading to the city from all points were choked with carts piled with timber and grain, fruits, fowl, vegetables, while alongside them wandered goats, pigs, calves, heifers, mules, and small children brandishing sticks drove flocks of raucous geese – all of them trudging, creaking, meandering steadily towards the burnt city. Day after day these processions passed through the charred gates as if they were so many living threads being wound in from the forest and the fields. And with the sound of hammers, saws, chisels, adzes, buckets, curses, cries – bursts of singing even – Angers began to be reborn from its ashes.

Sebrand's release overwhelmed Hersende with joy, and she fell upon him with a passion that scattered all the restraints the two of them had imposed upon themselves. The tragedy of Elizabeth and the plight of her beloved sister were quite displaced from her mind as she clung to him. Sebrand kissed her and held her tightly in his arms. Then he held her from him for a moment, and as he gazed at the invitation of those green eyes his hands very gently travelled down her neck and shoulders to the lacing of her dress. Her eyes closed and she felt his fingers gradually loosen the material to explore the abundance of her breasts and the softness of her belly. They made love as she had dreamed of making love in the sunlight of her lofty room every day since she had first set eyes on him riding into the castle in the swagger of his hunting clothes. For the first time she could feel the body of a man, and she gave Sebrand her own body, and her love, her life, all her future; and if there had been more she would have given it. And Sebrand, as he moved inside her, knew that he had never experienced such a hunger of desire, and that her flesh around and beneath him was the sweetest of all things. He gave Hersende his body and his longing, and if this was love then he gave her his love. His wounded spirit was healed, and there was no thought in his mind of tomorrow or of anything beyond his joy in this creature lying in her full nakedness beside him.

Nowhere else was there any such nest of love. While Sebrand lay sleeping amid the scent of hair in the sunlight, Rollo stalked the castle, angry and distraught. No one knew where Milesende had been taken. No one could throw any light upon why she should have been removed. Only the Count knew and he was mad, raging in his rooms, seen by no one except his chamberlain. Even Audemand could only look wistful, and pronounce upon the wild condition that had settled on Fulk since the birth of his stillborn son. Did the Chancellor know that the Count had sent a man to kill him? Rollo asked. Audemand looked weary. No, he did not know, nor could he offer any explanation why that should be. Rollo could sense a deep tiredness in Audemand which settled like a mist over the events of the past week. He seemed more stooped as he walked away, and the corridors longer. Rollo was suffused with helplessness. Might Fulk have sent her to be married? Might he have put her to death – secretly? How would he ever know? No one cared: they all had something more urgent to occupy their thoughts. Even Sebrand! Rollo reflected with indignation that one minute he had been lamenting for his friend as he languished in Fulk's dungeon: the next minute Sebrand was free and frolicking in paradise with the woman he loved.

Rollo lay on his bed and listened to the first rains of the autumn beat on the charred city: he wondered how the people of Angers were passing the night in the drenched wreckage of their homes; and he wondered where the slim dark girl he desired was spending that moonless night, listening perhaps to the same patter of rain and thinking – he hoped – of him. That thought gave him the only fragment of comfort in this evil place. If only he could ride out into the drenching night and carry her into the sun. But where was she?

A surprising sound broke with the dawn. It was the sound of an aged bell. Amid the scorched carcass of the city, lamps flickered within the blackened cathedral through jagged windows. A figure with a face as ashen as the city was tugging on the bell-rope in the dim light. No one clutching at sleep under their makeshift canopies had noticed Bishop Renaud pass by in the drizzle of first light and enter the cathedral through the burnt-out doorway. It was the first Sunday after the fire had died down. It was a day for the Bishop to summon his beleaguered flock to the presence of God.

The sound fell on unwilling ears within the castle. For Rollo it was the end of a night without sleep. His bleak mood was not improved by the consciousness that for Sebrand too it had probably been a night without sleep.

Nor would it have comforted him to know that others were lying unhappily awake and alone at that same hour. The Lady Ermengarde was no longer locked in, but her husband Bouchard continued to punish her by locking others out: she was unaccustomed to passing her nights alone. She spent her days giving what love she could to the Countess's bewildered daughter – who understood nothing except that her mother was not there. Ermengarde's heart bled for the child: having no children of her own she dreamed of fostering the girl, and took comfort in wrapping her in a little of that protective love that she would never again receive. But a nurse came and removed the child at nights, and it was then that the loss of her dearest friend became almost unbearable. She was alone: she could not even stifle her pain in the arms of her manservant.

She loathed Bouchard and turned her back whenever he approached.

'Go and count your gold!'

The Treasurer glanced at her angry back uneasily. He was almost as frightened of Ermengarde as of the Count.

'Go and stuff yourself with it,' she sneered over her shoulder. 'Then you can shit gold to your heart's content.'

He departed without a word.

The only comfort, apart from the child, was that Adelaide too was excluded from her company. She would have approved so eagerly of Ermengarde's celibate state.

The Lady Adelaide also heard the tolling of the cathedral bell alone. Her husband Roger was never one to frequent her room by choice, least of all at night. And that was relief. But her solitude at this moment was made the more uneasy by her meeting with the Count. It was not just that she had been rebuffed when she had longed to comfort him: the questions he had thrown at her troubled Adelaide profoundly. Hard as she tried, hard as she prayed, she could not dispel the fear that unwittingly she had betrayed the Countess. She had sought correction of Elizabeth's faults, nothing more. There was no one to turn to. The Lady Ermengarde was barred from her. Father Baudouin saw no one. She was confused and frightened. Her prayers seemed to lose themselves in the night air.

'Dear God, guide me!' she begged. But she felt no guiding hand.

As for Father Baudouin, the Chaplain was well accustomed to the antagonism of Fulk's court. On his pastoral rounds he had often felt set upon by robbers who would pluck him of his faith. Mockery was his companion. But now, in addition, he sensed in the Count a rejection of his spiritual counsel. The sufferings of his lord had warped Fulk's judgement: not once since justice was meted out on the Countess had the Count asked for confession. He was a soul in torment, and Father Baudouin's healing presence was excluded.

Only once had the Count sent for the Chaplain. This was to inquire of Baudouin in which area of unconsecrated ground the Countess's ashes had been laid. Fulk had muttered words about her spirit flying to heaven, to which the Chaplain had attempted to offer a correction.

'Silence!' the Count interrupted fiercely. 'Go about your business!'

Baudouin had left with an uneasy mind. He heard Fulk call for the chamberlain, and not long afterwards he observed the man leave the castle together with a servant who was carrying a spade and wooden box. The Chaplain felt disturbed. What did Fulk intend! What did he want with the Countess's ashes? And what had he meant by her spirit flying to heaven?

Father Baudouin took to spending much time in the Count's private chapel, praying for his lord's soul, praying that he be kept resolute. After one such evening spent on his knees, he was returning along the dark passageway when he heard laughter ahead of him. Suddenly two figures rounded a corner and hastened past him without a glance. One was the young High Constable, in bright clothing of a casualness he found distasteful. But the other disturbed him more deeply: it was Hersende, her face radiant and her body so indecently exposed that he could only gulp in horror. The pair disappeared into the lady's rooms, and as they did so Baudouin could not help but notice that Sebrand was clasping her bare breast in his hand. He crossed himself and hastened away, the serenity induced by his prayers quite dispersed. He sought for peace of mind in the solitude of his room, but none came.

The fine rain continued to fall on that Sunday morning. The cathedral bell sounded a second time, for mass. By ten o'clock the cathedral was full. People who had spent almost two weeks in the open fields and in the wreckage of their houses clustered together and sought a little warmth and, as they hoped, the comfort of the Bishop's words.

Bishop Renaud's sermons were rarely of the world they knew, or much understood. Rather, they led people's minds into a ferocious hemisphere populated by beasts quite unknown in the marketplace of Angers. It was a hideous and uncomfortable place of which the Bishop regularly spoke, but it was where all of them — he assured them — were destined to pass after this mortal life, and from it only a few would be released to enjoy the eternal springtime of heaven. Renaud's sermons had the principal effect of ensuring that everyone determined to cling to this present life as long as possible; and Sundays, after mass was concluded, were the occasion of much consulting of other gods and other spirits whose messages were more reassuring. No one contributed more than Bishop Renaud to the popularity of pagan worship in Fulk's realm, and many a day that began with fire and brimstone was concluded with feasting and much else in the privacy of the forest. The thirst after righteousness was usually well quenched before the Lord's day was over.

Not that there would be much feasting at this time. There was not an hour to waste in the rebuilding of houses, the reopening of workshops, the laying down of stores and food for the winter. Strain and weariness marked the faces of those gathered in that burnt shell filled with the smell of damp soot and damp flesh.

They listened, dazed and half-awake. Renaud glared, commanding that silence into which he prepared to hurl his words.

'We have been placed at the end of time!' he began, his

words spaced so that each flew like a dagger above the heads of the congregation.

There seemed a greater than usual fierceness in the Bishop's words that morning. He spoke of this poor suffering land held in the grip of wickedness; and as he warmed to his theme the tall, austere figure seemed to glow with indignation while his hands plucked out of the air the iniquities of man in these troubled times, crumbling them in his fingers above the bemused faces of the onlookers. He touched, as usual, on the avarice of rulers, on the corruption of secular powers and the manifold evils practised in the name of justice. But today his words held a sharper meaning for those standing silently before him.

'There is only one justice, and that is *His* justice,' he declaimed, holding an imaginary sword aloft so realistically that people strained their eyes in search of it.

As the Bishop continued on the theme of justice, even those who had not witnessed the terrible events in Angers were left in no doubt as to the meaning of his words. They listened and they wondered ... and they waited.

'And justice *will* descend!' he cried. 'Remember the promise of the apostle Paul – "The day of the Lord cometh like a thief in the night".'

The last words were almost screamed, and the sound carried down the length of the shattered cathedral and out over the ruins of the city. A long pause followed. As he gazed down over the congregation to that gaping wall it was as if the Bishop's attention had been caught by something unexpected. He drew a deep breath and began to speak with slow deliberation. He spoke of dreams, of manifestations, omens, signs. And he spoke of fire; and as he did so the Bishop raised himself erect and his arm rose before him, finger pointing.

'Antichrist is already come into this world!' he yelled, and his eyes were as hard as stones.

People turned to follow the direction of that pitiless glare.

319

A figure was standing motionless within the crumbled walls at the far end of the cathedral. His clothes were shabby, his hair tangled, and his dark eyes gazed at the scene in front of him with an expression of infinite sadness. In his arms he cradled a wooden box.

A murmur rose from the congregation as they recognized with astonishment the figure of Count Fulk. He continued to stand there quite still, with the box held before him. And as frightened eyes lingered on that solitary figure, the voice of the Bishop rang over their heads.

'Abimelech! Amelech! Assur! Belial!' Strange words rang down that blackened church, on and on like the tolling of a bell. The Bishop paused for a moment until the sound of his voice died away. Then he went on:

'The mountains will catch fire, no tree will be left standing on earth, the waters will run dry, the marshland swallow itself up, the sky become aflame with fire, the moon will fall and the earth burn, no stone will be left standing, and the Day of Judgement will drive through the land.'

There was another moment's silence. Then once again that sharp finger jabbed over their heads, and again the Bishop's voice rang out:

'I say to you as Our Lord said of the cursed — "Depart from me into everlasting fire!"'

Before the echo of the Bishop's words had died away, the solitary figure was no longer there.

Fulk's heart was heavy with torment and with terror. Few people in the charred streets on that Sunday troubled to notice the tall ill-kempt figure as he wandered past holding something clutched in his arms. His own city seemed to him like an image of himself — crushed by events too powerful to withstand. He did not know how long he wandered, or where. But eventually he found himself by the river. It was approaching dusk, and fine rain was still falling. Overhead.

a formation of white storks was passing southwards. Before long it would be another winter.

Several thoughts gripped Fulk's mind. The one dearest to him was Elizabeth – whom he had wronged, whom he had killed in his own madness. His most determined wish was to bury her ashes in holy ground. She would take her place in heaven, though he would never share it. He had hoped that the Bishop of Angers might find it in his heart to perform this service for the sake of the Countess's soul, but his heart had been stony. Then he would make further atonement, much much more. He would make a journey far from here, in poverty, in contrition. He did not know where, or whether he would return. But he would go. The pain of what he had done would never heal, but perhaps suffering would apply some balm.

Beneath the torment of Elizabeth's death a deep fear also lay within Fulk. Those words still rang in his ears – 'Depart from me into everlasting fire!' Christ's own words. From the depths of that fear the world seemed black. He would be excommunicated! He would be damned! There was no help. He would lose everything in this world, and he would burn for ever in the next. Fulk placed his hand to his forehead as if to stay the demons that raged there. He wondered if he would go out of his mind. That would be a release, and for a moment he longed for it.

Suddenly his eye caught the figure of a small boy ahead of him by the river bank. He was struggling with something in the water. As Fulk drew closer he saw that the boy was pulling at a fishing line which had become caught in the reeds out of reach. The boy looked up at him. It was growing dark. Fulk stepped into the river and waded out until it reached his thighs. He carefully disentangled the line and handed it to the boy. With surprise he found himself smiling. The boy muttered a word of thanks and ran off.

Following the river bank Fulk saw suddenly above the trees the dark outline of his own castle, and the sight of it began to piece his mind together. The castle had stood after all: the flames had not pulled it down. Like the castle, he had been scorched but not lowered. He straightened himself as he walked. And he remembered in that instant how, more than a year ago at Conquereuil, he had ridden towards death through his own folly, and had overcome. By his own blind will he had turned that tide. His wounds were deeper now, more painful, his enemies more implacable. But he would turn the tide again. The castle of Angers still stood.

It was almost night. A few lights shone in the windows of the castle. As Fulk made his way back through the crippled city he noticed men, women, children, rebuilding their houses in the soft glow of lamps. Stewpots steamed on small open fires. Everywhere there was life, and Fulk felt for the first time that there was still life in him. He would turn the tide — even against demons.

With astonishment people heard that Count Fulk had summoned the entire court. In the great hall bright with torches men and women gathered, not knowing what to expect or what kind of man they would see. Audemand had said simply that the Count wished to speak. It was late in the evening. Some had already retired to sleep and had had to be roused.

They waited. Then Fulk entered. He was dressed simply and without acknowledging anyone he walked the length of the hall towards his familiar chair, where he turned and gazed at the company. The court saw before them a murderer, and their lord. He remained standing, and people noticed that he stood on the very place where the Countess' seat used to be.

He spoke softly, but so quiet was the hall that every word carried. Even the servants were motionless.

'I have defiled and defamed an innocent lady,' he began. The entire hall seemed to draw its breath. They were hearing their imperious lord admit in public to having unjustly killed the Countess Elizabeth. The Count continued in the same soft, low voice. He had believed her to be guilty, he said, and he had been wrong. He had been out of his senses. She was as innocent as a child. No one was more spotless. There were others present, he reminded them, who had also believed her to be guilty, and he hoped that they too would understand how misguided they had been. But it was he, Fulk, who bore the responsibility, and who would carry the burden of guilt for the remainder of his days, in the knowledge that he had condemned to death the woman he loved more than anyone in the world, and whom all his grief could never bring back to life.

There was no lowering of his gaze, no hint of a quaver in his voice, no weakening of authority in his manner.

To Audemand, Fulk's words were an affirmation that the ship of state had been righted: the storm had taken its toll most grievously, but the storm had passed; the sadness in his heart was tempered by a deep sense of relief. To Roger the relief was still greater: he had neither known nor understood the Countess well, and took a slender and impersonal interest in wives generally, especially his own; the incident should not have occurred, but for reasons that were political rather than moral.

Rollo found himself gazing at a man he hated, who had ordered his own death, who had killed Elizabeth, and who had spirited away the girl he loved: it was loathsome to be standing here, and yet through that curtain of hate something close to compassion made its way to Rollo's heart as he listened to those unaffected, honest words and sensed within them intimations of pain deeper than any he could imagine.

Tense by Rollo's shoulder, Sebrand found it in him to forgive nothing: the mere mention of Elizabeth's name stirred in him such anguish that he almost choked; never again would he hear and set eyes on the most perfect woman he had ever known — it was as if much of his heart had been burnt with her.

For the women present the Count's words passed by more lightly: they had lost a lady who was one of them, and nothing the Count said could repair that damage. To Adèle, frail and frightened, it was as if she had lost her own mother, and now stood more alone in the world than ever. To Ermengarde, it was as if a part of herself had been ripped away: she grieved alone. For Adelaide, hearing Fulk speak what she already knew from her meeting with the Count only intensified the fear and confusion on her mind: somewhere within that trembling breast were awakened tiny stirrings of an awareness that she had played her part in removing a lady she dreamed of replacing, and never would replace because she was not of her mettle.

One person above all felt a shrinking within him. Father Baudouin did not view himself as the betrayer, but as the betrayed. Alone of that company in the great hall of the castle the Chaplain remained unmoved by what seemed to him grotesque fluctuations in the mind of the Count. He listened to Fulk's words with dismay and disbelief. Was not the evidence of the Countess's guilt blatantly visible? Had not three noblemen of Anjou accepted such evidence and passed unanimous judgement in consequence? It was inconceivable that all this should be set at nought without a morsel of further evidence and without even the briefest consultation with himself. He had offered himself as the prophet of the truth; now he saw himself cast as Judas. He recoiled. His eyes avoided Fulk while he spoke. And all around him he saw the flesh of women: he could smell the lust that the Countess had nurtured; and he could hear the mockery of her voice echo round the silence of the hall. It was as if she had never died.

Fulk went on to speak of his determination to bury the Countess's ashes in consecrated ground so that her spirit might rest in peace, and he invited the court to pray for her soul. He intended, he said, to seek the help and counsel of the Abbot of Corméry, who had been his spiritual father when he was a youth. He would depart this very hour, alone, by night, and he would undertake in penance whatever the abbot instructed, at no matter what cost. It was his intention to make a journey, he added, a pilgrimage: where he did not know. But he would leave the affairs of Anjou in strong hands – he looked at Sebrand, at Roger and at Audemand – and he hoped that in his absence they might offer prayers for him in consideration of those services which in the past he had performed for the good of Anjou.

Then he strode briskly from the hall, and a bewildered court was left standing open-mouthed.

The flames of lamps wavered across astonished faces turned in the direction he had gone. It was as if he had gagged them, had emerged from the madhouse in order to cast the spell of his authority over them.

In the seconds after the departure of the Count questions swarmed into the minds of everyone present in that great hall. But Fulk was not there to answer them. His stallion Moro had been waiting saddled, and the castle guard drew back to let their lord ride out into the dark. At dawn he would be at the abbey of Corméry, and then ... no one knew.

But one man had been able to speak to Fulk during that day: his oldest and most trusted friend – perhaps the only man whom the Count, in the cauldron of his pain, still felt able to trust. He was the Chancellor, Audemand. Fulk had sent for him on his return from wandering distractedly in the city and along the river bank. Audemand had listened to the Count's outpourings, and it had been he who persuaded Fulk to address the entire court.

'Rollo,' the old man called.

His slow footsteps drew closer to the Norman, who

waited for him in the dim passageway that led to his rooms. Rollo was distraught. He had determined to speak to Fulk that evening come what may. The man had first awarded him titles and lands in reward for saving his life. He had then tried to murder him: Rollo had no idea why. He had spirited away Milesende: again he had no idea why. And then Fulk had gone. Meanwhile he stood accused, unreprieved, and deprived of the lady he loved. All this without a word, not even a glance or a grasp of the hand. It was the stuff of madness. Very soon, he felt sure, he would go mad too. He could not leave without Milesende — he could not leave in any case without being pursued by murderers: but neither could he conceivably remain in this place of lunacy.

'Rollo!' The old man, breathing heavily, rested a hand on the Norman's shoulder. 'There are things I can tell you ... privately.'

And Audemand guided him further along the passageway towards Rollo's door. The two men went in. The candles had been lit and a fire was burning in the hearth. The Chancellor lowered himself wearily into a chair.

'I shall try to explain,' he said. 'Listen to me.'

The old man spoke as if he were conserving his energies. Through his own torment Rollo could detect the strain under which the Chancellor was labouring. And as he spoke Rollo understood how this elderly and weakening man was striving to hold together the very fabric of the state he had served for so long: if he let go, if he failed, Anjou might in no time cease to exist, be swallowed up, and his life's work break like a simple crock.

He had no idea himself until a few hours ago, Audemand said, what kind of madness had gripped the Count's mind. He had been allowed no access to Fulk; neither had anybody else — except, he added, for the Chaplain. At this Audemand paused and threw Rollo a glance that needed no words: Rollo understood from that look how much the Chancellor loathed Baudouin. But today the Count had bared his heart.

326

He, Audemand, had been horrified and moved – in equal measure. And he told Rollo the tale of how Fulk had come to believe in his wife's infidelity: of the potions, the poison, of the strange woman who had attended Adèle, the death of Bernard of Combourg, the supposed plot between Elizabeth and Milesende, and – Rollo by this time felt his head begin to reel – his belief that it was Rollo who acted as intermediary between the woman in Langeais and the Countess.

Did he understand now, Audemand inquired in a quiet voice, why Fulk had sent a man to track him and kill him?

Rollo nodded. He sat gazing into the fire, bemused by so extraordinary a tale.

'And because of this madness,' he murmured, 'the Countess is dead.'

Audemand looked at him, and the sadness in his eyes told Rollo how deeply grieved the old man had been. They sat in silence. The fire and the candlelight – the peace of this room – it all seemed inappropriate to the horror of Audemand's story. The Countess was dead because of the whim of a jealous man fed by the evil mind of a servant of God. What kind of God did such a man serve? Rollo wished it could have been Baudouin whom he had strangled on that terrible night under the moon. Rollo found it hard to believe he would never hear the laughter of Elizabeth again. The laughter; the smile; the little tendernesses; the warmth; the wit that made fools of the stupid; the openness that alarmed the timid. In a way, Rollo thought, the Countess was a victim of herself: she was too silken for this rough place.

'Yes.' The Chancellor gave a sigh. 'So often people's deaths are more undeserving than their lives, don't you think?'

Then a shadow of that old wry look passed across the old man's face.

'But at least *you* are not dead, Rollo, even though you were supposed to be,' he went on. 'What's more, you remain – the Count assures me – the Viscount of Combourg. Fulk is mortified by the injury he has caused you, believe me. But he's not one to lower himself to say so to your face. He's had enough to lower him already: try to understand.'

'So where is Milesende, Audemand?' It was a question Rollo had been aching to ask, and dreading to ask. 'Is she safe? Tell me!'

He looked down on the old Chancellor with fear in his eyes. Audemand nodded.

'She's safe, Rollo. I'm sure of that. But I don't know where she is.'

'You mean Fulk never told you? How could he not?'

Audemand pulled himself upright on his staff and placed a gentle hand on Rollo's arm.

'Listen, Rollo. He sent her away when he believed her to have been involved in a plot with the Countess, and he believed you to have been part of that plot. All I know is that he sent her to Loches — to his cousin Hildegarde. A pious lady. It would be my guess that Milesende is being cared for in some convent.'

Rollo felt a mixture of relief and anger.

'But how could he not tell you where she was? She's innocent. Fulk knows that. And he knows I love her. He's given his agreement that I should marry her. How could he just leave without a word?'

Rollo's voice sounded bitter. The old Chancellor turned towards the fire and began to warm his hands.

'Because', he said firmly, still gazing into the fire, 'the Count had other things on his mind.'

He glanced back at Rollo, and his face had a severe look.

'Consider what has happened today, Rollo. The Count has had to admit publicly that he unjustly killed his own wife, whom he loved. Imagine that! He sought out the Bishop to ask for her ashes to be given a Christian burial; and the Bishop denounced him. He's threatened with excommunication: you know what that means. The Count is also a deeply religious man: he believes he will go to hell.

Think of that! He's in torment and he's fighting for his soul. This very night he's riding to visit the one man he feels can help him, the Abbot Gervais. And yet he knows the abbot must condemn him. Do you really expect him to have time to tell me about a girl – just because she happens to be a girl you love?'

Rollo was silent. He had never heard Audemand speak like this. He felt reprimanded, and at the same time made aware that the old man was Count Fulk's Chancellor before he was anyone's friend. He must not expect too much.

'If I were you, Rollo,' Audemand went on, 'I should take myself to Loches. See Hildegarde. That's all you have to do.'

Then quite suddenly the Chancellor's face took on the mischievous look Rollo had seen so often.

'It shouldn't be too taxing a search for a man of your ingenuity,' he said with a playful flourish of his staff. 'A man capable of tracking down a witch in the forest ought to be able to find a girl in a convent, don't you think?'

And he chuckled. Rollo felt slightly uncomfortable. How did he know about the woman in Langeais? The wrinkles round Audemand's eyes deepened and his mouth gave a twitch.

'Of course,' he went on, 'it would be tactless of me to inquire what you were doing in the house of that lady at night. I'm told that she's – how shall I say? – well favoured by handsome men. And Vikings, of course, do have a certain reputation. She would have liked that. One day I shall tell you who she really is. You must remind me ... And now, if you'll excuse me, I must retire. It's not been the easiest of days.'

And he moved towards the door. Then, as he was about to depart, Audemand turned and gave Rollo a look of surprise.

'But some time I would love to know how you managed to kill the man sent to kill you. Fulk must have appreciated that skill. Was it your own strength, I wonder, or perhaps ... a spell? Good night, Rollo!'

The Chancellor fluttered his hand in a gesture of farewell and departed with a further chuckle. Rollo could hear the old man's staff tapping vigorously along the passageway.

It was late. A half-moon shone mistily through the clouds. Rollo thought of Fulk riding through the night to Corméry. Tomorrow he would ride to Loches.

Abbot Gervais listened to Fulk with the well-practised silence of a confessor. When the Count had finished, the abbot sat gazing ahead of him, his bright boyish face alert with thought and his small fingers clicking against his thumbs as though he were rolling a pebble between them.

Fulk felt a great weariness descend on him. For more than six hours he had ridden; for a large passage of the morning he had talked. By the time he had said all he had to say he would willingly have committed himself to a rule of silence and poverty, a diet of bread and whey, and no matter what tasks imposed upon him, so long as he could be allowed to forget everything that he had been, and everything that he had done. His life was a burden, and he ached to put it down.

He sat in the small confessional room, its walls bare except for a plain wooden cross beyond the chair where the abbot was seated. Gervais turned his eyes to look at the Count, his fingers still fidgeting, and his face impassive.

'And what do you think I should tell you, my lord Count,' he said in a voice that was calm and expressionless, 'since you already know everything I might say?'

Fulk raised tired eyes towards the abbot and did not answer.

'We've talked many times in the past,' the abbot went on after a few moments. 'You have chosen a life of evil. One more great evil is one more stone in a boat already sinking. One more deadly sin upon another. You have chosen to be a tyrant.'

Gervais' forehead puckered as he glared at Fulk.

'*Rex iniquus* is how the Church describes a man like you.'

He paused again and breathed deeply. Then his expression changed and he looked at the Count almost with sadness.

'You see, here it matters nothing to us who serves whom in the world, or under what name. Every man is born to serve just as a bird is born to fly. Lord or serf, it is the same. All that matters is *how* a man serves. You, my lord Fulk, are a serf to your passions, and in that way you have lost your dignity – you have lost yourself. You are no more ... This life is a transitory state: those who abuse it for gain, as you have done, can expect an eternity not of bliss but of damnation.'

The abbot drew another deep breath. His fingers tapped at one another.

'For all that, my lord Fulk, I am a man as you are.' Suddenly Gervais' voice took on a kindly note. 'I have a heart. I'm not entirely free of my own passions. If I judge you, I also judge myself. I do not have the voice of your bishop.'

The abbot rose and went over to the small window.

'It was brave of you to come here. I had not expected it.' Then in the same kindly voice he went on: 'Do you remember, when you were a boy, we would walk here in the garden? I was fond of you. It was I who pointed out the oriole to you – the golden bird. And you said you would make it your bird. When I asked why, you answered that you would have liked golden wings. I corrected you, saying that the oriole was indeed golden but that it had *black* wings. You weren't listening, or so I thought at the time. Perhaps I was wrong. You've certainly learnt to spread your black wings.'

The smallest of smiles rested on the abbot's face as he gazed at Fulk sitting stonily across that empty room.

'So, my lord, what can I tell you? You know what you are.

You know who I am. If there's some help I can give you, I will give it. As man to man.'

Fulk raised his head and looked intently at the abbot.

'Teach me to read!'

The abbot looked startled.

'To read?'

'Yes,' Fulk went on. 'The Countess could read. She knew things I couldn't know.' He paused for a moment. 'If I had known them, she would still be alive.'

The abbot saw the Count's face cloud over with sadness.

'As a boy I was taught how to rule,' Fulk went on. 'How to handle a sword; how to defend myself with these hands. But never how to use my eyes to understand things. That was left to churchmen . . . and to women. As a result, I look at the world I rule, and I feel blind!'

'What is it that you'd like to read?' the abbot asked.

Fulk gazed at the bare wall in front of him as if into the far distance.

'I should like to know what great men have said.'

The abbot looked at him with curiosity, and he nodded.

'That would take a lifetime – but a lifetime well spent, certainly.'

'I should like to know what great men have said about . . .' – the Count paused and he lowered his eyes – '. . . about death! About judgement! About the end of the world!' He paused again, then looked up at the abbot. 'About the Antichrist!'

The abbot's keen eyes turned on Fulk.

'So you see yourself as the Antichrist, is that it?' he asked in a quiet voice.

The Count looked past the abbot and said nothing. Gervais stroked his brow with his hand and breathed in heavily.

'That is indeed a proud boast, my lord Fulk,' he said, gazing at the Count from beneath raised eyebrows. 'Knowing you as I do, I suppose I shouldn't have expected anything moderate. A proud boast, and a heavy burden.'

Then after a few moments the abbot continued more briskly.

'Forgive me for saying so, but the idea of the Antichrist learning to read in order to read about himself is – to say the least – novel. Believe me, I'm not indulging in levity.'

Fulk ignored Gervais' remarks.

'Tell me what has been said about the Antichrist.'

The abbot again began to play with the imaginary pebble between his fingers as he paced the small room.

'Well. Certainly it will be quicker to tell you what has been written than to teach you to read it. Perhaps that could come later.'

Fulk was waiting. His hands were spread across his knees. His mouth was taut, his black eyes sharp. The abbot stopped pacing the room and seated himself on the wooden chair. The midday sun made his bald head glow.

'It's a subject of much dispute. There is nothing certain. Only God knows what is certain, and we do not know what God knows. We can only listen, and try to understand.'

The abbot paused again, and folded his hands across his belly. Then he looked solemnly at the Count and made a few silent movements of his lips as if searching for what to say next.

'Some three hundred years ago,' he went on, 'one of the most learned of scholars wrote that there were six ages of man. Each was of approximately one thousand years, the six ages corresponding to the six days of Creation. The scholar was a priest in England by the name of Bede, from a celebrated monastery at Jarrow situated in a most barbaric land – at least at that time. But perhaps', the abbot added, 'no more barbaric than Anjou now,' and he gave Fulk a sharp look. 'Bede wrote that in the sixth and final stage man received wisdom through Christ, and that the thousand years would be concluded with the coming of Antichrist, the man of sin, the son of iniquity. Bede's source in this instance was the second epistle of Paul to the Thessalonians, which is mercifully rather short. I am not always in agreement with St Paul: he has been responsible for some very poor theology from later scholars, Bede among them in my view – though it may be we are less sympathetic to his scholarship now that the end of those thousand years is so nearly upon us. That is possible. There are, of course, scholars among us who take temporary comfort in the belief that the thousand years must be measured from the Crucifixion of Our Lord, not His birth – a stay of justice of thirty-three years. Not very reassuring in my opinion! There are even those who maintain that the early Church was poor at counting, and that many years have been added twice – though why too many should have been counted, rather than too few, is unclear to me.

'Personally I find these rigid prophecies trivial and meaningless,' the abbot continued, now well into his stride. 'I prefer the interpretation of my great forebear Alcuin – another Englishman, you will note – who argued on the evidence of St Matthew (a far more reliable source than St Paul) that no man can possibly know when Christ will return, but that it will probably be some time after the death of Antichrist – whenever that may be.

'All things are suitably vague, you see, my lord Count, the divine purpose being to keep us on our toes and not let us put off the correction of ourselves until tomorrow as though the Day of Judgement were some kind of festival of doom due to take place at a specified time in the future and meanwhile we can all get on with other things. It was St Augustine who pointed out that Antichrists are with us all the time, even here in the Church; and by that he meant perjurers, cheats, soothsayers, drunkards, usurers, slave dealers and the like – of whom, alas, we have many. The Church is a house of many rooms, and in some of them disgraceful things go on. I deplore it.

'So, my lord Fulk' – and the abbot leaned back and took a deep breath as if to refresh his lungs after so lengthy a plunge

334

into theology — 'it is unlikely that you alone carry the sword of Antichrist, or that the Day of Wrath will arrive with tomorrow's sun or even in a little over two years when, if our calculations are right, it will be the year one thousand. I'm not offering you comfort for your sins when I say this, only a corrective to your superstitions.'

The abbot paused at last. The Count began to sense an unexpected calm flow through his tired body. Gervais had not pointed to the lake of fire opening up at his feet and bid him jump into it. He was uncertain where in fact he did stand, but he was conscious of being soothed by the mystery of the abbot's words.

'Let us go to the library,' Gervais suggested firmly after a few moments of silence. He rose to his feet. 'There are volumes I can show you which may guide you more surely than I can.' And he led the way.

The library of the abbey of Corméry was famous throughout Europe. It had been founded by Alcuin himself, and rare volumes had accumulated there ever since through the generosity of popes and princes. Count Fulk's own father, Geoffrey Greymantle, had donated numerous precious things, as had Fulk himself, following his father's practice of relieving abbeys in conquered lands of their treasures in order to enhance the splendour of the abbey within his own realm. Fulk could not recall an occasion when any such gift had been refused, or any objection raised at the practice. He had often wondered what the abbot's view of the Church's need to withdraw from the world might be if he had had to endure a weak lord rather than a strong one.

The library rose around them like a city of books. An elderly monk bowed to the abbot as he entered, and threw a startled look at the Count. Fragments of daylight were thrown here and there from slits of windows, and lamps were set on long tables at which monks pored over volumes opened beneath them. The smell of dust and parchment filled the cavern of a room. The abbot spoke in a low voice to a younger monk, who nodded, holding one pale hand timidly in the other. He hurried away. One by one the other monks looked up cautiously from their studies, and then looked again for rather longer when they noticed the Count. A few excited whispers passed between the lamps.

'Do you remember some time ago I said we were like bees storing nectar from far and wide?' The abbot's whisper had none of the furtiveness of those all around. 'Well, this is our hive.'

He took a large leather-bound volume from the young monk and led the Count to a vacant table some distance from the others on the far side of the library. The monk followed them with a lamp and carefully set it down beside the book. The abbot smoothed the leather with loving hands, and as he did so he turned to the young man and said something else in a low voice. The monk nodded and hastened away.

'Do you recognize him?' The abbot looked up at Fulk quizzically. 'The brother of Roger, the lord of Montrésor. You have the shell; I have the kernel. And now' – Gervais' voice was quite matter-of-fact – 'if you think you are the Antichrist, then I shall show you the Antichrist!'

The abbot opened the heavy volume. Fulk looked down and his eyes filled with horror. The page before him seemed to writhe with living forms – there were serpents, dragons, beasts that were spotted and striped in brilliant orange and purple, creatures with tails that coiled around their heads, heads that gaped with fangs, fangs that spouted fire, fire in which human bodies struggled and grimaced. Everywhere monsters rose up to snap and howl. He was aware of the abbot's finger pointing at a serpent with seven heads rising from the sea: its body was spotted like a leopard and it had the paws of a bear. And all around it people were falling in worship. The Count felt a hand on his arm and he heard the abbot's voice:

'There is Antichrist!'

Fulk looked aghast into this page of nightmares. Then, as he stared, a face he knew seemed to emerge and lift its features clear of the monsters. It was the Countess Elizabeth's face, and she was smiling.

The Count fell on his knees on the floor, his face buried in his hands. He was sobbing. Now he could hear the echoing voice of Bishop Renaud, and floating before his eyes came that accusing finger stabbing at him across the gloom of the cathedral. And still the monster with seven heads hissed and snapped around him, and then again there was that beautiful pale face within its garland of red hair, smiling, smiling. And again that accusing finger, closer this time, and the Bishop's voice, and the hiss of those seven heads. Fulk's fingers dug into the flesh of his face.

'No! No! No!' he gasped.

When he opened his eyes he saw the abbot standing by the side of him, a hand reaching forward to rest on his shoulder. The book was closed. Fulk looked up at Gervais and shook his head. He felt more tired than he could ever remember.

'No,' he muttered. 'I am a man. Only a man. I feel pain.'

The abbot helped him to his feet and looked searchingly at the Count.

'Yes,' he said. 'And only through pain can you live as a man. For you who have sinned so grievously there can be no other way. But come ...!'

The young monk had returned and was standing modestly some few paces away, holding several more volumes in his arms. The abbot took them from him, and the monk bowed and hurried away.

'Before you rest,' the abbot went on, 'let me share with you the wisdom of St Augustine.'

With that he led the way from the library and across the courtyard by the abbey church to the same room where the two men had talked with Sebrand and Rollo almost a year ago.

The abbot set the books on the broad table by the win-

337

dow: for a while he lingered over the pages while the Count sat exhausted on a chair by the unlit fire. Finally he raised his eyes towards Fulk.

'St Augustine was a man of dissolute life for a great many years until he chose to abandon that life. He was a sinner who repented. He became the wisest of men.'

Gervais' eyes started to scan the pages on the table before him. Then he began to read, pausing every so often as he searched for new passages that he felt to be appropriate. As Fulk listened, gradually the voice of Bishop Renaud grew fainter in his ears, and words almost of comfort flooded in on him. ' "I classify the human race into two branches," ' he heard. ' "The one consists of those who live by human standards, the other of those who live according to God's will." ' There was another pause. Then the abbot read on: ' "The man who lives according to God and not according to man should be a lover of the good, and consequently he should hate the evil. Moreover, since no person is evil by nature, but whoever is evil is so because of a fault, he who lives according to God owes a perfect hatred to evil men." '

The abbot looked gravely at Fulk, who sat like a man bound to his chair by a rope. ' "By the sin of one man we have fallen into a misery so deplorable," ' he continued, ' "so by the righteousness of one Man, who also is God, shall we come to a blessedness inconceivably exalted. Nor ought anyone to trust that he has passed from the one man to the other until he shall have reached that place where there is no temptation." '

The abbot turned several more pages before his finger pounced on a passage which caused his eyebrows to fly up, and a particularly fierce glance to be thrown in the direction of the Count.

' "The whole human race has been condemned in its first origin." ' The voice was emphatic, and the abbot's hand became rigid in front of him like a claw. ' "Is this not proved by the profound and dreadful ignorance which produces all the errors that enfold the children of Adam?"' The abbot paused briefly for breath. ' "Is it not proved by his love of so many vain and hurtful things, which produces gnawing cares, disquiet, griefs, fears, wild joys, quarrels, lawsuits, wars, treasons, angers, hatreds, deceit, flattery, fraud, theft, robbery, perfidy, pride, ambition, envy, murders, parricides, cruelty, ferocity, luxury, insolence, imprudence, shamelessness, fornications, adulteries, incests, sacrileges, heresies, blasphemies, perjuries, oppression of the innocent, calumnies, plots, falsehoods, false witnessings, unrighteous judgements, violent deeds, plunderings ...?"' Abbot Gervais breathed heavily again, and his hand was raised clenched above the book as he read on with slow emphasis — ' "These are indeed the crimes of wicked men!"'

Having paused to allow Fulk to absorb such a catalogue of wickedness, he fixed his visitor with another sharp glance. And then, with a sudden change of tone, he said — still looking at the Count —

'Note, my lord Fulk, what the saint now says after this. "But" — writes Augustine — "God does not wholly desert those whom He condemns."'

Fulk became aware that the abbot's face had become almost gentle. As if he were being wrapped in something warm he realized that he was being offered what he had believed to be forbidden him; he was being offered hope.

His eyes met the abbot's, and he thought that he detected in them a glint of kindliness. The abbot turned back towards the table and his hands reached for a slim volume that so far had remained unopened.

'I shall read you just one further passage,' he said. 'It is from a celebrated sermon which Augustine delivered on one of the psalms — Psalm Thirty-One.'

The abbot found the page immediately, and began reading.

' "Supposing you are hoping for a right reward, I mean eternal life. You are godless."' Gervais' eyes rose towards

Fulk for an instant. '"Believe in Him who justifies the ungodly, so that your good works may really be good works. For I should not call them good as long as they do not proceed from a right foundation. Put your faith right, set your faith in order, set your life in order; and now if you have sound feet, go straight ahead without anxiety; run, you are on the right road; the faster you run the sooner you will get there."'

Fulk said nothing for a long while. But in his heart he felt something that was close to joy. He saw the sunlight flooding into the abbot's room and he wanted to embrace it. He knew what he would do, where he would go.

The abbot was standing with his arms folded. Fulk looked up at him and nodded.

'I shall go to Jerusalem,' was all he said.

Gervais made no reply, but walked over to the window and looked out. Then he turned to the Count.

'Before you do,' he said, 'bring me the ashes of the Countess. We shall bury them together.'

TEN

FEW PEOPLE SAW FULK AGAIN before he departed. He returned
to Angers by night, just as he had left by night. A servant
roused Audemand, and the Count presented detailed
instructions to the Chancellor for the period of his journey
to the Holy Land — certainly no less than eight months and
possibly much more. He intended to travel alone except for
two companions who would be carrying gifts for those
rulers on whose hospitality he would be leaning during his
travels — in particular the Caliph of Jerusalem, Hakem,
whom the Abbot Gervais described as the most cruel of all
pagan fanatics to follow the false prophet Mohamet. But
since the Caliph's reputation for avarice exceeded even his
taste for Christian blood, the Count felt confident that he
would gain access to the Holy City and not lose his life. To
this end he was taking with him a Koran of the most
remarkable intricacy originating from the Spanish city of
Cordoba, and which had been obtained by the Count's
father, Geoffrey Greymantle, in exchange for a Moorish
nobleman of high rank captured in Vascovia.

The Count then roused the Treasurer, Bouchard, and
spent a considerable time with him selecting treasures for his
journey. Bouchard parted with these most painfully: it
grieved him to see so much gold and jewellery wasted on
foreign princes of no importance to Anjou, particular Saracens who were in the process of desecrating the shrines of
Our Lord. But his great awe of the Count forbade him to say
so, and he bore his pain silently.

Then, even before dawn broke, Fulk set off saying good-
bye to no one. His companions bore one extra package; and

by midday Count Fulk and Abbot Gervais were engaged in a private ceremony in the abbey church at Cormèry. That afternoon the box containing the Countess's ashes was laid to rest in the graveyard within the walls. Fulk wept bitterly, and around the grave fell the soft leaves of autumn.

While Count Fulk and his two companions were riding southwards, another man on horseback was returning alone to Angers. He was disconsolate, and went immediately to see the High Constable, Sebrand.

'So, what news, Rollo?'

Sebrand was struggling to suppress his joyful mood in order to accommodate the Norman's gloom. The look on his friend's face told him that the visit to Loches had not been a success. Rollo slumped into a chair.

'The Lady Hildegarde departed yesterday for Aquitaine – to see her father,' he muttered without raising his eyes. Then, with a spurt of useless irritation, he added, 'Why on earth couldn't I have known that earlier?'

'Well – set off quickly and maybe you'll catch her up.' Sebrand realized the flippancy of his remark and wished he had not made it. Rollo gave him a withering look. Sebrand felt duly corrected. He tried again.

'Look, Rollo. Her father is Duke William. He has a splendid court. You are now Viscount of Combourg – no longer just a visiting master-mason from Normandy. You could go there and present yourself. Why not?'

'It's worse than that,' Rollo replied heavily. 'It seems Hildegarde intends to go into retreat out of respect for the Countess Elizabeth. She'll see nobody.'

'Oh God! All these women in convents everywhere. They should be on their backs, not on their knees.'

Again Sebrand wished he had not spoken, but this time Rollo took no notice.

'How long do people spend in retreat?' he asked with a sigh.

Sebrand shrugged.

'Hildegarde is a good and pious lady. Maybe months ... What I will do for you is this, Rollo. I shall send a messenger to Duke William asking if I may be informed immediately the Lady Hildegarde has finished her prayers. You can then ride to Loches and wait for her, and the key to the convent will be yours. How's that?'

Rollo sighed and muttered his thanks. Sebrand was grateful that his own lady was not buried away among a host of whispering virgins: the only veils in his life were those he eagerly removed from his mistress on every possible occasion. He felt insatiably in love with Hersende's body.

With Fulk's departure he felt freer in his mind about his relationship with Hersende. However deep the sense of outrage he harboured towards the Count, he had been uncomfortably aware that he remained the Count's vassal. Fulk's wishes for his marriage could not be overlooked except at his own peril. But now that Fulk had departed for many months, perhaps a year, a generous margin of time accompanied the progress of his romance, allowing him to delay any ugly consideration of its consequences. Ideally, of course, he would like to be able to mount a successful siege of the city of Nantes, and so recapture Hersende's titles and lands: he would then have a strong case to lay before the Count on his return, further strengthened by the girl's incomparable superiority in beauty, charm and (surely) child-bearing over the Count of Maine's sister. On the other hand, even if it were possible, a long siege would remove him from Hersende's bed for a mournful length of time. And if the siege failed ...? Sebrand was conscious that his martial nature was becoming softened by the pleasures of the flesh — but oh! they were such lusty pleasures!

Hersende herself was glowing with love, and filled with a need to talk about it. With the death of the Countess it seemed natural – as well as comforting to her grief – to seek the company of the Countess's greatest friend, the Lady Ermengarde. Hersende had always been a little frightened of the Treasurer's wife, as well as nagged by jealousy lest Sebrand be caught in the lady's capacious net. But those fears had diminished of late, and the sight of Ermengarde playing so tenderly with the Countess's daughter touched her and drew her close.

Ermengarde, too, found in Hersende's company some ease from the pain of Elizabeth's death, and gradually she began to feel something of her former spirits return. In this way, two people whom the Countess had loved kept the memory of her alive, and came to life themselves by sharing their memories of her.

Ermengarde could not long resist inquiring about Hersende's passion for Sebrand. At first the girl blushed at her friend's frankness; but very soon a longing to share her joy with another overcame her shyness, and she seized every opportunity to treat even the smallest aspects of her love as the most burning matter in the world. His glance, the meaning of each sigh, the precise hour of his arrival, the number of moles on his back – these towering monuments of passion reduced all other concerns of the day to mere triviality.

'It's so much easier talking to women who are no longer virgins,' announced Ermengarde, stretching languidly as the sun painted her hair dark shades of autumn. 'Virginity is such a barrier to conversation. When I lost mine for the first time it was like a torrent – and I'm not talking about blood, my beloved.'

Hersende blushed again.

'I love him!' was all she found to say.

'I can see that,' Ermengarde went on hurriedly. 'You blossom! Be careful you don't bulge as well before long. I can help you there: it's something I know quite a lot about. You already bulge most enviably in the right places, my dear girl: don't go and spoil the shape of it.'

344

Hersende looked down sheepishly at her breasts. Ermengarde in fact found these breathless conversations about love less overwhelmingly important than her young friend, and she missed the sharpness of humour that the Countess would have brought to the matter. Love was tedious to talk about – it was always the same: what she wanted to know was how good Sebrand was at it, and what he liked to do. Ermengarde found herself constantly embarrassing the silly girl.

'Is he big? ... But that's a stupid question since you've known no other. He probably tells you he is, but then all men like to think they are, and secretly fear they are not. The fact is, they're all much the same size – with a few exceptions of course, and you need an expert eye to know which those are going to be. It's a gift I've acquired, which might be useful to you one day. You only have to ask.'

A look of horror had crossed Hersende's face, and Ermengarde realized that yet another path of conversation had been blocked. Whatever could she talk to the girl about? She imagined the younger sister might be more sprightly to discuss things with when the time came, though Heaven knows how long that might be with the girl buried away in some convent – nobody knew where – and wasting her youth in prayers and tears. She wished she could find some means of locating her so that Rollo could carry her away; and she enjoyed the image in her mind of the tall Viking with a swooning nun in his arms as the good sisters scattered with little shrieks. Ermengarde felt sorry for Milesende, and even sorrier for Rollo who moped about the castle looking forlorn. She had several times tried offering herself in compensation, but in his present mood the Norman had shown himself to be impervious to her glances and accidental brushings of the hand. Another person boringly in love!

Rollo had resigned himself to a long wait. At first he had determined to make a search of all the convents within a reasonable distance of Loches until he found Milesende. He had even approached the Lady Adelaide, who he thought would know about such things. How many were there? And where? Adelaide, paler and more drawn than ever, at first found it hard to address herself to the question; then she said that there were countless places where virtuous maidens sought spiritual protection, and a man such as himself would – she trusted – be given access to none of them.

The Lady Adelaide had no further thoughts to offer; neither did she suggest who else might. Rollo, she made it clear, had no alternative but to wait for the return of the Count's cousin Hildegarde.

'And even then I hope she will not tell you,' Adelaide continued rather waspishly. 'I'm sure the young girl is in the best possible place for her own good. To be a nun is a divine calling.'

Rollo pointed out sharply that Milesende had not been called, but abducted, imprisoned. Adelaide bridled, and the lines around her mouth described a downward curve. Her face looked papery and wan. She must have been beautiful such a very short time ago, Rollo thought; but she seemed to have fed on life as if it were vinegar until she was nothing but sourness. As he bid her brusquely good-bye he glanced at her little body so stiffly held, and a malicious picture came before his eyes of the bull-like Roger, hairy and reeking of wine, forcing those rigid limbs apart on their wedding night. What pitiful prayers to the good saints there must have been, murmured through clenched teeth!

Audemand was waiting for him.

'Rollo.' The Chancellor was making bold shapes on the floor with the point of his staff. He glanced up with a mischievous look before adding a last flourish to his invisible design. 'Those plans for the cathedral which you showed the Count: you still have them?'

Rollo nodded. Audemand had quite recovered his good humour.

'It still stands, then, does it? Your genius hasn't come up

with something entirely new? Your soul hasn't been entirely corrupted by building castles?'

Rollo waited until the Chancellor had finished enjoying himself.

'Good! Because it's the Count's wish that you build it. He woke me to tell me so — among other things — before he departed. A glorious cathedral.'

A sudden weariness overtook Rollo. More than a year ago he had worked on his plans for the new cathedral with all the excitement of a fresh life. On his very first meeting with the Count, Fulk had looked at them and then had ordered him to build castles. Not a word had been said about the cathedral since that day. Now the Count had departed like a thief in the night, and his Chancellor was telling him to build a glorious cathedral. Rollo knew himself to be the servant of whim.

'And the Bishop?' he asked.

Audemand's mouth made several extravagant movements in silence. Then he nodded.

'Indeed! You have hit on the obstacle, Rollo.' The Chancellor's eyes narrowed as if he were peering into the sun, and he made further silent movements of the lips.

'The Bishop,' he said, and sucked in noisily through his teeth. 'Well! The Count has left *us* to deal with the Bishop. As you can imagine, he had no wish to deal with him himself.'

'And how can one deal with the Bishop?' Rollo inquired.

'With difficulty.' Audemand's face had taken on that expression of diplomatic cunning that Rollo had seen many times. He waited for the old man to produce his solution.

'What you have to understand is this. The Count is in grave danger of excommunication — as you know. The Bishop detests him for having seized his father's lands. Hardly surprising, I have to admit.' The Chancellor's eyebrows rose sharply; then he blew out his cheeks so that his moustaches bristled. 'And now this tragedy of the Countess.

Undoubtedly he will be sending his report to Rome where Fulk is already none too well favoured on account of several – what shall I say? – irregularities. You, who were brought up within the Church, know what excommunication means. It can be the end. No authority. No rights. No friends.'

Audemand paused as if to allow Rollo to feel the full weight of what he was saying.

'On the other side,' he went on, 'Renaud is a proud man – proud on behalf of God, maybe, but proud none the less. His family is a more ancient one than the Count's. He will tell you that when the Count's ancestors were chopping trees and being bandits, his own ruled these parts, built churches, brought Christianity to the people – though I must say I don't always see much sign of it. But that's beside the point.'

The Chancellor was enjoying himself again.

'The point is that the Bishop is proud, and it's hard to feel proud in a cathedral that looks like a broken-down barn. He would dearly love a new one, and he cannot build it without Fulk. So . . . now do you begin to see?'

'What you are saying is that if I build Renaud a new cathedral he may temper his report to the Vatican.'

'Just so! How sharp your mind is, Rollo!' The Chancellor's eyes were crinkling again, and his lips twitching. 'The only problem is – will you and the Bishop see eye to eye on what is to be built? From what I recall, your ideas are very advanced. With respect to the noble Bishop, I would never describe him as a man of advanced ideas – at least not in matters of faith. Your cathedral – am I not correct? – was to be flooded with light. I seem to remember you telling Renaud how you believed that a church should enable men's spirits to rise up. I think you may encounter disagreement there. If I know the Bishop, he prefers men's spirits to be kept well down and quaking in fear. He may want a church that suits such a purpose.'

'He already has one,' Rollo answered sardonically.

The Chancellor merely smiled. Then he added, rising to leave:

'Well. The Count wants a new cathedral. The Bishop wants a new cathedral. You may just have to build what is required, and if it crushes your spirit, then leave your spirit out of it, as you did with the Count's castles. I can see that you're just as proud as the Bishop.' Audemand's face had a slightly taunting smile, and he tapped his staff as if to emphasize his point.

'One thing I can tell you, Rollo. The Count has already hinted at it to you: he intends to found a great monastery near Loches. His cousin Hildegarde has already chosen the site. The place is called Beaulieu. You should go and look at it – if, that is, your business should take you to Loches.' And the Chancellor chuckled. 'You will be the builder of it, and unlike the Bishop, Count Fulk thinks of himself as a man of the future. At Beaulieu you could show him the way. But if you'll take my advice, leave Angers down on its knees in the dark. We'll talk again.'

And with that Audemand departed, humming contentedly to himself.

It was exactly as the Chancellor had foreseen. A few days later Rollo managed to see the Bishop, and he unrolled the plans for the cathedral before him. Rollo said little, preferring to wait for Renaud to comment. He saw the Bishop's eyes tracing the line of the nave vaulting, and when they reached the very top, where the vaults crossed over and there was a dove embossed in stone at the highest point, he saw the Bishop frown heavily.

'Insolence,' he muttered, without looking up. 'An image of the Holy Spirit for men to gaze up at.' Then he turned fiercely to Rollo. 'The Holy Spirit cannot be seen; certainly it cannot be copied. That would be blasphemy.'

'The crucifixion is represented on churches, and that isn't blasphemy,' Rollo retorted. He could feel the Bishop freeze with anger.

'That, young man, is to remind us of man's great sin, for which we shall all be punished. You may be a fine builder, but it's clear you are entirely ignorant in theology.'

Rollo found it hard to conceal his own irritation.

'The cathedral of Chartres has a tympanum above the entrance showing Christ in Majesty, with the symbols of the four apostles all around. I've never heard it described as blasphemous, or as bad theology.'

The Bishop swept the plans for the cathedral on to the floor. He opened his mouth to speak, but no words came. He was shaking.

'This is *my* cathedral, young man; you shall build it as *I* want,' he said eventually. 'Show me a church that will humble a man.'

Rollo picked up his plans where they lay scattered, and took his leave. So, he must build a cathedral for the dark, he thought; a cathedral to humble a man – at the command of the least humble of men!

The winter settled – a gentle winter, to the relief of the inhabitants of Angers. A year ago they had starved; a few months ago their houses had burnt to the ground. Rebuilding had gone on apace, but there were still roofs to be finished, timber walls to be lined with wattle and river-mud, and there had been little time to collect fuel against another winter such as the last. But it remained mild right through till March, and by the time a late snow covered the city people were more or less ready; soon the young shoots would provide food for the animals, and the long evenings time to forage. A blessing had at last fallen on the city: it was because the Count was away, they said.

But no sooner had they said it than there were many who longed for the Count's return. The enemies of Anjou learnt of Fulk's absence, and as soon as winter passed began to profit from it. In the west, Conan and his sons mounted raids from Rennes and from Nantes. The smoke of burnt villages drifted across Anjou on the Atlantic winds. Pirate boats ventured up the Loire. Pillage, looting, rape, the slaughter of livestock, the murder of anyone not agile enough to flee: stories of horror and misery flooded into Angers. The High Constable, Sebrand de Chemillé, levied soldiers from the Count's vassals, and led counter-attacks and punitive raids into Breton territory; but the Bretons seemed to melt away like mist as if they knew already where the Angevins would attack. For Roger de Montrésor, Sulpice de Buzançais, Archambaud d'Amboise, Giraud Berlay, the sons of Audemand and for many other viscounts of Anjou it was a hard spring always on the move, and more often than not too late.

Moreover, as if by some magic signal, whenever the Angevin soldiers were drawn westwards towards Brittany, raids from Touraine broke out in the east. Gelduin of Saumur harassed the garrisons at Langeais and Montbazon, and plundered their lands. Geoffrey de St Aignan besieged Archambaud's castle at Amboise. Word reached Angers that the late Count of Blois' two eldest sons, the young Odo and his brother Tibalt, had returned from the king's court to Tours and were threatening terrible vengeance for their father's death.

For many people in Angers it was like the bad days again, before Fulk became a man; and they feared for their small state.

Worse news reached the castle. The late Countess's father, Bouchard the Venerable, had left Vendôme for Paris in his grief, filling the young King Robert's ears with accounts of his daughter's murder. The King's father, Hugh Capet, had been an ally of Anjou and an opponent of the Count of Blois: now the situation was reversed.

Worse still, word came to Angers that the late Count Odo's widow, Berthe, had married the King. Audemand knew the lady and shook his head gravely at the news.

'For the King to have taken her as his mistress was a shock. To have married her is a disaster!' he announced to Roger and Sulpice.

'Why on earth', muttered Roger, 'should the King of France choose to marry a widow with six children? Could it be, perhaps, that she is expecting a seventh?'

Audemand shook his head.

'That may be so. But if you knew Berthe, you might understand. She's a lady of extraordinary beauty and great intelligence. And by no means ancient as you might think. She was a mere girl when she married the Count of Blois. A dark goddess, she was, and I'm told she still is. As for the king, he's a good man, but soft.'

The three men stood in silence for a while by the fire in the great hall.

'How on earth can we fight them all?' asked Sulpice, more to himself than to Roger and Audemand. 'Brittany on one side; Touraine on the other; and now the King!'

The Chancellor breathed heavily and smoothed his white beard.

'One matter at a time, my friend.' And they noticed a gleam in Audemand's eye. 'On the question of the King's marriage there's something that can be done.'

The other two looked at him intently.

'You see,' he went on, 'Robert has been married before. It's talked about as little as possible, for good reason. She was an Italian princess, very much older than he, and she led him a dance, I understand. He was little more than a boy. Then he repudiated her. He obtained an annulment somehow. But Rome frowned; and when Rome frowns ... well, we know enough about that. This means that Robert cannot expect a sympathetic ear, which he is going to need when it's pointed out to the Pope that his mistress — I mean his wife — Berthe is in fact his cousin, which as you know is not permitted. At least, it's not permitted in kings: others may get away with it.'

Sulpice and Roger were listening with the closest attention.

'It would not go amiss, my friends,' the Chancellor continued, 'if His Holiness were to be informed of this family connection, do you not agree?'

Roger slapped his thigh vigorously, and his grin shone with broken teeth.

'But there's still more to it.' Audemand gazed upwards as if he saw there even more devious plans for the King's future misery. 'Robert may be King, but he's exceedingly poor. Berthe with her six children will bring him little: besides, her eldest, young Odo, is now Count of Blois and will be most unwilling to pay for his mother's lover, even if he *is* the King. So ... once the marriage is declared illegal Robert will need another wife. There's nothing to stop him continuing to enjoy the favours of the Lady Berthe, but he will need a queen who will bring him a fortune.'

The two men knew the Chancellor well enough to be certain that the long skein of Audemand's thoughts would lead to a promising candidate being named.

'It so happens that such a lady is available,' he went on. 'William, the Count of Toulouse, has only one child — a daughter, by good fortune. The Count is one of the wealthiest men in all France. His daughter Constance is said to be just as beautiful as Berthe, but of course a great deal richer.'

Smiles were spreading across the faces of Roger and Sulpice.

'But ... as much to the point is that the Lady Constance is a cousin, not of the King, but of Count Fulk!'

Sulpice clapped the Chancellor on the back, but Audemand held up his hand for a further audience.

'All this is long-term strategy. As it stands, we have to remember that the King is married to an enemy of Anjou, and it's this marriage which must first be pulled down. If that can be achieved, then the moment has arrived to present Constance as quite irresistible. You can be sure that the

Count of Toulouse would be happy to part with some of his wealth in exchange for his daughter being Queen of France. ... But one note of caution, my friends.' And the Chancellor's face again took on an expression of wry amusement. 'Heaven help us if the King should become acquainted too closely with the Lady Constance before he is committed to her in marriage. Beautiful and rich she may be, but those who have met her assure me that she is the most abominable and evil woman who ever lived.'

Spring blossomed in Anjou with some unexpected news that raised the spirits of all Angers. Sebrand had led a surprise attack on the soldiers of Gelduin, the lord of Saumur, who were encamped between the castles of Langeais and Montbazon. He had divided his own small force and struck from two flanks simultaneously. It was said that his own sword cut like a scythe through the enemy knights before they had a chance to strike back, and the Angevin horsemen following him wove a pattern of death through their bewildered ranks. The army of Saumur scattered in disarray while Gelduin stood helpless. He himself had the indignity of fleeing into the forest with a small body of knights — and the two Angevin garrisons were once again relieved.

This setback for the mighty Gelduin, whom even Fulk feared, was the first cause for celebration in the castle of Angers for many months. Though the shadow of the Countess's death still lay heavily over the court of Count Fulk, spirits managed to rise into laughter and feasting almost as if it were old times, and the absence of the Count himself removed from the rejoicing company the living presence of guilt.

The triumphant return of Sebrand coincided with the arrival at last of a messenger informing the High Constable of the return to Loches of the Lady Hildegarde. Her retreat in mourning for the Countess Elizabeth was at last ended.

Rollo's own long winter was over, and with his head full of the prospect of tomorrow's ride to Loches he joined in the feasting. Within a short time, he felt sure, Milesende would be in his arms.

But first he found himself having to evade the arms of the Lady Ermengarde. Waving a goblet in a manner which suggested it had been filled a great many times already that evening, the lady intercepted his return to his rooms like an amorous spider.

'Rollo! There you are! Drink from love's cup,' she chanted in a confusion of sounds that seemed to do battle with her tongue, and at the same time took a step forward which propelled the rest of her at him like a felled sapling.

He caught her, along with much of the wine, and as he did so her legs gave way altogether and her arms hooked themselves round his neck. She was singing wordlessly in between hiccups and plunging kisses which fixed on whatever area of his face they happened to encounter. Her breath was formidable and her saliva profuse. Rollo carried her in this fashion through her open door which he closed with his foot behind him, immediately wishing he had not done so because with a yell of delight Ermengarde announced to the four walls, and perhaps many walls beyond, that she was going to have the pleasure of a huge Viking and for once Adelaide was not present to pray for her soul.

'Adelaide!' she bawled. 'Adelaide! I'm about to sin most grievously!' Her words lurched and wound about each other as if they were leaves in a gale. Rollo stumbled through the darkness to where he imagined her bed to be and, locating it, pitched her on to it, struggling to disentangle her arms.

'Adelaide!' she roared. 'You'd love it, Adelaide, except you wouldn't know where to put it!' and her voice rose to a high-pitched shriek, mixed with gasps of laughter. Rollo, imagining that Adelaide might well appear at any second, and possibly the entire castle, wrenched himself free of

Ermengarde who slumped backwards with a muttering sound; and by the time he had reached the door he could hear only the burbling noises of sleep.

He passed the crepuscular figure of Father Baudouin and, behind him, the veiled shape of what Rollo imagined to be the nun who seemed to haunt the Chaplain in these corridors – on their way no doubt to some candlelit mumblings in the private chapel of the Count. Rollo looked the other way in disgust and the two shadows slithered past. Sounds from the dovecot below were rising in bursts of song and drunken laughter, and he could distinguish the familiar voices of Roger and Maurice until a wave of shouting drowned them in a confusion of noise.

Rollo closed his door and slept more peacefully than for many a month.

There was a glimmer of frost as he rode through the early-morning fields the next day, and the dark stumps of vines shone purple in the moist sunlight. The Loire ran swift and swollen, its current twisting among hidden sandbars and its surface milky with snow-water from the distant mountains. Debris battered against the boat as the four boatmen struggled to keep the craft from spinning out of control. Rollo had been compelled to pay heavily for them to take him across. They grumbled as they pocketed the silver, and Rollo's horse fretted with frightened eyes.

He took the long route southwards on the advice of Sebrand, keeping clear of Saumur and not risking the road through Langeais and Montbazon in case any of Gelduin's men still lingered there, prowling for revenge. He passed through Doué and Montreuil, and by midday he emerged from the dense oak forests around Chinon and followed the River Vienne to L'Ile Bouchard – through acres of further vineyards where peasants were sowing grain in the strips of newly hoed soil between the vines. Rollo paused at a tiny inn for an hour while his horse was fed and rested, and the innkeeper brought him a pitcher of pinkish wine which he drank thirstily in the sun while the villagers peered at him curiously. Some of them drew close and gazed at his eyes, then drew back whispering and pointing. He munched coarse black bread and strong goat's cheese, and the wine made him sleepy. He realized that it was Ermengarde's husband the Treasurer who was the lord of this place, and marvelled that there was any wine left here to be drunk. Perhaps they hid it in those limestone caves he had passed.

Rollo rode on through the cool afternoon. The Vienne flowed more gently than the Loire and he crossed it at a ford. As he did so he heard a faint swishing sound above him, and looking up Rollo saw the entire sky was streaked with birds in formation, like so many dark rivers in the firmament flowing northwards towards the sea – towards Normandy. The storks had returned for the spring, and Rollo remembered with a sweet sadness the birds that used to nest on the very church he had built at Jumièges, and how one year when a winter gale tore the nest down he had climbed the church-tower and erected a platform and tied the nest to it. The storks had nested as usual; perhaps it was even a pair out of these hundreds passing out of sight now above the vast forest. Rollo followed their flight until the last specks had vanished from the sky. Then he turned his horse eastwards.

Soon the oak forest became swamp; after a while the swamp in turn dried into heathland that was golden with gorse. Finally the castle of Loches stood before him emblazoned by the last of the sun. As Rollo approached, the sunlight on the massive walls gradually burnt out like a dying candle, rising and rising until only the highest stones still caught its rays. And then all was grey. He rode through the city gate under the tall tower of the Church of St Antoine whose deep bell was tolling the fall of night.

It was too late to seek an audience with the Lady Hildegarde, so Rollo sought out an inn where a fire warmed his tired body and a suckling pig sated his hunger. Tomorrow, he reflected with an excitement that he could scarcely contain, he would find Milesende after so many, many months. He would obtain a horse, lead it to wherever she was held, and take her away. Rollo's head was full of dreams, and as he slept his dreams were full of Milesende.

The Lady Hildegarde received him the next morning at once, and most graciously. She had heard much of him, she said, extending her hand softly; her cousin the Count had spoken of his gifts and of the debt Anjou owed to him. She herself had never visited Normandy, but she had been told by Abbot Gervais of the beauty of Jumièges, and that it was one of the wonders of Christendom: she was honoured to meet the man who created it, and how happy she was that Rollo had been ennobled in reward for his services to her dear cousin. She made no mention, Rollo noticed, of the late Countess, nor of her death and the long period of mourning she had herself undertaken; and he wondered whether she was being tactfully evasive, or whether – as it seemed from the dove-like calm of her manner – she had simply resolved in her mind to set the tragedy and her cousin's guilt behind her and lay the whole matter to rest.

Hildegarde was not beautiful, Rollo thought, but she had about her a composure that reminded him not a little of the late Countess. And, like the Countess, she was clearly an educated lady: she chose her words with the precision of someone accustomed to an environment of fine manners and the discussion of polite subjects. Rollo doubted, talking to her, whether the lady possessed the wit and sharp tongue of Elizabeth, but he felt sure that she was not one to be lost for a correct phrase: it was hard to imagine that feelings or tempers could ever be ruffled in her presence, or that her own temper was ever anything but smooth. She was, after all, as Rollo recalled, the daughter of the most polished of men, the Duke of Aquitaine.

'And to what do we owe this delightful visit, my lord

Rollo?' she asked once the rather extended politenesses had been concluded.

Rollo was taken aback — not by the question, but because no one had ever addressed him as 'my lord Rollo' before.

'I am anxious to inquire about the lady Milesende,' he replied. Hildegarde nodded, and her face told Rollo nothing. She waited for him to continue.

'I should like to take her back to Angers, my lady. We are' — Rollo was unsure what precisely he should say — 'to be married, with the approval of Count Fulk.'

Hildegarde's face retained the same serene smile: only the pause before she replied hinted that something might not be entirely in order.

'She is in my care, my lord Rollo,' she said with just a hint of firmness in her voice, 'entrusted to me by my cousin.' Rollo began to detect an intransigence within that calm, gentle manner, and his heart began to sink.

'My lady,' he went on, 'Milesende was as you know suspected of a certain conspiracy — unjustly as it turned out — and for that reason she was removed from Angers by the Count, as I understand. I wasn't there myself. But that suspicion is no longer laid on her: she's of course entirely innocent.'

'I understand that,' replied Hildegarde in a quiet voice. Again she waited for Rollo to go on.

'Then she can surely be released.' Rollo was aware that his own voice was becoming hard, and that Hildegarde was conscious of it. Her own face still registered no change of expression, but her eyes appeared sharper. He noticed that they were iron grey.

'I'm afraid that is something I cannot do,' she went on. 'Innocent as a lamb she may be: that is not for me to decide; nor was I ever concerned with her guilt. My cousin entrusted her to my care, and only my cousin can relieve me of that trust.'

There was an air of such finality about her verdict that

Rollo was left with nothing he could say. Worse, he could see that Hildegarde's stance was entirely reasonable — at least, it was reasonable for someone as impeccably correct as the lady, and as devoted to her cousin as she clearly was. What Rollo could not say to her was how grossly inhuman her correctness was, and at what tiny cost to her own propriety would be the simple decision to use her own discretion in the matter. Could the lady not appreciate that the Count, when he had entrusted Milesende to her, had been in a state of jealous revenge of short duration, and furthermore that he had had no thought at the time of departing for months — maybe years?

Why could he not say these things? The Lady Hildegarde continued to look at him in a firm and kindly way that somehow precluded all further argument. She had the inflexible strength of someone who was certain she was right. Rollo himself knew that he was in the weak position of believing he was both right and wrong.

'I hope you will visit me again,' she said extending her hand towards him. He kissed it, and hated himself for doing so.

The gracious smile accompanied him to the door, and he departed with a numb, blind fury rising within him. It was hard to believe that such a slender door had just been shut in his face, and he had not even been able to lean against it.

Rollo returned to Angers in a black mood. Without seeing anyone he set off the following morning for the stone-mason's yard which he had established beside the cathedral and where he had been working daily most of the winter. Frustration, disappointment and despair overwhelmed him. But at least it was some relief to return to his craft, to be using his hands and his eyes instead of the swordplay of words. Crouched here over blocks of stone he could feel himself coming back to life, and the duality of his existence began to seem more than ever ridiculous to him. What other viscount — possessing castles he had never visited and titles that had nothing to do with him — had ever sat in a mason's yard chipping blocks of stone with tools which he had designed and made himself? What other orphan brought up in a monastery stoneyard had become a nobleman in a foreign court?

He looked up and to his surprise he saw Sebrand standing only a few paces away.

'I thought I would spy on the master at work,' he said with a bright smile. 'At least you're not swinging from trees.'

Then Sebrand noticed Rollo's dour expression and enquired about the visit to Loches. Rollo told him the story.

'Sanctimonious bitch!' Sebrand exclaimed when Rollo had finished. 'Hildegarde is one of those women who are all virginity. She thinks Fulk is God the Father while she waits trembling for his favours — like Adelaide, only rather more ladylike and cunning. I bet you all those months she spent in mourning for the Countess she was on her knees praying that she might replace her.'

Rollo looked at him, surprised.

'You mean that?'

'Of course I do! She's always loved Fulk. That's why she's never married. The Countess's death is her great chance. She might have willed it. You wait! The moment the Count returns, she'll be here, being gracious and attentive with that sweet smile of hers. She may be his cousin, but she's only a distant cousin, and with her wealth and influence that distance will soon be made wide enough to marry him.'

'Will she succeed, do you think?'

'Who knows? The daughter of the Duke of Aquitaine would do Fulk no harm, if the Duke can be persuaded to agree. We'll have to see. My God! It would be like having a Mother Superior as Countess.'

Sebrand's eyes turned to the stone Rollo had been carving.

'And what are those?'

Rollo brushed the stone-dust off the block beside him.

'Beaks! To go round the door of the cathedral.'

'Why beaks? To peck at the Bishop as he enters?'

Rollo laughed.

'It's a Norman design. An arch of beaks. I used them at Jumièges. I admit I'm using them here because Renaud, if he knew they were Norman, would loathe them. He thinks all Normans are barbarians, especially me. But he won't know because he doesn't know anything that's ever happened outside Angers.'

'And those?' Sebrand was pointing to some small blocks of stone with the outlines of faces roughly drawn on the surface.

'Ah, well!' Rollo hesitated. 'They're my secret. But I'll tell you so long as you keep it to yourself.' He smoothed his hand over one of the blocks. 'You see, churches in Normandy sometimes have faces high up on the outside of the wall, just under the eaves. It used to be said at Jumièges that they were grotesque because it was like warding off the Devil – keeping him from entering the church. But stone-masons now give them the faces of local people, just for fun. And so I thought . . .'

But Sebrand was beginning to laugh.

'So you thought you would amuse yourself in a place where no one but you would ever know. I like it, Rollo! Show me! Who's this going to be?' And he pointed to a face with staring wild eyes and a mouth turned down like a hound's, but the ears of a pig.

'I don't think the Bishop will recognize himself, do you?' said Rollo, picking up a piece of charcoal and adding a few lines of emphasis to the frown.

Sebrand, hands on hips, was chuckling with pleasure.

'Wonderful, Rollo! And the others?' And he bent down to peer at the head of a nun, with eyes raised and mouth wide open like an idiot. 'Don't tell me! Adelaide! . . . And what about him?' Sebrand pointed towards the face of an old man with resplendent moustaches and the most knowing of grins splitting his entire face. 'Obviously Audemand! ... And what about me? Can I be on the cathedral too, with my sword – or perhaps my prick? And Hersende! You must have Hersende. Two enormous breasts with a face above them.' And he roared with laughter.

'I thought you were supposed to be in love with the girl?' Rollo asked, looking up at Sebrand.

'Ah! But you did say that no one could see these things. So it would be a very private joke. And she does have the most enormous breasts, Rollo. I rather like the idea of them pointing out over the city for ever. Perhaps I'll tell her one day when we're making love.'

'She might insist on posing for me, you know, and how would you feel about that? If you're prepared to share them with the entire city then you can surely share them with me.'

'Not necessary, Rollo. Not for a man with your imagination. Besides, I remember you once thought you loved Hersende. Peering at her breasts might rekindle it. Or at least rekindle your lust. Talking of which' – and Sebrand's eyes widened – 'where's Ermengarde? You can't leave her out.'

Rollo smiled and picked up another piece of charcoal.

'And what part of her anatomy would you choose for the cathedral, Sebrand?'

The two men burst out laughing while Rollo drew on a stone an intimate detail of Ermengarde's body.

'That's also from my imagination, by the way,' he added, 'though there must be plenty of men who could verify if it's correct.'

The appearance of one of the junior masons ended the frivolity. Rollo dipped a rag in a nearby bucket of water and wiped away Ermengarde's anatomy.

'There's my artistic genius gone for ever,' Rollo said with a sigh as he rose to his feet. And the two men walked away from the stoneyard in the direction of the castle.

Rollo's heart felt less weighted after the joviality of his

meeting with Sebrand. He had waited six months for Milesende: he was becoming resigned to waiting a few more. It was Audemand's view that the Count would return during the summer. How Audemand knew Rollo had no idea, and neither did Sebrand when he asked him, but both men agreed that the old Chancellor seemed to have access to all kinds of information about the world without ever stepping outside the walls of Angers, and in an uncanny way he was generally proved right. The inflexibility of Hildegarde was infuriating, but it was a sentence of only a few more months. As they walked through the rebuilt alleys of the city Rollo described to Sebrand how Hildegarde had addressed him as '*my lord* Rollo', and how uncomfortable that made him feel. It seemed entirely unreal to him, he explained, to be a lord of a place he had never visited, and to be considered wealthy without ever having seen any signs of his wealth.

'Let me tell you, Rollo,' Sebrand answered. 'The truth of the matter is this, at least according to Audemand who knows the Count's mind better than anyone. It's perfectly true', he went on, 'that Fulk felt a deep gratitude to you and was determined to reward you. It's one of Fulk's virtues — one of his few virtues — that he's generous towards men who are loyal to him, though not, alas, towards women. A nobleman you are, and there are lands that are yours: but *which* lands is another matter.'

Rollo looked at him, puzzled. Sebrand went on.

'It seems that a cousin of the late Viscount Bernard was pressing Fulk to award him Bernard's titles and lands, and that legally he had a strong claim. But the man was a vassal of the Count of Maine, and there's nothing Fulk dislikes more than to lose control of a territory — especially a territory so vulnerable to attack by Brittany. Do you begin to understand?'

Rollo felt that he had heard this kind of devious tale many times before.

'So – the Count needed someone to whom he could award Bernard's titles: someone loyal, and who would not be entirely outraged if he later removed those titles. Let's say that Fulk *lent* them to you for safekeeping. In Audemand's view, the Count will offer you something in compensation, so that you will still be one of us – and you will have lands and wealth – but you will not be expected to administer great territories, command castles, raise armies, and all that. Does this offend you, Rollo?'

'Far from it. I feel relieved,' Rollo replied. 'The Count chose his man well. I am, after all, a builder, Sebrand, not a soldier.'

'Then I'm relieved too. There have been enough crimes and insults committed by the Count already. Heaven forbid that he should have committed another against so honourable a man as you – who are also so good a friend.'

And he embraced Rollo. The two men entered the castle gates and went their separate ways.

There was still no news of Count Fulk.

It was almost summer. Sebrand had led another successful attack – this time on a party of Breton soldiers who had advanced up the Loire from Nantes and seized the town of Champtoceaux. Together with Roger de Montrésor and Giraud Berlay, Sebrand led a mere two hundred men by night, circumventing the town so that at dawn they approached the gates from the west. They waited in hiding until the night guard was being replaced, and the gates were open to allow a fresh group of Breton soldiers to take up their positions. Being the flank from which no attack was expected, the Bretons were casual and in no hurry to close the gates. Roger, Giraud and Sebrand rode straight at them, followed by twenty other knights. Roger killed the captain of the guard with a single blow, and the knights forced their way into the town. The Bretons panicked, and the Angevin foot-soldiers slaughtered them as they tried to flee. It was all over in a matter of minutes.

Hersende watched Sebrand's return from the castle walls. The early sun glowed on his bright armour and she all but fainted with love. Next to her, the Lady Adelaide watched as her own husband, Roger, rode through the city gates behind Sebrand, and she shivered.

As Hersende fled to greet her lover, Adelaide turned to the Lady Ermengarde — whom Hersende had persuaded to watch the triumphant return — and placed a hand through her arm. This, the closest that Adelaide ever came to intimacy, Ermengarde knew to mean that some corrective observation was imminent.

'That girl is shameless,' she said. 'Her manner, her dress, everything about her provokes.'

Ermengarde forbore to say that with Hersende's shape it would be hard for a dress not to provoke: her eyes took in the unrelieved flatness of Adelaide, and she tried to imagine any garment short of one bolstered by two turnips in which the lady might be considered provocative.

'At least', Adelaide continued, 'it's a relief that the younger sister is safe in that convent with such pious sisters. To have the spectacle of two wantons at large would be more revolting than I could bear.'

Ermengarde looked at her incredulously.

'You mean . . . you know where the girl Milesende is being kept?' she asked, her voice strident with accusation.

Adelaide's face was suddenly even paler than normal, and she stuttered a few meaningless syllables. Then she turned away to descend the stone staircase. Ermengarde grabbed her arm.

'You know where Milesende is!' she repeated loudly. Adelaide's mouth became thin and she turned away again towards the staircase. Ermengarde pulled at her arm roughly so that she was jerked off balance against the wall.

'And you've known all the time! More than six months!'

Ermengarde's face was taut with anger. 'Where is she?' Adelaide's eyes were still lowered. 'Where is she?' she screamed. Adelaide shook her head in feeble defiance.

'I can't . . . I can't tell you,' she murmured. 'I owe it to the Lady Hildegarde not to say.'

'You little monster! I always believed you had a warm heart underneath all that primness and piety. But you're heartless.' And Ermengarde's other hand slapped Adelaide hard across the cheek. 'You worm!'

Adelaide was shielding her face with her arms, and her eyes were moist with tears. Then she raised her head, and her frightened little face glared at Ermengarde.

'I promised! Don't you see, I promised!' Her voice was sharp and quavering, and her cheek was red where Ermengarde had struck her. She rubbed it with her hand and gazed at Ermengarde.

'Not everyone in this place betrays a trust,' she added in a sulky voice. Ermengarde's hand struck her again.

'How dare you!' she screamed at Adelaide, her hands clawing the air in fury. 'How dare you talk about betraying a trust!'

Suddenly Ermengarde's voice became controlled and low.

'You grovelling hypocrite!' she said icily. 'You betrayed the Countess and she died for it!' A look of horror came over Adelaide's face and she burst into tears. 'You just can't bear any other woman to have what you can't have. You're poisoned with jealousy, and you call it virtue.' And Ermengarde pushed her way past the weeping Adelaide and hurried down the stairway into the castle.

'It's not true! It's not!' She heard the defiant sobs of the Lady Adelaide grow fainter as she hurried away quivering with anger.

The sounds of Ermengarde's outburst met some astonished ears, and before very long there were few people in the castle who were unaware that something dramatic had taken place that morning. Fulk's court passed the even-

367

ing celebrating the return of Sebrand, Roger and Giraud; but under the raucous sounds of welcome as many people were engaged in discussing the battle between the two ladies as there were discussing the battle against the Bretons. Only Rollo, who had worked early and late in the stoneyard and knew nothing of either battle, remained ignorant of the fact that the Lady Adelaide was concealing the whereabouts of the lady he loved.

Sebrand himself was too tired to seek out the Norman that evening. Hersende tended a very small wound in her lover's leg with a devotion worthy of Andromache lamenting the corpse of Hector. Roger ignored his wife Adelaide even more scornfully than usual, and later the sounds from the dovecot matched the celebrations of victory in the hall.

The following morning Sebrand went to seek out Rollo with the news about Adelaide, and to share with him his excitement over the battle at Champtoceaux. But his rooms were empty. Neither was he at the stoneyard. Rollo had in fact risen early and ridden over to the quarry some half-hour's distance from the city. Sebrand returned to the castle, and later that day was observed emerging with Roger from Adelaide's rooms, after which the two men talked for some time with dour looks on their faces before making their way to the great hall. Here, it was said, they sat consuming large quantities of wine. They were last seen rolling drunk and battering on Adelaide's door demanding to be let in.

It was the next day before anyone saw Rollo. Sebrand found him standing with — of all people — Bishop Renaud. They were in the stoneyard close to where he and the Norman had been talking some weeks earlier. Sebrand noticed with amusement that the pile of carved stones, which had grown considerably since that day, was now carefully covered with layers of sacking. He smiled, and waited at a discreet distance while the Bishop and mason remained deep in discussion. Finally the Bishop turned from Rollo with a proud nod of the head and made his way to where a low foundation of pale-grey stone was all that marked the rebirth of his cathedral. Renaud looked about him thoughtfully, peered closely here and there, and departed.

'Rollo!' Sebrand called out. 'I have news for you.' The two men embraced warmly, and Rollo looked at his friend expectantly.

Sebrand told him of the storming of Champtoceaux and Rollo shook his hand vigorously. He listened to his friend's account of the battle, full of admiration and respect. He felt his own life to be mercifully calm by comparison. Sebrand could have died in the brief time since he last saw him, Rollo pondered, while all he had done was carve a few lumps of stone.

'But that's not all, Rollo,' Sebrand went on, and his face brightened as he spoke. 'I know where Milesende is held.'

Rollo was speechless for a moment. Then he threw his arms round Sebrand, lifting him off his feet in excitement.

'Where?'

'Stay calm, for heaven's sake! Having survived the Bretons I don't want to be crushed to death by a Norman! She's in the convent of Genillé, which is in the forest of Loches, near Montrésor. So as it happens she's in Roger's domain, and not Hildegarde's, which is fortunate. You have Roger's permission to free her – I've spoken to him.'

Rollo could hardly believe his ears. He thanked Sebrand again and again.

'But tell me,' he asked eventually. 'How on earth did you find out? Who told you?'

Sebrand became hesitant suddenly.

'I'm not going to tell anybody that,' he said, looking away rather uneasily towards where the pile of carved stone lay covered in sacking. 'Let me just say that I was extremely drunk, and that you owe it to Roger.'

Rollo felt bewildered and overjoyed.

'But you can tell me who knew, surely. Presumably if Roger found out, then he found out from Adelaide,' he added. 'Yet Adelaide swore to me months ago that she had no part in it.'

'Well, she did,' said Sebrand quietly. 'It was Ermengarde who discovered that.'

Then Sebrand became more at ease as he related the quarrel between Ermengarde and Adelaide – which took place, he explained, at the very moment when he was riding back into the castle expecting to be embraced by the loveliest ladies of the court for his bravery, instead of which they were much more interested in the fact that Ermengarde had struck Adelaide on the cheek. Sebrand laughed. The substance of the quarrel, he went on more earnestly, was that Adelaide let slip that she had known all along where Hildegarde had hidden Milesende, but refused to say where it was.

'And Roger got it out of her. With a little help from you – and a good deal of wine.'

Sebrand nodded. Then his mouth puckered.

'I feel rather ashamed,' he said, avoiding Rollo's gaze. 'It's not that I did anything; but ... I was there, and I was very drunk. Roger even more so. Adelaide, as you can imagine, not at all.' He paused, still looking around him rather wistfully. It was obvious that Sebrand longed to talk about it but could not bring himself to do so.

'I can tell you one thing,' he said. 'Adelaide can be quite beautiful. You'd be surprised.' There was another pause. 'I think if Roger hadn't always been quite such a brute,' he went on, 'she might not be as she is.'

The two men walked away from the stoneyard in silence. The noises of a street-market echoed around them.

'I'm sorry,' said Rollo after a while. He laid a hand affectionately on the Angevin's shoulder. 'You've been made ashamed for my sake. Whatever happened, I am grateful to you – deeply grateful.'

Sebrand smiled.

'Well,' he said with a sigh. 'Maybe we shouldn't lose sight

of certain things.' And he looked at Rollo with those sharp dark eyes. 'You've been made to suffer unbearably and quite unjustly. You came close to losing your life, and you've been deprived of the woman you love. If it hadn't been for the Lady Adelaide neither of those things might have happened. And the Countess might still be alive. So, don't feel too sorry for her – or for me.' He paused. 'There are jokes that go sour, that's all,' he added.

Then, with the warmest of smiles he went his way. Rollo was left with the deepest affection for the young Angevin. There were few men of his mettle he had ever met. Thanks to Sebrand he could now prepare for the journey he had begun to fear he might never make. It was as if his life were truly about to begin again.

ELEVEN

IT WARMED INTO A SUMMER in which men and women felt themselves to be blessed. While the days were still lengthening, a gentle rain sweetened the meadows and the forests. Never had the markets been so laden with produce, nor the animals so fat. And then, as if by divine command, from the day of midsummer the clouds were banished and the moist earth burgeoned. Each day the sun rose in mother-of-pearl and set in sapphire; at midday from horizon to horizon the sky rested like a polished canopy over the land. Between the hills of Maine and the swamplands of Aquitaine, Anjou was a jewel of green bound by the silver Loire.

And there was peace. People could not remember when there had ever been such peace.

In the burnished heat of that high summer, Count Fulk was returning. From Cyprus, to Rhodes, to Crete, Sicily, then up the western shore of Italy and along the Ligurian coast heading for Marseille, a small merchant vessel would be seen entering harbour with a strange cargo that brought people from their houses to gather on the quay and whisper, wonder and point in amazement. An enormously tall, emaciated man in foreign clothing would step ashore; and behind him carrying sea-chests would follow three men almost as tall as he – but blue-black like the night sky. The ghost-thin man wore a heavy, straight sword which he would lay before him on the ground as a gesture of peace, and bow low. He would then wait until word of his arrival had reached caliph, prince, governor or bishop; and before long the curious procession would pass along dusty streets and disappear within gates held open by wide-eyed guards.

The Count of Anjou — the words ran through the town, eyebrows were raised; 'Count' they understood — their visitor was an important figure — but 'Anjou'! What could such a place be where the leader was so tall, and the servants and slaves the colour of night? And those huge sea-chests — what did they contain? Rumour spread that they held treasures from the far end of the world, from the east, beyond the desert, from where camels brought spices and silks and jewels deep-red as wine. But a count — a prince — travelling from so far, with so small a retinue! From the look of him, people said he had escaped some battle: but then — those laden chests! Count Fulk left mystery and many tales behind him during those months of burning summer heat as the ship moved from port to port.

Fulk knew that he was fortunate to be alive. None of the rigours of his past life — battles, wounds, combats of strength — had prepared him for such a sustained trial of his own body and his own will. That he had survived could, he felt, only be because divine power had intervened to protect him, or perhaps had preserved him in this world so that he might endure yet further trials to come.

The story Fulk carried with him to tell was this.

On the outward journey he and his two companions had chartered a ship at Marseille to take them as far as the coast of Asia Minor: the ship's captain was fearful of the savage Moslems and would agree to convey them no further. After a week at sea the ship encountered a tempest so severe that they were compelled to furl all sails and drift at the whim of the gale. All night they feared for their lives, and at dawn found themselves being swept towards a rocky coast close to a village set high on a promontory above the crashing sea. They were helpless: the white spume and the thunder of the rocks drew closer. The seamen tried to row into the shelter of a bay, but the oars snapped like twigs. They ran up a small sail aft, part-reefed, and it tore as if by the wind's fingers. Then, in what they believed to be their last minutes on earth a stormy sun peered above the promontory, and as the waves lifted the ship and held it there before hurling it on the rocks they saw a beam of sunlight strike the white flank of a chapel high above them. They prayed in this final moment before their death, and as they did so the giant wave spun the ship round and round through a curtain of white spray. Clinging to the timbers they waited for the dreadful tearing of the rocks and the sucking of the water; but none came, and the ship skidded along the back of the wave like a smooth shell fixed to its surface, on and on, until before them a beach seemed to rise out of the wrath of the sea and catch them from the water. And as the giant wave was sucked back into the ocean the ship lay quite still on the shingle. Above them rose the high cliff and the small white chapel in the sun.

They blinked as if unsure whether they were truly in this world. They touched the timbers, and they were real. The sun began to warm their drenched bodies, and as it rose higher the gale softened into a mere wind, and then a breeze. All was peace again.

As soon as they recovered their senses Count Fulk insisted on climbing the promontory alone to the village perched above. Entering quite unarmed he found the villagers gathered to greet the man who had come out of the storm unscathed. They spoke a language he could not understand, but they led him to the priest and the two men knelt in prayer together in the church while the villagers gathered round whispering and pointing at their huge visitor, his clothes and beard streaked with salt, and his eyes like black torches fixed upon the altar.

Then Fulk placed his hand on the priest's arm and led him to where the little chapel could be seen clearly in the sunlight on the nearby cliff-top. Below the cliff they could see the ship, safely beached amid the grey foam of the storm. The priest cast his eyes from the one to the other, from the ship to the chapel, and once again to the ship; then he nodded as i

he understood. 'San Nicolo,' he said. 'San Nicolo di Myra.'
And with his hands the priest indicated the storm and the
little ship, and with his eyes he spoke of a blessing from
Heaven. 'San Nicolo,' he said again, and crossed himself.

Fulk turned to face the village church, and with a cere-
monious gesture placed into the priest's hand a jewelled
cross which he had carried with him from the ship. The
priest's eyes widened in disbelief and a gasp rose from the
crowd gathered round them. Then the Count bowed, kissed
the priest's hand, and departed the way he had come.

The sea had calmed, and they continued on their voyage.
As the ship pulled away from that rocky shore Count Fulk
gazed back at the chapel shrinking into a white dot on the
headland, and he vowed that if he returned safely to Anjou
he would found a religious house at the same distance from
Angers as that tiny chapel was from the village – and he
would dedicate it to Nicholas of Myra, the saint of sailors.

After a further month they reached the coast of Asia
Minor. Winter was setting in, and the chill winds from the
mountains buffeted the three men as their mules picked a
light-footed path through olive groves and the stony fields.
They bought furs and wrapped them to their bodies as they
rode eastwards; and on their right the sea lay sometimes
blue as lapis, sometimes dark as thunder.

At Antioch they rested. It was a city of many languages
and many costumes. Familiar words could be heard in the
jostling streets, and eyes met eyes searching for compatriots
among the bustle of merchants and soldiers, moneylenders
and adventurers, custodians and cut-throats. There were
Frenchmen in the crowded taverns, and the talk was all of
the Caliph. It was Hakem who had seized their possessions
and their lands to the south, and they had fled north carrying
what they could rescue from the fury of the Moslems. He
should go no further, they warned Fulk: death carried a
curved sword in Palestine.

The Count waited and watched. There were Frenchmen

here who spoke Arabic, he noticed; men who moved with slippery ease from the company of their compatriots bemoaning their lost lands to the Arab souks where the air was perfumed with spices, and ivory dice rattled on the tables. They were the in-between men who shifted with the winds of politics, and fanned their own small fires by knowing where to build them. These were the ones he would need, Fulk perceived, if he were ever to get to Jerusalem — and back again alive. These were the ones he would have to pay. He approached a group of them alone at dusk, and they looked him over with cold eyes. Then they glanced at one another in silence. Fulk waited, and they waited. Quietly he laid some gold on the table. They looked at each other again, and back at him — more sharply this time. Fulk put the gold away and rose to leave. A hand on his arm dissuaded him, and one of the men nodded. What did the foreigner want? Fulk told him. There was another silence before the man raised his head towards an elderly Arab on the far side of the room who seemed to have been waiting for such a signal. He came over and words were exchanged that Fulk could not understand. Then, in French, the man said to him — Yes, the Arab would supply twenty men to escort him to Jerusalem. And he named a sum — an enormous sum. Fulk said he would see the men first, and would pay according to how much he liked them — half now, and half on their safe return to Antioch. He would see them here the next morning, and they were to bring their weapons so that he could test their skill, one by one.

The man looked at Fulk hard; then he looked at his sword, and at his purse. His companions had melted away and the three of them were alone — Fulk, the Arab and the in-between man. The Count laid some gold pieces on the table for the second time, and nodded towards the Frenchman. 'A token of trust,' he said. And with the same hand he grasped a pewter goblet, raised it before him, and slowly crushed it like a dead leaf. The eyes of the two men widened.

Fulk gazed at them impassively, and smiled. 'If trust should be broken,' was all he said. And he rose, laying the remains of the goblet among the gold pieces on the table. Then he departed without glancing back.

Two weeks later, in early February of the year 998, Count Fulk with his companions and their escort of twenty rode over the last hill and came in sight of the city of Jerusalem. Fulk was seen to weep with joy: he dismounted and fell on his knees. He rubbed dust in his clothes and in his hair, and he prayed aloud.

Slowly the party descended towards the great walls of David's city. But as they approached the northern gate the Arab guard barred their progress and the gates were bolted in their faces. Fulk's escort tried to bargain with the Moslem soldiers, but they were adamant. The Caliph's orders, it was explained to Fulk, were that no Christian might enter the city. The leading escort made discreet gestures to the Count with his eyes and his fingers, suggesting that money – much money – could perhaps melt Hakem's resolve; and at this stage Fulk called one of his companions to unpack the magnificent Koran from Cordoba which he had been keeping for such a moment. He turned the pages slowly in front of the guard, whose eyes grew round with astonishment. One of them pointed at the Arabic script, and his lips moved. Then Fulk closed it again, handed it back to the companion, and to each of the Moslem soldiers he presented a silver amulet, showing them that it was no less fine than the one he wore himself. They took the amulets very cautiously and turned them over in the palms of their hands, until one of them found the courage to slip his over his wrist, twisting his arm this way and that in wonder. In a gingerly fashion the others followed suit, staring at each other and at Fulk alternately. He gazed at them gravely, and then, taking the Koran from his companion, he tapped it with his hand and spoke the Caliph's name – 'Hakem! Hakem!' The soldiers whispered amongst themselves, and three of them unbolted the huge gate and disappeared inside.

Fulk and his party waited for several hours until once more the gate was opened and a group of men in white robes stood staring at the Count. Fulk bowed and very slowly advanced towards them. As he did so he began to unbuckle his heavy sword-belt. He laid the belt and the sword at their feet and bowed again before turning to his companion and asking for the Koran. Fulk held it out before him and again spoke the Caliph's name – 'Hakem! Hakem!' The men nodded, took the Koran and indicated to Fulk that he should follow them, first pointing to the sword and gesturing to Fulk that he might bring it with him in his hands. The party entered the Holy City.

One week the Count remained in Jerusalem as the guest of the Caliph. Every courtesy was shown him: water to wash, new clothing, fragrant meats and fruit to eat, servants to attend him. But the Caliph himself never appeared. Instead, a young man of extraordinary beauty stood one morning at the entrance of the Count's chamber. By this time Fulk had decided that he was certainly a prisoner here: each time he walked out into the courtyard he saw soldiers gazing at him balefully, their hands resting on the hilts of their swords. His own sword had been removed. He was entirely at the Caliph's mercy, but the powerlessness of his situation made him feel curiously at ease. And now this young man stood before him. He was unarmed, and dressed in a simple pale garment that seemed to be wound about him. The man bowed; then to Fulk's astonishment he spoke – falteringly – in his own language. Hakem, he said, accepted with gratitude the gift of the Koran. The Caliph was indisposed, the young man explained: he was his son, and was at the visitor's service. What, he asked politely, was the purpose of his visit? The Caliph admired his courage in venturing so far with so small a retinue. And what, the son inquired almost apologetically, should he inform his father was the name and title of the visitor who had brought so

378

handsome a gift? And was he himself, perhaps, a Moslem?

Fulk explained the reason for his journey — often repeating his words when he saw the young man's brow begin to furrow. He had come in peace, he said, and in penitence. As a Christian he wished more than anything in his life to visit the Holy Sepulchre of the Lord Jesus and to do so in humility and in reverence.

The young man gazed at Fulk for some time; then he smiled, and slowly nodded. He understood, he said. He would ask his father, and return as soon as he had obtained an answer. And he departed with a bow.

On the following day a scene took place such as no one in that city had ever witnessed. As a chill wind swept the narrow streets of people a strange procession made its way towards the holy tomb. Astonished faces peering out of doorways and slatted windows saw a huge man who was naked except for a loin-cloth and bound on a hurdle. With him were two companions. One had a rope coiled round his shoulders like a halter, and he was dragging the hurdle behind him along the dusty streets. All the time, the second companion was walking alongside beating the bound man across his bare torso with a switch. Streaks of blood marked the man's body as the switch rose and fell, rose and fell. But he made no cry, only the occasional moan as those huge shoulders tensed under the pain of the lash. Crowds began to gather behind the group of men, following them as they passed slowly through the city. Then, as they reached the Church of the Holy Sepulchre, the bound man cried out; and those few who understood the language he uttered heard him call — 'Oh Lord, have mercy on treacherous and false Fulk. Jesus, Jesus, pardon my entreating soul!'

His companions unbound him at the door of the Church and he rose proudly to his feet. His chest and shoulders were raw and bleeding. But he seemed not to notice the pain. He stood there like a king, taller than any man they had ever seen. Who was he? they whispered. A prince of enormous wealth from far away, it was understood. The story of the magnificent Koran, and of the silver amulets, had spread through the city like a legend. People pressed around him, water was brought to bathe his wounds. Then, to their amazement, the son of the Caliph himself appeared carrying fresh clothing, and oils for his tortured body. The young man bowed as if he were the stranger's own servant, and with his own hands gently wiped the blood from the prince's body. Dressed in white robes, the stranger then embraced the Caliph's son and kissed him on both cheeks, and together they entered the Church of the Holy Sepulchre. The crowd pressed around the entrance, not daring to enter, but those in front could see the tall visitor fall on his knees by the tomb, and lower his head until it touched the stone slab. They said he was weeping.

Two days longer the stranger remained in the city, and several times he returned to the Church to pray. Always the Caliph's son accompanied him, as if devoted. On the last occasion the foreigner was seen to emerge carrying a piece of stone, which he gave to one of his companions very carefully. Then the Caliph's son led him to a house which, it was said, was lived in by a Christian monk who had remained in Jerusalem after his compatriots had fled; and eventually the group of men emerged carrying a small box which they took back with them to the Caliph's palace. No more was seen of them after that, until the stranger departed with his escort of Moslem soldiers in the earliest light. The city gates opened for them, and the Caliph's son embraced the stranger like a brother. People saw the tall prince offer something to the young man, and they swore it was a huge red jewel on a golden chain. Then the strange procession made its way across the stony hills among the olive trees in the direction of the sea.

They made for the port of Sidon. The Caliph's son had sent an envoy to accompany the Count, and to arrange a ship that would take him westwards in safety. At Sidon

Fulk paid off his escort, and the three men boarded a Phoenician ship that was making for Alexandria. From there, the envoy assured them, merchant ships could be found carrying spices and ivory to the ports of Cyprus, Italy and North Africa. Then as soon as the wind was fair they set sail: to their left a winter sun coloured the receding hills of Palestine.

Fulk's own cargo was modest. He brought with him a small iron box: in it lay a fragment of the True Cross, wrapped in silk – it had been offered to the Count by a monk who had asked a price appropriate to so holy a relic. Next to it were several decayed pieces of thong which the same monk had been able to reveal were those that had bound Our Lord's hands at the Flagellation. Then there was a somewhat larger container – this time of wood. Inside was a piece of stone that appeared no more remarkable to the ignorant eye than the thongs and the fragment of wood: yet this slab was from the stone of the Holy Sepulchre itself. Fulk's companions vouched that it broke on the impact of the Count's tears as he kissed the sacred tomb. Only some years later was it learnt that after Fulk's departure the Caliph Hakem had destroyed the Church of the Holy Sepulchre entirely. Some said it was in the zeal of his fanaticism, others that it was in fury at the respect and devotion shown by his own son towards a penitent French count whose humility had turned the young man's heart towards Christ.

In Alexandria, Fulk found no difficulty – as the envoy had predicted – in securing the services of a ship's captain who was trading silks, spices, jewels and ivory to Italy. But on the day before the ship was due to sail a fever struck the Count. He lay in a pool of his own sweat for several weeks in a humble inn, tended only by his faithful companions. Then, one after the other, they too succumbed to the illness. They could not eat, only sweat and groan and cry for water. The innkeeper left pitchers outside the door, fearful of entering: ten more days passed before the Count's own delirium lifted sufficiently for him to be able to drag his emaciated body out and seek help. The two companions died on the same day, and Fulk spent a further month in the house of a Coptic merchant who tended him lovingly and was handsomely rewarded for his care. The Copt procured him another vessel that was sailing to Cyprus, and thence to Rhodes and Crete. The merchant also purchased for him three slaves from Nubia, all of them men of huge stature and physical strength. Between them they carried the Count — little more than a skeleton — to the ship, along with his possessions and precious relics.

By the time the ship reached Rhodes, Fulk was able to walk and to take regular food in small quantities. Only a man of extraordinary physique could have survived such an ordeal, the ship's captain maintained to his crew, his voice reflecting the disappointment of one who had observed what riches of gold, silver and jewels his guest carried with him. Had Fulk's slaves not shown so powerful a loyalty to their master, the Count's body might have been found swept on to some lonely beach by the same spring winds that bore the ship rapidly towards Crete.

In Crete, Fulk discovered another Phoenician vessel that was sailing — miraculously — to Genoa with a cargo of the rarest silks dyed with the purple murex shell. The captain was an affable man, and became even more so when the Count agreed to purchase from him his entire cargo at a high price on the condition that he continue his voyage as far as Marseille. A few words only — the names of ports — accompanied by gestures, much laughter and the passing over of many jewels, concluded the deal as the ship lay at anchor off Messina. Thereafter the voyage continued lazily into the heat of the summer, and by the end of July the vessel slid quietly into the broad harbour of Marseille.

Fulk stepped on to the quay eight months after he had stood at that same spot wondering if he would ever see his country again.

He was still thin, but his vigour had returned and his spirits were buoyant. For a further week he remained in Marseille feeling the strength returning to his legs. People gazed at the lofty, proud figure still dressed in oriental clothing and accompanied by three black giants in pale blue robes. Then one day they were seen riding northwards, together with a small escort of armed men. The tall prince was wearing a light tunic of linen and no longer looked oriental, and a huge sword dangled from a belt at his waist. But the black giants were still in the pale blue of their desert robes, and as they rode their costumes billowed in the wind like sails, and their daggers glinted in the sun.

Count Fulk was riding home. His heart was full of joy and he saluted all who passed. Children would escape their parents' fearful grasp and rush to him, and he would sweep them into his saddle with a laugh, and gallop up and down the village street; then dismount and let them struggle to draw his sword. Those who succeeded he rewarded with a coin, and the children dragged the heavy blade through the dust towards their anxious fathers like puppies with a bone, the coin clutched tightly in the other hand. Sometimes he would stay and eat with the villagers, drink and dance, and in the morning they would escort him on his way, kiss his hand and return to tell tales for ever of the mighty prince who slept under their roof one night so very long ago.

While the endurance of Count Fulk was being tested by tempests, Saracens and disease, Milesende was enduring the solitude of a convent whose prospect — at least in this worldly life — was a horizon of forest.

For much of each day the silence of the place was interrupted only by the rustle of garments outside her cell and the thin tinkle of a bell. Conversation of a whispered nature was permitted only in the cloister, and the scope of such exchanges was shrunken to those areas of experience shared by the hooded figures who walked there. These were for the most part confined to breathless speculations appropriate to ladies instructed to view their time on earth as a fragile perch from which the soul would soon flutter into the afterlife. There were novices of Milesende's own age whom she met in the refectory, where they ate in silence at a table set apart for them to the accompaniment of textual readings by the prioress or one of her juniors. Milesende knelt beside them in chapel and listened to the humble monotony of their prayers; and she sometimes walked with them in the cloister where they would entreat her to join them in their novitiate, and touchingly understood her tears to be the dew of innocence and the dowry of a bride of Christ. If she had not been long accustomed to her own company, Milesende would have found her loneliness spilling into the blackest despair as the months passed and nobody ever came.

It was not knowing anything which was hardest to bear. Why was she here? Where was Rollo? Perhaps he was banished, married, dead. She knew only that she had been led to this place without a word — with no messages, no good-byes, nothing. At Loches a lady who introduced herself as the Count's cousin had spoken to her about dangers, without explaining what these might be, and about her need of protection, without suggesting for how long or for what purpose she was being protected. She had then talked to her of the spiritual life and the balm of Christ's presence. And that was all. She was received here — quietly, graciously, knowingly even, but when she asked the prioress why she was here there was no reply, and there had been none since. She wondered in the early months if she might go mad, and if this might not be preferable to the torture of her solitude and her removal from the man she loved.

Spring brought tiny buds of comfort. One of the nuns spoke to her occasionally of life beyond the convent walls, and as Milesende responded eagerly the lady began tentatively to speak more of the world she had left behind, and the circumstances in which she had left it. One day Milesende noticed tears on her face as she talked. Instinctively she held out her arms to the nun, who at first drew back but then held out her own arms and they embraced. Milesende felt her body reawaken at the contact with another being, and she wanted to hold the woman close to her like a drowning spirit. The two women wept together; then suddenly the nun pulled herself free and was gone.

But from then onwards there was a look of sharing between the two women when their eyes met. Some days afterwards the nun again came to Milesende's cell. It was early. First prayers were just over, but Milesende as a pre-novitiate was excused services until mass. She was still in her bed when the nun arrived and quietly closed the door behind her. She had been crying: Milesende could see her cheeks and eyes were red. She sat on the narrow bed and, as if she could no longer contain what was in her heart, she began to speak of a man she had loved and was to have married. Then he had died. She had no recollection of her life after that – until she was brought here. She had been here at Genillé for ten years. Milesende reminded her so deeply of what she had been like, she said. At first she had imagined she would leave – but for what? A dead lover! She could imagine nobody else she would want. And so she had stayed; had taken her vows; and until Milesende came she had thought she was happy. Now she felt she was reliving her pain. And she wept again – such a deep well of pain threw up those tears.

After a while the crying ceased and she gazed at Milesende almost hopelessly, shaking her head.

'My life has become dry, like a crust,' she said. 'Dried up.'

Very gently she reached out a thin hand and slipped it beneath the open neck of Milesende's nightgown until her fingers touched her breast and she held it within the cup of her hand.

'How lovely you are,' she said, her eyes downcast. 'How

wonderful to be so soft, and so young ... it's so long since I touched anything warm.'

She held her hand there, still not looking at Milesende. After a little while she drew it back and raised her head.

'My life is over.' Her voice was flat. Then she added sadly, 'My body was as beautiful as yours ... Don't stay here, whatever you do.'

That was all she said. Milesende could feel her withdrawing into her fate as she rose from the bed and smoothed her habit over that quite invisible body. Then she departed.

Milesende was surprised at how the touch of the nun's hand had awakened her senses. She felt her breasts glow and her nipples were hard. For the rest of that day she moved differently. She thought of the nun's words – 'My life is over'; and she knew that she had not known until now that her own life was still to be lived. It was as if Rollo's hand had held her breast.

That evening the nun spoke to her again in the cloister. Milesende felt a new spirit rising in her while she walked in that quiet place. Beyond the convent she could hear the song of nightingales and they sounded like the song of love.

'Now it's summer you could go out for an hour if you wished.' The nun's voice was low and she never raised her head as the two of them walked slowly side by side. The light was beginning to fade. Any minute the convent bell would ring for prayers.

'I've spoken to the prioress,' she went on, 'and she agrees – provided you don't stray too far. She's breaking a rule, but she trusts you.'

It seemed like a prison door opening. Milesende looked at the nun with grateful eyes.

'Thank you,' she said. 'I should like that.' And she thought of the walks she used to steal in the summer evenings at Angers; the flowers she would gather; the dreams that would walk with her. She felt young again.

'Tomorrow if you like. Just ask me. I'll watch for you

coming back.' The nun glanced up, and Milesende could see that she had been crying again. 'One day, I think, you'll never come back,' she added. 'And then I shall be alone.'

The bell sounded. Silently the nuns and novices filed into the dark chapel. In gratitude Milesende accompanied them, and she kneeled beside the nun. Only she was aware that as the woman clasped her hands in prayer her teeth held the skin of her thumb as if in a trap, and her eyes were locked tight against the world of her prison.

Milesende was free now for an hour or so each day. She came to know the forest around the silent convent as intimately as though voices talked to her there. She imagined her body naked among the trees, sunlight warming her legs, her belly, her breasts. She let her hair flow loose and tossed it across her shoulders like a foal; then removed her shoes and felt the cool moss caress her feet and the grass draw tiny fingers past her ankles as she walked. There was a stream within the forest where wagtails bobbed yellow among the rocks, and gnats rose and fell on invisible threads among the sunbeams. She stood with the cool water stroking her legs, and she thought of the stream where Rollo had found her: he was bare to the waist, and his huge chest was splashed with moisture. She had felt faint at the sight of his body almost naked, and he had carried her in his arms across the water, her arms round his neck, his beard against her bare shoulder.

She shivered, and the woods felt empty.

It was two days from her sixteenth birthday. She was standing near the stream feeling inconsolably alone, her eyes following the movement of the water almost mechanically. All of a sudden she became aware that someone was close by, and she turned to see a woman leading a horse down the steep bank to the stream some twenty paces from her.

As the horse drank, the woman looked up at Milesende and smiled. Then she tethered the horse to an alder and approached her. She was roughly dressed and her hair tangled. Her face was handsome and big-boned, and her hands large and strong. Milesende felt startled.

'Milesende,' the woman said.

She nodded, amazed.

'I thought I should find you here,' the woman went on. She was still smiling, and her face was gentle under the tousled hair. Milesende wanted to ask who she was and how she knew her name, but no words came.

They were standing by a tall rock beside the stream. It was late afternoon and the sun shot spears of gold among the trees around them. Milesende could hear a chorus of nightingales in the woods above.

The woman reached out and gently grasped her arm.

'I have something to tell you,' she said. 'Your lover is coming.' Her voice was low and warm. Milesende rested against the rock, trembling.

'What do you mean?' was all she could say.

'He's coming!' the woman said again emphatically. 'I promise you.' And she laid both hands on Milesende's shoulders. 'Tomorrow ... Be ready!'

Milesende burst into tears. She could feel the woman's strong arms around her, but her eyes were closed and it was as if a dam had given way within her and she was being swept far away, helplessly crying, crying.

Tomorrow! He would be here tomorrow!

She clung to the strange woman as though he would never come if she let go. She felt frail against her powerful body, and the arms still held her.

'Who are you?' she managed to say after a while between sobs, her head on the woman's shoulder. There was a pause.

'Never mind who I am,' she heard the woman say, 'but I'm telling the truth.'

Then firmly she pushed Milesende away and held her at arm's length, looking at her with those large pale eyes.

'Yes, you are very beautiful. I knew you would be.' The woman went on gazing at Milesende. 'You always were,' she added.

'You know me?'

The woman nodded. 'A long time ago,' she said.

'Then why won't you tell me who you are?' Milesende grasped her hand as though she were frightened the woman might vanish.

But there was no answer. Instead the woman reached into her rough clothes for a piece of linen and very tenderly began to wipe the tears from the girl's cheeks; and as she did so her loose garment revealed the deep curve of her breast. For a second before the garment closed a vivid red scar caught Milesende's eye; numbers appeared to have been branded there on the skin.

The woman saw the startled look on her face, and she smiled.

'You *will* know who I am,' she said, 'but it's better now that you don't.'

With that she turned away and walked towards the horse, swishing its tail at the water's edge. She untethered it and gracefully mounted.

'For Rollo's sake, and your own, don't say anything to him about me,' she added over her shoulder as she pulled the horse towards the bank. 'Be here tomorrow ... You're lucky, Milesende. Very lucky.'

She guided the horse up the steep bank and along the ridge above the stream. She never looked back, and Milesende's eyes followed her as she disappeared into the forest. For a moment she thought she caught sight of a large grey animal that crossed the path and turned in the direction they had taken, but when she looked again there was no sign of it. The only sound was the song of the nightingales. The sun had dipped low among the trees, and in a bewilderment of joy and apprehension Milesende clambered up the bank and hurried towards the convent through the warm grass. The nun was waiting for her anxiously outside the entrance, and as the little gate was locked behind them they heard the ring of the chapel bell.

That evening she prayed for tomorrow, and for the rest of her life.

The extreme heat of summer cast a careless lethargy over the castle of Angers. The absence of the Count, and the absence of any word of him, intensified the state of inactivity which hung over the place. The women of the castle had never, in truth, been much prone to activity of a vigorous nature, except on occasions when there was a fine hunt, or when the dancing in the great hall became unusually buoyant with music and wine. But now it was simply too hot for anyone to exert themselves more than was necessary, and such energy as was not soaked up by the heat became directed towards engagements that required no movement of any kind, except the movement of the tongue. In the cauldron of July and August only gossip failed to wilt.

One subject above all exercised the tongues of the castle, and that was the affair of Adelaide's secret, and how on earth she had been induced to reveal it.

A few bald facts were known to all. Adelaide had let slip that she knew the whereabouts of the young Milesende. Ermengarde had struck her in fury. Roger, outraged at his wife's duplicity, had demanded to know where the girl was, and Adelaide had bluntly refused. Roger and Sebrand had then conferred while imbibing a lake of wine, after which the two of them had lurched towards Adelaide's rooms where they remained for some considerable time. As a result the information had been extracted. Rollo, who had been absent all this time, was told by Sebrand that Milesende was at the convent of Genillé. Roger, in whose domain the convent lay, had granted the Norman permission to abduct the girl whatever the prioress or Lady Hildegarde might wish to the contrary. And now Rollo had departed to do the deed.

All this was thrilling enough to those with appetites for small scandal, which in Angers was everybody with the exception of the Treasurer and perhaps the quivering Adèle. But it was nothing compared to the excitement of speculation aroused by the crucial missing fact. What had actually happened in Adelaide's rooms?

If Roger had been there alone with his wife, speculation would have been muted. He might have screamed at her, beaten her, browbeaten her, ordered her: none of this would have been out of the ordinary for Roger the Devil. But he was not alone. Sebrand was with him. Both were exceedingly drunk. And neither would say anything at all about the incident. Roger looked as he always looked, like a black bull menacingly unaware. Sebrand on the other hand seemed ashamed. Not even Rollo had been told how the information so beneficial to his wellbeing had been obtained. So, what had happened?

The Chancellor Audemand, who knew everything, was cornered by all; but he would wave the question away like a tiresome mosquito not to be allowed to interfere with matters of state. The smile with which he did so, however, left a strong impression that he was intimately aware of what had taken place; though, when the questioners had departed empty-handed, they formed the opinion that he had not the faintest idea but was hugely enjoying his reputation for omniscience. Even if he were to be the last to know Audemand would certainly radiate the air of one who had known all along. He had enjoyed years of practice at the art.

'It seems to me a matter of small importance,' he said to the group of lords gathered in the great hall late one evening. 'Very small.' And he left them with his mouth working rhythmic patterns of deceit.

'Good night!' he added with an exaggerated flourish of his staff.

Archambaud, Sulpice and — more drunk than the others — Fulk's brother Maurice, all three had exhausted the subject of Adelaide's revelation long before they had exhausted the wine. It was a hot, sweaty night. The litter of roast pig was being gnawed by dogs. Servants lingered in the shadows, waiting for their masters to make their way to their wives or to the dovecot. Archambaud, the taciturn brother of Sulpice, was rather mistily eyeing a servant-girl laying a basket of fruit on the long table before them.

'Where's Sebrand?' said Maurice unsteadily. 'Why won't he tell us what he did to Adelaide?'

'You know where he is,' muttered Archambaud gloomily, his eyes wandering after the servant-girl as her ample rear receded towards the kitchen. 'He's with Hersende, the lucky devil!'

They were bored. Soon they were joined by Giraud Berlay, who was unmarried and had the air of one lost in love while in fact having no one to love at all. His company was no cheer, and one by one they made their way listlessly to whatever bed was due to receive them. Married or unmarried, the young men of Fulk's court shared a strong disinclination to seek the company of the women available to them. Magnificent at war, profligate with wine, outside those two activities they were dispossessed. The focus of their discontent, especially at these late hours, was the collective dream of Hersende whose glorious flesh they would never enjoy. Their envy of Sebrand bubbled sourly.

In fact Sebrand was alone, and most uneasy about being alone. The tears and anger of Hersende, on hearing of Sebrand's excursion to Adelaide's rooms, had come as a shock to him. Plead his innocence as he might, there was no denying that he had been present with Roger when the information was extracted; and since he was unwilling to disclose what had taken place, Hersende took the view that it must have been disgraceful and a breach of trust. She had not let him touch her since.

That evening she had sought the company of the Lady Ermengarde. No one, in these last few days, had enjoyed more colourful speculations of the Adelaide affair than Ermengarde. It seemed perfectly clear to her that Sebrand, encouraged by Roger, had at the very least threatened to rape the woman. Ermengarde had been long convinced that such a fate was what Adelaide secretly pined for, and that having failed to provoke it from the Count she was happy to settle for his High Constable. What a triumph to lure him from the lovely Hersende whose youth and shapeliness Adelaide could scarcely match!

Exploring this delightful line of thinking, Ermengarde envisaged the occasion in the following way.

Roger and Sebrand barge into Adelaide's room blind drunk. The husband announces to his frigid wife that he has brought her a saviour at last. Sebrand is then thrust forward by Roger to play his part. With drunken bravura he announces that he will rape her unless Milesende's whereabouts are revealed, expecting the lady to shriek in horror and tell all. Alas, no! Instead, Adelaide's eyes shine with desire as she awaits her fate. Sebrand is compelled to remove her clothing, and then his own. By now she is in ecstasy. She will offer the vital information only *if* she is raped. Sebrand is trapped. Distaste for his task is accompanied by awareness that wine has set it beyond his powers. No encouragement from Adelaide or expletives of desire succeed in raising the High Constable's organ high enough. Finally, in pity (because Adelaide has a warm heart somewhere), she offers to reveal Milesende's whereabouts, but only on the condition that Sebrand return in a more sober condition to perform what he has failed to perform so far. And if he should not agree to the bargain, and fulfil it, she will announce the disgraceful scene to the entire court.

Clearly, Ermengarde reflected as she held the hand of the tearful Hersende, Sebrand had much to be ashamed about, and it was hardly surprising that he should refuse to disclose what had taken place to anyone. She prided herself on the certainty that, had she been in Adelaide's place, the High Constable's standard would have been raised in triumph, and the unfortunate Sebrand would have been spared all this indignity as well as received a few timely lessons in love from which this tearful girl would no doubt profit.

'How can he love me if he behaves like that?' sobbed Hersende. 'How could he?'

'I'm quite sure he did nothing,' replied Ermengarde in a soothing tone, tactfully not expanding on why she felt sure he had done nothing, or what he might be compelled to do very soon. 'He was also very drunk, it seems,' she went on, endeavouring to imply that such a condition was unfamiliar to her.

'He cannot possibly love me,' Hersende continued.

Again Ermengarde was unable to say what was in her mind. It was clear to her, and she would have thought clear to anyone not entirely blinded by infatuation, that men by and large did not *love* like that. They enjoyed love, just as they enjoyed fighting, or eating, or getting drunk. Men needed women to love them, and to be available to them – by preference exclusively – but that was different. Love did not come naturally to men, particularly if they got what they wanted without it. Clearly Sebrand got exactly what he wanted without it, and looking at this gorgeous creature, all curves and tears, Ermengarde could easily understand how much he wanted it. No, women had to employ their own weapons if men were to be induced to love them.

'Then you must make him jealous,' she replied.

Hersende raised her tear-stained face and gazed wonderingly at Ermengarde.

'How would I do that?' she asked with such apparent innocence that Ermengarde laughed aloud.

'My dear girl, but you've done it before. With Rollo. What could be easier? There's not a man in Angers who doesn't lust after you – my husband excepted. Just choose your victim. Choose your moment. And, of course, choose your dress. In fact I'll design it for you.'

With that she placed an arm fondly round Hersende, and Ermengarde's imagination began to work with great fertility. By the time she had finished, she had no doubt, Sebrand would be crying at the girl's feet, a slave, while some other young fool would be wandering lost in love – and be much in need of comfort from herself. She must pick a man she fancied to be Hersende's victim, Ermengarde decided.

But while she was reflecting on the downfall of lovers, a scene that would have amazed even Ermengarde was taking place nearby.

The boredom of the court was finding its usual relief in the dovecot, and sounds especially raucous were drifting from the little courtyard at the rear of the castle towards the dark, curtained passageways that wound along the upper floors.

In addition to Roger, Maurice, and several minor lords of Fulk's court, the male company on this night was swollen by a young man of robust appearance who had been introduced as a fine scholar visiting Angers from Toulouse. In fact, unknown to others, the Chancellor had invited him. The young man was part of his plan to interest William, the Count of Toulouse, in proposing his daughter Constance as a future wife for King Robert – just as soon, that is, as the king's present marriage to Odo's widow Berthe was annulled, which it surely would be. The young man was indeed the Count's nephew.

In a short time he had impressed all who met him, not only with his learning but also with his conviviality. On this particular evening Roger had introduced him to the pleasures of Angevin wine and of the dovecot, his fine mind being apparently no bar to other delights. It became a night of exceptional revelry and licentiousness, in which the young man from Toulouse joined wholeheartedly, and more than one of the girls serving wine on that hot summer night discovered that the reputation of the Gascons for free behaviour was entirely justified. Furthermore, he enlivened the revels with appropriate tales, poetry, and the reciting of passages from learned texts whose authors would have been surprised at the context given to

395

their spiritual labours, and at the laughter they provoked.

It was one such recitation which provoked the event that was to make this so memorable a night in the castle of Angers. While several of the company were openly enjoying the pleasures of the dovecot, the young man began to offer a ribald version of a holy text which concluded with the exhortation 'Raise up thine eyes and thy spirit to the Lord!' Duly obeying, eyes were raised, only to observe a curtain twitch violently above them.

Roger looked surprised; then he turned to the young man.

'I didn't expect the Lord to be behind a curtain! I wonder what He looks like.'

Three men were already making their way quietly up the staircase to the curtained passageway. From the darkness they found themselves gazing at two dark-robed figures who were just visible in the torchlight of the passage. One of them was a woman – a nun, they were astonished to realize. Her dress was quite open in the front and she was wielding something in her hand. The second figure had his back to them, but as they drew closer they could see he was holding up his robe before him, and whatever was in the nun's hand appeared to be beating him vigorously. The three men paused in astonishment. Groans and sighs were coming from the figure with his back turned, and the nun's hand kept descending sharply. Suddenly she looked up and saw the men approaching. She dropped what was in her hand and fled. The robed man tried to restore his clothing and follow her, but he was too slow and his pursuers overtook him. They dragged him struggling down the staircase into the courtyard. And in the light of the lamps they saw the gulping, terrified figure of Father Baudouin.

An extraordinary silence fell.

'Bring him here,' commanded Roger quietly.

The Chaplain struggled as two men seized him. Then his eyes bulged and his lips drew back in a snarl.

'I was observing your sins,' he screamed, 'so that I might

pray for your immortal souls!'

A mutter spread across the courtyard.

'And that was why you and your nun were half-naked, was it?' exclaimed one of the young lords who had caught him. 'And why we found this?' He held up a lash.

'Disrobe him!' ordered Roger.

The two men tore at Baudouin's robe, and as the lamp-light revealed his pallid flesh he screamed out again even more loudly.

'Don't dare touch a servant of God! You will be ...!'

But his final words were muffled under the robe as rough arms pulled it over his head. And as they did so a gasp arose among the people gathered in the courtyard, for amid so much sallow and sagging flesh rose a member of grotesque proportions veined with streaks of blood.

The gasp turned into a murmur of horror. Then horror turned to a sick fear as Roger slowly picked up a carving knife from the table and walked forward to hold it under the revolting organ. People averted their eyes. The Chaplain whimpered in a choked voice.

'For that thing,' said Roger, 'the Countess died!' And he looked at Baudouin with an expression of cold loathing. 'You've polluted this place in the name of God,' he went on. 'And in the name of God I say you'll pollute it no longer!'

And Roger gazed around him.

'What shall we do with this foul priest?' he called.

Then, quite unexpectedly, anger dispersed into laughter. From the darkness of a doorway came the shout of a woman's voice blurred with the effects of much wine, and staggering into the centre of the courtyard came the corpulent figure of the cook. With some difficulty she raised her hand for an audience.

'I'll have him!' she called out. And without further ado she advanced unsteadily on the Chaplain, removing her own clothing as she did so. The two grotesque bodies met and, under the cook's weight, tumbled to the floor.

Cheering rose from around the courtyard as they watched this most bizarre coupling of flesh. Roger stood aside, his own fury replaced by a grin of jagged teeth. People urged them on and began to clap to the rhythm of the cook's buttocks. Scarcely anything of Baudouin could be seen beneath that gigantic dough except his face, which those closest to the pair swore had a look of agonized rapture.

Meanwhile the young man whose recitation had provoked this festivity leapt on to a table and began to proclaim in a ringing voice – ' "I will show unto thee the judgement of the great whore that sitteth upon many waters: with whom the kings of the earth have committed fornication, and the inhabitants of the earth have been made drunk with the wine of her fornication." ' And then, even louder – ' "I saw a woman sit upon a scarlet-coloured beast, full of names of blasphemy, having seven heads and ten horns." ' The cheering was redoubled. ' "And the devil will ascend into the mother of the Antichrist and completely fill her," ' he shouted, ' "surround her completely, fill her completely both inside and out, so that she will conceive through a man with the cooperation of the devil." '

By the time the young man had finished, Roger was so convulsed with laughter that he could barely stand. The cook was now lying quite still, and onlookers were beginning to peer in order to see if anything of Baudouin remained alive beneath.

The young man turned to Roger with a smile.

'See what an aid to life scholarship can be,' he said solemnly. 'Who would have thought the words of St John the Divine and Abbot Adso would rouse such healthy passions!' And he too burst out laughing.

'Take him, then!' Roger called out to the cook, who by now had risen to her feet and was pulling on her clothing with the most satisfied of smiles. 'We spare you, Baudouin, by the grace of this fine lady.'

And he slapped the cook's huge thigh with his hand.

'Lead him from here in his shame, naked!' he went on. 'And use him well, Cook. Should he fail you, return him to us and we shall deal with him. I imagine the Lord Bishop would be interested to hear how one of God's servants conducts himself in private.'

Roger pointed a finger menacingly towards the far door of the courtyard.

'Go, Baudouin!' he commanded. 'Take your hypocrisy with you. Consider yourself fortunate that you still have a member to play with. You've found someone more generous than you deserve. Go!'

No one had ever heard Roger speak like this.

The gulping figure of Baudouin, eyes blinking with tears, shuffled across the courtyard, his hands hiding his shame. People withdrew to let him pass, and he said nothing. The cook grabbed his hand and pulled him after her through the doorway, waving her other hand above her head and cackling with merriment. A small procession formed behind them as the party advanced towards the castle gate, and astonished guards gaped at the sight of the naked cleric as they stood back to let the company file out into the midnight street, singing and cheering all the way to the ramshackle hut where the cook lived. People woke from their dreams and gazed out at them as they passed, and imagined themselves to be still dreaming. There were strange tales in the city at dawn of a naked man with the member of a horse being led from the castle, and no one who had not witnessed the sight believed them.

Within the castle there was much clapping of hands and raising of goblets, and the company broke into song, led by the young man whose store of verses was still unexhausted when the night sky began to pale.

So it was that learning was brought to the dovecot, and Father Baudouin departed from the castle for ever. The Lady Ermengarde never forgave herself for not being present at such an enlivening occasion.

TWELVE

IN HIS LEATHER WALLET Rollo carried the small gold key that
Milesende had once given him. It was the only memento he
had of her, and since her disappearance he had looked at it
over and over again, laying it in the palm of his hand,
turning it, raising it to his lips, looking at it again. Sometimes it was too painful to recollect the moment when he
had placed the key in the little golden heart that hung from
her neck, and opened it. Then he had locked within it a piece
of his own hair and laid it gently back on her skin: it was as if
the shape of the golden heart had been moulded by the curve
of her breasts.

Today, besides the key, two further objects lay in his
wallet as he rode. One was a silver ring – a heavy, man's ring
set with a jewel engraved as a seal.

'Take this, Rollo,' Roger had said. 'Show it to the prioress
and tell her that she is to release the girl.'

Rollo may have looked doubtful because Roger had
laughed.

'She's my sister!' he said. 'She will know this seal. My
brother you've met already, at Corméry. As you can see,
they've shared God between them, and I have all the rest.'
And he laughed more raucously. 'Or maybe', he added, 'I
drove them to it.'

Roger had departed chuckling earthily.

The other object was also a ring – small, quite plain, and
of gold. Hersende had lent him one of her own for the
craftsman to match for size.

'Milesende has hands exactly like mine, I promise you,'
she had assured him.

'Not everything of Milesende's is your size,' added Ermengarde slyly. Hersende had blushed, as she was intended to do. 'I'm only jealous, my dear girl,' Ermengarde had gone on. 'Both of you have bodies far more beautiful than mine, and Milesende is a virgin as well.' Hersende looked down awkwardly. 'Goodness, by the time I was your sister's age I'd lost my virginity more times than I could count, and the only man who gave me a ring was my husband who never took it.'

Rollo had left Hersende to Ermengarde's reminiscences about her imperishable virginity.

He decided to rest the night at the inn at L'Ile Bouchard where he had once broken his journey on that spring day when he had travelled to meet the Lady Hildegarde. For the moment the heat was ferocious and his horse too weary to continue. So, as the light began to fade Rollo strolled along the banks of the Vienne, his mind occupied by Milesende. Anxiety was rising in him. So much had gone wrong. Might it go wrong again? Then Rollo checked himself from exploring the hazards that might intervene. He reassured himself that nothing could now forestall him. Roger had even told him where he might purchase a horse for Milesende, outside Loches. In this way he would not even have to enter Hildegarde's city. After that the seal would release her, and this time tomorrow the one he loved would be riding beside him. He would place the ring on her finger. Perhaps he would take her back to Normandy before the winter. She would be his bride — the loveliest of brides.

He stood and gazed at the violet sky. After the opaque heat the evening light was liquid, and below him the silent river dragged at strands of waterweed like combed hair. This peace, Rollo thought; why could there not always be this peace? Nightingales filled the woods with pearls of sound. Then, as he looked across the water a thread of gold looped between the alders, trailing its flute-call. Fulk's golden bird with black wings. Rollo found himself thinking about the absent Count, and the traumas of working in his service. Why, he wondered, should it be necessary to owe so much to another man in order to achieve anything at all in his life? And to owe it, what was more, to a man who would pull down so wilfully what he had himself struggled to create, as if birth and death rode with him together in harness? There lay the enigma of Count Fulk, it seemed to him: such rage to create, such fury to destroy; so much power, with so much pain. And yet he, Rollo, as a builder for God, ought to be able to understand that enigma, he felt. Was it not true in his own experience that man could only love and respect what he was prepared to endure great pain to build? That he must indeed rend his own soul and body to prove his love? Did not Christ need to be crucified in order to be born again as God?

Rollo was beginning to understand something about Fulk which had always eluded and mystified him. To create anything was a kind of birth, after all; and to conceive there had to be a fusion of male and female elements. This Fulk could not do: the gentle and the strong in him could never blend. He could never align those softer parts of himself with his own strength. The two were always in conflict. Fulk longed to create, yet because of this conflict he could create only pain, grief, war: he was for ever on some road to Golgotha; a troubled soul. Rollo thought of the Count's pilgrimage to the Holy City; then he thought of his deformed child – and shuddered. Was deformity perhaps all he could create, just as his golden bird would always have black wings?

It was twilight as Rollo made his way back to his horse and rode to the inn. The sky spread like a dark jewel over the town. He would sleep peacefully tonight, and tomorrow Milesende would lie with him.

The innkeeper approached as he entered. With a mystified expression on his face he explained that a visitor was awaiting him in his room. A woman, he said. Rollo was perplexed. Could it possibly be Milesende? But that was inconceivable. He took a lamp from the innkeeper and climbed the stairs. The curtain was already drawn back and the light of a candle glowed within. A figure in coarse clothing was standing with her back to him, and he knew immediately who she was. His heart sank. What did she know? What had she come to tell him?

The woman turned as he entered.

'I wanted to see you,' she said in the soft, calm voice he remembered. Her eyes were fixed on him, and she had that same knowing smile with which she had greeted him when he came across her in the forest of Langeais.

'What's wrong?' asked Rollo almost brusquely. The woman shook her head, still smiling.

'Nothing is wrong.' She placed her hand on Rollo's arm, and for a moment the look she gave him was a reminder that they had been lovers. Then she lowered her eyes.

'I've seen Milesende – this afternoon!' she went on. Rollo started. He was about to rain questions on her, but she placed her fingers over his mouth and softly pressed his lips. 'Wait! ... She's well. And she's waiting for you.' Relief and joy flooded Rollo's body. He felt weak, and he wanted to embrace the woman.

'But why I've come is this, Rollo. Whatever you do, don't go to the convent. The prioress will never release her.' Rollo felt in his wallet and pulled out the ring with Roger's seal.

'I have this from Roger de Montrésor,' he said.

She shook her head.

'The prioress hates her brother.'

'But the convent is in his domain. Isn't that so?' The woman nodded.

'Even so,' she answered, 'the rules of a convent are not made by Fulk's lords. The prioress obeys her abbot, and her abbot is Gervais de Corméry.' She looked at Rollo knowingly. 'Gervais would go to hell rather than take orders from Roger. You would have to take Milesende by force, and that would not be good for you if you want to marry the girl. *Do you want to marry her?*'

She looked intently at Rollo, and when he nodded she lowered her eyes. She said nothing for a moment.

'What you must do', she went on in the same calm voice, 'is go to where a stream skirts the forest a short distance beyond the convent. Tomorrow afternoon. She'll be there. ... And now,' she added abruptly, 'I have to go.'

As she turned away to leave the room Rollo took her hand.

'Tell me. Why do you do all this for me?'

The woman stopped. For a moment she looked away. Suddenly she smiled and without a word took his hand and placed it under her garment on her naked breast. She held it there ... and then she stepped back. Rollo's eyes followed her as she moved swiftly to the door, and a few minutes later he heard the sound of hooves growing fainter until they were lost in the gathering night.

Who was she? Audemand had suggested that one day he would find out. But he did not even know her name.

The next morning Rollo rode as if on air.

By noon he was with the horse-breeder Roger had recommended – a swarthy and expansive man who invited Rollo to his house to share his food and wine, surrounded by a tribe of women and children who gathered round him like bees as the two men seated themselves in the cool kitchen and began to cut off hunks of pork sausage, goat's cheese and dark bread. Roger was good to him, he said when they were alone, and always came here for his horses: the two of them would sit there – just as now – eating, talking, laughing, getting drunk together. Or they would hunt boar in the forest. There were not many lords like him, the horse-breeder assured Rollo. Straight, earthy, a man you could talk to as a man. Yes, he knew Roger's sister slightly: a timid woman, fragile-looking, startled, hands quivering and twitching ... so! And he narrowed his own hands into two beaks pecking at one another nervously in front of his face. Then he laughed. Too much prayer, he said; nothing between her legs!

The man inquired why Rollo should want to go to Genillé, and why he needed another horse when he possessed such a fine one already. Rollo told him his story in brief and the man's eyes widened with delight. He laughed again heavily. A mare for a beautiful lady, eh! he chuckled. A lady with black hair and black eyes, you say. And he led Rollo to a stable behind the house and pointed to a dapple-grey horse, small in stature and graceful, with a long white mane. A most gentle creature, he assured Rollo; just imagine her seated there!

The two men made the deal and Rollo rode off along the path the horse-breeder showed him, the grey mare following obediently behind, tethered by a length of rope. The man wished Rollo luck and called out to him to return if he ever wanted to rescue another lady from the convent. Rollo heard the breeder's heavy laughter behind him as he made his way along the narrow track. In an hour, the man said, he would be at Genillé.

The silent heat of the afternoon enveloped Rollo as he rode. Occasional quiffs of dust rose from the dry fields where grapes were already ripening amid a splash of scarlet poppies and the spikes of bugloss. Then the track led through an oak-forest and a welcome cool rose from the dense grass. A deer darted this way and that ahead of him before vaulting away among the trees. Rollo felt tension gripping him as he sensed that any minute he would catch sight of the convent. Head off to the left, the horse-breeder had said, and soon you will hear the ripple of water.

Before long his ears caught the thin sound of a bell. Rollo paused to locate it. Then as quietly as he could he guided his horse and the dappled mare through the undergrowth at an angle from the track. There was only the crackle of twigs underfoot and the persistent hum of insects. Streaks of sunlight caught the grey crust of oak-bark and, for a second, the blue fleck of a jay's wing between the trees.

It felt like the first day of a new world, and all the fears of the unknown crowded in on him. More than nine months had passed since he had set eyes on Milesende, or heard a word from her. Rollo clung to what the woman had said at the inn – 'She's waiting for you!' Would she have changed so much? Would their love still burn? Nothing at that moment could seem more unlikely than that she should be here, somewhere in this unknown forest, by an unknown stream.

But she was standing by a rock among the trees, and must have heard him coming because her face was turned towards him. She was dressed in a plain white garment of linen fastened high to the neck, and her dark hair strayed over her shoulders almost to the waist. Rollo looked at her in wonder and he saw that her face was damp with tears. In that moment as their eyes met he knew that their hearts were rejoined, and there was nothing that needed to be said. He loved her.

She did not even smile, but slowly placed her arms round him and pressed her face to his chest. His tears fell on her dark hair, and hers on his warm skin. They held one another in silence as all those months of parting healed like a wound. All around them spread the whispering forest and the gentle murmur of water.

'Carry me, Rollo,' she said at length.

Her body was so light. He held her in his arms and her moist eyes gazed at him as he climbed the slope to where the two horses were grazing quietly.

'Carry me away from here.'

They said nothing as they rode, side by side. Rollo did not even know where they rode. The sun was still high, shuttered by dark branches. The dry heat of early evening scented the land. Their fingers touched and entwined, and they rode softly over the sandy earth, their eyes sharing the nearness of each other's face, the distance between their two bodies filled by what had no need to be spoken.

They arrived at an expanse of open heath, baked dry, with narrow ravines which opened before them among the stretches of heather and seemed to disappear for ever into the darkness of the hill. Gingerly they made their way round these sudden chasms until they came to a ridge. Beyond, the ground dipped away steeply through trees to a river half-hidden that hugged a wall of limestone below them, through which the track descended down a narrow cleft. The trees closed above their heads as the horses picked their way cautiously among giant slabs of white rock. Tiny rivulets spouted from the mossy earth, and suddenly the air was moist. The sun, huge and orange, had sunk just low enough so that it shone beneath the tall canopy of trees cloaking the river, and was staining the black water with fire. They dismounted, and the horses drank thirstily while Rollo and Milesende gazed about them at this secret place plunged deep in the damp summer woods under the high rock. A stream stroked the surface of a deep cushion of water-plants beside them, breaking into minute specks of sunlight as it flowed. He turned her to him and kissed her, and her body pressed against him. Then, her lips still almost touching his, she smiled for the first time, and her eyes were as deep and dark as the river.

'I love you,' she whispered.

They removed their sandals and stepped into the cool water, their feet and ankles lost within the soft cushions of green. She waded ahead of him towards the high cliff and began to pull herself up on boulders, agile as a cat. Her feet and hands felt for the surface of the rock as she climbed, and her hair spread in a dark curtain across her face and her white dress.

He gazed at her, enchanted. She looked down, her face radiant, and as he approached she gave a little laugh and leaned over to kiss him. Then she turned and let out a cry of pleasure. Before them lay a pool held within the rocks, and beyond it a cascade of water seemed to hang suspended from the cliff, sending up a mist that quivered and drifted in the sunlight.

Rollo watched as Milesende stepped lightly from rock to rock around the edge of the pool, her arms outstretched to steady her balance. She was laughing and calling to him, the sun playing on the movement of her body. She drew close to the waterfall, hands held out to catch the spray, hair tossed back. Water speckled her arms and face as she edged forward. Suddenly the laughter stopped and she closed her eyes. A breeze was blowing the drift of water across her hair and clothing until her white dress began to melt before him into a transparent veil caressing the nakedness of her body. She stood perfectly still, showered by the sunlight and the waterfall, as he stepped towards her. His fingers touched her, and he peeled the damp skin of her garment from her shoulders, her breasts, hips, thighs, ankles; then Rollo lifted her and laid her on the cool cushion of grass in the shallows of the pool. Her eyes opened and lingered on him as he removed his own clothing, and she curled her body, a little frightened, as she waited for him to come to her in the sunlight of that green bed of water.

The sun was low above the horizon when they rose and stepped on to the warm rock. Rollo raised her face and kissed her lips so softly that they scarcely touched and his hands stroked the damp of her shoulders and her back. Her fingers furrowed in his hair, and they could feel the warmth of the air and the rocks wrap their bodies.

'I love you,' he said very quietly. She gazed at him, and such trust lay in those dark eyes that he felt his own tears rise. A surge of joy swept his body and he swung her round and round in his arms until both of them collapsed in a rapture of laughter on the warm rock.

'Look', she said after a while. He looked where she was pointing, and a short distance beyond them in the steep cliff he could see a cave, like a dark mouth within the rock.

They spread their damp clothing in the last of the sunlight and picked their way cautiously along the base of the cliff, their bodies drying and their bare feet tender on the rough stones. As they approached, the ledge in front of the cave mouth was no more than shoulder-height above them: Rollo lifted Milesende and then clambered up after her. They gazed around them. The cave was larger than Rollo had imagined – perhaps twice his own height and as wide as a large room.

Suddenly Milesende gripped his hand and started back. 'Don't let's stay here! Let's go, Rollo!'

Around them the floor of the cave was littered with bones.

'Wait,' he said, holding her hand firmly. And he bent down. The bones were dry, and crumbled in his fingers. Rollo looked around, and everywhere he looked there were bones. Then among them he noticed there were piles of small flints: he picked some of them up and laid them in the palm of his hand. They were chipped so that each had a blade, and some of them a point and a shaft.

'What are they?' Milesende peered closely at the objects in Rollo's hand. 'But they're weapons! Stone weapons!' And she looked up at Rollo with a puzzled face.

He nodded, and gazed about him.

'I wonder how long ago people lived here.' And as he looked his eyes caught sight of something in the shadows by the wall of the cave.

'Look,' he said.

They peered into a dark recess in the rock, and lying there was a tusk as long as a man, but curved like a horn almost in on itself.

'What creature did that belong to? Can you imagine?' He gazed at Milesende, who grimaced and looked away.

'I don't think I want to imagine.' Then she tugged at his hand and pointed. 'Rollo, do you see?'

The sun was throwing its last rays deep into the cave, filling the vault beyond them with a deep orange light. It seemed to go on and on until the cave melted into the far shadows. Milesende had shed her terrors and was led as if enchanted into the heart of the cliff. The sun painted her naked back a warm gold and threw a slender silhouette of her body on the walls as she passed. He saw her raise her head and look about her, and heard her draw breath.

'Rollo, where are we?'

As he came close to her his eyes followed the faint shafts of sunlight over the walls of the cave. Rollo gasped. Everywhere he looked there were creatures painted on the stone, and they were creatures he had never seen. High above him ran a herd of deer with antlers as long as the branches of trees; close by, moulded by the shape of the rock, was a beast like an ox but with a vast head coated with fur; another creature on the farther wall was no more than a few black lines on the bare stone, but with savage eyes and a pair of curved teeth which thrust from its mouth like daggers. And then, almost lost in the shadow, rose a mōnster shaggy all over with hair, and from whose head protruded two gigantic curved tusks. Dwarfed at its side was a group of miniature human figures who were aiming spears towards it.

'There it is!' Rollo exclaimed. 'The tusks! Look!'

They stood in wonder. Whoever they might have been, these people from another time who lived in the hillside and hunted with flint arrows, they described their world with a skill greater than anything Rollo could ever have imagined. He felt shaken – the thought that he, a craftsman, should be gazing in awe at a craft from a lost world: it was as if he knew the man who had drawn these living creatures, even though the beasts had vanished along with the people who hunted them and drew them. Rollo felt humble and proud at once.

'I wonder if what I've made will be looked at when we're all gone,' he said.

Milesende glanced at him curiously, not quite understanding. Then she shivered and pressed her body to him. The sunlight had gone, and the creatures around them were fading into the darkness of the cave.

They turned to leave. But as they did so they noticed that one shaft of light still lingered by the farthest wall of the cave. A single patch of daylight. Milesende went closer. Then she looked up, and Rollo's eyes followed her gaze. Far above them was a bright streak of sky. He remembered the sudden chasms they had avoided as they crossed the heath. There had been scores of them: this cave must go on and on through the hillside, he thought.

'Rollo, look!' And she gripped his hand tightly.

Low on the rock wall, and lit by that blade of daylight, were drawn two figures – a man and a woman, sticklike, with round heads and fingers outstretched. Her only other features were two pointed breasts: his was a long member erect.

'It feels strange,' she said, staring at the figures. 'People live on so long after they're dead.' She paused, then she looked up at Rollo. 'They're just like us.' And she laughed, and ran her hand down his body. 'Perhaps they made love by the same pool.' She shivered again. 'It's cold, Rollo.'

They made their way to the mouth of the cave. The sky was all fire, and the heat of the evening embraced them as they stepped over the smooth rocks towards the pool and the waterfall. They stood watching the twilight gather around them, and there was only the sound of water and the soft breathing of the woods.

'Let's stay here tonight – where we made love,' Milesende whispered. 'It's so warm. I wish we could stay here for ever.'

She was gazing at the waterfall, almost black now against the luminous white of the cliff.

'I used to bathe in a waterfall like this,' she said. 'And I used to dream of making love to you.' Then she slid her arms round his neck and laid her head against his chest. He ran his fingers through her hair and down her back. 'When they

took me away,' she went on without looking up at him, '[
used to think of that waterfall every day. And every day [
cried!'

He held her close to him, and she snuggled her fist withir
his hand so that he enclosed it.

'Tomorrow's my birthday. All my birthdays will be witl
you till we die.' And she raised her head and gazed at him
He kissed her throat, and his tongue traced the curve of he
breasts. 'Make love to me – here!' she said. 'And alway:
make love to me.'

In the middle of August – that roasting August – Count Full
returned. The people of Angers had grown accustomed tc
their lord returning amid dramatic splendour: they had also
grown accustomed for the greater part of a year to his being
away. It was a surprise, then, when he reappeared; and th
manner of his reappearance was even more surprising.

Around midday, as peasants were trekking from marke
to their farms and villages, four horsemen were seen ridin
slowly through the vineyards towards the city. People stop
ped and gazed as they drew closer – not at the rider in fron
whose head was bowed and who wore plain garments dust
with travel, but at the three who followed him. They wer
dressed in pale blue clothes that billowed as they rode, an
their skins were black as night. Even the guard failed at firs
to recognize the gaunt, weathered figure of their Count
their eyes passed rapidly to his extraordinary entourage
and they stared agog at the three huge men in monk-lik
robes with faces and hands the colour of no human they ha
ever seen. A sharp order brought their attention back to th
shabby figure who accompanied them – and suddenly on
word began to speed through the city and the castle. Fulk

He had returned. No one, knowing their lord, had been i
much doubt that he would return, even from so hazardous
journey. But there was no triumphal entry: he was just ther

among them once more. Gradually during the following days his adventures became pieced together, and the amazement of his listeners was enhanced by the constant attendance upon him of the three black servants, whose huge dignity seemed in no way touched by the stares and whispers they aroused.

It was strange having him with them as though nothing at all had happened. He gave orders as before; he summoned Audemand, Sebrand, Roger, Bouchard, as before; and he appeared from time to time in the great hall, only to depart again quite suddenly, just as he always had. But it was strange none the less; and it was some days before those around him began to understand what it was that they found almost disconcerting about his presence. Then they realized that he had changed. He had become — there was no other word for it — gentle! Perhaps there was suspicion among those accustomed to his storms that this eerie calm might presage an eruption of unprecedented violence. Or perhaps the quiet gaze he awarded to those who approached him with some request instilled less ease of mind than the fierce glare which they had come to expect. Formerly people knew where they were with Fulk, even if they did not like it: now they were not sure at all. It was as if he knew more about them than he used to, and was measuring them.

The Chancellor, more than anyone, appeared to relish this state of calm.

'I have news for you, Sebrand,' he announced some four days after the return of the Count. Sebrand was making his way to the mason's yard by the cathedral to talk to Rollo, whose joyfulness since his return with Milesende had become a delight to him. Audemand was approaching from that very direction, and had hailed him with a flourish of his staff.

'First of all,' he said, placing a hand on Sebrand's shoulder, 'you will be grieved to hear that the Count of Maine's sister is no more.'

413

Sebrand stared at the Chancellor in bewilderment. But before he had time to absorb the news Audemand continued, his face showing every sign of relishing the effect of his words.

'Since this unfortunate death releases you from a duty you have never shirked' – and he paused while his mouth worked its way in and out of a smile – 'I took it upon myself, with the privilege of age, to approach the lord Fulk about another marriage.' And he peered aslant at Sebrand, whose face suddenly looked as if it had been struck by a gale.

Sebrand opened his mouth to speak, but Audemand raised his hand firmly.

'I thought it wise not to mention that in his absence you had been enjoying some of the sweets of marriage for some time.' Sebrand began to look irritated, and his foot tapped the ground nervously. 'For which I don't blame you in the least,' Audemand went on, ignoring the expression on the young man's face. 'I did precisely the same, I may tell you. Love can't always be constrained within these formal ceremonies. D'you not think so?'

The muscles in Sebrand's face were taut with exasperation.

'What did the Count say, Audemand?'

The Chancellor raised his eyebrows in surprise.

'He agreed!'

Sebrand closed his eyes and let out a long, deep breath.

'He talked – rather surprisingly – about love,' Audemand explained. 'I believe going to Jerusalem has melted him. It would have killed me, mind you; but then I've never felt the need to suffer for my own good. There's quite enough suffering as it is ... Fulk did add, I might say, that the city of Nantes was likely to remain in Conan's hands rather temporarily in his view.' Audemand looked at Sebrand quizzically. 'He seemed to think that you would be playing your part in restoring it to Anjou before very long, after which your bride would be a lady of some ... reckoning!'

The Chancellor made a move to depart. He mopped his brow. Then, with a cloth still held before his face, he added:

'It's not that the marriage is conditional, you understand; but Fulk did think you might make an admirable Count of Nantes. He's been regaled with your military triumphs in his absence ... My God, I've had enough of this summer, Sebrand.' And he mopped his brow again.

Sebrand was reeling. He could marry the woman he wanted. He might become lord of Nantes. These favours from a man who had flung him in prison and then departed for nine months without a word. If it made sense it was not sense he could grasp at this moment.

Audemand was raising his staff in farewell.

'By the way,' he added, 'I assume you're on your way to see our master-mason. In my own eyes the likeness of myself is more flattering than that of the Lady Ermengarde — depending of course on one's point of view. You'll find Rollo cheerful enough. Fulk has confirmed his permission to marry Milesende. He suggested that you might even be married in the same ceremony, in the Count's chapel — though as you know we have at present no chaplain. Father Baudouin is apparently well employed doing what no one knew he could do, least of all with such equipment.' Audemand chuckled. 'The Count was rather surprised at that.'

And then, as if quite another mood had been touched by the thought, he said half to himself:

'There are men of God, Sebrand, who would be seen as devils if their clothes were different. The Count has suffered much from that disguise — his chaplain, I mean of course. Count Fulk has endured more pain than you or I.'

Sebrand watched him make his way towards the castle gate, still wiping his brow and tapping the ground a little feebly with his staff.

He found Rollo in precisely the frame of mind the Chancellor had described. He had never seen the Norman so elated, and the two men passed an hour in the sun assessing the remarkable changes in their fortunes. Rollo had expected, he said, to find himself stripped of every privilege he enjoyed for having abducted Milesende and defied the orders of the Lady Hildegarde. Instead, the Count had summoned Milesende and himself and offered them his blessing, adding his deep regrets at the trials imposed upon Milesende. He even commented on how lovely she was. He had then inquired about progress on the cathedral, adding that he hoped Rollo would soon be able to delegate that work to some trusted subordinate since he was anxious to proceed with the abbey of Beaulieu – this was to be his life's work, he stressed, the finest building in Christendom, and to be dedicated to the Holy Sepulchre, a fragment of which he had brought with him from Jerusalem. And he had shown Rollo the chunk of stone, together with the piece of the True Cross and the cords which had bound Our Lord's hands.

Sebrand looked startled.

'You mean, Fulk brought back such things? I never knew. I thought he went as a poor penitent for the good of his soul.'

Rollo smiled.

'And what better medicine for a man's soul than to possess such powerful relics? – at least in the eyes of the Church! Fulk is not a man to miss such an opportunity, Sebrand – you must know that!'

'It will certainly make Beaulieu a place of insufferable pilgrimage: and I suppose the Count will profit from that too.' And Sebrand laughed. 'Well, never mind, so long as we stay in the sun, my friend.' He placed a hand on Rollo's arm. 'I'm truly happy for you. And I shall be intrigued to see what blessings he showers on you for your wedding.'

Rollo looked at Sebrand wistfully.

'I think I want nothing from Fulk,' he said. 'Except his trust.'

'Ah! That may be the thing he finds hardest to give,' Sebrand replied with a wry smile.

'Then I would settle for being left in peace.' Rollo bent down and picked up a stone-chisel, turning it over in his hand. 'Because *this* is what I am, and what I want to do. To build, and to live with the woman I love. That's enough.'

Sebrand gazed at Rollo thoughtfully, and nodded.

'You're a lucky man. What I do is fight. That's what *I'm* good at, and that − I suppose − is what I am!'

'Would you rather exchange with me?'

Sebrand was silent for a few moments. Then he laughed. 'No!'

Celebrations to mark the Count's safe return were delayed in accordance with Fulk's own wishes. Exhaustion after his voyage and illness compelled him to rest: and for the Count to need rest was so remarkable that people assumed his ordeals to have been worse even than he was prepared to relate. Word reached Angers at this time of a group of noblemen from Aquitaine who had been butchered on their arrival at Jerusalem after requesting from the Caliph permission to venerate the holy shrine. That Count Fulk should have survived, had even received hospitality from the same Caliph, seemed more than ever a miracle.

Then, some three weeks after his return, a procession of closed waggons arrived at the gates of the city, and the Count's chamberlain was commanded to arrange for the huge chests they contained to be brought into the great hall. At the same time it was announced that the long-delayed feast would take place two days later. The Count, it was made known, would preside, and would personally reveal the nature of this unexpected cargo.

It was to be the first occasion that the entire court was to assemble in the company of its lord since before the tragedy of the Countess Elizabeth almost a year before. Lords who had passed the summer on their lands with their families were summoned by messengers who rode out from the city across the whole of Anjou. The labyrinth of the castle began to fill with faces normally seen only during preparations for war.

One entirely new face – except of course to Audemand – was that of a most handsome young man by the name of Hubert. There was much fluttering of eyes on his appearance until it was revealed that the young man was in fact a priest, and was likely to become the Count's new chaplain.

'I can't see a man as beautiful as that being allowed to keep his vows very long,' observed the Lady Ermengarde to Hersende as she cast an interested eye towards where a group of young women were being entertained by the newcomer. 'That's the end of celibacy in one house of God,' she went on. 'And I don't imagine he'll need a nun with a lash to hoist his standard.'

Hubert, it emerged to everyone's surprise, was a cousin of the late Countess Elizabeth and a nephew of Count Bouchard the Venerable – her father. Since the noble count had now retreated to a monastery in Paris in his grief, the young man's father had become the lord of Vendôme. It did not need any unusual perception on the part of Fulk's court to understand what must have taken place under Audemand's skilful diplomacy. The only outstanding answer to be supplied was – what high post had been promised the young man in return for the loyalty of Vendôme which had been so shattered by the death of the Countess Elizabeth? The position of chaplain would certainly not be enough to expunge such painful memories, it was thought.

'Perhaps we should remember that Bishop Renaud is not a young man,' observed Sulpice, standing with Roger, Maurice and Archambaud some distance from the female circle round the beautiful Hubert. 'The Bishop is also far from well,' he added.

The others nodded. So, the young man with the ladies fluttering around him was to be a rather temporary chaplain, and before long Angers might acquire a bishop of a very different character from the austere Renaud.

While the arrival of a handsome chaplain was diverting many of the ladies from their customary boredom, the Lady Ermengarde was more than usually alone. She still missed the bright company of Elizabeth, who was irreplaceable in her life. Without her the court of Count Fulk was a hollow place in which she could share few of her intimate thoughts and little of her appetite for intrigue and gossip. She was ageing, she realized – becoming drawn and flaccid – without children – without a husband to speak of – discontented with lovers. Even Adelaide she missed: since the business of Milesende the two women had scarcely spoken. One of Ermengarde's few pleasures was to be with the little girl, Elizabeth's daughter: she would play with her by the hour, teach her songs, laugh and hug her. She even spoke to the child of her mother, and they would hold one another and weep until a nurse would appear anxiously – and quietly leave with tears in her own eyes.

It was an entertaining diversion to think of Hersende and her indignation over Sebrand's escapade with the Lady Adelaide, and it gave Ermengarde some pleasure to plan how to make the young man sick with jealousy on her behalf. She already had with her the dress she had designed for Hersende to wear for the occasion – and what better occasion than the feast to celebrate the return of Count Fulk? The only question was: who should be Hersende's victim?

'It must be someone suitable,' she explained to the girl on the afternoon of the great feast.

Hersende nodded shyly. Her misery of the past month lifted a little when she thought of Sebrand falling contrite and adoring at her feet. She hoped that the suitable young man would prove easy to please, and when she tried on the dress she blushed to realize that he would almost certainly be so. Ermengarde stood watching with envious admiration.

By 'suitable', Ermengarde of course meant suitable to herself, since she had every intention of profiting from the occasion by consoling the young man afterwards. Given a free choice she would have selected either Sulpice – the young Adonis – or the beautiful newcomer, Hubert. But the former was married and the latter a priest; and while neither condition was a barrier to her personally, she did have to consider the reputation of Hersende. Ermengarde's dilemma had not been eased by the arrival of the three enormous black servants of Count Fulk; and she had already expended some charm on the Count in endeavouring to persuade him to part with one of them as an act of kindness. She was still hopeful, and the prospect quite rekindled her interest in the male sex. Meanwhile, as the object of Hersende's charms she had decided on Giraud Berlay – who was neither black, nor married, nor a priest, but who did have very fine thighs and the most gentle charm.

'All you have to do is to gaze at him,' she explained. 'Occasionally lower your eyes as if the pain of love is too heavy to bear. The dress I've made for you will do the rest.'

'Are you sure?' said Hersende.

'Of course! Young men like Giraud are just waiting to be slain by love. Fine soldiers always are.'

'But Sebrand's a fine soldier,' replied Hersende uncertainly.

'Exactly!' retorted Ermengarde. 'And once you've shown him you can't just be pushed over by his lance he'll be yours for ever. And then, my dear, you can let him use his lance as much as he pleases.'

Hersende blushed, and Ermengarde thought what a very pretty and foolish girl she was. And the two women parted to prepare for the evening.

The sun set, and it became a night of torches and splendour. No one could remember seeing so many men and women in fine clothes in the great hall of the castle. Jewels glistened on silk and on soft shoulders. Minstrels sang between the bouts of dancing, and the finest wines were raised in silver goblets to toast the Count who had returned safe from across the world. Among those in the company of the Count some recognized the Lady Hildegarde, pale and graceful, wearing the smile of a woman who found herself supremely happy — as she had good reason to be. Only she, apart from Fulk himself, knew that she was shortly to become the Countess of Anjou, though it is probable that a good many people in that company guessed as much just from looking at her.

Fewer people, it is true, were looking at the Lady Hildegarde than at two younger women who were dancing in the torchlight with the freshness of flowers. Milesende, her hair shining like black water against the whiteness of her shoulders, moved with the grace of a faun, her red gown shimmering and a golden heart resting in the valley of her breast. A plain gold ring adorned her left hand. She danced with the ease of a woman in love, unaware and uncaring of all eyes except those of the tall Norman who gazed on her continuously and held her fingers as she turned, holding them sometimes to his lips.

But if it was obvious that Milesende was in love, it was less clear what state guided the movements of the other girl upon whom eyes were fixed. She glided like a swan among the other dancers, and as she passed all heads turned to follow her in a silence of envy or of longing. The gown she wore held her body in outline as if laid upon it like a white skin, so that although she was as modestly covered as a nun she appeared to be covered by nothing at all. Her lover, Sebrand, was never far from her side, yet she seemed hardly to notice him, and she danced most of all with the slim Giraud Berlay whose shy and gentle face was coaxed into the softest of smiles, and his eyes when they met hers were tender and warm.

To her confusion Hersende found herself responding with pleasure to the young man's silent company. He danced as though his movements were his own, and his hands when he touched her might have been playing inaudible notes on her body. She danced closer to him so that he might touch her again, and she felt a tremor of excitement in her skin. It was as if, when he gazed at her, he knew her very well and had always known her. Since she loved Sebrand she could not understand what this might mean, and she longed to rush away and ask someone – her sister – except then this moment would be lost and she did not want to break it. So she danced, and her body moved to the rhythm of his gaze.

Late in the evening the Count called for silence. The music and the laughter ebbed and all eyes turned towards the tall figure of Fulk. People remembered the last time he had spoken to them in this hall, and some of them shuddered. They waited, and as he stood there before them they realized to their astonishment that he was nervous. It was such a surprising awareness that people felt quite disturbed, and then – unexpectedly – moved. His face seemed more lined, his eyes and mouth less sure of themselves.

He said little at first, speaking as if anxious to get the occasion over as quickly as possible. He was happy, he announced, to be back among faces he knew and loved. Then he stretched out a hand towards the Lady Hildegarde: he wished to welcome his dear cousin from Aquitaine, he said. Rather mild applause rose from the hall, and there were some sharp exchanges of looks. Finally he called two of the black servants to unlock the huge sea-chests that stood behind him, explaining that he wished to make a gift to every lady in the court. A more enthusiastic murmur arose and people began to press forward to see what the chests might contain. Then there was a gasp as the Count raised before them a length of woven silk which was of a colour no one in that hall could remember ever having seen. It was a red more brilliant than rubies, and where it fell in folds the shadows were a purple darker than amethyst.

People stood amazed as gradually the vast sea-chests,

fifteen or twenty of them, were emptied of their treasure —
until finally the long tables at the far end of the hall became
buried under that blood-red sea of silk.

The Count grew jovial as he watched the treasure pour
around him.

'There!' he said at length, spreading his arms wide. 'I
wanted the women of my court to wear the most beautiful
silk in the world.' And he beckoned them forward.

There were ladies unaccustomed to leaving the shadows
of their husbands: suddenly they found themselves embraced by their Count and then swathed in gorgeous silk.
Fulk appraised each one graciously, sometimes turning to
Hildegarde for approval, sometimes laughing, jesting, and
now clearly enjoying himself enormously. Even those who
had lived in fear or loathing of Fulk discovered their feelings
towards their Count to be quite altered, and in a short time
there was hardly a man or woman present who did not feel —
even if reluctantly — the peculiar magic which the man could
wave over them. He told them, during this strange ceremony, how it had been told to him in Jerusalem that the
rarest and most prized of all dyes could be found in the city
of Tyre where it was made from a seashell discovered only in
those waters: how he had met a Phoenician ship's-captain in
Crete who was travelling northwards with — as it turned out
— a cargo of silk that had been dyed with this very colour:
how the captain had intended to sell it in Genoa from where
it would have found its way to the court of the Holy Roman
Emperor to adorn his majesty: and how he, Fulk, had persuaded the captain to sell the entire cargo to him instead.
The royal colour, the Emperor called it — according to the
ship's captain: no one else might wear it. But now, Fulk
went on proudly, when kings and dukes visited Anjou, they
would depart in envy.

It was the first time the nobles of Fulk's court understood
that their lord saw himself as a king.

The Count received the Lady Ermengarde with a specially

423

affectionate embrace, whereupon she insisted that Fulk's small daughter receive a similar length of the rare silk: and there were tears in Ermengarde's eyes, and in many others, as the Count raised the child high in his arms and kissed her.

Hersende he embraced too, with much applause from the men in the hall, especially two men who had looked at no one else but her all evening – one of them dazed with love, the other racked with jealousy.

Her sister, Milesende, followed more shyly, to equal applause. The Count kissed her most fondly, but there were several pairs of eyes in that hall that detected in the impassive smile of the Lady Hildegarde a certain tightening of the lips.

Maurice's timid wife, Adèle, advanced and retreated without raising her eyes; and there followed the wives of Audemand's sons, and of Sulpice and Archambaud. Finally it was the turn of the Lady Adelaide, who had been waiting in the farthest shadows praying that some miracle would prevent her moment ever coming. She looked paler than ever, almost a ghost. Nothing in the Count's manner betrayed the least coldness towards her, but as she turned away carrying her unwanted burden of silk her face was a grey mask upon which fortune had engraved its wounds.

The feast was over, and the company dispersed with a sobriety which rather disconcerted those accustomed to turning their backs on a rubble of flesh and goblets. Perhaps it was the pained exit of the Lady Adelaide which lowered the spirits. Perhaps it was the very unexpectedness of the Count's manner. Or perhaps it was the presiding sobriety of Fulk's cousin Hildegarde who, it was already hoped, might not appear too often at such gatherings.

There was one figure of the court who had left the festivities some time before, without his departure being noticed. The Chancellor Audemand was accustomed to keeping one ear sharply tuned to sounds beyond those of the company he kept; and early during the evening the lightest of coughs had informed him that his presence might not be so urgently required at the feast as at some more private place.

Still wearing that smile of cunning benevolence which hid anything Audemand wanted it to hide, he had slipped away from the hall. Audemand rarely needed to be told much, only led to whatever figure it was who sought his company. There were many such figures: none of them knew each other, and all they had in common was that each man carried with him the seal of Anjou, and each was handsomely rewarded for his services. Few people other than the Count knew that the keenest weapon of the Chancellor's diplomacy was the presence of these figures in every court of Europe, from Winchester to Cordoba, Rome to Constantinople. They were not precisely ambassadors because Audemand had these as well, more prominently displayed though rather less well provided for. They were referred to, if at all, as 'friends': the Count and the Chancellor, between themselves, talked about 'our spies'.

Audemand was happy to see that the figure waiting for him in his rooms was from Paris.

'Well, Gilbert.' He poured out a goblet and handed it to the young man. 'You must have been missing our Angevin wine.'

And he lowered himself carefully on to a couch with his hands folded over the handle of his staff. The visitor emptied his goblet appreciatively, poured himself another and sat facing the Chancellor.

He had come from the royal court at Dreux, he explained, where the King and his bride had passed the summer. Now they had just returned to Paris – for reasons of some urgency. The day before their departure a legate had reached Dreux from the Vatican. (Audemand's eyes widened.) The King had received the papal legate alone and talked with him for several hours. He had emerged looking deeply troubled and had immediately gone to speak to the Queen: they had remained together for the rest of that day.

'Do I need to ask you the nature of the message from Rome?' Audemand's moustaches were betraying the suggestion of a smile. 'It cannot be that you don't know, Gilbert.'

The young man's face remained expressionless, and he spoke just one word.

'Anathema!'

The Chancellor whistled through his teeth like an astonished snake. And then he nodded his head repeatedly, his fingers excitedly tapping the handle of his staff.

'Well, well!' And he breathed out heavily. 'Who would have thought we could have done our work so well?' he added, his moustaches twitching again. 'Presumably, Gilbert,' he went on, 'the order of excommunication applies only if the King refuses to have his marriage to Berthe annulled.'

His visitor nodded in agreement.

'And is the King permitted time to disentangle himself from the marriage?' asked Audemand.

'That I don't know.'

'We must hope there is not too much time.'

The suggestion of a frown settled on the young man's face.

'The King loves her deeply,' he said with a sigh.

Audemand looked at him sharply, and then smiled.

'But perhaps not so much as his kingdom.'

There was silence between the two men for a few moments before the Chancellor made moist sounds with his lips and gazed at Gilbert from beneath his eyebrows.

'So what do you imagine he will do?'

'One thing I know,' the young man replied.

And Audemand listened attentively as Gilbert explained how the King intended to call his dukes and his counts to meet him before the autumn was out: the purpose, he assumed, must be to gauge their loyalty to him. Audemand looked at Gilbert in surprise.

'Loyalty to him if he's excommunicated!' The suggestion of a laugh came from the Chancellor. 'I think it would be a high price to pay for a man such as the Count who has narrowly escaped excommunication himself. Loyalty, what's more,' he went on, 'to a king who's just married the widow of his deepest enemy. Oh, Gilbert, what a very simple king!'

Audemand rose and poured the young man a further goblet of wine.

'And do we know where this lordly gathering is to be?' he went on. Gilbert took a sip of wine.

'Orléans, I believe. And very soon!'

Audemand looked away.

'I see,' he said after a moment. 'So the Count can expect a royal summons.' And he nodded. 'Well, we shall have to prepare our thoughts. What, I wonder, must we do to obtain the King's loyalty to *us*? Now, that will test our skill!'

And a contented smile spread across the old face. Nothing rejuvenated Audemand more keenly than the challenge to outwit those in a stronger position than he. Or was the King in a stronger position? he wondered, as he bade good-bye to his visitor and prepared for sleep. The King had his lover and his crown: he stood in some danger of losing both.

There were others within the castle of Angers who slept less well than Audemand on that September night.

Hersende still barred Sebrand from her rooms, and tonight she wished she still had the company of her sister Milesende to share with her the delicious confusion of her tears. Hersende had prayed that tonight would be the fulfilment of all she had longed for, and Sebrand's whole love would be hers – and from her lover's face while she danced a few hours ago she knew she already had what she wanted. But now she did not know if she wanted it, and when she closed her eyes it was another face that smiled at her. His eyes opened her like a new flower. It was as if she were listening to music for the first time, and all the old tunes were forgotten.

Sebrand's own state of mind was as dark as the night. The joy of knowing he was free to marry Hersende had withered with the first gaze she had turned on Giraud Berlay. He could not understand what had happened, nor what he felt. Jealousy was a new pain to Sebrand and he was like a man shipwrecked. There was nothing he could cling to that would hold: the bright stars of love that had always appeared such gay and pretty things to grasp now felt far and inaccessible. He paced the room a hundred times, and rehearsed a hundred times the events of the evening, hoping to reveal some clue, some explanation, which would lift the torment. He could not understand – and misery, resentment and anger churned within him. As dawn broke he could bear it no longer. Calling a servant, he ordered a horse to be saddled. Before the sun rose the city gates were opened and Sebrand rode towards the forest without glancing back.

Amid the tremors of that night there was one person in the castle who slept quite unaware of the intrigues and the pains. The Lady Adelaide, once she had closed her eyes, would never open them again.

THIRTEEN

ON A SILVERY MORNING late in September two young men
scarcely more than boys rode side by side westwards
towards the city of Rennes. They were dressed in plain
garments as if they were hunters, yet a group of armed
horsemen formed a loose cordon around them as they rode,
keeping a keen watch on the forest and the clearings through
which they passed. Woodcock swerved low through the
undergrowth and deer bounded among the trees, but no one
raised a bow and there were no dogs to unleash in pursuit.
The party of men continued at the same pace: they avoided
the villages and farmsteads, and they crossed river-fords
cautiously. After a while the riders came to a stretch of
sandy wasteland between two belts of oak forest. It was a
bleak, abandoned place, and the young men decided to cross
the open ground rather than make the long detour among
the trees. Apart from tufts of heather and stunted gorse the
ground was parched and bare, and ahead of them a low
bank cut across the wilderness from forest to forest.

Suddenly one of the riders reined his horse and the others
heard him call out. They gazed around them and their
bodies stiffened. Thin furrows had been carved by the wind
like waves, and in the troughs between the ridges of sand the
men looked down on to a sea of bones. It was as if the
ground beneath their horses' feet were a gigantic carcass
which the wind had partially stripped of skin.

'Where are we?' exclaimed the elder of the two young
men. His voice sounded hoarse.

'Conquereuil,' answered one of the soldiers – a Breton
who had been sent to escort the two visitors from Touraine

429

to Brittany. 'I've heard of this place ... We should leave,' he said uneasily. 'It's damned.' And he wheeled his horse and rode off. The others followed him, their horses' hooves slithering on that windswept carpet of death.

The two young men could remember their father talking of Conquereuil and the slaughter of the Bretons by Count Fulk, and how Conan had managed to slip away; how he had never recovered from the shame of that battle – a kind of madness had overtaken him and his hair turned white. Then their own father had died before their eyes: they remembered the giant Fulk advancing towards him with his sword drawn, and Odo's face a mask of pain as his eyes widened like white stones and his knees collapsed without a blow struck. And they had fled in terror. Their mother had hastened them away from Tours by night towards Paris, and everything had been confusion and fear. 'Avenge your father!' she had said to them when they were a little older. 'Join with Conan and crush him!'

Conan was waiting for them as they reached Rennes the following day. The scarred, white-haired figure advanced towards them in the courtyard and shook the hand first of the young Odo, then of his brother Tibalt. His eyes were grey as frost and his lips moved without a smile. Even his rooms, where he led them, seemed cold as winter on this early-autumn day.

He had invited them, he said, because the time had almost come to fulfil a vow he had made many years before. Together they would kill Count Fulk and sack the city and castle of Angers. He and their father, he explained, had determined to crush the lord of Angers and divide Anjou between Brittany and Touraine. But Fulk had armed himself with powerful allies and had proved too strong. (Conan's eyes narrowed like a man wincing at the sun.) And then Count Odo had died, and their position was even weaker. So he had decided on another plan. (He paused and took a deep breath, gazing at the two young men with those hard

430

grey eyes.) First he had retaken the city of Nantes and killed the imposter Judicael. From Nantes, gradually he had been able to throw invisible cords round Angers. It had taken time. But now there were four Bretons within the castle undetected: one of them was in contact with his eldest son Budic, held prisoner there; another was a member of the castle guard; a third kept watch at the main gate of the city; the fourth had obtained a key to the armoury.

Odo and Tibalt listened to Conan's plan without a word. The weathered features seemed to quiver with energy as he spoke, and his wrinkles flowed into the scars on his face.

'The King, your stepfather, has summoned his lords to meet him in Orléans – as you know.'

He paused again, twisting an amethyst ring on his finger. Then his mouth gave a twitch which sent a ripple across the furrows and scars of his face.

'Fulk will be there,' he went on quietly. 'And so will you and I, Odo. And there we shall destroy him.'

The eyes of the young men grew round. Their only memory of Count Fulk was of a huge figure striding forward with his sword raised. How to kill such a man? And in the presence of the King? Conan saw the expression on their faces and held up both hands as if to ward off their thoughts.

'Of course we shan't kill him. We don't need to do that, because he will be ours. All we have to do is to detain him. And I shall have the means to do that. Then ...'

There was a pause while the lean, sallow figure of Conan gazed about him as if surveying on the walls of that bleak room the scene of Fulk's ultimate destruction. He looked at his visitors.

'Now, listen,' he said. And he began to outline what was in his mind. The objective, he explained, was the crushing of Anjou – an upstart state which threatened both Touraine on one side and Brittany on the other. To achieve this, two things had to be accomplished simultaneously. The city of Angers must be taken; and Fulk must be held. This was why he had waited for this moment; otherwise he could have struck while Fulk was away in Jerusalem. But Fulk was half the strength of Anjou, and he would have returned and roused his allies. Now it was possible to have them both — Fulk and Angers — separately but at the same time.

'This is what we do,' he went on. 'I shall raise a small force in Nantes; and you, Odo, will do the same in Tours. Once Fulk has left for Orléans, those two forces will move stealthily to within striking distance of Angers — from the east and the west.' Conan's hands moved together like two claws. 'If detected, they'll seem like small raiding parties and disappear into the forest. My sons will lead the Bretons. Gelduin de Saumur and Geoffrey de St Aignan are already alerted to lead the Tourangais with you, Tibalt. With those two fine soldiers you'll be in good company: don't fear! Everything is arranged.'

Conan's plan had the polished detail of long workmanship, and he laid it out before the young Count and his brother like a treasure every jewel of which had been measured, fingered lovingly, weighed. It had been the sole occupation of his mind for more than two years, ever since he had dragged himself from the graveyard of Conquereuil and locked himself away in this high room without food or company, only the burning pain of his hate.

He explained with calm precision how a message would be smuggled into the castle of Angers as soon as it became known when the King would reach Orléans. While Fulk was waiting to greet his monarch, the two forces of Brittany and Touraine would converge on Angers. The four Bretons within the castle would then play their part. Budic would be released, the gates of both the castle and the city would be opened at an exact hour, and the armoury set on fire. The defenders would be taken by surprise, and with no weapons to defend themselves.

For the first time in many years Conan smiled — like a wolf baring his teeth at a trapped kid. The Count of Rennes turned to gaze from the high window over his ancient lands, and it was as if he could hear the music of a harp blowing from the distant sea and the drowned city of Is.

Count Fulk and his entourage departed for Orléans in a manner appropriate to a summons from the King.

The proud figure all in red on the black stallion Moro led his knights and his bodyguard majestically out of the city gates at first light on an early-October day. They rode through the laden vineyards as harvesters were beginning to congregate with deep reed-baskets strapped to their shoulders. Heavy dew glistened on the horses' legs as the riders passed by. People watched with expressionless faces until the party of men became no more than a cluster of coloured dots moving towards the forest: then they bent to their work, and the procession of laden baskets started to move to and from the tall carts drawn up along the edges of the fields. Pale sunlight began to part the mist into long threads strung between the trees and across the grey river. Within the forest it flowed like a chill liquid among the oaks beginning to glow golden with autumn. The faces of the riders were damp, and their hands cold.

Riding with Fulk were three knights, including his High Constable, Sebrand. The two men had exchanged only a few words since the latter's return from Chemillé, his domain, the evening before. Apart from Fulk, Sebrand had seen no one else except the Chancellor, Audemand, who had greeted him and made an offhand inquiry about his sudden departure and disappearance for almost a week.

'I'm told your lady has been quite distraught,' Audemand had added.

'That surprises me,' Sebrand had replied. 'I imagined she would have plenty to occupy her mind.'

But even as he said it Sebrand felt a spurt of joy. He had spent a week of misery at his old home in Chemillé which he had scarcely visited since the death of his father Barthélémi more than two years ago. Never before in his life had he moped; but for a week he had done little else. The image of Hersende had pursued him, always out of reach: Hersende asleep in his arms for all those months when they had been lovers; Hersende laughing with love in her eyes and her arms reaching for him when he returned from battle; Hersende in a white skin of a dress, her wonderful body turning to the fingers of another man as she danced. Hunger and pain lunged at Sebrand like daggers, and he had no armour against them except to flee.

And now – to hear that she had been distraught! For all his relief and joy, a sullen pride held him back from seeing Hersende, boosted by a fear lest Audemand be wrong and Hersende might at that moment be lying sated in Giraud's arms. So he left with Fulk for Orléans without even having set eyes on her. But she rode with him in his mind.

Count Fulk seldom spoke while he rode: to anyone with him it was as if it was his thoughts that were travelling, encased in the silent shell of those long features. And on this journey Fulk had many thoughts to fill his mind. There had been moments in his life when he had felt another hand to be guiding his own, and that he was capable of steering where no one else had sailed. To others who were aware of it, this sense of destiny accounted for much of the aloof glory of the man: a dark star guided him, drawing him into the light.

He was aware that another such moment was very close, and, as before, that half-blurred vision of light was accompanied by intimations of great risk, unknown danger. He did not know what, but he knew that it was there, and that he had to pass through that danger in order to attain his goal. He had felt it at Conquereuil as he leapt the ditch of death; he had felt it as the ship bearing him to the Holy Land slipped unscathed over the murderous rocks. And he felt it now.

For the first time he would meet King Robert. For the first

time off a battlefield he would meet the Count of Rennes and the young Count of Blois. Three enemies – whose hands he would shake in peace, but their eyes would meet in hatred.

'Sebrand,' he said as they rested that evening at Amboise, in Archambaud's castle. 'Watch Conan very closely. And watch who's around him . . . And when you look at the King, remember that his eyes are hiding what he believes I do not know.'

Sebrand looked puzzled.

'And what is it you know?' he asked.

'I'll tell you. Robert has been given six months to annul his marriage to Berthe, or else' – and the Count's eyes looked upwards as if contemplating some judgement poised there – 'he'll be excommunicated. Six months. That's all. Audemand heard it from Rome only two days ago. Our Chancellor has done his work well.'

Fulk rose and poured them both a goblet of wine from a pitcher on the table.

'That means he will be pronounced "anathema". No one may serve him, support him, befriend him. He will have no rights, not even the right to his own life should someone choose to take it.'

He laughed, and Sebrand blinked in astonishment.

'So what do we do?' he asked.

'There's nothing we need to do,' Fulk replied, and his voice was quietly triumphant. 'That's the joy of it. We can be most truly loyal, and just wait for it to happen.'

Then Fulk's face became serious.

'Sebrand,' he went on, 'when the King's stepson is your enemy on one side of you – and on the other side stands his closest ally, Conan – there can be no room for kindnesses . . . We have to play Judas. We've delivered the kiss, thanks to the Pope. Now our role is to smile . . . and wait.'

Sebrand looked thoughtful.

'Do you imagine the King will desert Berthe, if he loves her as they say?'

Fulk gave Sebrand a rather patronizing smile.

'There's the voice of a man in love. He doesn't have to desert her, Sebrand. He can go on loving her as much as he likes. I'm not talking about love, but about marriage.'

Sebrand was reminded of the ruthlessness of Count Fulk, and of how much he had at times loathed him. As the Count talked cynically about love, the face of the Countess Elizabeth rose before his eyes and he felt a twinge of pain. When Fulk had last played Judas, it was she who had died for it. And he thought of Hersende and their nights of love together, and of Rollo and Milesende. Sebrand wondered if Fulk could possibly understand that kind of love, and if he did what on earth he would do if it stood in conflict with his ambitions. And yet . . . Sebrand could not help but be aware of the truth of what the Count was saying. He too would be crushed if Odo, Conan and the King were together to squeeze the neck of Anjou. And where would love be then? Kindness would be a beautiful act of suicide.

'There's something else, Sebrand,' said Fulk calmly. 'Berthe is carrying Robert's child. That's another secret his eyes will be trying to hide.' He paused and drained his goblet, and seeing that Sebrand's was also empty he refilled them both, cradling his own within his huge hands as he gazed thoughtfully across the room.

'That complicates matters a great deal for Robert,' he went on. 'Even with the marriage annulled he will have to support her – and who knows? The child could be the future King of France.' He smiled wryly at Sebrand. 'The point is, Robert has no wealth, and almost no lands. And this is where, when the time comes, we can be his saviour.'

Sebrand was listening with morbid curiosity to the underground workings of Fulk's mind. He sipped his wine and waited for the Count to explain.

'Robert will need to remarry,' Fulk continued. 'And he'll need to marry someone very wealthy indeed.'

Sebrand understood. The fragments of story he had heard

from Roger and Sulpice now fitted together, and he saw Fulk's strategy clearly.

'Your cousin Constance?' And Fulk nodded.

'What nobody knows except Audemand and myself – and now you – is that the Count of Toulouse has agreed to cede his lands to the crown on his own death if his daughter becomes Queen of France. That means the whole of Gascony!' A glint appeared in Fulk's eye. 'Robert will not be able to resist that. And once Constance is queen she may have to share her bed with Berthe, but I assure you she'll share nothing else with her. She'll hate Touraine because of Berthe, and we shall have a grateful ally behind the throne of France. As for Conan, we'll see how we can deal with him once and for all.'

It was a long speech for Fulk, and Sebrand was surprised. He was aware of having been initiated into the devious rites of diplomacy, and they made his own role as a soldier seem a rather straightforward business.

'Conan', he suggested, 'seems to be a man easier to defeat than destroy.'

Fulk scrutinized his goblet as if it held the secret of the Breton's downfall.

'This time he must be encouraged to destroy himself,' he said knowingly without explaining what he meant.

Rollo was a contented man. As summer slowly cooled into autumn he began to use every hour of daylight working in the cathedral stoneyard until his back ached and his hands became rough and chipped. Milesende washed the stone-dust from his body and massaged his tired shoulders; and she would pretend to complain when he rolled over and stroked her breasts until her nipples were as hard as dark buds, and he would pull her down on to him until he felt her whole body convulse and she would collapse in his arms with a sigh. When the candles burnt low he would call a servant to bring food and wine; and afterwards, while Milesende slept naked in the black veil of her hair, he would light a lamp and work deep into the night on his designs for the abbey of Beaulieu. And in the early mornings he would be half-wakened by her body twisting against his, her face burying itself in his neck and her hand feeling for his to close round it. This was the hour of paradise — while the day awoke around them.

The cathedral was taking shape. The west door with its arch of carved beak-heads now led into a nave whose walls rose to more than half their full height, broken by a row of small, round-topped windows on either side, and plain square columns whose capitals, decorated with a pattern of leaves, still lay on the ground waiting to be hoisted into position.

Discreetly concealed in the stoneyard were the carved figures and heads destined for the exterior, high under the roof and — as he hoped — invisible to the Bishop's eye. Rollo was uneasy about how these corbels might possibly be put in place without Renaud noticing. He prayed that when the time came the Bishop might suffer some illness for several weeks. In any case they would have to be set in the wall with great speed: thankfully, there would be no lack of helpers since there was hardly a man or woman in all Angers (with the exception of the Bishop) who did not know about them. At times the stoneyard was like a fairground, crowded with laughing and giggling townsfolk all pointing and making jokes, and Rollo was assured that he was the most popular man in Angers. Even the Count had appeared one morning demanding to see these grotesques which he had heard so much about, he said. He had peered rather solemnly for a while, and then leant back and roared with laughter, slapping Rollo heftily on the back. He wanted his own face there, he announced (his *face*, he emphasized with a broad smile). Rollo obliged, and Fulk had laughed even louder. Suggestions for fresh subjects arrived almost hourly, and in

438

this way Rollo learnt more about the intimate habits of the citizens of Angers than the Bishop would ever know. The most popular request was for a portion of Father Baudouin's anatomy: the new cathedral, it was felt, would be incomplete without a representation of the former Chaplain's now famous member. It seemed that the fat cook spoke of it loudly and with reverence. When Rollo insisted that there was no space for further carvings around the roof-line, he received the imaginative suggestion that the clerical penis might be a most effective water-conduit for the nave roof in times of exceptional rain.

Rollo began to wish he had left the idea safely in Normandy, and continued to concern himself with how to evade the Bishop.

Gradually he released more and more of the responsibility for the building work to an under-mason he was in the process of training. Rollo had employed him during the construction of the castles of Langeais and Montbazon, and had come to respect the man's understanding and love of stone. Rollo carved his own head on one of the corbels, and the under-mason became his devotee. He was a man Rollo could trust.

This left him increasingly free to begin the enormous task of planning the abbey of Beaulieu. Rollo spent days in discussion with Count Fulk, and later they sought the opinion of the Abbot of St Aubin close by. The scale was to be colossal. There was to be room for four hundred monks and one hundred and fifty lay brothers. Rollo's own experience at Jumièges was invaluable: even the abbot knew nothing about so large an establishment, while Fulk himself knew only that it had to *be* very large. Nothing small would do. It had to be worthy, he insisted, to receive the fragment of the Holy Sepulchre and the other potent relics he had brought back from Jerusalem. But apart from that consideration, he was happy to leave details to the abbot and master-mason. Such 'details' included refectories, kitchens, cellars, dormitories, a chapter-house, a guest-house with quarters for visiting bishops and abbots, as well as accommodation suitable for men of differing status — lords, monks, clerks, beggars. Each guest-house had to have a separate oratory. There had to be a school; also outbuildings to shelter the abbey's vassals in troubled times; as well as workshops and homes for people of numerous trades — cobblers, smiths, coopers, parchment-makers, founders, masons, carpenters, wood-carvers, brewers, bakers, butchers, clothiers, cooks, gardeners, and so on.

And — of course — the abbey church. This, Rollo explained after a visit to Beaulieu to measure and survey the terrain, was to be one hundred paces long, with a nave span of eighteen paces, the roof to be held by twenty interior supports. There were to be twin western towers — octagonal as at Jumièges — surmounted by steeples. At the eastern end would be a third tower, and below it three or even five apses for private prayer, the exteriors to be adorned with sculptured arcades and friezes, the interiors painted, like the nave. Into the western face of the abbey church was to be set the most handsome portal ever devised, with elaborate bands of sculpture — vividly coloured — representing biblical themes of a moral nature; perhaps the abbot would like to choose which, Rollo suggested. And in the centre, above the west entrance, there was to be a tympanum of Christ in Glory flanked by the symbols of the four evangelists, which he — Rollo — would undertake to carve entirely himself.

In the final meeting with the abbot he produced numerous drawings of all these details as he referred to them, and Count Fulk and the abbot said not a word.

Finally Rollo turned to the Count and reminded him of certain strange buildings that had so astonished him — he had said — on his journey to the Holy Land, and which he had expressed interest in reproducing here.

'I have two ideas, my lord Fulk, based on what you have told me.'

And he unrolled in front of the Count a large sheet of parchment that showed a roof viewed from below. Fulk's eyes widened in surprise, and he looked at Rollo, still without speaking. The entire roof of the nave, between the western and eastern towers, consisted of octagonal pyramids, one after the other, hollow within, and each rising to a point like a tall hat. Between each pyramid the drawing showed a broad arch spanning the width of the nave.

The Count stood up, his face blank with surprise.

'I told you about pyramids, and you give them to me for my church!' And he shook his head in bewilderment. Then he turned to the abbot.

'I should explain, my lord Abbot. The pyramids in Egypt are the largest buildings in the world. They are monuments of a grandeur I never expected to see. Our master-mason proposes to offer that grandeur to God.'

He turned back to Rollo.

'I don't know what to say. I'm overwhelmed! ... But if you can build them, do it.'

And he placed a hand on Rollo's shoulder.

'One thing!' And a hint of laughter rose in his voice. 'The pyramids in Egypt have *four* sides. You've given me *eight*. Is it that you're trying to outdo the pharaohs?'

'My lord Fulk' – Rollo's eyes betrayed the smile he was trying to conceal – 'the men who made the pyramids had the advantage of building on the ground. This is a roof. The weight has to be distributed between the walls and the arches that bridge them.'

Fulk looked hard at Rollo, and nodded.

'And now tell me about your second idea. Is it another pyramid?'

'Yes, in a way it is.'

Rollo could see the Abbot of St Aubin looking ever more bothered. He wished it was Abbot Gervais instead of this humble figure whose life had been spent protecting the blessed relics of St Albinus. Gervais would have understood what he was trying to do, even if he might not have agreed. This man, he knew, was going to close his eyes and resist.

Fulk's eyes on the other hand were bright with anticipation. He was like a child enchanted by a magician, and Rollo had a satisfying feeling of power.

'You talked about fountains, and how the courtyards in Jerusalem were fresh with water. And you described how the Moslems would wash themselves from such fountains to purify themselves.'

Fulk was looking at him intently, but said nothing.

'I thought', Rollo went on, carefully avoiding the eyes of the abbot, 'that you might have such a fountain for the abbey cloister.'

Fulk stared down at the last drawing which lay unrolled before him. The fountain, Rollo explained, would be shaped like a pyramid, but again eight-sided so that it echoed the roof of the church. And it would be raised upon columns. In this way the fountain would be many times higher than a man, and the water would cascade down the outside of the pyramid and fall round the columns into a basin – like a curtain.

The Count's fingers traced the cascade on the drawing before him; then his forefinger tapped the parchment at the apex of the pyramid.

'And how do you propose to bring the water up here?' he inquired. Fulk looked at Rollo out of the corner of his eye, and his mouth gave a slight twitch of amusement. 'In a bucket?'

Rollo heard a swallowing sound from the abbot.

'Exactly as the Romans used to do it,' he explained. 'Beaulieu is low-lying. The land there floods every winter. So we have to bank up the River Indre, and at the same time we can run an aqueduct direct to the abbey. This will provide water for the entire community, and part of it can be controlled through sluices to run beneath the cloister. The pressure will raise it up the hollow central column of the fountain, and a pipe from the water-basin will then run it back again into the channel underground.'

The abbot's timidity at last cracked.

'It seems to me', he said with a look of nervous concern on his face, 'that this may be a monastery for the Devil, not for God.'

The Count looked at him in astonishment. The abbot, having spoken, now seemed uncertain how to continue, and his small mouth opened and closed without a sound emerging.

'But where are the Devil's quarters, my lord Abbot? I don't see them in the plan.' The mockery in Fulk's voice goaded the abbot to reply.

'Everywhere! I see the Devil everywhere!' His face was contorted with anxiety as he spoke, and his hand swept across the leaves of parchment that lay open before him. 'Pyramids, fountains, mosques. Romans, Egyptians, Moslems.' He looked about him as if he were in some quite unfamiliar place. 'I'm not a learned man, my lord Count,' he went on almost pleadingly, 'but I believe I can recognize the hand of the Infidel. Would your mason have us follow Mohamet?'

Fulk turned to Rollo, eyebrows raised.

'And what do you say to this charge, Rollo? Are you leading us to the Devil?'

Rollo could see anguish on the abbot's face, and he knew that he had bruised some of the man's most cherished convictions. Here was none of the haughty arrogance of Bishop Renaud or the iron severity of Abbot Gervais. Before him stood a simple man of God.

'My lord Abbot,' he said gently, 'I see nothing devilish about a fountain! When I think of water I think of baptism; of Christ in the River Jordan; of the Magdalene washing Christ's feet.'

The abbot began to look flustered, and his mind seemed

443

to be struggling to find words. His eyes blinked repeatedly as if he were trying to clear a mist from his head.

'Where Christ was baptized was . . . just a simple stream in Galilee.' He spoke in little jumps and rushes, losing his breath repeatedly. 'Not . . . a great aqueduct . . . from the Romans . . . Nor a fantastic fountain given to us by the Infidel . . . Where is your simple stream?'

There was a shy strength in the abbot's face as he spoke, and Rollo warmed to him. He could not help feeling respect for this man. And yet if he were to share the abbot's views he would spend his life building churches that were nothing more than little boxes to God. Nothing would ever change, and no light would ever be let in. The Count was still looking at him quizzically, expecting an answer.

'My lord Abbot,' Rollo went on, 'let me try to explain. As an abbot you take men by the hand and lead them to God. If I build a church or a monastery that is also what *I* do.' Rollo noticed the abbot's eyes resting on him, scarcely blinking. 'But whereas you lead men through prayer, a builder does it through physical things – things of beauty. It was St Augustine who said that all beauty is proportion and unity, and that it points to the perfect proportions and unity of God. So, by contemplating beauty – whether in nature or in man's artistry – one approaches God.'

He paused. The abbot was staring at him with amazement, and Fulk's eyes were shifting curiously from one man to the other.

'You see,' Rollo added, beginning to roll up the sheets of parchment before him, 'when I talk of pyramids, or fountains, I'm not talking of paganism. As a builder, I want to use whatever is beautiful in the world, because its beauty does honour to God.'

There was silence. The abbot was gazing down at his fingers which were tapping nervous messages to each other. Finally the Count gave a heavy grunt.

'My lord Abbot,' he said firmly, 'I have been to the Holy

Land and returned with relics of the life and suffering of Our Lord. Am I to believe they could be robbed of their power by mere stones and mortar? After all, they managed to survive in the Jerusalem of the Infidel.'

And with that he rather peremptorily kissed the abbot's hand and turned to leave. Rollo followed him, and they heard a soft rustling sound as the abbot gathered his habit about him and departed through another door.

'There are men of God, Rollo, who are frightened by the slightest breeze,' Fulk muttered as they made their way back through the city. 'If they were all like him the Church would have been blown away before the first stone was laid.'

'And yet without men like him, my lord Fulk, the Church would have sunk into corruption. They are also the rock.'

Fulk looked at him hard, and checked his pace. Then he pursed his lips and nodded.

'Perhaps,' he said. 'Yes, perhaps.'

Lamplight was flowing from the huddled houses as they passed, and the dusk was gathering around them. The black wall of the castle seemed to hang above them.

'Do you think I'm a man of God, Rollo?' Fulk asked suddenly, his voice so quiet that it was scarcely audible.

Rollo was taken aback. He could just make out the Count's eyes turned towards him.

'As much as I am, my lord,' he answered, 'but I'm not certain how much that is.'

In the deep dusk it was impossible to see the expression on Fulk's face, and they walked on in silence.

It was that evening when the Count received his awaited summons to Orléans; and on the following morning he departed.

Rollo knew now that he would build Beaulieu, and that it would take much of his life to build. Fulk had given him his life's work.

*

Life became abnormally quiet at the castle of Angers: it was as if the place had been hollowed out. Fulk and Sebrand were at Orléans awaiting the King's arrival. Roger, Sulpice and Archambaud were also absent: no one seemed to know where — except Audemand, who was not saying. At night only the rough laughter of the Count's brother Maurice could be heard echoing up from the dovecot. Rollo was scarcely ever seen except on his way to or from the stoneyard, or leaving on horseback at dawn with two armed soldiers in attendance, heading for Beaulieu. The women of the castle were still more invisible. Ermengarde spent even larger amounts of her time with the Count's young daughter or — less willingly — with Hersende, upon whom a pall of gloom had descended. Adèle was seen only rarely, teaching her baby son to walk. Hildegarde showed no signs of returning to Loches, but since the evening of the feast had kept to herself. As for Milesende, she and Rollo lived a private existence away from the rest of the court, though every so often the raven-haired girl — ever more radiant and lovely — was noticed making her way to the late Countess's garden where she would sit in the sunshine under the tree that was golden with autumn and crowned with white doves. People envied her: she was the only woman who appeared to know what happiness was; as if the clouds parted only for her.

The air of stillness was also due to the shock of the death of Adelaide. How she had died, why she had died, no one knew. It was as if she had shrivelled away in the night like some plant deprived of what it fed on; perhaps it was because she had been so entirely unloved that her death stirred such unexpected feeling among those who had not loved her — she had died of *their* neglect, however much she may have invited that neglect. People had thought of Adelaide as mean, proud, vain: she as much as anyone had contributed to the Countess Elizabeth's death. But now, with the grief of sentimentality, they saw her as a sad figure from whom all hope had simply drained, who had walked alone towards her own death and nobody had stretched out an arm to hold her back.

Sebrand had said just one thing to Ermengarde before he departed.

'She had such a beautiful body. I desired her.'

Ermengarde had been astonished, and surprised to find herself moved: she understood now why Sebrand had remained silent. And she imagined Adelaide, stripped at last of her veils of self-protection, suddenly desired and desiring. Hence Sebrand's awkwardness. Lust and shame on a tide of wine. All the anger drowned. And so Adelaide was rejected – just as the Count had rejected her: everyone rejected her. And she died.

None of this Ermengarde chose to pass on to Hersende: she had no wish to add further miseries to the girl's life; least of all did she intend to prolong the heavy hours she already had to spend listening to the girl's tearful agonies.

'Hersende, do try to understand,' she said wearily after more than a week had passed following the circles and loops of the girl's misery. 'Sebrand loves you or he would not have gone away. And because he loves you he'll come back.' Ermengarde tried to conceal a sigh of irritation. 'So, you had a beautiful flutter one evening with another man who touched your heart, and you longed for him to touch your body. How wonderful and how lucky! Those are the best moments of your life. When they come less often you'll regret it.'

Ermengarde felt like adding – but did not – that Hersende had the heart of a butterfly and would most probably spread her gorgeous wings before every new man who glanced her way with a sad face for the rest of the summer of her life. She wanted Sebrand and Sebrand alone only while he kept some part of himself apart from her. Once she had it all, as Ermengarde was certain she would, then the eyes on those sumptuous wings would open to the sun whenever a new bright day shone on her. Ermengarde also felt like adding –

and did not — that the consolation she had herself offered to the wounded Giraud Berlay had been welcomed with such a hunger of gratitude that she hoped Hersende might have this effect on beautiful young men more often. Certainly, the dreamy young man was a lover more subtle and more tender than Sebrand could ever be, she felt sure.

'Remember how long you've loved Sebrand, Hersende. Two years! More! One night of dreams can't touch that, my sweet girl.'

Hersende nodded and even smiled a little through her tears, as if what Ermengarde had said was a revelation of truth — which it was not: one night of dreams could touch everything, tear up all promises, render the daytime a mere interval between dreams. But that, Ermengarde thought, was something Hersende would have to find out for herself. Let her first marry her Sebrand; then the dance of dreams could begin.

'Thank you, Ermengarde. Thank you!'

And Hersende threw her arms round her friend's neck.

'You're so wise.' Then she added, 'Please will you see Giraud, and explain? I couldn't bear it! I should cry.'

'Yes, of course I shall see him,' Ermengarde replied. 'I'd do anything for you, my dear!'

The King was to arrive at the end of a week. The Duke of Orléans played host to more noblemen than had ever been assembled in France under one roof. From Provence to Picardy, Brittany to Roussillon, Champagne to Poitou, dukes and counts gathered with the most forced of politenesses — and waited. Each had a private motive for being there; each believed that no one else was aware of what that motive might be; and each laid elaborately false trails which by and large were seen to be elaborately false. Fulk towered above the rest in stature, an advantage which he employed to full effect towards those who feared him, or despised him. Conan was smaller, more shrunken, than he remembered: their eyes rarely met. Young Odo was absurdly youthful, and the anger in his eyes had a petulant look: Fulk made no acknowledgement of his presence.

Then there were the archbishops, trailing their reputations like their robes. The Archbishop of Tours, the pederast, whose hands fluttered as if they were feathers when he talked to the young Count of Blois; the Archbishop of Paris, a man upon whom gloom rested like the tablets of the law; and the infamous Archbishop of Reims, the most debauched figure Fulk had ever set eyes on, whose entourage was the principal subject of conversation among those lords who felt able to talk to each other. He alone was not staying in the castle, but had taken over an entire inn — to be closer to the cathedral, he let it be known.

After two days a messenger arrived one evening in Orléans from Angers. Sebrand went immediately to greet him, and beneath the rough cape and hood he recognized one of the sons of Audemand. The man nodded as he saw Sebrand and the two of them made their way as unobtrusively as possible to the Count's rooms.

Sebrand had been anxious lest this final link in the chain should snap. The risks seemed to him enormous, and as a soldier he found restraint hard to bear. But he looked at Fulk listening to Audemand's son, and he could only admire the icy calm of the man.

Finally the Count nodded, and let out a cold laugh.

'So,' he said, flexing his fingers and gazing down at them as he did so, 'they would take Angers by stealth, and have me too!' And he laughed again. 'Now, Sebrand, we shall start to outflank them. We must leave first thing in the morning. Put it about that we have gone hunting for boar and may be away several days.'

He returned to Audemand's son.

'You remain here and assure everyone that we shall return before the King arrives.'

Then he looked at Sebrand again, and placed a hand on his shoulder.

'You and I, Sebrand, shall indeed go hunting. The King arrives at Chartres tomorrow. I think as a token of our respect' – and Fulk gave a mocking bow – 'we should seek to tell him a few things in advance about his stepson and the Count of Rennes, and how they behave when his loyal subjects' backs are turned.'

With that, Fulk adopted his familiar proud stance in the middle of the room, hands on his hips, legs wide apart. He looked like a man preparing to bestride the world.

'And then', he went on, 'we shall have the hardest ride of our lives – to Angers!'

Sebrand took stock that evening of everything that had passed. He felt dazed and rather out of his depth. Fulk and Audemand had kept their secret well, and his own lovesickness in Chemillé had left him entirely ignorant of the Count's plans until their arrival in Orléans. Now he learnt how, on the night he had spent agonizing with jealousy over Hersende and Giraud Berlay, the Chancellor had been called to speak to a servant whose task it was to take food to prisoners in the dungeon at Angers. The man was bound, and his back soaked in blood. He had been overheard talking to Conan's son Budic in his native tongue, Breton. After some persuasion he had confessed to being a serf of the Count of Rennes. Further persuasion had elicited the fact that he was one of several informers insinuated into the castle by Conan, and that he was awaiting a message telling him of the precise day on which Budic was to be released, the gates opened, and the forces of Brittany and Touraine pour into the defenceless city. This was to coincide with Fulk's absence in Orléans, when any alertness to danger would be diverted by the solemn business with the King.

It had taken the Chancellor only a short time to convince the by now gibbering servant that his life hung on one thread. If he co-operated he might be freed: it was as simple as that. The man's head had nodded frantically even before Audemand finished, and he was promptly placed under discreet surveillance by a guard until the messenger should arrive with the final, vital piece of information – when? In the meanwhile Roger, Sulpice and Archambaud were preparing an ambush for the attacking army.

It had been a matter of keeping one's nerve. The trap was sprung.

And now the message had come. The attack was to be in four days.

Sebrand found it hard to sleep. And when he did, dreams shook him awake with their violence. Anjou was being swamped by giant waves, and on the water rode men with wild eyes, screaming, their horses pawing the waves and treading underfoot the floating houses, trees, churches, people vainly struggling, animals like flotsam swirling by. Then, before Sebrand had time to feel fear there rose a man, tall as a mountain: with one hand he turned back the water, and all the horsemen were sucked towards the far horizon in a froth of limbs and a long, terrible cry. The man, he knew, was Fulk; and around him spread a beautiful green land laden with blossom and fruit both together. He, Sebrand, was walking there in the heavy stillness of summer when a woman came towards him, bare to the waist, and she carried a child at her breast. The woman smiled, and as she did so he knew her to be Hersende. He woke with a start, and her voice rang in his head, loud and loving. 'Your child,' she said.

He rose in a bewilderment of happiness. Was Hersende really bearing his child? It was dawn. From his window Sebrand could see the Loire drifting silently between long islands of sand. It would pass in that same steady drift westwards through Touraine, Anjou, Brittany – through the landscape of his life, to the sea. Today his life felt all of a piece, threaded, as if that river held it unbroken. It was the dawn.

He never heard Fulk enter. To his surprise, as he turned, the Count put out his arms to embrace him.

'Today will be the beginning of great things,' was all Fulk said.

The two men rode hard all day. The Count had left his black stallion Moro in Orléans to await his return. Sebrand left his grey. The two horses they purchased from the Duke of Orléans' stable they changed for two further mounts at midday, halfway to Chartres, pausing only long enough to make the exchange. Well before dusk they reached the palace of the Bishop of Chartres where the royal party was due to stay. Guards were already lining the road near the approach to the palace: the King, they were told, was expected within the hour. Fulk and Sebrand found rooms at a nearby inn, and waited.

The two servants they had brought with them produced their finest clothing – red, the colour of Anjou. Sebrand noticed that the Count wore a sleeved garment of the rich silk he had brought with him from the East. 'The royal colour', he remembered Fulk had described it, and he wondered if the King would understand his visitor's presumption, and if the Count intended him to. Probably, Sebrand thought.

'So, it's not only the women of Anjou you bought it for, my lord,' he said. Sebrand realized that it was the first time he had ever felt able to tease the Count, and it pleased him. Fulk glanced at him sternly at first; then for a second the shadow of a smile crossed his face.

'It's not only women who are vain, Sebrand. And remember, peacocks are male.'

They made their way to the palace to wait for the King. People turned to stare at the two brilliantly dressed strangers – the immensely tall figure with the fierce black eyes, and the lithe dark-haired man walking beside him. They bowed to the Bishop, introduced themselves, then joined the party assembled in the palace courtyard to welcome King Robert.

And as dusk was beginning to gather a chill autumn mist around them, the royal party came into view.

King Robert was a strikingly handsome man of about the Count's age. His features had an almost feminine softness, and his beard was light in colour and in growth. His teeth when he smiled were strikingly white, and his smile had a charm about it which was instantly captivating. He talked easily to all who greeted him, and his presence seemed to warm those around him. There was an ease and a polish about the man which Sebrand found himself admiring. He watched the King move from guest to guest in the company of the old Bishop, who shuffled as Robert stepped smoothly. But Sebrand noticed that between talking to those he met the King kept glancing towards the resplendent figure of Fulk; then he saw Robert whisper something to the Bishop, who also glanced at Fulk a little uneasily. Clearly Robert was anxious to know who his aloof visitor might be, waiting in the background, confident that his presence needed no further prominence.

'Count Fulk,' the King said eventually, after he had spoken to all the others assembled in the courtyard. Even in the fading light Sebrand could see that Robert's smile contained none of the warmth he had shown to the others.

The Count knelt on one knee and kissed the King's hand. Then he rose and made the most of his superior height and gravity. Sebrand had never been more aware of the power of the Count's presence, and of how intimidating was the eloquent silence which he maintained.

Fulk's silence compelled the King to speak again. He inquired why the Count of Anjou had come to Chartres and not to Orléans. Fulk explained that he hoped he might enjoy a few words with the King without the company of his other lords. Robert looked puzzled and a little nonplussed. The others in the courtyard fell quiet, and Sebrand noticed that they were gradually retiring a little, leaving Fulk and the King a circle of space.

The Count then pledged the King his loyalty, and bowed his head. Robert began to seem more pleased, though a look of surprise still lingered on his face. And as a token of his loyalty, Fulk went on, he hoped the King would accept a small gift. And with that he produced – to Sebrand's astonishment – a magnificent golden amulet studded with jewels which gleamed like dark-red eyes in the dusk. A gasp rose from the company looking on, and the King took the object almost timidly. Sebrand remembered what Fulk had said about the King having almost no wealth, and felt a touch of admiration for the Count's diplomacy. He had obtained it, he said, in the Holy Land which he had recently visited as a poor pilgrim.

The King was by now looking more than a little disconcerted. Was there anything he could do for the Count? he asked. Fulk paused, and then lowered his eyes which until now had been fixed on the King's face. No, Fulk replied, but there was something *he* wished to do for the King. Fulk paused again. He looked hard at Robert. Was his Majesty aware that even as his lords were gathering at Orléans to swear their loyalty to him, two of those very lords were plotting to sack the city of another lord while he was in attendance on His Majesty?

A hollow silence filled the courtyard. Lamps from the palace lit up startled faces. The King looked at Count Fulk, then away from him as if searching for a reply.

'Who, my lord Fulk?' he said falteringly.

Fulk gazed at Robert for a few seconds.

'The one who is threatened, Your Majesty, is myself,' he replied in a calm voice. 'The two lords whose armies are about to attack my city are the Count of Brittany and' – Fulk hesitated – 'the Count of Blois, your stepson.'

Sebrand saw the King step back as if he had been struck. He fingered the golden amulet in his hand, and Sebrand wondered if he might hurl it to the ground. Then he spoke very quietly.

'You ask me to believe they would take advantage of my authority? I cannot accept that.'

Fulk went on looking at him. He knew he was looking at a frightened man. Robert's authority had a fragile face at that moment.

'My Constable and I leave tonight,' Fulk replied coldly. 'I shall bring back something to prove it to you.' Then, in order to make that face look even more fragile, he added, 'The King, your father, would never have doubted my word.'

Sebrand could hear people draw their breath. Fulk bowed, and left. Dimly lit faces in the courtyard turned to follow the tall figure of the Count as he strode into the twilit street. The dark hulk of the cathedral rose against the violet sky, and the only sound was the hooting of an owl.

'We'll sleep for four hours; then we'll ride as you've never ridden before.' Fulk glanced at Sebrand as they entered the inn, and there was a distant smile on the long, austere face.

When the jaws of a trap close, it is all over in a second. Fulk's plan was clean and deadly.

The preliminaries were unobtrusive. It was after dark when the Count and his High Constable rode through the city gates of Angers. For two dawns and two days they had been on the road, and four times they had changed horses. Audemand was waiting for them. So were five Bretons — in chains. One was the servant who had informed on the others. One was the messenger who had brought the news that the attack was to take place the following morning. The other three were the remaining spies identified by the first.

Within twenty-four hours the bodies of four of them would dangle above the river from the castle walls; the fifth would be shivering in an iron cage beside them.

But by then much else would have happened, so that the people of Angers would scarcely trouble to glance up at the carcasses and at the naked man. They would be too stunned, too joyful, or too drunk; and the fields around the city would be lit by a hundred fires by which figures danced and sang through the mists of an autumn night.

It all happened during the course of a single day, beginning two hours after dawn.

A party of horsemen in armour galloped out of the forest, heading straight for the main gate of the city. People scattered in panic as they passed. As the horsemen approached the gates they drew their swords, and those in front let out a cry. And then ... nothing happened! Figures who had fled peered out from behind bushes, low walls, from doors, ditches, barns. But the gates did not open. Again the cry went up; and the gates did not open. The horsemen turned as if bewildered. The horses wheeled, some reared. A third time the cry went up, longer and more strident. But the gates remained closed.

Without warning, from left and right, from copses and from below the river bank, some fifty knights converged on the group of horsemen clustered outside the city gate. There was no time for them to escape. They were pinned against the wall like flies, and within a minute the white stone was flecked scarlet with their blood, and the ground littered with their helmets, their heads, their limbs. From the fields all that people saw were arms and swords beating downwards, horses falling, men falling; and the only sounds were the screams of terror and dying.

Suddenly the attackers drew back, and from that churning hillock of bodies a few figures staggered away from the gate. Two of them collapsed, blood overflowing from their helmets and their armour. The others were led or carried away. Their horses cantered wild through the deserted fields – all, that is, but one, who was whiter than snow except for the blood spilt by its rider across its flank and neck.

Count Fulk grasped its reins and guided it over the mound of carnage and through the city gates. People watched agog as he passed by.

And then they listened.

It was as if the very forest had let out a long cry. From far away it came; how far no one could tell. But on and on it sounded, out there somewhere in the direction from which the Breton knights had ridden, out there within the woods where dark birds were already gathering, wheeling lower and lower until the trees seemed to swallow them.

Finally all was silent except the breathing of the wind.

A herdsman who led his cows to water in a clearing some distance away drew back when he saw the stream flowing red. A farmer's dog returned from hunting and presented his master with a man's arm. A forester wounded a stag with an arrow and pursued it until it leapt into a ravine; when he looked over the edge he thought he was gazing into hell.

It was several hours before the truth became known to the people of Angers. Two armies lay slaughtered in that forest. Scarcely a Breton or a Tourangais escaped: they were trapped in a gorge where they had lain hidden, expecting to follow up the knights who were to secure the gates of the city and the castle. But a force of Angevin archers and foot-soldiers – led by Roger the Devil, Sulpice and Archambaud – was waiting for them. Arrows fell like a dark waterfall from the rocks above. Those who managed to flee were struck down as they panicked and struggled through the neck of the ravine. The sun had scarcely cleared the trees when the attack began, and it seemed hardly to have moved by the time all life had been squeezed from that gorge.

As dusk gradually drew a skein of mist over the fields, the fires began to be lit and the silence of death was overcome by jubilant voices.

But by that time Fulk and Sebrand, with a small force of armed knights, were already heading eastwards for Orléans. Behind the Count rode a manservant leading a stallion that shone like moonlight long after all around it had melted into the darkness of the forest. Its former rider lay headless outside the walls of the city he had failed to take. Two of his brothers were dead beside him. The two who had survived set eyes on their eldest brother, Budic, for the first time in twenty-eight months — behind the prison bars that were now the landscape of their own little world, where there would be time enough to dream of the beautiful, drowned city of Is.

The lords of France were waiting to greet their king. The early-November sun shone brightly on the roofs of Orléans, and on the river and the castle, and on the great courtyard emblazoned with the colours of the noblemen gathered there. They stood like so many flags waiting to be unfurled. Finally the gates swung wide.

The royal party had made stately progress from Chartres, and the King had continued to charm all he met. After the uneasy encounter with the Count of Anjou there was no further discord; and now in the courtyard of the castle of Orléans the lords of France eyed and summed up their monarch with a composure that matched the manner of King Robert. The absence of Count Fulk was noted by Robert and rested heavily on the minds of his stepson, Odo, and of Conan. It seemed unlikely to the lord of Brittany that Fulk's love of hunting should have overruled his need to impress the King with his loyalty, and Conan felt a twinge of concern that something had indeed gone wrong, though he could not imagine how that could be. His planning had been meticulous.

It was midday. The great assembly of lords was preparing to escort the King into the hall of the castle where a banquet lay spread for the occasion. Suddenly the sound of a hunting horn diverted the attention of all. Fulk had chosen the moment of his arrival well, and as the eyes of all the lords of France were turned back towards the courtyard, the castle gates swung open again and a figure resplendent in red rode slowly towards them. His hand calmly patted the neck of his white stallion as he dismounted; then he advanced and bowed low before the King.

Only one man was distracted from the sight of those two men facing one another. Conan barely noticed them: he saw only his own son's white stallion, and if anyone had been gazing at the Count of Rennes at that moment he would have seen the muscles of his face grow slack and his mouth quiver. A hand rose to his forehead as if to support its weight, and the hand was shaking.

'You doubted my word, Your Majesty,' they heard Fulk say. 'Here is the evidence I promised you.' And he directed the King's gaze to the stallion motionless in the centre of the courtyard.

The King looked mystified. He looked at the horse, then back at Fulk.

'The rider of this horse', Fulk went on without shifting his gaze from the King, 'was killed while he and his knights were trying to seize my city. The Count of Rennes will tell you who he was.'

As the King turned to follow the direction of Fulk's raised arm, the lords assembled in that courtyard saw Conan double up as though in pain, and a sound like a low hiss emerged from his gaping mouth. 'My son!' they heard him murmur. 'My son!'

But Fulk's eyes were on the young man standing close to Conan, with the look of someone trapped.

'Your Majesty, I have something else for you,' Fulk said, without shifting his gaze from the young Odo.

And as he spoke Fulk held out a hand towards the King. In the centre of his open palm lay a ring. Sebrand saw Odo start, and the other lords turned to look at him.

The King took the ring reluctantly, as if it might burn him, and turned it between his fingers. Then he looked at Fulk inquiringly, and there was fear in his eyes.

'The man who owns this ring lies wounded in the castle of Angers. He was luckier than Lord Conan's son: it was his horse that died.' Fulk stood quite motionless, a huge figure in red with the eyes of everyone upon him except those of the King. 'Your stepson there will recognize his brother's ring.'

Then, as heads turned towards the young Count of Blois, Fulk added in a voice loud enough for all to hear –

'Since we're gathered here to pledge our loyalty, may I repeat, Your Majesty, that at least you can be sure of mine!'

With that Fulk bowed again and withdrew among the company of attendant lords. Only Sebrand noticed the tiredness in the look of those dark eyes and in the set of his mouth.

It was a subdued gathering around the King in the great hall of the castle. Few words were spoken for the remainder of that day, and much of the wine was left undrunk. Fulk never spoke again to Conan or to Odo before his departure. The Count of Rennes moved slowly, as if he had no strength, and his eyes were like dead fires. All was dark before him: instead of a vision of his great and ancient land, now he saw only his own tomb beckoning. Three sons dead; three imprisoned. His shame and grief could take no more. He would leave here tomorrow: at least it would be his own soil that would wrap him in its eternal silence. Only the unheard whisper of a curse would blow for ever on the Atlantic gales eastwards towards Anjou.

It was a gentle journey homewards through the bronzed forests of autumn. Fulk, who usually travelled in the simplest clothing of a peasant so that only the great sword and the great size of the man caused eyes to turn, now rode in his proud red that shimmered on the glossy flank of Moro, his black stallion. Fulk had trimmed his own hair and beard, and Moro's tail and mane were plaited with scarlet threads. A golden medallion rested on the white star of the horse's forehead, a parting gift from the King, and a royal ring glittered on the Count's hand as he loosely held the reins. In villages and fields, and by the river bank, people stopped their work and stared as if the King himself were riding by.

A few paces behind Fulk rode Sebrand on his favourite grey, and Audemand's son on a handsome roan. Never had they ridden in such peace, and never had Sebrand known the Count to be at such peace with the world.

Fulk had surprised him before they left Orléans. Refusing to see Conan, he had instructed Audemand's son to bear a message to the lord of Brittany. In respect for Conan's grief, he said, he would release to him the three surviving sons now held in Angers. He even added that Budic, Conan's eldest son and heir, had impressed him by his stoic courage and his unfailing dignity: it was Fulk's hope, the message went on, that when the time came for the young man to become Count of Rennes there might even be friendship between Brittany and Anjou, sealed perhaps by a bond of marriage. The generosity of the victor was coupled with a single condition, on which Fulk awaited Conan's reply: that he return the city of Nantes to Anjou. Fulk proposed that his High Constable, Sebrand de Chemillé, accompany Conan's three sons to Nantes within a week, and the young men would be returned to their father on the formal submission of that city to him.

Audemand's son had returned within the hour. Conan had barely raised his head, he reported. Nor had he spoken a single word. But when the Angevin had made Fulk's offer to return his three sons, the Breton had nodded, and there were tears on his cheeks. When he had raised the condition – the return of Nantes – Conan had moved not a muscle for several minutes: then again he had nodded, just once. But when Audemand's son had expressed the Count's hope for friendship, Conan's face had remained as still as a skull.

'Very well,' Fulk said. 'But Budic may not feel so proud. Conan will not live long. He has only his bitterness to live on, and that won't sustain him.' And then, to Sebrand's further surprise, he added, 'Conan has been

461

a great warrior, but he's never had my luck.'

For three days Fulk, his two lords and their attendants rode on through the forest and the yellowing fields. At the end of the second day they reached Langeais, and the young governor received them warmly. They dined royally in the hall of the castle where Fulk had passed so many weeks with the sound of Odo's army stirring beyond the walls and the palisades. They drank and feasted before the fire, and gradually a great exhaustion settled about them. They slumped, with their legs towards the fire, goblets of wine held before them.

'Your father will be pleased with his work, the old fox,' Fulk muttered without turning his gaze from the fire. 'He's very dear to me,' he added.

Sebrand could see Audemand's son smile contentedly, and something of his father's wry look pass across his face.

Still without raising his eyes from the fire, Fulk went on speaking – almost to himself – between sips from his goblet which he then refilled, his hand feeling for the pitcher by his side.

'So, Sebrand,' he said, 'when you return you will be Count of Nantes.' Fulk was still staring into the fire. 'You'd better make Hersende your Countess very soon,' he added almost carelessly. 'Otherwise I'll have to lock her up before she makes all the men in Angers mad.'

He turned his head for a moment and grasped Sebrand's hand.

'Perhaps Rollo would care to marry her sister at the same ceremony,' he went on. Fulk's hand released Sebrand's and filled his goblet.

'In fact, why not make it three?' he said suddenly, glancing again at Sebrand. 'Hildegarde is to be my wife ... and what better than to marry her in the company of friends!'

Sebrand blinked – with the wine and the fire and the Count's words. A few moments later he saw that Fulk was asleep.

FOURTEEN

IN THE NOVEMBER NIGHT anyone lying awake heard it — and hearing it, continued to lie awake. There was nothing strange about the cry of wolves in the distant forests around Angers, but few people could remember a howl so near. Gusts from the Atlantic flailed at roofs and windows, paused between breaths, then the houses shuddered again; and as the wind rose and fell, and rose again, so the sound was at one moment far away and at the next so close that it made the heart thump in fear.

Then, as dawn broke, the wind dropped altogether and there was not a further sound: the sky was like the reflection of a silent sea, and the sun bathed the woods a pallid gold. The creature, wherever it had been, was gone — or sleeping.

The very last of the summer warmth still lingered in the sheltered vineyards where farmers had cut back the forest, patch by patch, deeper and deeper every year; the scent of woodsmoke hung sweetly on the air now the harvest was over and further clearing could begin. The day echoed with the rhythm of the saw; and this autumn — for once — people were not afraid of raiding parties.

It was at dusk that Sebrand rode back from Nantes. People raised their heads and watched him and his attendants pass by as they made their way homewards, saws, axes, scythes and hoes over their tired shoulders. They recognized Lord Fulk's High Constable in the half-light, and could make out the smile on his face and the arm raised in welcome as he rode by. They liked him, and talked among themselves of the Breton girl they had often seen out hunting with him in her shining furs and buckskin, her face bright with laughter. They were to be married any day, people knew.

And very soon they knew that Sebrand was now the Count of Nantes. The city was taken without a blow. There would be no more pirate boats in the murderous dawn. That era was over.

That same evening Sebrand knew that his dream about Hersende was true. She was carrying his child. His happiness overflowed, and his arms around her dismissed the tears which Ermengarde had wearily nursed for so many weeks. Hersende believed herself the most contented woman alive, and insisted that as soon as the ceremony was over she would travel with Sebrand to Nantes, which she had left three years earlier as an orphan and an outcast. She wanted to feel what it was like, she said, to ride into that city as a lady. Not just a countess, but *the* Countess. Already she had visions of the castle of Nantes as a place that sparkled, just as the beloved Elizabeth used to describe the castle of Vendôme as a court where the most wonderful people would gather, laugh, parade their brilliance. In Angers it was only wine that flowed now that Elizabeth was dead: she wanted eyes and wit to flash and she, Hersende, to gather that brightness around her, and to shine in it like a jewel.

Giraud Berlay was not so much forgotten as irrelevant. It had been exactly as Ermengarde had promised. Now, when she gazed at Sebrand, she knew that he was entirely hers. Her spirit was as free as a bird's, she exclaimed to Ermengarde, and hugged her.

And where would the bird fly next? Ermengarde wondered. Before whom would she next fluff out her pretty feathers?

The Chancellor, Audemand, felt his own head to be tediously full of marriages. Why in old age, he pondered, was one supposed to be so expert in arranging such things? The only novelty was that these marriages appeared to be about love. With Sebrand, as with Rollo, this hardly surprised him. What young man could not love the radiant Hersende or her dark-eyed sister? If he had been younger he would have loved them both. But Count Fulk! Audemand found it hard to imagine a man falling in love with the Lady Hildegarde, unless love were to exclude the heat of passion. He smiled as he remembered Ermengarde's comment —

'Hildegarde possesses everything a man might desire in a favourite dog!'

But the Count did love her; of that Audemand had no doubt.

'After Elizabeth, where does a man turn for a wife?' Ermengarde had added a touch scornfully. 'If you've had the best, and sent her to the stake, then perhaps a faithful dog is the one to settle for. She'll never bite him ... and the Count does want a son. I'm sure she'll breed.'

Then Ermengarde's eyes had lit up as she saw the Count's small daughter running towards her, and she hugged the child.

'I shall never have one like you,' she had said. And Audemand noticed tears in Ermengarde's eyes.

The Chancellor discussed the details of the three weddings with Hubert, the Count's chaplain; then at length with the Count and the Lady Hildegarde, with Sebrand and with Rollo, and their brides-to-be. Hildegarde was precise, Hersende effusive, Milesende shy.

'One thing I should tell you,' said Audemand quietly, drawing Rollo aside and glancing around to make sure Milesende was out of earshot. 'There will be someone you don't expect present at your wedding.' And he placed a hand on Rollo's arm as he saw the look of alarm on the Norman's face.

'There's a good reason,' he went on. 'And I shall explain to you afterwards — when you're a married man.'

Rollo saw the creases round the Chancellor's eyes deepen, and his mouth give a familiar twitch.

He might have known, Rollo reflected after the Chancellor had departed, that even his own wedding was unlikely to escape one of Audemand's schemes. He heard the sound of the old man's staff tapping down the passage, and decided that he had more important and much more delightful matters to think about.

The bells of the cathedral of Angers had not rung out like this since the Count's triumphant return from the siege of Langeais. They were new bells – three of them; the founders had given them their final polish only a few days earlier, and Rollo had commandeered all help to have them raised and set in the belfry in time for the occasion.

The unfamiliar sound spilled across the city and the surrounding fields, and brought people to their doors to listen – and to learn that on this bright November day Count Fulk was to be married.

This week no tithes were to be paid; taxes were waived, punishments lifted, pardons and petitions granted, and gifts distributed to all who worked in the service of the Count, however remotely.

At mid-morning a slow procession made its way through the tangle of alleys where the roofs all but joined overhead, and across the cobbled market-square. Fulk walked at the head, swathed magnificently in a red cape, his hand grasping that of his bride who walked as if in his shadow, eyes lowered. Behind them was the Count's young daughter, her hand in the Lady Ermengarde's; and the child's red hair reminded many onlookers of her late mother, and a chill of memories dampened their joy as the procession passed by. And as Fulk and Hildegarde came close to the cathedral on their way back to the castle and the Count's private chapel, other memories were stirred – of that evening when the Bishop's curse had echoed down the crumbled nave towards the distraught figure of Fulk standing there holding the box with the ashes of his wife. Those were the blackest days, lit

466

only by the fires of hell. And now ...! It would have been hard to believe the sun could shine again on their Count, or that he could walk so proudly through his rebuilt city.

Above the procession the half-built cathedral lay open to the sky. The roof-line projected like the rim of a cup awaiting its lid; and the sunlight caught its fresh stone.

Rollo was aware that Sebrand, walking beside him, kept glancing upwards: then there was a barely audible laugh.

'I see you got them up,' Sebrand murmured. 'How did you do it?'

Rollo made certain those around him in the procession were out of earshot.

'The Bishop was on a pastoral visit,' he said in a low voice. 'He was unaccountably delayed.' Rollo heard Sebrand chuckle again.

'Where have you put Ermengarde?'

Rollo glanced around him cautiously.

'Facing the marketplace, naturally!'

Noises bubbled from Sebrand's throat, but Rollo kept his eyes firmly ahead of him. What he was unable to see was that the entire procession behind him was walking with eyes elevated towards the roof-line of the cathedral. Rollo's much-discussed corbels were receiving their first public acclaim amid the sanctity of Count Fulk's wedding parade; and, as they passed beneath, those with sharp eyes strained for a glimpse of their lords and ladies, neighbours and friends, revealed in their most intimate natures – while the bells tolled, and the Bishop was tending his flock in quite another town.

Hersende, as she knelt in the dark chapel, watched the ceremony of the Count's marriage with no more than a distant curiosity. Within half an hour she would herself be married. Her thoughts were on the unborn child within her, and on the brighter world into which it would be born. She wished her own wedding could have been a more splendid thing, with the eyes of all Anjou turned upon her and upon the man whose countess she was about to be. Her face glowed at the prospect of that golden world of pleasure and delight that would shortly be hers.

Milesende's eyes saw the colours and movements of figures in the chapel as if they were no more than patterns woven on a transparent curtain; beyond lay the endless forest where invisible birds sang and streams flowed between banks of wild flowers. There was only Rollo, and he was naked with her in the water, holding her; nobody knew where they were, nor would ever need to know. 'Love me!' her lips said silently: 'There is only love.'

Their own turn came, and in the lamplight they stood together, two and two, as if they were already standing in their own history and the present was asleep. Voices and figures moved about them, hands were raised in blessing, and they kissed. There was an exchange of rings. Slowly Sebrand and Rollo walked down the aisle of the chapel, their brides on their arms. The Count and Countess were waiting to embrace them.

'This is my happiest day,' was all that Fulk said.

'This evening we shall all rejoice together,' added Hildegarde, her smile more gracious than ever, and the most pure happiness in her eyes.

Rollo knew that he too was happy, but at this moment he could feel almost nothing. He was aware of Milesende's hand firmly on his arm, and of the faces all around. There were colours, and lamps. Hands shaking his own. People embracing Milesende. How lovely she was! His bride!

Faces lingered on in his mind as he found himself walking almost aimlessly by Milesende's side down endless passages where it felt as though he had never been before. Now he knew that he was in the great hall: it was bright with banners and there was music playing. The same faces were here around him — all except for one. And suddenly he recalled having seen her in the shadows of the chapel, without realizing at that moment who she was. She was partly hooded, looking at him aslant, and then at Milesende.

And she had gone.

In the shock of recognizing who she was Rollo felt himself to be stepping into the present as if through a screen, and everything was in that instant real – was as it had to be – the end of a journey that could have led to no other moment. Milesende's arms were around his neck, her lips pressed to his cheek. People were applauding. He was talking, laughing, embracing Milesende, embracing Hersende. His arm was on Sebrand's shoulder and his other hand held a goblet of wine. All round the hall goblets were raised in a toast. Then the Count was toasting them all – happy as Rollo had never seen him before.

'We shall rejoin tonight,' he called out. And with that he led the Countess slowly from the hall, and the faces began to disperse.

Rollo and Milesende found themselves alone on their wedding day.

'My bride, I love you,' he said.

'Her name is Rosamund.'

For several moments that was all Audemand said. The Chancellor was seated in a large oak chair by the fire in his room – that panelled room that had guarded so many secrets for so many years. His face was unusually grave, and his fingers tapped the head of his staff as he appeared to be reflecting on the precise manner in which he would unfold this particular secret he had been keeping for so long, or perhaps reflecting on how much of it to unfold. Rollo and Milesende waited patiently. Rosamund. Who was she? And how did Audemand know who she was?

The Chancellor gazed into the fire. Not even his moustaches moved – only his agile fingers that continued to drum on the staff. Then he sniffed.

'She has something important for you both,' he went on.

'But first let me tell you how this has come about. But you must be patient. I'm an old man and I tell stories slowly.'

Audemand's lips twitched just a little, and he glanced at the other two with eyes crinkled against the heat of the fire.

'Her mother was a simple woman. A beautiful woman. Her husband was killed when she was very young.' There was another pause, and Audemand looked grave again.

'Then she met a nobleman who fell in love with her ... He was already married ... Before very long she gave birth to his daughter. The nobleman loved the child and wanted to adopt it as his own. But the mother refused. Instead he installed her in a house some distance from where he lived, and visited her as often as he was able – always in secret. His own wife never knew ... And so it went on, and the child grew up.'

Again Audemand turned his gaze towards Rollo and Milesende, who were seated on a low couch beyond the fire, listening attentively.

'The nobleman had plans to marry his daughter well. But again the mother refused. There was a reason. The child had strange powers – already, at three or four. She could see things that no one else could see. She had visions. She would scream at night: it was always when the moon was full. And the next morning she would tell her mother things that later turned out to be true. The mother was frightened, and wanted to keep her away from the world.

'Then something else happened,' Audemand continued. 'The nobleman's wife bore him a son – whom he adored if anything more than his daughter. The mother was distressed and felt neglected. She refused to see the nobleman any more. But he still loved her – more than he loved his own wife. And he continued to provide for her, and for the daughter, and begged her constantly to let him return to her. For year after year she refused ... until one day when the daughter was about thirteen the child vanished. The mother discovered that a priest had seized her as a witch, and that she was to be burnt. In terror she sent a message to the nobleman, asking for his help. The girl was freed ... and in gratitude she agreed to receive the nobleman again as before.'

Audemand raised himself with the aid of his staff and walked slowly to the window behind Rollo and Milesende, gazing out.

'A year later,' came his voice from behind them, 'another daughter was born. A child of extraordinary beauty. The nobleman was overjoyed, and for several years more he continued to spend as much time as possible with the mother and his new child. And then, one night, the elder daughter had a vision. She screamed and tore at her skin, and collapsed in a faint. In the morning she was still shaking with terror. She would never say what she had seen. But a week later her mother was dead.'

Audemand was still gazing out of the window. Rollo and Milesende both turned to look at him, and his eyes seemed far away.

'There are a few more pieces to the story,' he went on without shifting his gaze from the distant landscape. 'The nobleman was stricken with grief. For a year he hardly spoke. He passed his time with his own son, and people said he looked an old man. The elder daughter he was anxious to protect. She was now seventeen. She needed to be taken from the place where she was known; but she wanted to live alone as a simple peasant. That way she would be safer. So he found her a plot of land and built her a small peasant hut. And there she went to live – all alone.'

Audemand paused, and his face looked weary suddenly. When he spoke again his voice was still far away.

'The younger daughter was barely three when her mother died. The nobleman had a friend who lived very freely – with a great number of people who came and went. There were always children about the place: often nobody knew whose children they were. He took the child gladly, and she was brought up in his house by a kindly woman who had a daughter of her own – the man's own daughter – only a little older than the child she took on . . . That man was Alain, the Count of Nantes.'

Audemand was still gazing out of the window. He did not need to turn to know what expression was on Milesende's face. There was a moment of silence: then she went quite white. Rollo held her in his arms.

The old Chancellor returned to his chair by the fire, and peered at Rollo and Milesende over the top of his staff.

So that was Audemand's secret, Rollo thought. He could not help wondering why he had kept it a secret for so long, and why he had chosen to reveal it now – after their wedding. He was sure that there was something more the Chancellor had to say, and that he was keeping it until Milesende had absorbed the shock of what he had just said. He held her to him. She was gently sobbing. At length she raised her head and brushed her hair from her eyes.

'Rosamund is my sister. And Hersende is not,' she said, her dark eyes wide with amazement. Then – 'And who is my father?' she added, almost vehemently.

Audemand continued to look into the fire.

'He died a few years after your mother. I don't think he ever recovered from her death. I knew him.' Audemand's voice sounded hesitant. 'He was a fine man.'

'But who was he?' Milesende asked fiercely.

Audemand did not answer. He took a deep breath as though he had discharged his duty, and rose from his chair, beginning to tap his staff in a manner which invariably suggested that he was proceeding to some other matter.

'The practical point of all this', he added lightly, a smile returning to his face, 'is that you, Milesende, have a house which is yours. Rosamund has been keeping it for you. The house where you were born. She will tell you about it, and I shall have you conducted to where you may find her. And you, Rollo' – Audemand turned to face him with the most knowing of looks – 'are to enjoy a change of titles. At least, the Count hopes you will enjoy it. Fulk is of the view that it would be impractical for you to be the lord of one place while your wife is mistress of another.'

It was in this way that Rollo learnt – just as Sebrand had predicted – that his title of Viscount of Combourg had indeed been no more than a loan, and that he was to be granted the lands and titles around the house which was to be his wife's.

Audemand gave his staff a flourish and his face twitched mischievously.

'Since I understand you enjoy performing feats with water, Rollo, you should enjoy your new home. It's in the middle of water! Perhaps when you invite me to visit you,' he added, seizing a hand-bell which he proceeded to ring, 'I shall find it a miracle of fountains and a bathing-place for the Infidel. I should enjoy that.'

And as he continued to chuckle, a servant entered.

'This man will lead you to your sister,' he said, placing a hand affectionately on Milesende's shoulder.

Too bewildered to do more than nod to Audemand, Rollo and Milesende left the Chancellor's room of secrets and followed the manservant along the quiet passages of the castle until they came out into the courtyard which led to the stables. They waited while horses were saddled; then the three of them rode out of the city gate and along the quiet river bank.

It was a bright November afternoon, and golden leaves spun on the current across the reflection of the clouds. As Rollo gazed down at the water a vast skein of birds passed in a cross-current among the drifting leaves and the mirrored clouds. The three of them looked up and watched the migrating storks flying southwards, and Rollo remembered his spring journey in search of Milesende when he had gazed at the same birds filling the sky on their way northwards. The cycle was completed. The storks had flown to Normandy –

to Jumièges, to his own church even — and had now departed for the sun. He looked at Milesende and felt a stir of happiness that was also a stab of sadness. He would never go back to Jumièges.

'Your eyes!' she exclaimed. 'Why do they change colour? Just now they're like the sky.' And she laughed.

Lovely Milesende! She was watching the birds become a dark stain above the horizon, and as she raised her head Rollo could see the golden heart resting below her neck. He leaned over and kissed her.

They were still within sight of Angers when Audemand's manservant guided his horse down from the river bank to follow a track that led round a swampy field among willows. At the edge of a wood ahead of them Rollo could see what looked like an animal shelter — reed-thatch supported on rough poles, open on the side facing the river. Suddenly he was reminded of the hidden field near Langeais, and the woman's hut set among the trees. And even as the memory came to him he saw a beast stir at the entrance of the shelter, and raise its grey head. He took Milesende's hand.

'Don't be alarmed.'

'What is it?'

'It belongs to Rosamund. It's . . . a wolf.'

Milesende gave a start and reined her horse. She looked at Rollo suspiciously, but when she saw him dismount she nervously did the same. The creature yawned, and stretched itself comfortably by the entrance to the shelter. The three of them approached, and the manservant called out her name.

'Rosamund!'

They waited. The wolf eyed them dolefully. Then it rose and turned its head towards the interior of the shelter. And at that moment a figure appeared at the entrance. Rollo gave a start. It was Rosamund. Her feet and head were bare, as he had known her; but she was robed entirely in red. Jewels were on her wrists and fingers, and draped about her shoulders hung a shawl the colour of rubies that shimmered as the sun caught it and darkened into the deepest purple in the folds where it fell. As she moved towards them Rollo saw there were pearls in her hair – and then he noticed that round her neck was a thin golden chain from which hung . . . a golden heart.

She stretched out her arms towards Milesende, and the two sisters embraced. They cried and laughed, and looked at one another with their hands on each other's shoulders. Rollo saw the manservant discreetly lead his horse towards the river where he seated himself beneath a tree to wait.

Rollo felt bemused. There had been so many surprises, and there were so many questions unanswered. How did Audemand know so much about Rosamund? How did the manservant know where she was? The rich clothing. The golden heart exactly like Milesende's. It could only have been their father who gave one to each sister. Why had Audemand not told them who he was? Rosamund must know. Would she tell Milesende? Would she tell her who she was?

Rosamund embraced them both. She must leave, she said. She had wanted to be at their wedding, but now she must go. Milesende must have the house, she insisted. She had kept it for her – for the day she would be married. Their mother's house – not far from Langeais. When she had died Rosamund had travelled through the forest and across the river to live where she was safe. But she returned every so often: for thirteen years she had returned to tend the place. It was Audemand, beloved Audemand, who had always kept servants there, so that one day she could give it to Milesende. This was what their father had wanted. He told her that before he died.

'The house is outside a village,' she explained. 'Azay. The river runs round it. Our father used to come by boat – often at night. He loved you. And he loved our mother.'

Milesende burst into tears.

'Who was he? Tell me!'

There was silence for a moment. Then Rosamund looked at Rollo, and at Milesende again.

'Don't you know – from these clothes?' she said.

Milesende gazed at her sister, and at the jewels and the shimmering silk. And at that moment Rollo knew. But Milesende still shook her head.

'Audemand gave me this silk,' Rosamund went on. 'You must never tell anyone that – because it would give away Audemand's deepest secret. Not even the Count knows. Nor does he know what I'm about to tell you.'

Rosamund again laid her hands on her sister's shoulders.

'Your father – and mine – was Count Fulk's father,' she said in that calmest of voices Rollo remembered. 'Geoffrey Greymantle. You and I are Fulk's half-sisters.'

'Something's come to an end, Rollo. It's time for new things to be born.'

It was two days after the wedding. Audemand had found the Norman by the cathedral, and was gazing sceptically up at the arch of carved beaks above the west door. He had wanted, he said, to make sure all was well with Milesende and Rosamund, and to stress that the Count must not know what had taken place with his father so long ago. Fulk knew only that Milesende's father was some nobleman who left her a house.

The Chancellor looked about him. Rollo thought he was probably searching for his own likeness, but did not like to say so. There was thunder in the air. Audemand was in philosophical mood, and he looked tired.

'After I've gone Fulk may learn one day, I suppose. I hope he won't think ill of me.' Then he turned to Rollo. 'Old men shouldn't be allowed to go on too long,' he said, tapping his staff and looking up again at the beak-heads. 'We're like these.' He raised his staff and pointed to the carvings. 'A menace and no bite. We become too affected by our own infirmity, and begin to believe it to be the normal condition of life.'

He sighed wearily and the folds of skin on his face seemed to sag.

'We're driftwood, Rollo; just driftwood,' he went on. 'If we're lucky we catch on a sandbank and history grows around us for a while — until the floods come and we're swept away for ever.'

He stepped through the open door into the nave of the cathedral and looked around him at the high walls that still ended in the sky; then he went on talking as if the building itself were his audience.

'There are those who believe in what they do, and those who just do it because it can be done. I don't know which I prefer: both can be very dangerous. But to do nothing at all is worse because we leave nothing behind — except children who will also do nothing. We might as well watch the sun and the stars turn around us, then go to sleep till we die.'

He turned to look at Rollo, who was standing watching him from the doorway. There was another peal of thunder.

'I like people who leave something behind them — even if it's only foolish hopes. Or vineyards. Or a pile of stones ... You're one to understand that, Rollo.'

The old face had a softness about it that Rollo had rarely seen. Beloved Audemand, Rosamund had called him. He realized how much he too had grown to love the old man.

And then the rain fell as if it had been waiting all year to fall. Audemand gave a deep growl.

'Damned Viking! Used to the open sea! Why don't you put a roof on this thing? I thought you were supposed to be a master-mason.'

He pulled the hood of his cape over his grey head and hurried to join Rollo in the shelter of the doorway. They gazed out as the rain flailed across the open square.

'When I said that something had come to an end, Rollo, I didn't mean the end of the world.' He chuckled. Rivulets of water were trickling down the furrows of his face, and Audemand mopped his cheeks with a cloth. 'Mind you,' he continued, 'there are many who believe it soon will be the end of the world.'

Rollo saw that Audemand was still in a mood to air his thoughts.

'And if they're right,' he answered, 'then next year will be the last. There's hardly any point in my putting a roof on the cathedral, Audemand!'

Rollo noticed an amused look on the old man's face. But then he remembered Fulk's terror on the road to Langeais, and the questions – those desperate questions – the Count had put to him in the governor's house on that same evening. The year one thousand! Fulk was undoubtedly one of those who believed. And Rollo thought of Father Baudouin and how the Chaplain had convinced Fulk that his stillborn son bore the mark of the Devil. What anguish the Count had endured, and what suffering there had been to others as a result.

The Chancellor's face was serious again.

'There are many kinds of churchmen, Rollo. Good and evil. And a lot in between. They wield a frightening power over men who can't read – because if you can't read how can you tell the difference?'

Rollo knew the old man was thinking of Fulk.

'Does the Count still fear he'll be damned?' he asked.

Audemand's eyes crinkled, and he shook his head.

'No,' he replied. 'I'm sure not. Something changed him on that journey to Jerusalem: maybe it was a feeling that the world has only just begun. I don't know. Besides,' he added, and Rollo saw the lines round Audemand's mouth begin to twitch, 'our priapic Chaplain has now found other employment.'

Then he looked solemn again.

'And don't forget there's somebody else to reassure him now. Let me be indiscreet and say that the Countess Hildegarde may not be everybody's taste, but she's right for Fulk ... And if she should bear him a son ...!' The Chancellor raised his eyes. 'Goodness, we'll be in heaven – if I'm not there already by then.'

The rain had stopped as suddenly as it began.

'Come. I have things to do. I've been enough of an old philosopher for one day.' And with a determined flourish of his staff he stepped into the open square.

The sun shone on to broad pools of water as the two men steered a course among the drying cobbles.

'So tomorrow is the great departure – for a while at least.' And Audemand gave the cobbles a resounding tap with his staff. 'Sebrand to Nantes with full pageantry! And you more unobtrusively to Azay, I imagine!'

They were approaching the castle gates. Rollo felt the old man's hand on his shoulder.

'Not that the Count will let either of you stay long. Fulk has plenty of plans for Sebrand which will keep him away from his pretty lady. As for you' – and the Chancellor drummed his fingers on Rollo's shoulder – 'I must warn you that Beaulieu isn't the only monastery he plans to build. The Countess Hildegarde intends to have a nunnery. She likes nunneries. You're lucky Milesende has been spared. The Count wishes to dedicate it to St Nicholas – who saved Fulk from shipwreck on his journey to Jerusalem.' He paused, and then added with barely detectable sarcasm, 'There are many ladies in Angers, it seems, who are in need of being saved from shipwreck.'

The two men entered the castle gate and went their separate ways. Rollo looked up at the gaunt black walls. From tomorrow, he reflected, he and Milesende would have a place to live which did not scowl darkly on the world.

It was as though all the colours of Angers were on the move. The city gates opened and a procession of red and gold, blue and bronze, orange and silver, pennants, plumes, tassels, cloaks, streamers, fur and finery – to the accompaniment of clarions, horns, bells, cheering and laughter – all passed in a brilliant cavalcade before the eyes of the city in the sharp sunlight of that November morning.

They moved across the fields and gradually the forest closed around them, until those watching from the high walls could see no more than specks of movement merging one by one into that dark band of trees stretched between meadow and sky.

In the midst of the cavalcade were two women riding side by side. One was fair, the other dark, and their heads were forever turning towards one another as they rode. From time to time laughter rose from them: they would reach out and clasp hands, and their sleeves would form a loop of black and red across the centre of the forest track. Behind them at a little distance were two men – a tall, powerful figure in pale buckskin, and his smaller companion resplendent as a fighting-cock. They rode together mostly in silence, reins held relaxed and their eyes enjoying the sight of the two graceful creatures in front of them: but every so often they would exchange a word or a gesture as if acknowledging a bond formed by many such journeys.

After a while the forest gave way to a stretch of heathland stained bright with heather, and the track divided – one way westwards through oak woods to a distant river, the other east across the open heath towards another forest. Here the cavalcade paused and the two men dismounted. They stood for a moment at the meeting of the roads and gazed about them, until the slighter of the men stepped towards the other and the two of them embraced. Then they remounted and both raised their hands in salute before the larger party of horsemen turned to ride westwards with their bright pennants and flowing cloaks, to the sound of horns and the click of hooves on the stony earth. The tall figure in pale buckskin watched them go before wheeling his own horse towards the

480

other path. He leaned from his saddle and placed a hand on the arm of the dark-haired girl. She looked up at him, and the sun caught the black stream of her hair and the golden heart below her throat. The two of them set off across the silent heath.

Count Fulk gazed out over the river and the empty meadows long after the cavalcade had disappeared from view. Beyond, and far beyond, lay the forests where his ancestors had cleared their fields; and as he listened he imagined the wind carried with it the ring of axes. He had built Anjou with the blade of an axe and the blade of a sword: blood, wood and stone. He looked down at his own hands. The blood had been washed from them: hands that had held a sword, held his own child, held his wife's ashes, held his own tears.

It felt like a time of thanksgiving. He had been carried over rocks that should have destroyed him; and suddenly in his mind there rose before his eyes the tiny chapel above the cliff, white in a shaft of sunlight. He had made a vow to St Nicholas, and he would keep it.

Beside him a hand was pointing, and he heard the voice of Hildegarde.

'Look!'

A flock of white doves was circling above the river, turning in the sunlight. Wider and wider they circled; then they tilted on the wind and Fulk watched them fly far over the fields until they reached a small copse where again they turned in the sunlight before settling like snow among the branches.

He looked at Hildegarde.

'Let us build there!' he said.

Author's historical postscript

Count Fulk III (or Fulk Nerra – 'the Black' – as history has dubbed him) ruled Anjou for a further 41 years. Some of the events I have related took place outside the period of $2\frac{1}{2}$ years which this book spans, there being a limit to the number of passing seasons I wished to describe. The bare facts of his early career are more or less as I have described them, but those facts being rudimentary I have allowed myself to weave threads of fiction into them.

Fulk died in AD 1040 on the journey back from his third (possibly fourth) penitential pilgrimage to Jerusalem; and from this it can be deduced that his brilliant and rather monstrous mode of life did not greatly change. But history contributes some interesting *addenda*. His second wife Hildegarde duly bore him the son he craved, Geoffrey Martel, who was Count of Anjou for twenty years after the death of Fulk 'the Black'. Geoffrey died without an heir. But Fulk also had a daughter, and the title passed to her son who became Fulk IV, and subsequently to his son, Fulk V, who was not only Count of Anjou but also King of Jerusalem. It was Fulk V's son Geoffrey who was nicknamed 'Plantagenet', supposedly because of his habit of wearing a sprig of broom in his hat. As a mere youth Geoffrey married the Empress Matilda, widow of the Holy Roman Emperor and daughter of King Henry I of England. Their son, Henry Plantagenet, became King Henry II of England, father of Richard Coeur de Lion. So Count Fulk 'the Black' was in fact the great-great-great-grandfather of the first Plantagenet king of England. Fulk's dreams of a crown were to be fulfilled.